D0044171

# THE
# WORLD
# OF
# PONDSIDE

## BOOKS BY
## MARY HELEN STEFANIAK

NOVELS

*The Turk and My Mother*
*The Cailiffs of Baghdad, Georgia*
*The World of Pondside*

SHORT-STORY COLLECTIONS

*Self Storage, and Other Stories*

Mary Helen Stefaniak

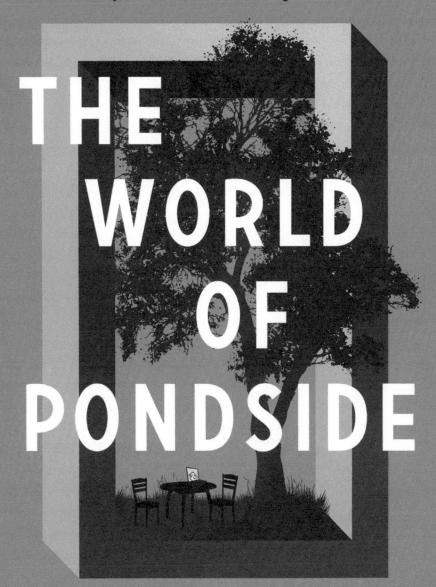

# THE WORLD OF PONDSIDE

BLACK
STONE
PUBLISHING

Printed in the United States of America

First edition: 2022
ISBN 978-1-7999-0971-2
Fiction / General

Version 2

CIP data for this book is available
from the Library of Congress

Blackstone Publishing
31 Mistletoe Rd.
Ashland, OR 97520

www.BlackstonePublishing.com

*For Sarah Lamb*
*In memoriam*

"Although I am no better than a dead man, still let me see the light of the sun."

*—The Epic of Gilgamesh*

It was pretty sad when you had to go outside to warm up, Foster thought. In October, no less. You'd think the geezers were already dead for how cold they kept the place. "I'm taking a break," he announced to Jenny, the breakfast and lunch cook. They were the only two in the kitchen at this hour. "It's like a meat locker in here."

"If you put some meat on your skinny little butt," Jenny said, "you might not feel the cold so bad."

Foster was supposed to come up with something clever to say in response. Normally, Jenny Williams was one of the few people on staff that he could talk to. This morning Foster was too pissed and too sad to talk to anyone. He'd thought it was a mistake when he first saw it: Robert Kallman on the "pureed" list.

"What the hell is this?" Foster had asked Jenny.

She'd looked up, with a frown, from the great stainless steel pot she was filling with uncooked oatmeal. Jenny didn't like cussing. She said it was a way to let the devil sprinkle a little poison into the course of human events. (That was the way she always put it, Declaration of Independence style.) She looked at the spreadsheet taped to the wall next to the "All Employees Must Wash Their Hands" poster over the sink. "You appear to be looking at the diet list," Jenny said. She resumed pouring oatmeal into the pot.

"It says Robert's on pureed. Robert Kallman."

"That's new," Jenny said lightly, as if it wasn't a death sentence or anything.

"He's mechanical soft," Foster argued. He knew this for a fact. Clearing supper tables last night, he had to wait, as usual, while Robert cleaned his plate. Spaghetti and meatballs, garlic bread (no crust), coleslaw, the works. Robert had eaten it all. Some staffers complained about Robert taking the whole day and half the night to finish eating, but Foster didn't mind waiting for him. Whenever he could, Foster took a break from clearing and sat down to eat dessert with the man. Robert Kallman had an impressive career in the military before he got hit with ALS. He had been all over the world: Germany, Iraq, Afghanistan, Japan, China. Plus, he knew everything there was to know about computers. He had created the game, for God's sake. *The World of Pondside.*

"He had mechanical soft at supper last night," Foster said. "I was there."

Mechanical soft was one giant step above pureed. On mechanical soft, there was plenty a person could eat: pasta, meatloaf, all kinds of cooked vegetables and fruit, eggs, hash, mashed potatoes, ice cream, even pie. Eating was the one thing Robert had left. He'd been diagnosed in his midthirties, and in the decade or so since then, ALS had crippled his hands and arms, wasted his leg muscles, weakened his neck and back until he needed specially designed cushions and supports to keep upright in his wheelchair. It had muddied his speech so that only a listener as dedicated as Foster could understand him. But his left hand could still grip a fork or fat-handled spoon and bring it slowly to his mouth. He could dump it with a turn of his wrist onto his tongue, and then chew, chew, and chew, and trickiest of all, swallow it, swallow it hard, the right muscles sending the food down the right hole, getting it down and then remembering how to open up and take a breath. Just thinking about it made Foster's jaws and throat ache, but, like Robert said, what else did he have to do?

*Pureed*, on the other hand, meant eating nothing thicker than what you could suck up with a straw. At Pondside, that meant a plateful of normal food run through the food processor. Foster had seen the dinner "chef" puree a salad and send it out: iceberg lettuce turned to green slush.

Jenny reached for a wooden spoon. She raised an eyebrow in Foster's direction. "What were you doing here at supper last night and now you're here this morning? You been working twelve-hour shifts again?"

"Wait a minute," Foster said, suddenly all too certain that he had figured it out. "It's Thursday." Speech therapy came through on Wednesdays. "You think they reevaluated him? Knocked him down to pureed?" *The bastards*, Foster thought.

"He should've got pureed at supper then," Jenny said. "Somebody slipped up."

Foster pulled the paper kitchen cap off his head in disgust. His hair sprang free.

He stopped at his locker to pick up a cigarette on his way outside. Employees were strictly forbidden to carry a pack in any visible pocket. He punched the four digits plus pound sign on the pad beside the heavy glass door, waited for the click, and threw himself gratefully outside into thick warm air, currents of it you could almost see snaking into the building behind him, like the arrows that mark a storm front rolling across a TV weather map.

Outside it was just getting light, the trees and the cornfield and the Heartland Trucking warehouse emerging from the darkness beyond the parking lot, frogs trilling their last-chance love songs down by the pond. Pondside Manor had the look of a medium-priced motel: three redbrick and fake-stone wings guarded by a phalanx of stunted evergreens, with an atrium wrapped in windows up front. It sprawled on its own frozen lake of concrete in the middle of the kind of nowhere that exists at the edge of most midsized towns in the Midwest, where you might spy a horse or two nibbling some grass in the shadow of a giant billboard or discover an old fishing pond hosting its ducks and bluegills in a glacial depression behind the box stores that line the highway. Foster crossed the concrete, tacking through a smattering of employee cars. He kept his eyes on the prize that lay at the edge of the parking lot: a wooden bench under a tree overlooking the pond. He could see only one end of the bench as he approached; most of it was hidden by a border of variously successful spirea bushes that made a broken line around the parking lot.

At this hour, so close to the shift change, Foster expected the bench would be unoccupied, the sand-filled bucket beside it overflowing with butts. He was close enough to stub his toe on the bucket before he noticed the tendril of fresh white smoke rising from the hidden end of the bench.

"Hey!" he said.

"Hey, Foster," a husky voice replied. It was Tori, the first-shift RN. She didn't turn her head right away to look at him, but kept scowling down at the pond, her arms folded over her scrubs—it was light enough now for Foster to make out the teddy bear print—and her crossed leg bouncing on top of the leg that was jiggling up and down underneath it. Foster had never seen Tori sitting—or for that matter, standing— still. When she finally looked up at him, simultaneously blowing out a stream of smoke, she tipped her head toward the end of the bench—an invitation to sit. The loose topknot of her blond ponytail bobbed sideways, seconding the motion.

Foster sat. "What're you doing here so early?" He flipped his dumb phone open and shut. It was 6:32. Her shift didn't start until 7:00.

"I have charts to finish from yesterday." She sucked on her cigarette, held it, pursed her lips to exhale noisily. "Don't tell."

Foster breathed in the smoke that wafted toward his end of the bench and remembered harder times, before his latest employment at Pondside Manor, when he used to stretch out his cigarette money by positioning himself downwind of people on their smoke breaks. Usually, he didn't like to think about the fact that he was breathing in what had been inside somebody else's lungs. With Tori, he didn't mind that so much. He thought about asking her if she knew why Robert Kallman's diet got downgraded, but that seemed like too low a note to start her day on. Of course, now that he'd thought of that, he couldn't think of anything else to say. He inhaled one last secondhand breath and reached for the Camel in his pocket, surveying the pond.

"What do you think that is, down there?" he said.

He pointed to the end of the short wooden pier a farmer up the road maintained on the pond for fishing purposes. A couple of the old guys used it when they could get somebody to take them down there. Wheelchairs needed help getting over the bump where the boards met the shore. A curve of silver emerged from and returned to the water at the end of the pier. He could tell it was something that didn't belong there.

Tori looked where he pointed. "Is it a bicycle?" She stood up to have a better look. "Didn't yours get stolen from the rack?"

"Not lately," Foster said, and he stood up, too.

It was that time of the morning, right before the sun showed its true colors, when the stillness got whipped up into a distinct breeze. The leaves over their heads rustled and the pond suddenly scalloped into little waves. The frogs fell silent. Ducks bobbed into view from the reeds behind the pier. One of them stopped and plunged its head into the water and its tail into the air, the way ducks do, as if to have a look at the rest of whatever was out there, the part that was underwater. When the duck popped up again, the silver half circle behind it suddenly became to Foster's eyes what it had been all along.

He crushed his unlit cigarette in his fist.

Tori said, "My God."

Then they both took off at a run, Tori pulling out her phone and racing across the parking lot to the building, while Foster stumbled down the steep hill to the pond.

# CHAPTER 1

Laverne Slatchek had been hiding in her room since breakfast—not that she had eaten any. Who could eat breakfast with all those red and blue lights zooming along the walls in the dining room, and the food-service people gawking at the windows—blocking *her* view—instead of feeding Screamin' Jeannie and the others who moaned more quietly but could not feed themselves? Laverne had gotten a few glimpses of police cars, an ambulance, a fire truck—they always sent a fire truck, just in case. She asked a staff member what was going on, but the girl didn't seem to know anything. Or, if she did, she wasn't talking. Laverne had given up on getting any more coffee. She removed her clothing protector, which was actually a towel-size bib, and hotfooted it down the hall toward the library, where she found Duane Lotspeich already hunched over the computer in the corner. After cursing her luck loud enough to make Duane's narrow shoulders twitch, Laverne had taken a left out of the library and scooted down Hawkeye Lane toward her room.

All the hallways at Pondside Manor had street names. Laverne's room was in Boysenberry Boulevard, which was home to residents who were independently mobile, mostly continent, and fully aware of their circumstances. The last of these characteristics is what made Boysenberry Boulevard the quietest and arguably the saddest hallway in Pondside

Manor. Laverne had been living in room 2021B for two years now, ever since her son Joseph and his wife moved away to a western suburb of Chicago. Joseph couldn't bear to think of Laverne rattling around in her two-bedroom condo with no one in town to replace light bulbs or to take up the throw rugs she persisted in scattering all over her floors despite the well-documented trip hazard they afforded. Laverne had held out in her condo until one day she tripped, as predicted, on one of the rugs and broke something. "Fortunately, your arm and not your hip!" exclaimed Joseph's wife, whose name Laverne had only recently begun to forget for hours at a time. The arm, which was broken in two places, required a brief hospital stay followed by a lengthy period of rehabilitation, and it was a far, far simpler thing to check into Pondside Manor, where physical therapy was available *daily* on *site,* than to arrange pickup and delivery via Bionic Bus.

Somehow Laverne's slow but measurable progress in squeezing foam balls and reaching for the ceiling had stretched to fill the up-to-one-hundred days of skilled nursing care fully covered by her Medicare plan. She was just about to go Private Pay—an inheritance-guzzling prospect that had her son and daughter-in-law talking in low tones about turning their garage into a mother-in-law flat—when a stroke knocked out her right field of vision and, more importantly from a financial standpoint, put her back in the hospital for three fully covered weeks of acute care and rehabilitation. The hospital stay set her one-hundred-day skilled nursing clock back to Day One.

During her second hundred days at Pondside Manor—around Day Thirty-Seven, in fact—the right half of Laverne's world, nonexistent since the stroke, began to be populated by shadowy figures and the occasional cloud of bright light. By Day Sixty-Three, when she could discern the outline and contents of her whole dinner plate and no longer needed to turn it to find the hash browns to the right of the Salisbury steak, it seemed likely that she had recovered as much vision as she was going to recover.

On Day Seventy-One, the kind of bright Sunday in April that made visitors bloom like algae in the hallways and courtyards of Pondside Manor, Laverne took her visitors to a trio of rocking chairs on a porch overlooking the pond, and having carefully situated herself across from them with her son Joseph in her left field of vision and her daughter-in-law cast into semi-darkness on her right, Laverne informed them that she had decided to stay where she was until she moved on to her final resting place, or until her money ran out, whichever came first. (She had done the math, with the help of Pondside's business manager, and was pretty sure her funds would last a lifetime of reasonable length. She was already almost eighty-six.)

"But, Mother," the voice of her daughter-in-law came at once from the shadows, "we have the garage—the apartment, I mean—all ready for you." Her son Joseph was silent, his tall forehead beading up in the sunlight.

Laverne suggested that they might buy themselves a new car to put in there instead.

It was a shiny little moment of triumph that Laverne had lived to regret. By midsummer, she had listened to every audiobook in the library, watched all the videos (some of them twice), and made a lot of hand-crafted items (every pot holder and clay pot and macramé wall hanging a bit more developed on the left side than on the right). She had learned the names of all the plants in the front and back courtyards, and planted a few of her own. She had attended every ice-cream social and had taken what she soon decided was one too many field trips in the SeniorMobile. She was just about ready to consign herself to living out her days in a con-verted garage under her daughter-in-law's watchful eye when somebody donated three computers to the facility and, shortly thereafter, with the help and encouragement of the very Duane Lotspeich who was currently hogging the computer in the library, Laverne had started playing the game.

Only one of the three donated computers was powerful enough to play the game, although the skinny young fellow who worked in the kitchen intended to "upgrade" the other two, he kept saying. The game had been invented by the poor man across the hall who had Lou Gehrig's disease. Robert was his name.

Laverne could not begin to imagine how anyone could *invent* what happened when she clicked the little duck on the computer screen that had the words *World of Pondside* under it.

In *The World of Pondside*, Laverne Slatchek was not a former high school biology teacher, long retired. She was a neuroscientist at the University of California, Berkeley, a member of a team racing against the clock to crack the code that would put the kibosh on Alzheimer's and other dementias, once and for all, earning the team a nice pile of money in the process and maybe a free trip to Sweden. Laverne had always wanted to live in the Bay Area, ever since she and her long-departed husband Bill spent their twenty-fifth wedding anniversary there, more than thirty years ago. Sitting in the upper deck at Candlestick, where they could look right out over the bleachers to the sailboats in the bay, Laverne had been surprised every time she glanced at Bill by how young he looked (he was fifty-seven on their twenty-fifth) with his Giants cap settled low and shading his face, turning the yellow tinge of his skin back into a golden tan. His liver was halfway to gone then, although they didn't know it yet. In *The World of Pondside*, Laverne could see the Golden Gate Bridge from the glass wall of her beautifully decorated condo. She and Bill went to see the Giants play at Candlestick Park (not at Ma Bell or wherever they played now), and the notorious offshore winds were always in the home team's favor.

Surely Duane Lotspeich was finished with the computer by now. If not, she'd go ahead and ask him to log off and let her have a half hour or so, just to tide her over. Laverne poked her head into the hallway. Boysenberry Boulevard was empty of traffic, although there was still some commotion going on at the far end of it, where it opened on the atrium, which is what the brochure called the many-windowed and almost always empty front lounge. (Duane Lotspeich called it the Aquarium, due to all the glass.) It wasn't empty now—Laverne caught a glimpse of reflective tape on the back of a fireman's coat—but everyone's attention was directed at the windows. Nobody was looking down the hallway toward Laverne's room. She followed her walker (which she didn't *need* but often used as a kind of rolling handrail) in the opposite direction, letting it lead her past the deserted nurses' station and back down Hawkeye Lane toward the library.

The good computer—*Glory be!*—was free. Duane Lotspeich was nowhere in sight.

Laverne eased herself into the Easy-Up, Easy-Down ergonomic chair, her heart already beating faster and her fingertips almost tingling. She took the headphones out of the drawer—surprised that Lotspeich had bothered to put them away—and plugged the cord into the hole before she put them on. She experienced a moment of not *exactly* panic when she couldn't find the little picture of a yellow duck that opened *The World of Pondside*. The ducklink, they called it. Had Duane Lotspeich moved it? Or worse—had he stolen it somehow? She turned her head to search the screen with the good side of her brain—and there it was! Laverne maneuvered the mouse to bring the arrow over to the right side of the screen, where somebody—she supposed it had to be Duane—had moved the ducklink into a row of other little pictures: the camera, the fox, the wastebasket. Finally, she got the arrow to settle on the duck. This took a while of dancing all around it first. Reminding herself to breathe normally, she clicked once and waited for the arrow to become a little hand.

Mary McIntyre took deep breaths and tried to keep her heart from racing. She had heard the sirens but told herself that didn't matter. You could always hear sirens this close to the base—well, not always but often enough. Her sister Mildred said that if there ever really was an air raid, everybody's goose was going to be cooked because they had learned to ignore the sirens. Mary couldn't ignore them, unfortunately; they were making her head feel like it might explode, but she told herself that the sirens didn't have a thing to do with her. She told herself that she knew exactly where she'd left the baby. She'd left him with Mildred.

Mildred could be trusted to take excellent care of a baby, having already had two of her own—beautiful children, dark-haired and dark-eyed with creamy skin like Mildred's and wavy hair like their dad's. They had been so excited to meet the baby. They planted kisses on both of his fat cheeks at once. It looked like he might cry with all that smooching, but then they backed off and he changed his mind and gave them a big open-mouthed grin, sticking his tongue out the way he does, like a happy puppy. Blinking his big blue eyes. Looking like the world was his oyster.

Mary was not herself today, not at all. Something was wrong inside her head, she thought, looking up and down the street. How could she tell anyone that she couldn't find the baby? They would probably put her in jail. This place didn't help matters: one redbrick house after another, so close together they were almost connected, all of them with what Mildred called her "picture window" looking out at a front yard paved with pebbles instead of grass. A few sad-looking evergreens poking up here and there.

Mary wished she'd paid more attention to the evergreens. Hadn't she walked between a pair of them when she came out the front door? *Just like those two there!* she thought hopefully. She was almost sure that was the house. Mildred's house. Even the drapes were the same, Mary thought, what she could see of them anyway, hanging down on either side of the giant picture window. Maybe she would walk down the sidewalk, right on past the house, as slowly as she could without looking peculiar about it, and maybe then she'd catch a glimpse of somebody inside.

When Mary was right in front of the right pair of evergreens, she turned her head to look into the picture window. At first, all she saw in the open space between the drapes was the dark interior of the house—no Mildred, no baby—and then, all at once, from deep inside the dark interior, she saw a light, several lights, red and blue and white ones, spinning and darting, growing larger as if they were moving toward the window, coming closer, something big inside the house moving toward the window—no! The lights were a reflection, weren't they? She hadn't meant to stop as she walked by, but here she was, standing in the way of whatever was coming toward the window from behind her. She spun around, ready to throw herself out of its path, and ran smack into a policeman who appeared out of nowhere and said, kindly, "Ma'am? Are you all right? Can I help you?"

Mary could only look at him at first. He was not someone she knew, of that she was fairly certain, although the uniform made them all look—and even sound—more like each other than like themselves. She remembered how startling it was the first time her husband came home in the uniform:

the double-breasted greatcoat with Police Department patches on the sleeves, the flat-topped hat with the gold-and-silver badge over a shining visor. This one here was in blue shirtsleeves. He had a sweet, narrow face. The longer she looked at him, the more he reminded her of George. She felt something expand in her chest and rise in her throat and she knew: he wasn't here to lock her up! He could help her find the baby. She let him take her arm. If she told him, he could help. All she had to do was say it. She took a breath.

"Mary, honey!" said a husky woman's voice, and all of a sudden, there was a woman next to the policeman, peeking around his shoulder—a young woman in pajamas with her blond hair in a ponytail, like a fountain coming out the top of her head. "What are you doing out here in the parking lot? Are you looking for the baby?"

"Maybe your baby's inside the building," the policeman said then, just as kindly, but Mary had already turned herself to stone.

Foster Kresowik sat shivering in wet scrubs and a blanket in the arts and crafts room. He had dry jeans and a T-shirt in his locker, but no one asked him if he wanted to change. Two uniformed officers, a youngish man and a middle-aged woman who reminded him of his fourth-grade teacher, Mrs. Appelford, did the questioning. The first question—after he had given his name and position—was easy: What time had he arrived for work? He always looked at his dumb phone to see if he was late or not before he went inside. *It was 5:59 a.m.,* he told her. Did he see anything at all unusual in the parking lot upon his arrival? *It was still dark,* Foster said. But the lot was well lit, Mrs. Appelford pointed out. Where did Foster park his car?

He hesitated then. Both officers looked at him expectantly. Foster hated to admit that he didn't have a car. In the midwestern heart of this great land of ours, to be twenty-six years old and not own a car marked a man as a loser, if not a criminal or weirdo of some kind. At the very least, people assumed that your license had been revoked, but in Foster's case, it was economics, pure and simple. After wasting his money on three different vehicles, each of which ran briefly and would have cost more to repair than he paid for it in the first place, Foster had decided to save his money until he could afford the monthly payment, along with gas and insurance, for a car that wasn't just another piece of crap. He told them that he rode his bike to work and brought it inside the building through a service entrance at the back. The youngish officer wrote that down.

The questions got harder as they went on. Asked to describe exactly how he had discovered the deceased, Foster hoped that he was giving the cops the exact same details that Tori would give them about spotting a silvery half circle in the water at the end of the pier. Foster knew—because the officers told him—that a second body had been found, another one of the residents evidently, as yet unnamed. The officers wondered why neither Foster nor Tori had seen the second body at the edge of the parking lot. In fact, Mrs. Appelford expressed surprise that Foster hadn't tripped over the body on his way to the path that led down to the pond. He reminded her that he hadn't taken the path; he had charged directly down the hill from the smokers' bench to the water's edge. By the time it was light enough to see the shadowy reaches of the parking lot, Foster's attention had been focused elsewhere.

Then he was supposed to explain how and why he tried to extricate the body from the pond. What was his intention going into the water? At least ten minutes had passed, Foster himself had told them, between his arrival at the smokers' bench and his realization that the object submerged at the end of the pier was a wheelchair. What was he trying to do? What did he hope to accomplish? Surely it was too late—he couldn't be hoping to rescue Robert Kallman?

Foster had almost drowned himself, trying to get Robert out of the water that morning. He had plunged down the hill and splashed directly into the pond. The water was shallow, or would have been, if the mud underneath it had been less deep. Foster sank to midthigh in the water by his third or fourth step, and knew, too late, that he should have run along the path to the little pier, instead of splashing into the pond from shore. The mud almost sucked one of Foster's shoes off. It closed around his ankles and then his calves, making each step harder than the last. Somehow, though, he reached the pier. The wheelchair lay in the water at the end of it, tipped back and to one side. His first effort to pull the deeply mired chair upright had no effect whatsoever. He abandoned that, filled his lungs, held his breath, and went under to tackle the straps that not only kept Robert in the wheelchair but normally held him upright—so many straps! Foster pulled on Velcro and tugged at buckles. When the straps wouldn't budge, he had no choice but to straighten up, gulp air, and look down through four or five inches of water at the man in the tipped-over wheelchair. Robert's eyes and mouth were open, and his arms moved freely in the muddy currents Foster himself had stirred around the pier—more freely, in fact, than Foster had ever seen them move in the unaccommodating air.

Foster wanted to tell the cops, *Yes, I was hoping to save him. Even after all that time.* Instead, he shrugged. When Mrs. Appelford pressed him a little, he said, "I couldn't just leave him there."

Afterward, they offered to give him a ride home. Foster didn't know why—maybe to keep him from skipping town on his bicycle? Was he some kind of suspect? Whatever their reasons, his arms and legs were feeling rubbery, and he was glad to have a ride from anybody, even the cops. Mrs. Appelford spoke to the administrator about it while Foster went to change his clothes. Still shivering, wearing the blanket like a cape over his wet scrubs, he paused at the intersection of Iowa Avenue and Hawkeye Lane—both routes that led to the employee lockers—and chose the one that would take him past Robert's room.

The hallway was entirely deserted, the door to Robert's room not quite closed—which was just the way Robert used to leave it, open a hand's width, to signal that he was accepting visitors. Foster stopped outside the door and listened for a moment. He had to stop himself from saying, "Hey!" or, "Foster here," before he pushed it open.

Robert Kallman's private room was large enough to accommodate the standard adjustable bed with a space to park his wheelchair beside it, a Pondside dresser and nightstand, his mother's favorite armchair, and, taking up the length of one wall, a desk made out of two wooden doors resting on four short filing cabinets. The door-top desk was home to not one, not two, but three personal computers and four flat-screen monitors (two of them paired to make an extra-wide display), along with a variety of external hard drives and modems, a router, two scanners, the eye-tracker screen and digital speech generator that could be attached to the arm of Robert's wheelchair, and the powerful laptop that served up *The World of Pondside*.

There was something Foster hadn't told the police. Something Robert said not long ago. They had been alone in the dining room, Robert working on dessert and Foster clearing tables, when Robert's speech device piped up to say: "If something happens to me, I want you to give the server to my mother." Foster, who had never spoken more than two words at a time to Robert's mother, wasn't sure he'd understood. He stopped stacking plates and said something brilliant like, "What do you mean, if something happens to you?" Robert had given him the kind of look people give you when you've asked a question they know you know the answer to—ALS was a one-way ticket, everyone knew that—and then he responded with his own voice, pausing between words to get his lips and tongue in line. "You know howww it goes," he said. "I don't wwant that laptop to disappearrr."

Standing wet and cold in the doorway, Foster was all but overwhelmed by—what? He couldn't say. Sadness, strangeness, disbelief. The words "unfinished business" came into his head. Robert's room looked pretty much the same as it had the day before yesterday, the last time Foster was in here. The day before yesterday, Robert's wheelchair had been rolled up to the big PC with the paired screens, where they did their 3D modeling. Foster had been scooting back and forth between the big PC and the *World of Pondside* laptop, which they kept tucked between the flatbed scanner and the wall, beyond the view from the door. He took a few steps into the room, wet shoes squishing.

The laptop wasn't there.

He stood very still for a moment, as if that might make it reappear. Then he made a quick search of the computer desk, opening and shutting drawers as quietly as he could, and crouching to check underneath. Sliding open the closet door was harder—nothing but familiar-looking shirts, Robert's down jacket, two of his three fleece hoodies, and a pair of slip-on shoes that made Foster close his eyes and squeeze them tight to shut out the image of Robert's slipper floating like a little boat under the pier. Foster closed the closet door. He moved to the dresser: one drawer of socks and underwear folded with military precision, another full of Mrs. Kallman's balls of yarn and knitted scarves and mittens she worked on while she and Robert spent long evenings watching the wall-mounted TV. The remaining two drawers were stocked with packages of plastic tubing and waterproof Chux pads. There was no need to disturb the bed, which Robert almost never slept in. It was made up as tight as a drum, nothing but dusty floor underneath.

Foster straightened up slowly, clutching the damp blanket around his shoulders. Someone had taken the laptop. Probably not the cops, since they hadn't asked Foster anything about Robert's computers, and surely not Mrs. Kallman herself—someone would have called her, made sure she didn't show up for breakfast with Robert today. Maybe Robert had changed his mind about counting on Foster and asked someone else to take it out of his room.

Or maybe Foster was just too late.

Whoever took the laptop had left no trace. Foster looked down at his trail of muddy footprints. He dropped the blanket to the floor and wiped the shiny no-skid vinyl clean as he backed out of the room.

# CHAPTER 2

By lunchtime that Thursday, all the staff on-site and many of the residents at Pondside Manor Rehabilitation and Long-Term Care Center were aware that two bodies had been carried away from the grounds of the facility that morning. First, to the surprise of some and the dismay of many, there was Robert Kallman, age forty-eight, whose wheelchair was recovered from not quite three feet of pond water. The divers had found the wheelchair on its side, mired in the mud at the bottom and almost completely submerged, with only one wheel visible above the surface of the water. Robert, whose late-stage ALS had left him unable to sit upright without support, was strapped securely into the chair. The medical examiner's report would later confirm what seemed obvious at the scene: Robert Kallman's lungs were full of water, his death due to drowning.

The second body, discovered after the first responders appeared on the scene, was that of James Witkowski, an ambulatory eighty-seven-year-old who had collapsed in the parking lot, just beyond the modified school bus they called the SeniorMobile. Two fishing poles and a tackle box on wheels—known to be Witkowski's property—were found in the parking lot, not far from the top of the grassy hill leading down to the pond. Since Robert Kallman was known to have little fondness either for fishing or, frankly, for James Witkowski, a majority of the staff and a substantial number of residents were inclined to believe that James had probably left the building independently of Robert. It seemed clear to everyone that James had hurried up the hill and across the parking lot in search of help, and that this unaccustomed activity, perhaps combined with the shock and excitement of finding the wheelchair and its occupant in the pond, had proven too much for the older man's heart.

But how had Robert ended up in the pond? Everyone agreed that he *could* have maneuvered his motorized wheelchair down the difficult but not impossible asphalt path that began at the corner of the visitor's parking lot. From there, he would have had to make at least a half circuit of the path around the pond to reach the pier, but this, too, seemed possible, although he would have needed help getting his wheelchair over the bump onto the pier. As to whether he had gone into the water intentionally—the residents were of at least two minds about that.

Robert was, if one could pardon the expression under the circumstances, an odd duck. Despite the fact that he had all manner of high-tech paraphernalia in his room, he could be found using the computer in the library at almost any time of the day or night. Moreover, the third-shift staff could attest to many nights when Robert refused the help he needed to get from his wheelchair into bed, preferring to spend the night propped up in his chair. He also made frequent requests for assistance with the security code so he could get outside for a breath of fresh air or to see the stars, sometimes in the wee hours of the morning. (According to the third-shift nurse, he had made no such request last night.) Still, for all his late-night inclinations—and for all his hobbies and interests and ingenuity—Robert Kallman must have been keenly aware of his diminishing abilities. ALS was a cruel sentence for anyone, and Robert had been diagnosed when he was in his thirties, after experiencing his first symptoms while on active duty in the military. Who could blame him if he had chosen to avoid the finale of his inexorable and accelerating decline?

James Witkowski, on the other hand, had been in good shape—as good as any eighty-seven-year-old of sound mind might hope to be. He was at Pondside, he had explained to anyone who would listen, only because his son insisted that he sell the farm and put himself in the hands of someone who could cook and clean for him, give him his meds on time, and provide him with the social contact that was completely lacking in his life as a widower these past fifteen years. If he couldn't be on his farm, James had little interest in where he was, and the proximity of the fishing pond made Pondside Manor a little better than as good a place as any. And now, nurse Amelia Ramirez suggested to the Certified Nursing Assistants who came on shift that Thursday afternoon, James Witkowski had gone on to a better place.

"You *think* so?" one of them said.

The one person at Pondside who had actually seen Robert Kallman strapped in his wheelchair under the water was not on hand to take part in these early speculations. Foster T. (for Thomas) Kresowik, whose name most Pondside residents would not have recognized, had gone home for the day, excused from the rest of his shift. To the residents, Foster was the kitchen boy, the one to call when they wanted more coffee, or a fork, or a diet upgrade (which was *not* within his power to bestow but that didn't keep them from asking), or another mouthful of macaroni, or a different, less tired-looking piece of pie. If they disapproved of his abundant hair and his blurry tattoos, or the cigarette smell that clung to him, they kept quiet about it. Many of them called him the Kitchen boy the way they might have called a neighbor's child the Yoder girl or the Matthews kid.

"Did you see the Kitchen boy come running in here like a drowned rat this morning, dripping everywhere?" said those who had been in the dining room early, waiting for breakfast, to those who had not. "What do you think he was up to?"

# CHAPTER 3

In the front seat of the police van, Foster's wet shoes felt like cold lumps of clay on his feet. He found himself hoping that none of the residents had seen him getting into what the geezers would have called a paddy wagon. They would jump immediately to the worst possible conclusion. It irritated Foster that he cared if they did.

The younger cop attempted small talk. "You've had one heck of a morning, haven't you?"

"Turn left at the light," Foster said.

His efficiency apartment was on the second floor of a small, mostly commercial building that had somehow held on to one corner of what was now a multi-acre parking lot around the shopping mall just down the road from Pondside. This was the mammoth suburban mall that had decimated the bustling downtown shopping district of Foster's boyhood, home to the video arcade where his initials had topped the leaderboards on games that blinked and buzzed and dinged no longer, games that were probably moldering in a landfill. Foster felt bad sometimes about living in a building surrounded by the killer mall, which was itself in decline, but there was no arguing with zero transportation costs. His seven-minute back-road route to Pondside steered clear of the mall and the highway and the Costco that was giving Sam's Club a run for its money these days, according to the NPR station that Robert Kallman listened to—*used to listen to*—in his room.

"I can get out here," he told the cop at a stop sign in front of Panera Bread Company, which occupied the first floor of the commercial building.

"This is it?"

"I'm upstairs."

The young cop retrieved Foster's bicycle and stood at the back of the police van while Foster rolled the bike over to the apartment entrance. He fumbled with the key, partly because he had to balance the bike against his hip to free both hands, and partly because the cop was watching him, as was the guy wiping off tables behind the big plate-glass window at Panera.

*Great*, Foster thought. *Just great.* With a shove from his shoulder, the door finally opened, and he carried his bike up the stairs.

The first thing Foster did—after standing at the window and watching the police van drive away—was to sit down at his computer. It was a souped-up Dell that Robert had given him two years ago when they started working on *The World of Pondside*. Robert Kallman had an advanced degree in computer science that he'd earned between multiple deployments in the Gulf. He'd spent most of his military career in and out of Iraq, he told Foster the first time they met in Robert's room to talk about the game. "In 2005 I was supposed to be collecting data for self-driving supply vehicles," Robert told him, "but I ended up commanding a Humvee escort team. Somebody's tour was up. It was pretty ironic anyway, talking about AI in the same breath as those patched-together Humvees."

Robert had much better speech two years ago.

He told Foster he had worked out the game design and created some templates for the portals. (It was Foster who came up with the duck-shaped icon for the game.) Robert envisioned the game as a cross between an alternate-life simulation and the *you-are-there* point of view of a first-person shooter—without the shooting, in most cases. To eliminate worries about security and personal information, the game could be locally networked, at least to start, with access limited to a few IP addresses and

Robert's new laptop—fortified with graphics cards and multiple processor cores—as the server. "A much-less-than-worldwide web," he liked to call it.

Foster didn't think geezers would go for a computer game, but Robert said, "Who needs an alternate reality more desperately than people in a nursing home? All the real world has to offer is a life sentence of institutional meals and fluorescent lighting."

"I thought you liked the food here," Foster said. It was the first time he had been in Robert's room, and he was trying to look as if he weren't astounded by the array of computers and things on the door-top desk. All Foster had then, before Robert fixed him up, was a PC he bought at a garage sale for twenty-five dollars.

The secret to success with the senior population, Robert believed, was a personalized game, a world built of materials gathered from the player. He'd start with an interview, followed by the collection of photos, documents, the occasional audio recording or video, anything at all that could be used to digitize a person's memories and daydreams and desires. He had begun by working on a prototype for none other than the Pondside Manor administrator, Kitty Landiss.

"Why *her*?" Foster said.

Robert did the little neck stretch that was all he had left of shrugging his shoulders, even two years ago. "Because she is the key to the bank."

He had already wrangled one upgrade in the library from Administrator Landiss in return for development of her portal, which is what he called each customized environment. Before he knew it, Foster was spending a lot more time than he would have preferred to spend scrolling through *Vogue* and *Vanity Fair* to expand the administrator's wardrobe.

He was looking forward to working on Duane Lotspeich's "Black Ops" portal, which sounded like it would be more up Foster's alley, until he found out it was a dance studio! Robert told him that Lotspeich had been a dance instructor at some point in his life—presumably before the point where he lost his leg—but he had also been a US Marine. The old man kept changing his mind about which life to revisit in *The World of Pondside* until Robert, inspired by a wedding he'd witnessed in Afghanistan, came up with the idea of a dance hall in the middle of a combat zone. Naming the portal "Black Ops" instead of, say, "Duane's Dance-More" was the old man's choice.

Foster pretended to know what Robert was talking about when he said he had a Natural User Interface (he called it the "Nooey") that could do skeletal tracking on one or two moving subjects. The Nooey would have been perfect for a dance game, Robert said, but Duane was too wobbly on his one leg plus prosthesis to dance in the sensors' field of view. Instead, the on-screen dance moves of an exceedingly debonair two-legged Duane were made by the pressures his thighs and backside exerted on a cushion pressed into the seat of his wheelchair, together with the movements of his shoulders against the cushion behind his back.

"Dancing is all in the hips and shoulders anyway," Lotspeich explained one time while Foster was adjusting the position of a sensor inside the seat cushion.

"Right," said Foster.

"People think it's the feet," Lotspeich said, "but the feet are incidental."

*Good thing*, Foster thought.

In terms of input, Duane's Black Ops dance studio with its cushion sensors was the most sophisticated portal they had created for the residents so far. Most of them worked with arrow keys and typing in text boxes.

Laverne Slatchek had the most personally detailed environment, due to the wealth of raw material she was able to provide. On top of about a thousand photos, she had home movies of Christmases past that were transferred to VHS, a 16 mm of her husband Bill at bat in 1967, and—the jackpot—a bunch of audiotapes that Bill made for her while he was on the road with a San Francisco Giants' farm team. Robert figured that there was a sample of every word Laverne's husband had ever uttered to her on those tapes. All they—meaning Foster—had to do was transfer the data from analog to digital, cut it up, and reassemble the words to make every kind of greeting, reply, suggestion, and term of endearment that Bill was likely to say in response to almost any situation Laverne's *World of Pondside* portal could present. From "That was no strike!" and

"What a catch!" to "I sure miss you, sweetheart," and a half-dozen slightly different versions of "I love you" that rotated through their conversations randomly, like banner ads at the top of a web page.

All of this and more was on the *World of Pondside* server, the laptop Foster had failed to keep from disappearing. It occurred to him that Robert would have backed it all up, but Foster had no idea how or where.

When the Dell booted up, illuminating Foster's tiny apartment with its cool glow, the yellow ducklink was right where it was supposed to be: in the middle of his cluttered desktop. Foster's highly affordable internet service was the finest, fastest broadband Panera had to offer— available daily from five thirty a.m. until ten p.m., which is when the coffee shop closed. Foster didn't understand why they couldn't leave their router turned on after hours. He'd suggested it one time on a "Help Us Serve You Better!" card, to no avail. His finger was on the mouse, a microsecond away from double-clicking the ducklink, when he stopped to consider what might happen, under the circumstances.

If whoever took Robert's laptop had turned it off, then he should just get a "Server Not Responding" alert. But what if the laptop was on and waiting for someone to show up? Foster couldn't think of any reason why he or the *World of Pondside* server should be the target of anybody's cyber schemes, but he sure didn't want to be one of those idiots who clicked on a link and subsequently found their hard drive erased. With the *Pondside* server in unknown hands, even opening the browser suddenly seemed risky. He resolved instead to prowl his local desktop directories—opening folders and closing them again, maybe doing a bit of housekeeping, anything that would keep him away from the ducklink—at least until he had some idea of who had the server and what was going on. He opened the folder labeled "Kallman" and selected a JPEG with the file name "Turban."

The soldier in the picture was wearing battle fatigues and a white turban and also a big grin, his teeth extra white in his dusty face. If you looked hard, you could see that the soldier in the turban was Robert Kallman, the same Robert Kallman who had to be Velcroed into his wheelchair. One time, Robert told Foster, on his first tour of duty, when they were going door-to-door someplace, they caught a guy by the dangling tail end of his turban as he tried to sneak out a window. Foster was surprised to learn that those turbans they wear are really a long strip of cloth wound around and around and tucked in certain ways. Why would they go to all that trouble?

"Because a turban keeps your head cool," Robert had said, and then he had pulled up this photo. In it, Robert was holding his hands in the air while one of his men pointed a rifle at him, like he was about to shoot Robert, only it wasn't supposed to be Robert but some terrorist in a turban. Foster could feel the hair on the back of his neck stand right up the first time Robert showed him the picture. It was too easy to imagine the other soldier's gun going off and blowing a hole through the middle of Robert Kallman, who wouldn't even have time to wipe the grin off his face before he fell. Foster was very good at picturing calamities. He had taken a test in high school, one of the useless tests the guidance counselors made everybody take. The test confirmed that Foster was a visual person, rather than a verbal one. That was why his grades in English and history and things like that had always been in the toilet.

Foster closed "Turban" and opened another photo. In "R. on Humvee," Robert was posing on the hood of a Humvee that appeared to be made of plywood and sandbags. It was parked in front of what was left of one of those sand-colored, flat-roofed buildings that look like they are made out of dirt. This one had most of its roof caved in and half the walls blown out. Foster's military experience was limited to playing *Call of Duty: Zombies* in the Teen Room at the public library. He liked picturing Lieutenant Kallman in grimy but heroic fatigues, his M16 cradled in his arms, trigger finger at the ready, squinting in the desert sun, as he was doing in this photo, or leading his men from house to house in an old part of Baghdad where the streets were so narrow the sun couldn't reach the darkened doorways.

All the pictures of Robert came from before he was stricken, which is how he always referred to the onset of his condition. ALS had struck him, like lightning—insidious, low-key lightning: a sudden weakness here, a clumsy moment there—while he was still on active duty in Iraq. The

first time it happened, Robert told Foster, he had laughed. He'd *laughed.*
He was bringing a bottle of water to his lips, just getting a sip of water,
and the bottle bumped into his cheek instead—he'd missed his mouth!

"It was like that movie where the pilot has a drinking prrroblem,"
Robert said, enunciating very deliberately. They were alone in the Pondside dining room. Foster had finished clearing all the other tables, and
Robert had finally come to the end of his second piece of pie. It was
more than a year ago, Foster thought, closer to two, back when Robert
could tell a story in his own voice—no eye-tracker or speech device
needed—and Foster could understand every word.

"His drinking prrroblem," Robert had said, "is that he can't ffffind
his mouth."

"That's in *Airplane!*" Foster had said. "My grandpa loved that movie.
He had the video."

When the bottle hit his cheek, Robert said, he had thought of that
movie—the glass smacking against the guy's forehead and the drink running down his face—and he'd laughed. Only then did he notice that
the reason the bottle missed his mouth was that his arm wasn't working right. He barely managed to get the water bottle to the counter. His
arm—both arms? mostly his right—was feeling heavier, slower; it was
losing power, like a car running out of gas. It was enough to make him
sit down and put his hands, suddenly heavy and useless, in his lap. Now
his arms were beginning to ache, too, and he was beginning to feel—not
alarmed, not even terribly concerned, but surprised and puzzled. Something seemed to be happening to him that had never happened before.

And then it went away. Just like that.

The heaviness and the ache were gone. Robert lifted his hands from
his lap and waved them around, then he tried swinging the right one up
to touch his nose with the tip of his finger. Off target the first time but
the second time, right on the nose. That made him laugh again. *Come on,*
he scolded himself. *This is not funny. This is serious business.* Sudden weakness—wasn't that a sign of stroke? He was awfully young for a stroke, at
thirty-two, and his blood pressure and cholesterol were top-notch, but you
never knew. His father had died of a stroke in his late fifties—age fifty-eight,

to be exact. The fact that the sudden weakness in his arms had gone away after only a couple of minutes was reassuring, but there were those *T*-some-things—those temporary strokes. Could it have been one of those?

Robert wasn't sure why he didn't tell anyone. If he had been state-side, or even in Germany, he supposed he would have gone for an MRI, like the time he fell off his bike in Stuttgart. Here, they'd send him to Riyadh. The claustrophobia of an MRI was bad enough when you were sure that everyone in the room was your friend. But here, on the Ara-bian Peninsula?

A week went by, then another, and then it seemed like it would never happen again.

The next few times it happened, he didn't know it, not right away. He tripped, that's all, and while there was plenty to trip over around the bunkers they had repurposed as their forward operating base—chunks of concrete, depressions in the sand, all kinds of crap—when he looked back to see what he might have caught his foot on, there was no obvious culprit. Only later, answering the doctor's questions and thinking about this sudden clumsiness that had the CO calling him Twinkletoes, did he learn that tripping over your own feet was not always a joke, that sometimes it was a condition known as *footdrop*—a persistent difficulty in lifting the toes and the front of the foot. Some-times it was a symptom of a disease more terrible than anything Robert could have imagined.

The next time it happened, he knew it all right. It was a good thing he'd always been extra conscientious about the safety on his M16. When the rifle butt hit the ground, he hardly flinched. Nobody even saw him drop it, he caught it so fast with the other hand, or if anybody did, they were all too busy climbing into their vehicles to give him any shit about it. This time, it was more like numbness than weakness, or maybe a combination of the two, but the problem was, this time it didn't go away. The supply convoy was moving out at 0600, and his team was in the escort. He climbed in. He was the driver of the lead Humvee; they were ready to move out, one huge tanker truck at a time, and all of a sudden, Robert couldn't keep his right hand on the wheel.

Mahoney, at the computer in the seat beside him, noticed this. "Robo," he said. "What's with your hand?"

"I don't know." They both watched Robert's fingers slide off the steering wheel a second time. His right hand floated, numbly, to his lap. To get it back up, he gave it an assist with his other hand. He tried to curl the fingers around the wheel.

They could hear the giant tanker truck engines warming up and the Humvees growling their throaty growl, a threatening don't-mess-with-me sound played against the trucks' deeper rumble.

"You can't drive like that," Mahoney said. He was truck commander today, which meant he was riding shotgun with the computer on his lap. Robert was driving. Except for the gunner, the driver sat in the most precarious position their team's Humvee had to offer. This was a 2003 vintage Humvee, still trucking in April 2005, wearing a lot of plywood and sandbags for armor. Because the driver needed room to move his feet, and because the steering wheel had to clear his knees, the driver had the thinnest layer of sandbags under his seat and none at all—only a piece of three-quarter-inch plywood—under his feet on the floor. On the plus side, the driver was the least cramped, most freely mobile man in the vehicle, but if an IED exploded directly under the driver's seat, the odds of his survival were not good. Even the gunner, in his sand-bagged turret-nook, had a better chance in the event of an IED. As team leader, Robert Kallman had made the assignments; he was the driver, and now his hand refused to grip the wheel.

"We better switch," Mahoney said, and after the smallest of hesitations, with the tanker trucks and Humvees roaring up such a racket it was almost impossible to think, Robert agreed. In seconds, he and Mahoney had hopped out of their respective sides of the Humvee, run around the front of it, and hopped back in.

"What the fuck are you doing?" somebody on the ground yelled. Mahoney stuck his arm out the driver's-side window and flipped him off.

This was the moment that plagued Robert afterward, when his numb arm was getting stitched up and the doctors, first in Riyadh, then in Virginia, and finally back in Iowa, were listening with interest as he listed the times he had dropped something or missed the mark or inexplicably tripped. They were testing him for a variety of possible neurological disorders, a list that at first seemed endless—he was smart, they said, to suspect a stroke—and then began to narrow relentlessly. No, it wasn't a stroke. It wasn't MS. It wasn't a tumor.

They weren't a hundred yards out on the highway when an IED exploded directly under the driver's seat. It blew Mahoney's face off, and most of his right hand, and his legs, below the knee.

Robert didn't see or hear a thing. He flew out of the truck commander's side of the Humvee, propelled as if by a great and invisible hand. When he could breathe again, he picked himself up and stumbled around to where guys from the squad's Bravo team had pulled what they thought was Robert's bloody, faceless body out of the driver's side. There was the terrible moment when they all looked up in horror and confusion from mangled Robo on the ground to Robo standing dazed and bleeding beside the Humvee. Somehow those seconds of grisly confusion made everything, already unspeakably horrifying, so much worse. "It's Mahoney!" Keith the gunner boy cried when he understood. "You switched places—it's Mahoney!" And he began to curse and sob, as if a terrible trick had been played on him.

Robert had told this story to Foster in a voice that slowed and grew more labored as he grew tired, giving Foster all the time in the world to see and hear the scene unfold in even more vivid detail than Robert himself could have reported. It was not the blood and gore that bothered Foster. It was Keith the gunner, the way his outrage suggested that the other man's death would be the greater loss, Robert's survival a dirty trick. Robert tried to explain that wasn't what Keith meant—the dirty trick was the surprise, the adjustment everyone had begun to make even before their ears had stopped ringing suddenly overturned, the suspicion that they could be fooled at any time, and also, the reminder that another man's death could so easily have been their own.

For Robert, the dirty trick was something else altogether, something much more specific, and, at the time, unforeseeable. It was not only the trading of another man's future, as it were, for his own. It was knowing,

Robert said, as time went on, that the other man had paid such a price for nothing, for worse than nothing. He had paid it so that Robert could wind up like *this*. What Robert came to regret most about switching places in the Humvee, he told Foster, word by slowly enunciated word, was the loss of that opportunity to go out in a blaze of—"maybe not glorrry," Robert would say, his sluggish tongue and soft palate working hard on the *r*, "but not, at least, as a two-perrrrson assist to the can."

# CHAPTER 4

Dakota Engelhart, Certified Nursing Assistant, worked odd shifts—some weekdays, some nights, some weekends—to accommodate his classes at the university, where he was a senior. He was still officially premed, although he'd already broken the news of his decision to Erika. She had not taken it well. "Did you tell your dad?" she asked him in the same sharp tone that she might have said, *Are you happy now that you've ruined our lives?*

Dakota spent Thursday at home in Marengo, talking to his parents, so he'd missed all the excitement at Pondside Manor that morning. By the time he arrived for work on Friday afternoon, the only signs of the previous day's trouble were the grid of muddy tire tracks in the parking lot and a lone police car out front. He parked his ancient Nissan around the back of the building, per the administrator's instructions, so that visitors wouldn't have their first impression marred by the rust bucket his father had sold him for a dollar the summer after he graduated from high school. ("You can upgrade when you get your MD," Dad had said.) When Dakota spotted a pair of first-shift CNAs coming out of the building—which meant that he was late again—he waved them down, nodded toward the police car, and asked, "What's going on?"

For Dakota, the worst part of the news was James Witkowski. He had intended to *apologize* to Witkowski today for Wednesday night's shower. Sure, Dakota had a lot of things on his mind that night, but that was no excuse. *Why* did he let the old guy get to him? Witkowski had asked him the same irritating question, in his trebly old-guy voice, at least a dozen times before.

"What the hell kind of name is Dakota?"

Dakota had said, "James, could you please sit down?"

"I mean, it's fine for an Indian tribe. Or a place, like South Dakota. But what kind of name is it for a carrottop like you?"

"James, I can't turn the water on until you sit down."

"I mean, are you some kind of hippie? Seems like the kind of name a hippie might like."

"You'd have to talk to my parents about that," Dakota had said, and then, because James's bony bare butt had finally made contact with the white plastic seat, Dakota turned the water on, full force, and, he would have to admit when Amelia Ramirez came to see what all the racket was about, somewhat cooler than James was used to.

Less than twelve hours after that last shower, the old guy was dead, having expired, apparently—or at least possibly—while trying to get help for someone in worse shape than he was, someone he didn't even like. If James Witkowski had set out deliberately to make Dakota—and all the other staff members he had spent the last few years of his life annoying—feel guilty about their lack of generosity and patience for an old man with little more to look forward to than a few hours of fishing once or twice a week and a nice hot shower every other day, he couldn't have picked a better way to do it.

Dakota confessed every damning detail of James Witkowski's last shower to the pair of cops in the conference room who had returned specifically to question him, Dakota being the last person known to have spoken to Witkowski. ("I was?" he said and felt even worse.) When Dakota repeated for the third or fourth time that he couldn't remember ever feeling worse about anything in his life than he felt about Witkowski's last shower, one of the officers, an older woman, told him he should consider himself lucky in that case. She asked him if he knew of any bad feeling between James Witkowski and Robert Kallman. Dakota thought for a moment and told her no. James seemed to dislike everybody about equally.

After the police were finished with him, Dakota had nowhere to turn with his burden of guilt. He couldn't tell Erika how bad he felt, not only because they were taking a little break, he and Erika, but because he knew that she would agree with the policewoman. Erika would say something like, "You work in a nursing home, Dakota. People are going to die on you." She would say this gently, reasonably, meaning to console him but also to suggest that it was something he had to get used to, people dying on a regular basis, people he knew by name. He passed the nurses' station on the way to his locker, and Tori, the first-shift RN, waved him over. "More good news for you, Dakota," she said. "You've got Mary McIntyre today."

"What do you mean, I've got Mary McIntyre?"

"We're taking turns," she said, hanging a clipboard on the meds cart.

Mary McIntyre had been at Pondside Manor for less than a week, and already she was legendary. When Dakota came to work on Monday, which was her first full day on the premises, Mary McIntyre was sitting on one of the seldom-used couches in the atrium, weeping, begging her daughter—who was sitting beside her, also weeping—to take her home. The poor old lady looked harmless, even (deceptively) frail, but at the nurses' station, Tori was warning the oncoming shift of CNAs about her. "Among other things," Tori said, consulting a fat spiral binder on the counter, "she pulled out a total of six IVs during her last five days in the hospital. Also, it took three nurses and an aide singing 'You Are My Sunshine' to make her put down the portable heart monitor she yanked off and was trying to use on the nurse's aide like a—" Tori hesitated. She looked up from the page. "What's a cat-o-nine-tails?"

That night, when the CNAs tried to give her a shower, Mary McIntyre had grabbed the showerhead with both hands, lifted her feet up off the floor, and pulled the shower right out of the wall. She spent Tuesday and most of Wednesday zonked out, although she did manage to sweep a bowl of pureed spaghetti off the table and onto James Witkowski at dinnertime on Wednesday. (*That was the old guy's last meal, too*, Dakota realized.) And then, Tori told him, the police found Mary wandering around among the emergency vehicles and personnel in the parking lot yesterday morning.

"Nobody knows how she got out of the building," Tori said. She pushed the meds cart past the counter. "Don't let her out of your sight."

Dakota found Mary in Arts and Crafts, the last one left at the long table, her head bowed over a heap of Popsicle sticks. It looked like she was zonked again. "She's all yours," Stephanie, the activities director, said. Dakota wheeled Mary out to the lounge area between the nurses' station and the supply closet and parked her in front of the TV. "Well, Miss Mary," he said, crouching in front of her bowed head, "what do you think? Game shows or MeTV?" She had no opinion. He aimed the remote. "All right," he said. "*I Dream of Jeannie* it is."

He was lining up towels on the cart they called the Shower Tower, hoping that the CNA who was missing from this shift hadn't decided to quit, when somebody spoke up behind him.

"I wonder if my daughter knows I'm here."

Dakota turned around. He was looking at the back of a wheelchair topped by a fluffy gray head and narrow shoulders. He put down the towel he was folding and turned the chair around by one handle. "Mary!" he said. "You're back!"

She lifted her head and drew a bead on him with her eyes. "Are you a doctor?"

"No, ma'am."

"You look like one. You got doctor clothes."

"Oh—everybody around here wears scrubs."

"All trying to look like doctors," she grumbled.

"Ma'am," Dakota said, "you may have something there." He reminded himself that this was the same wisp of a woman who had pulled the showerhead out of the wall the other night.

"This is a nursing home, isn't it?"

"Yes, it is." He was sorry to have said it, she looked so sad. "Can I get you something? Are you hungry?"

"I'm always hungry."

"Well," he said, "we can take care of that! Do you like pudding?"

"It's okay. Not chocolate."

"Not chocolate—got it. I'm going to go get the pudding. Don't go anywhere. Wait right here."

Dakota ran to the storeroom, which he hoped somebody had left unlocked so he wouldn't have to wait for the nurse to bring the key. *Let there be vanilla*, he thought as he pulled open the refrigerator door. *Aha*. There was nothing *but* vanilla, except for one lonely banana flavor. Everyone else wanted chocolate. He snatched a vanilla and the banana and hurried back down to the nurses' station, half expecting that Mary would be gone—either physically gone, wheelchair and all, or shut down again, with her head bowed low—but no, there she was, sitting calmly with her hands folded in her lap and her face looking—well, at least not scared and not vacant either. He wished there were someone around to witness this side of Mary McIntyre—not wild, not weeping, not semicomatose—that no one here had seen before, as far as he knew. Not that moments of lucidity were unknown in dementia patients, but this was a transformation you had to see to believe.

"Here we go!" Dakota said cheerfully. "I brought two flavors for you to pick from."

"Thank you," she said. "Where's the spoon?"

He had forgotten a spoon.

"Well," she said, "can I just use one of those?" She pointed to a quart-sized cup prickly with white plastic spoons on the meds cart in the middle of the nurses' station.

"You sure can," Dakota said. He watched her work on opening the pudding and when she had trouble, he said, "May I?" and peeled the top off for her.

"Thank you," she said again and smiled at him, which made him wonder if he could get her teeth brushed. First, though, he had to show her to somebody so they would believe him when he said how polite and cooperative she was. After she finished the second pudding, which she had gotten open on her own, Dakota asked her if she wouldn't like to see the library.

"I guess," she said without much enthusiasm. She allowed him to turn the chair in that direction and told him, "I already read all the books."

Not thinking, Dakota laughed. "I don't think you've been here long enough quite yet to read them all!"

"I said I did."

Things went downhill from there. Not that Mary McIntyre went berserk on him or anything, but he could feel her slipping away from his grasp. When they got to the library, she looked around nervously. Somewhere in the world a baseball game was being played, doing its best to fill the quiet room with the usual crack of the bat and roar of the crowd. Three wheelchairs were arranged in front of the large-screen TV, their occupants dozing. The only other person in the room was Laverne Slatchek, who was in her middle eighties but sharp as a tack, as she'd be the first to tell you.

Laverne was sitting at the best of three aging PCs in the Computer Corner, looking despondent. She was making slow circles on the tabletop with the mouse, watching the little arrow make corresponding circles on the screen, which had a picture of the activities director's pit bull on it. In spite of the babushka on its head, the dog appeared to be smiling—as pit bulls do. Laverne sat up straight when she saw Dakota rolling Mary into the room.

"Ha!" she said, getting to her feet with surprising ease, Dakota thought. She looked like a white-haired deejay or an air traffic controller with those big headphones curled around her neck. "Finally!" she said. "I was beginning to think there was nobody left but me and the zombies." She nodded toward the trio facing the television. "I need help." Although she had been approaching Dakota, Laverne backed up a little when he aimed Mary McIntyre's wheelchair in her direction. "Is this the one who broke the shower?" she asked warily.

Dakota said, "Laverne, this is Mary McIntyre. Mary, Laverne."

It was a nice try, but Mary's politeness had disappeared. She was wringing her hands together, craning her neck to look around. Laverne didn't seem very interested in social niceties herself. "I need help," she repeated.

"What's up?" Dakota asked lightly.

"I can't find my condo."

Dakota didn't know what to say to that. He would have to let the RN know that Laverne Slatchek, smart and cocky Laverne, might need a neurological reevaluation. He was about to remind her, gently, that her room was in Boysenberry Boulevard, that she was a resident of Pondside Manor. Nobody had a condo here.

"*Pondside* isn't working," Laverne told him earnestly. "The ducklink is down. You can't get *in*."

Perhaps she'd had a stroke. She threw her hands in the air—both hands, he noted. She wasn't favoring one side over the other.

"Oh, never mind," she said, pulling the headphones off entirely. "I can see you don't know anything."

She left the library without looking back or turning off the computer, which, also, was not like her at all. She'd left her walker, too, Dakota saw, and he ran to the door to call her back. She was holding the built-in handrail as she scurried down Iowa Avenue, so he let her go. The television roared.

"Get me out of here!" Mary McIntyre suggested vehemently.

Dakota was happy to oblige.

That night, Laverne lay wide awake in her bed. The light in the courtyard outside her window seeped through the blinds, even though she had pulled them shut as tight as she could, and the bright glow of the corridor leaked into the room from under the door. What was worse, she could feel the memory of whatever unpleasant thought had awakened her hovering in the corners of her mind, threatening to make itself known.

There had been a time in Laverne Slatchek's life when she had to resort to all kinds of strange tactics—shaking her head or humming a song or babbling some nonsense—to drive away an unpleasant thought, which is to say, to *keep* herself from remembering it. What a struggle it used to be to put out of her mind the way she'd sighed dramatically before answering some poor student's question, or to forget some smart-alecky thing her son said to her, or to stop thinking—this was the worst one—about the very last time Bill called her at school to remind her to get home early because a full harvest moon would be rising at dusk. Bill kept track of such things. If it weren't for him, Laverne might have gone to her grave without ever seeing a full moon rise, huge and red as a tomato on the horizon. She had lost track of time that evening, putting the finishing touches on her Meiosis vs. Mitosis bulletin board for an upcoming unit on the Life of the Cell. When she finally got home, the darkened living room was bathed in silver moonlight. "Never mind," Bill had whispered. "Other moons will rise."

It used to take her breath away every time she remembered it.

Now, though, now that remembering required considerable concentration and forethought, *forgetting* things had gotten easier and easier to do. These days, Laverne had no trouble forgetting just about anything—including unpleasant or inconvenient things. She'd gotten really good at it, in fact. So it was especially annoying to wake up in the middle of the night and find that her encounter with Mary McWhatsit in the library had reminded Laverne of something she would have preferred to continue to forget. It was something she had seen earlier in the week and hadn't mentioned to anyone, not even when the administrator—Lovelace? No, that wasn't it—had encouraged them to speak to the police officers if they had anything at all to share about poor Robert, who had Lou Gehrig's disease, and now on top of that, had drowned in the pond.

One thing Laverne had seen but hadn't said anything about (because it was really none of her business) was Robert talking to the new girl in the atrium lounge on Monday night. She was sitting on the couch in there, where nobody ever sat, crying a blue streak about how she couldn't find her baby. It was the poor woman's first day at Pondside and her daughter had finally gone on home. Robert had rolled his motorized wheelchair right up to that couch and sat there making noise just like he was talking to her. Laverne never could understand anything poor Robert said unless he used his robot voice, but the new girl acted as if she understood whatever he was trying to say, nodding her head at him and taking a Kleenex from the box attached to the arm of his wheelchair, which she seemed to find interesting—the wheelchair, not the Kleenex. She stood up and took hold of the handles for a moment when he turned the chair, and Laverne thought she looked disappointed when it rolled away without her.

Plenty of other people must have seen Robert talking to the new girl, so Laverne didn't feel too guilty about not mentioning *that* to the police.

But the next day—or maybe it was the day after that—here comes poor Robert's mother to have breakfast with him, as usual, and she's brought along a doll, a life-sized baby doll wearing a pink dress and bonnet and looking all cozy in a basket like a little bed. Laverne just happened to be coming out of her room for breakfast at the time, and although Robert's mother, who was hurrying down Boysenberry Boulevard with the basket on her arm, didn't seem especially glad to see anybody, she had said, "Good morning, Laverne." (Robert's mother knew everybody's name, despite her own advanced age.) At first, she had switched the basket to her other arm, as if hoping that Laverne wouldn't see what was in it. Then, she seemed to change her mind about hiding the doll. In fact, she stepped closer to Laverne, tipping the basket to show her, and said, in a confidential tone, "It's for the new resident—Mary? Robert thought it might help her through this difficult time, getting used to things, you know." Laverne didn't doubt Mrs. Kallman's (or Robert's) good intentions, and they had been known to give presents to people before—the whole *World of Pondside* was a present from Robert!—and yet Laverne was uncertain about the wisdom of giving a doll like this to Mary McWhatsername. The poor woman had been crying because she couldn't find her baby. Wouldn't the doll be as likely to keep reminding her of what she'd lost as it would be to console her? Of course, there was no way to say all that to Mrs. Kallman, who had already patted Laverne's arm and was scooting across the hall into her son's room.

The very next day—no, it was the day after that—Robert had drowned in the pond. Laverne had neither seen the doll nor heard a word about it since. And Laverne was a good listener. In the past few days, she'd heard a lot of things—like those two nurses talking about how they wished the police would just leave everyone alone and call poor

Robert's death a suicide, which the one with blond hair thought it obviously was. Laverne had listened to the two of them, especially, thinking they might have something to say about finding a baby doll in a pink dress and bonnet somewhere—maybe out in the parking lot (if Mary McSomething had taken it with her when she went wandering around outside) or in the pond or even in Robert's room, where it still could be if Mrs. Kallman never got a chance to give it to Mary at all. Sadly, Robert's room was all locked up now so Laverne couldn't take a look herself. (She had peeked, only peeked, into Mary's room.) Laverne was beginning to feel as if she had *imagined* the doll, and you can be sure that she had no intention of drawing anyone's attention to *that* possibility. It was really none of her business anyway. It was none of her business at all.

Laverne squinted at the bedside clock with the extra-large display that Joseph and his wife gave her last Mother's Day. (Never mind that she already had a clock—the kind with hands—on the wall above her TV.) The numbers glowed, red and menacing, from the nightstand: 2:27. Hours remained before Laverne could reasonably get up and start the day. She raised her head, flipped the pillow over to the cool side, then laid her head back down. There was nothing to do, she thought, but try to fall asleep and hope that all would be forgotten in the morning.

When Mary McIntyre woke up that night, she found herself in a strange bed in a strange room. She knew it wasn't the squealing that woke her because the squealing had only started after she got out of the bed. If she had been at home, in the bed with her sister, she would have thought it was somebody killing a hog for Christmas—but here, wherever "here" was, she wasn't sure what to make of it.

She did her best to ignore the noise as she dragged herself through semidarkness toward a doorway filled with light. On the other side of the doorway was—a bathroom? Since when was there a bathroom in the house? Daddy had tried to talk the landlord into putting an indoor toilet and a bathtub in the mudroom of this old place when they first moved in—there was already a water pipe in the wall for the kitchen sink—but Mr. Johnson said if Daddy wanted an indoor toilet he was just going to have to pay for it himself. "And the minute I do," Daddy said whenever Momma or one of the girls brought up the subject of the bathroom again, "then that old son of a gun will be raising the rent on us on account we live in a place with a inside bathroom!" That had always been Daddy's last word on the subject. And yet here it was: a bathroom. No bathtub in it, but a nice, new-looking toilet and a sink with a mirror. Either Daddy had changed his mind or she was someplace else entirely. That was it, wasn't it? She wasn't home at all. Wherever she was, she was glad to have the facilities so close at hand, although it took a while to find the button on the top for flushing the fancy toilet.

Afterward, she enjoyed washing her hands thoroughly in the lovely warm running water. Then she rested for a moment, supporting herself by holding onto the sink, and that's when she looked up to find an old woman giving her a frightened look. What she'd thought was a mirror above the sink wasn't a mirror at all—it was a window! Mary let go of the sink and stepped back. She moved to the doorway, watching fearfully over her shoulder as the old woman stepped away from her window, too. Mary climbed back into bed before anything else could happen. She pulled the covers over her head and waited, with her eyes squeezed shut, for that hog to stop squealing. Finally, it did.

# CHAPTER 5

"Okay," Jenny said when Foster returned to work on Saturday, "now you look like you come from the land of the living."

On Friday, she'd told him to go home. "Boss told me you weren't coming in today," she said. "Don't you never check your phone?" He'd flipped his dumb phone open and there was the message. In what was either an unexpected show of understanding or—more likely—a calculated move to get him out of the way of residents and their loved ones and the local reporter, Administrator Landiss had given him Friday off. A personal leave day. He'd slipped down Boysenberry Boulevard on his way out of the building and found Robert Kallman's door closed and locked. Foster wondered if he was the only one who knew the laptop was missing. Apart from whoever took it. He had one heart-stopping moment when it occurred to him that Robert might have taken the laptop with him down to the pond—the mud was at least ankle-deep on the bottom—but he found he couldn't picture Robert doing any such thing.

Foster spent most of his personal leave day on his bike. He cruised multiple times past the big house on Summit Street where Mrs. Kallman lived all alone, although he supposed she might have visitors to keep her company at a time like this. Robert had called the house a

*Victorian monstrosity*, but Foster thought it was pretty cool. One front corner of the house was a stack of three round rooms with curved glass windows, one on top of the other, from the ground floor to the attic, with a witch's hat of a roof on top. Foster wondered what it would have been like to live in a house where you could hide out, flee to, and sleep in a room with no corners, dark or otherwise. He also wondered if—in fact, he hoped that—someone else had already given the laptop to Mrs. Kallman, even though that might mean he would never again set foot in the *World of Pondside*. Virtually speaking.

He was shoving his hair under the elastic band of a new paper cap on Saturday, when he became aware of a wavery figure reflected in the gleaming stainless steel refrigerator door, someone all in black coming up behind him. Foster's heart rose in his throat until he saw that it was only Administrator Landiss. He considered pretending not to know she was there. Instead, he turned around.

"The police want to talk to you, Foster," Landiss said, and added, "again." She looked over the menu notes scrawled on the whiteboard by the milk machine. The last item on the list was still "R. Kallman. Pureed: NEW!" She reached for the eraser, then set it down again, as if having second thoughts. "Now, please," she said briskly, and just as briskly left, the double doors swinging behind her.

Jenny, who was peeling brown-skinned bananas on the butcher block, said, "Take that thing off your head before you go."

Foster glanced at her. Jenny wore her salt-and-pepper hair in tiny braids that peeked out here and there from under her paper cap. Foster's hair was an unkempt wilderness by comparison. He pulled off the cap and stuck it in his back pocket.

A pair of detectives were conducting another round of interviews in the conference room, where Landiss usually met with the sons and daughters of prospective residents—a homey room where they could sit at a polished oak table in the sunny window bay. These two detectives looked much younger than the ones who had questioned Foster on Thursday. *Junior detectives probably got stuck working weekends*, Foster thought. They were dressed up for the occasion in business suits and heels (on her) and a tie (on him), like Scully and Mulder on *The X-Files,* every episode of which Foster had seen at least twice.

He wondered if there was some rule for cops about gender, like you had to have two on hand to ask questions behind closed doors. The girl cop was sitting at the sunny table with a legal pad in front of her and a pen in hand. The boy cop, who had opened the door, led the way to the table and pulled out a chair. Foster sat down. He reminded himself that there was no reason for anyone to think that he had taken the laptop out of Robert's room. The girl cop introduced herself as Officer Zowalke, it sounded like, and the boy cop as Brooks. With a minimum of prompting, Foster stated his name and his job at Pondside. "Kitchen boy," he said. "And feeder."

The girl cop consulted a sheaf of papers on the table next to her legal pad. "It says here that you are a dietary aide."

"I was just breaking the job down into its two major parts."

"I see. Thank you." She looked at Foster. "You work in the kitchen with Ms. Williams—Jennifer Williams—is that correct?"

Foster nodded, hiding his surprise. What did Jenny have to do with anything?

"Looking over our notes we found a mention by Ms. Williams that you seemed concerned about Mr. Kallman on Thursday morning, shortly before the body was discovered. Specifically, she said"—she had been shuffling papers and now she stopped and read—"'I could tell Foster was feeling bad about his friend Robert.' When we looked through your earlier statement, we didn't find any use of the word *friend,* and so we just wanted to check with you and see if you were in agreement with Ms. Williams's choice of words. Were you a friend of Mr. Kallman, would you say?"

"Yes."

"Did you know Mr. Kallman before he was a resident at Pondside?"

"No."

"It says here, in Ms. Williams's statement, that you felt Mr. Kallman had reason to be despondent in the hours, or perhaps the day, preceding his death."

"Jenny said that?"

"Yes, she did." The girl cop waited, and when Foster didn't say anything more, she asked, "Was there a particular reason for Mr. Kallman to be despondent? Had he mentioned something to you?"

For a second, Foster could only look at the woman across the table, with her pen poised above the legal pad. "The man had ALS," he said finally. "He lives—lived—in a nursing home."

The girl cop leaned ever so slightly toward his side of the table and tried to sound sympathetic. "But he had been a resident at Pondside for more than two years, and his diagnosis was something he'd known, I believe, since 2006." She smiled, sort of, doing her best to look as if she cared.

All of a sudden, Foster knew exactly what kind of girl this cop was. He sat near someone like her on the bus from Wisconsin one time. He had gone there to visit his grandfather, the only living family member who remained on speaking terms with him after he dropped out of high school. The girl on the bus was in the window seat across the aisle and she kept leaning toward him, over her backpack and things, to ask if he needed something for that cough of his—she had drops, if he wanted one, and even some cold medicine, etc., etc. He had finally taken a cough drop. She shook it out of the bag into his hand and smiled so happily that he began to think she was actually a nice person. But when a pile of people got on the bus in Chicago and he tried to sit next to her so this lady and her kid could have his seat, oh no. She needed the aisle seat for her backpack and computer and every other goddamn thing. He had given up his window seat for nothing and ended up sitting on the aisle next to a big guy who really needed a seat and a half, all the way to Des Moines.

The girl cop pretended to consult the sheaf of papers she was shuffling. "There was something in particular that morning," she continued, "a change in Mr. Kallman's condition, evidenced by his diet. Let's see, who told us about that?"

"Probably the speech therapist. They put him on pureed."

She looked up from the papers, interested. Concerned. "And the significance of that—"

"The *significance* is, they just downgraded him to pureed food."
What else was there to say? She kept looking at him, though, as if he
was supposed to keep talking. Suddenly, Foster felt like slapping the look
of concern right off the carefully arranged features of her prom queen
face. That would probably be a felony, to slap her. Maybe she would
shoot him. (If she had a gun, he didn't know where it was.) Or maybe
her partner would. Foster had never in his life wanted to do something
that would make somebody else—somebody right there in the room—
possibly likely to shoot him. He was surprised by how it made him feel.
Not powerful, exactly, but—significant.

He said, "The *significance* is that ALS is a disease where you deteri-
orate over time. Once you lose something, you don't get it back. Robert
already had trouble with talking and eating, and now it was taking him
so long to chew and swallow that they put him on *pureed*. Did you ever
see a pureed salad? Green mush. Pureed lasagna? Orange glop. It's baby
food, is what it is. Oh, they'll say it was for *his* benefit, because of the
choking hazard and pneumonia and calories consumed versus calories
spent, but Robert already signed a waiver about the risks—which you
can do, sign a waiver—and he didn't mind sitting in the dining room,
chewing, for as long as it took. The man loved to eat." To his horror,
Foster heard his voice rise sharply on the word *eat*. His nose prickled
and his eyes burned. This was not where he meant to go at all!

He called up a great surge of anger to staunch the tears and aimed
it right at the girl cop, sending her a look that stopped her hand from
reaching sympathetically across the table, stopped it in midair and lowered it, lamely, to the oak veneer. She wrapped things up by asking if
there was anything Foster wanted to say about Robert Kallman's relationship to the other deceased, James Witkowski.

"What relationship?" Foster said scornfully. "They probably didn't
even know each other's name." The truth was that Robert had spoken
more than once about making a *World of Pondside* portal for Witkowski so the old guy could fish year-round instead of acting like an asshole
all winter.

Foster felt a little thrill, lying to the police.

Back out in the hall, he realized what it was all about, this second round of interviews. How could he be so dense? He had played right into their hands, so to speak. "Wait!" he said aloud, causing Edith Cole, who was trucking past on her usual morning tour, to look up sharply from the collection of stuffed animals in the basket attached to her walker. "They think Robert committed *suicide*? No way," said Foster to the question-mark curve of Edith's rapidly retreating back. *No way, no way, no way.*

He was back in the kitchen, stuffing his hair under the paper cap, before it occurred to him that neither cop had said a word about the laptop missing from Robert's room. *They don't even know,* he thought. *Stupid, stupid cops.*

Back at the oversize desk in her office, Kitty Landiss—chief administrator of Pondside Manor, a locally franchised entity of Simply the Best Care, Inc.—lifted the silvery lid of her laptop as if it were a jewelry box and pressed the button to power it on. She wished she had sent someone else to fetch Foster Kresowik for the police interviews. It was particularly annoying that scrawny, unkempt Foster had put himself in the limelight by discovering the body in the pond and plunging into the water as if he could rescue the guy, making such a scene about it. Kitty Landiss hated encountering Foster, with his ratty hair and scraggly goatee, and usually took care that their paths wouldn't cross any more than they had to. In fact, she would have liked to fire him, if only they were not so seriously understaffed. She kept a list of his infractions, like using foul language and smoking within sight of the building, for the day when she could let him go. The real reason she disliked the sight of him was not on her list.

Foster Kresowik was the only current employee (apart from Kitty Landiss herself and the physical therapist, Ruth von Maur) who had worked at Pondside when it first opened eight years ago. He had been a boy back then, one of several hastily trained youngsters, the majority still in or just out of high school, who made up most of the staff of the newly opened Pondside Manor. Kitty Landiss, who had been hired as activities director, was one of the few whose education and training (an MSW from the state university) matched up even remotely with their job descriptions. Somebody at the SBC corporate office had turned a blind eye to the attempts of the first Pondside administrator to open the doors of a brand-new facility on the shoestring budget the bottom line required, and when staffing violations came to light, they fired him and closed up shop to reorganize. Three years later, corporate recruited former employee Kitty Landiss, luring her away from a low-to-mid-level position at a nearby hospital, to be chief administrator of the new and improved Pondside Manor.

Kitty had gone through some changes herself by then. These included an expensive wedding paid for by herself, one year of ignorant bliss with an insurance salesman who claimed to love her just the way she was, two years of heartbreaking deceptions and infidelities on his part (he wasn't even a real insurance salesman!), a rigorous weight-loss program that she hoped would save her marriage, and finally, a no-fault divorce that left him with the Lexus and the condo she never wanted to set foot in again. The divorce left *her*, she liked to say, with a whole new self—slimmer, stronger, smarter than before.

Understandably, her new self did not wish to be reminded of her old self. Foster Kresowik always looked at her with a kind of sneer that made her recall dumb things her old self had done, the worst of which was a Christmas Eve at the original Pondside Manor, after the party was over and the residents put to bed, when she kept pouring rum and Cokes for herself and the skinny kid with all the hair (no goatee then), not even noticing that the rest of the staff had gone back to work or home to their loved ones. She kept pouring her lonely heart out, along with the rum, to a kid who probably couldn't believe his good fortune: free alcohol and female flesh, both available in such abundant quantity. He was (just) eighteen, thank God, and probably weighed a hundred and twenty pounds. She was thirty-four and close to her top weight of a hundred and ninety. When he passed out, she hoisted him into a wheelchair and rolled him to an empty room on Boysenberry Boulevard, where she sat with him all night to make sure he didn't puke and die. Merry Christmas.

Today, at the age of forty-three, Kitty stood five foot five-and-a-half and wore a mere size ten. If she was willing to pay for an upscale label (or if she got lucky at her favorite resale), she could find herself an eight or even a six that worked in certain styles. Like the pencil skirt she was wearing today. She smoothed the black linen-cotton blend over her thighs and pulled the bandless waist up. The skirt was an Eileen Fisher, size small—take *that* all you store-brand mediums!—and she looked good in it, especially standing up.

Kitty watched her index finger make lazy circles on the trackpad of her laptop. It was her own personal machine. On the screen, the cursor arrow roamed, now aimlessly, now in a melancholy circle around the little yellow duck located dead center on her desktop. In her *World of Pondside* portal, Katherine Landiss was a top-dog fashionista, like Meryl Streep in *The Devil Wears Prada*. She spent her days in size-zero designer outfits, trying on clothes and ordering people to bring her skinny lattes. The *skinny* part of the skinny lattes was just for show, though, because the best thing about *The World of Pondside* was that size-zero Katherine Landiss could eat as much of anything she wanted as often as she liked there.

It seemed like a particularly cruel twist of fate that the ducklink was down and she couldn't slip into *The World of Pondside* today, when she needed it most, with all of the terrible business going on about Robert Kallman, with the corporate office and the DIA inspectors and the LTC ombudsman *and* the police department all breathing down her neck. Everybody wanted to know how two residents could have left the building in the wee hours of the morning—or at any time, for that matter—without anyone being aware that they were gone. If Kitty could calm her nerves with a latte at the brasserie on the ground floor of her ritzy Manhattan office building, she wouldn't need to have one here, she thought, as she reached for her steaming carry-out cup.

# CHAPTER 6

According to the handwritten note on cream-colored stationery that appeared on the Things-To-Do bulletin board at Pondside Manor, a funeral service for Robert Kallman would take place on Monday at ten a.m. in the Forest Park Chapel at Englert & Sons Funeral Home. There would be a visitation Sunday evening, the note said, starting at five o'clock.

Foster, who saw the note after breakfast on Sunday, had been to only one other funeral in his life. He was too young to travel alone to his grandmother's funeral back in Wisconsin, and by the time his grandfather died years later, Foster had lost touch with the boy who used to play cribbage and chess with Gramps on the porch. The one funeral Foster had attended was for one of his former classmates, the kid who drowned the summer before senior year. Foster had been kicked out of high school—well, all right, suspended—for vandalizing that very kid's locker when they were juniors. The kid had made a career out of mocking Foster for pronouncing words correctly in French class that year. It was the only class in which Foster participated with some regularity, mostly out of sympathy for the teacher, a young woman from what she called "francophone Africa," which was pretty cool in itself; plus, she was the only teacher in the school who actually appeared to know something that was, at least potentially, interesting.

Somehow, one day, *fumer* had set the kid and his friends to trailing after Foster all afternoon pretending to puff on pens and pencils which they held between thumb and forefinger in a manner they considered to be *très français* and thus, in all their asshole stupidity, "gay." All Foster did to the kid's locker was blow smoke—a half pack of cigarettes' worth of smoke—into the vents on the door, the opening edges of which he had meticulously caulked shut beforehand to seal the smoke in. Foster nearly passed out doing it. He was hoping that a cloud of smoke would poof out of the locker when the kid finally got it open—that was the special effect that he was going for—but the smoke had dissipated, a lot of it absorbed by the asshole's clothes, including a cashmere coat that belonged to the kid's father. Foster's suspension was supposed to be temporary, but he never went back.

A year later the kid was dead, after a long day of drinking and tubing on the Peshtigo River up north—an informal class trip planned by the popular kids to celebrate their new status as seniors. Foster saw the story in the paper. He couldn't help but notice that not one of them got thrown out of school, or even suspended, for bringing the booze that made the kid pass out and slip right through the middle of his inner tube. It occurred to Foster at the time that they would have gotten in a lot more trouble if there had been no tragedy, if the kid *hadn't* drowned. They all might have been suspended for that "class trip" instead of being interviewed on the local news about the prayer vigils they had organized at the hospital while the kid was in the ICU. He was brain-dead for a while before they pulled the plug on him. Pretty much the whole school had attended the asshole's funeral. The line of people—surely some of them were merely curious like himself, Foster thought, rather than feeling bereaved—stretched from the funeral home entrance to one-and-a-half times around the block.

Foster wasn't sure he wanted to attend Robert's funeral visitation, but he was afraid nobody else would. Well, maybe not *nobody*—Robert's mother would be there—but someone who had spent his last years in a nursing home with a debilitating disease and had no visitors that Foster had ever seen, apart from his mother, might have found it challenging to keep up his social contacts.

Even before he opened the double glass doors inscribed with *This is the way* on the left side, *and the truth and the life* on the right, Foster could see that he needn't have worried about attendance. The place was packed. Among the ordinary-looking people like himself were several men and women in military uniforms—including an honor guard of eight soldiers flanking the closed casket up front—and maybe a dozen people, mostly men, wearing PALS T-shirts. *PALS* meant Persons with ALS. Robert had last worn his PALS shirt at the Ice Bucket Challenge the Pondside CNAs put on last summer, partly to raise money for research and partly (according to Duane Lotspeich, as he stuffed dollars into the jar) to give the geezers a glimpse of some girls in wet T-shirts.

A few of the PALS who were present at the funeral looked pretty ordinary, too, upright and walking around. They would be the more recently diagnosed, the ones who still believed, as Robert Kallman had believed at first, that they would beat this thing. If you looked, maybe you could see that they favored a leg or dragged one foot a little, maybe one arm looked underrepresented when they gestured or held onto the back of a chair. Three of the PALS were in wheelchairs, with headrests and braces to keep their heads from falling to the side, straps and Velcro to keep their torsos upright. One man had a breathing device—something that required a corrugated plastic hose and a compressor packed under the seat of his wheelchair, going *sshh-kunk* with every assisted breath.

A long line of people snaked back and forth around and among the rows of chairs set up for the service, waiting to offer their condolences to Robert's mother. She was sitting in a wing chair up near the closed casket. Foster bypassed the guest book and little envelopes in the foyer and joined the line. From his spot, just inside the doorway, Robert's mother looked like a queen or something, half hidden by giant flower arrangements and backed by the honor guard, her subjects approaching one by one, bending toward her, bowing their heads.

All that Foster knew for sure about Mrs. Kallman was what Robert had told him, namely: that she was almost forty when Robert was born (which made her close to eighty-eight now, although she looked, even to Foster, more like a person in her seventies); that she raised him on her own after his career-army father was killed in an airplane crash; and that she used to be a psychiatrist or a psychologist or something, an actual doctor, Robert said. This was back when women doctors were few and far between.

What Foster knew firsthand about Mrs. Kallman was that she had spent a good part of every day at Pondside Manor during the two-plus years that Robert was a resident there. Her usual pattern was to arrive before breakfast with an insulated picnic basket that contained two hot breakfasts, each in its own Tupperware serving container, which she would set out on their regular table near the front windows in the dining room. In the early days, she brought pancakes and French toast, waffles, biscuits, sausage, bacon. Back then, she used to come extra early so that the aroma from her insulated picnic basket wouldn't set the other residents to complaining enviously about the quality of *their* breakfasts, which weren't that bad.

Later, when a mechanical soft diet was all that Robert's compromised jaw and throat could handle, she brought foods that were appropriately soft and easy to chew but no less delicious: scrambled eggs and cheese omelets, hash browns with fried onions, pancakes precut into bite-size pieces, sliced strawberries, orange sections, bananas. She tried blending orange juice and peaches and other more challenging fruits into a smoothie, but soon found that smoothies tended to coat the back of Robert's throat in a way that made him cough. (You didn't want to cough at mealtimes, especially on Wednesdays when the speech therapists were around, ready to swoop in with their clipboards and record your every cough and wide-eyed swallow, every throat-clearing *ahem*.)

Mrs. Kallman knew the ropes as well as anyone did. She would fill two cups from a thermos of coffee, one cup outfitted with a special top and a base that not only kept the coffee hot for the whole time it took Robert to drink it, but also raised the cup to just the right height for him to catch the built-in straw with his teeth. She laid out the fork and spoon with the easy-grip handles (later augmented with elastic bands to keep them in hand), and when all was ready, she would sit with her back to the window and wait for Robert to come rolling down the corridor in his motorized wheelchair, which he would pilot expertly to the opposite side of the table using what strength and mobility he still had in his left hand and wrist.

The sight of him rolling down the hall in the wheelchair—his body held up by a pair of wide fleece-lined straps that went across his chest and under his arms and around the back of the chair, his head fallen to the side like a wilted flower, and his face arranged into the lopsided smile he mustered as he got closer to her—just about broke Foster's heart every time he saw it. He couldn't imagine what it did to Mrs. Kallman's.

From his place in the line of mourners, Foster watched Mrs. Kallman lean forward in her chair next to the casket and take both hands of the man with the breathing apparatus.

Foster was well past the middle of the line when, to his surprise, a Pondside crowd showed up, delivered to the visitation by the Pondside SeniorMobile, which was visible through the glass doors in the vestibule. They all hung together at first, clumped near the door—Foster spotted Laverne Slatchek, Duane Lotspeich, and Edith Cole with her lap full of stuffed animals in a wheelchair pushed by wholesome, handsome Dakota Have-a-Heart, Certified Nursing Assistant. Foster concealed himself as best he could in the line of mourners. He would have ducked out of the line and fled—he had a straight shot to the vestibule—but feared that would only make him more conspicuous. It occurred to him that he was hardly recognizable in a shirt and tie (and without his kitchen cap). Not a single Pondside resident had spotted him. To keep it that way, he turned to face the front.

Mrs. Kallman was standing now, accepting a hug from Amelia Ramirez, who must have come to the visitation on her own, not with the Pondside contingent, since she was ahead of Foster in the line. He wasn't too surprised that he hadn't noticed her before. The crowd was thick, and she had her curly waterfall of hair twisted up under a scarf. Even so, Foster was impressed by the way all eight members of the all-male honor guard, standing at ease alongside the casket, kept their eyes aimed over the heads of the crowd as Amelia Ramirez walked past them in a pair of raspberry-sherbet-colored scrub pants that curved, neat and snug, over her backside. She was probably going straight to work from here.

Suddenly, he was next. Mrs. Kallman was still standing in front of her chair. "Foster!" she said, with feeling. He almost looked down at his dress shirt to see if the pocket had sprouted a name tag. Mrs. Kallman took both of his hands in hers. "You've done so much for Robert. How can I thank you?" she said.

All Foster could think of was that he had never been this close to Robert's mother before—she looked pretty ancient, close up—and that she had quite a grip for an eighty-eight-year-old. Neither of those was a thing he could say, and it suddenly seemed obvious that this was not the time to find out, no matter how politely or indirectly, if she knew what happened to Robert's laptop. He'd half hoped that the laptop might be *here*, set up as a kind of memorial to Robert, *The World of Pondside* launched and running. Robert would have liked that. There was a projector set up on a table at the front of the row of chairs, as if they were going to show a video or a slideshow, but the Lenovo laptop next to it wasn't the *Pondside* server.

Mrs. Kallman must have assumed that he was too choked up to speak. She squeezed his hands. "Foster," she said, "you know better than anyone how many people depended on Robert to give them hope." She thanked him again and added, "Bless you, Foster Kresowik."

Now he did glance down at his shirt pocket. When he looked up again, the eyes of one of the honor guards were aimed right at him. They looked away immediately. Mrs. Kallman gave his hands an extra squeeze, then released them. He recognized this as the signal that he should move on, and he did.

Flustered as he was, Foster forgot that he was going to walk right out the door without talking to anyone else. Instead, he followed the general traffic pattern away from Mrs. Kallman and the honor guard toward the rows of chairs that faced the casket, filing into the next open row. There he had the misfortune of sitting down, heedlessly, next to Duane Lotspeich, who had apparently decided to skip the reception line and find himself a seat. Lotspeich, thank God, did not seem to recognize Foster. The old man was barely recognizable himself in a shirt and tie and the below-the-right-knee prosthesis that he claimed was uncomfortable enough to be worn only on special occasions. Foster couldn't see the prosthesis itself, of course; only that Duane's pant legs were both fully occupied.

If you asked Duane Lotspeich—or even if you didn't—he would tell you that he was at Pondside for rehab only, that as soon as he got used to the prosthetic leg he would be going home to his bachelor pad. (The old man made sure everybody knew that he'd been married and divorced three times—proof, somehow, of what a stud he was.) If he really had come to Pondside, of all places, for rehab, Foster thought, then Duane Lotspeich and/or his family were seriously deluded. Pondside Manor— with Ruthless von Maur constituting the PT department—was the last place anyone looking for competent, regular physical therapy should be. All it took was a peek into the "gym" between nine and eleven a.m. if you wanted to see what kind of hand-tailored, personally prescribed therapy was being administered to the geezers who qualified for it, insurance-wise. Duane Lotspeich spent most of his time in there sitting in his wheelchair alongside a semicircle of other Medicares, Medicaids, and Private Pays, all of them apparently working on their pectorals with one of those giant rubber bands you stretch out like an accordion. How this was supposed to help a person manage with one leg, Foster couldn't say.

"You need strong arms to catch yourself and keep yourself from falling, don't you think?" perpetually optimistic Amelia Ramirez pointed out one time when Duane himself complained about the uselessness of the exercises. "*Everyone* needs to work on avoiding falls," she added. Foster, who overheard, suspected that Duane Lotspeich was too smart to buy a line like that, even from Amelia Ramirez, but the old guy merely harrumphed and let her wheel him from the library to the gym. Not that he needed help with that. With all the rubber band training, Lotspeich had the arms to wheel himself to Kansas. It was just a way to keep the pretty nurse and her rose-petal scent nearby for a few minutes longer. Watching her shiny black curls bounce on her shoulders as she rolled the old guy down the hall, Foster wondered if she believed the lines she handed out. It was hard to tell with Amelia Ramirez, who was as earnest as she was smart. Tori seemed to think Amelia was okay, and that was enough for Foster to give her the benefit of the doubt.

He wondered if Tori would show up at the funeral, or if she was running the show for Amelia tonight. There were only four RNs at Pondside to cover all of the shifts. Sunday night was usually Amelia Ramirez's. By the time she got out to the edge of town, it would be too late for Tori to get back here. The row in which Foster had seated himself was slowly filling with Pondside people. Here, for example, came Edith Cole, her wheelchair pushed into place at the end of the row in front of him by one of the suits that obviously came with the funeral chapel. Edith was clutching a purple bunny, holding it against her face, her lips moving as if she were murmuring in the bunny's ear. (Why the hell Have-a-Heart brought Edith Cole, who spoke only to her stuffed animals, to Robert Kallman's funeral was anybody's guess.) When Laverne Slatchek lowered herself into the chair on Foster's right without so much as turning her head in his direction, he hoped that he was correct in thinking that no one would recognize the kitchen boy without his kitchen gear. He would wait until the service got started and then he would slide his chair backward—the chairs were not linked together, he'd checked—and make his escape. Just then he felt a stirring and a leaning on his left, a gust of atticky breath on his neck.

"*Black Ops*," Duane Lotspeich growled into Foster's ear.

The old man gestured conspiratorially with his chin, aiming it toward the casket and the honor guard. *What*, Foster wondered, *was that supposed to mean?* Mrs. Kallman was still accepting condolences from the last of the people in line, while a couple of suits set up a screen and fooled with the laptop on the table in front of the casket. Before Foster could ask Duane Lotspeich what he was getting at, a bony elbow poked him in the ribs from the other side. Laverne.

"The ducklink's down," she whispered.

So they both recognized him. Foster glanced at Laverne. He had often wondered why old ladies thought it was a good idea to smear bright patches of pink stuff on their cheekbones. Tori the RN called it war paint. When Laverne Slatchek's watery blue eyes met his without wavering, Foster suddenly saw Tori's point.

"Didn't you know that?" she said, and she leaned forward as if she were trying to catch the eye of Duane Lotspeich, who had his hands on his knees and his back ramrod straight and his eyes trained on the business that was going on up front, where one of the suits was stepping up to a podium rolled in from somewhere. After several seconds of being ignored by Duane Lotspeich, Laverne sat back in her chair. She turned to Foster again. "We can't get *in*," she said. "Don't you *play*?"

He didn't have to answer because the funeral director up front was asking everyone to take a seat for the memorial service. A fellow with a lot of braid and medals decorating his uniform joined him at the podium, behind which the screen had lit up. The funeral director introduced him as Lieutenant Robert Kallman's commanding officer. Foster didn't hear the captain's name, or if he did, he couldn't remember it afterward. As much as he wanted to hear whatever Robert Kallman stories the captain might have to offer, Foster could tell from the way his throat tightened at the first image that he would not last long. There on the screen, a little larger than life, was the very same shot that Foster had pulled from the *Pondside* folder on his desktop multiple times in the last few days: Robert posing in dusty fatigues on the hood of the Humvee, a grin on his suntanned face.

"Who's *that*?" one of the geezers whispered too loudly.

"That doesn't look like him at all!" another one said.

"I didn't know he was in the war! What war was it?"

"That poor man, no wonder he—you know."

Foster extricated himself from the middle of the row of chairs and threaded his way through the standing-room-only area behind them to reach the vestibule.

"Are you all right?" a deep voice asked beside him. Foster was startled to find one of the suits, an older man, holding the first glass door open for him, his tie perfectly knotted and his round face darkened by fake concern.

*Fuck you!* Foster either thought or said—he wasn't sure which, nor did he care—as he plunged through the vestibule and out into the autumn evening.

Pondside Administrator Kitty Landiss did not ordinarily return to work in the evening, and she tended to avoid the place entirely on the weekend, so it was more than just unusual for her to show up there on a Sunday night. It was unheard of. She had come from the gym in her yoga pants and oversize sweatshirt (worn inside out to hide the Guns N' Roses World Tour 2000 schedule on the back). Her gym bag hung, heavier than usual, from her shoulder. She was hoping to slip in the front door, take a sharp left into the administrative area, and shut herself in her office without attracting any attention. The vestibule, the atrium, the hallway, and the corner of the dining room that she could see from outside the door all looked clear. She punched the numbers on the keypad and gave the heavy safety glass a push.

A buzzer buzzed insistently. She had forgotten the after-hours alarm, armed only when there was no receptionist on duty in the front office. By the time she pushed the reset code on the inside keypad, she expected to face—well, somebody—but the hallway remained deserted. Kitty thanked her lucky stars and scooted down the short hall to her left past the closed doors of the business manager's office and the social worker's office, hugging the gym bag to her chest.

In her own office, with the big windows overlooking the deserted parking lot, she plopped the gym bag on her desk, pulled out her laptop, and flipped it open. It was already on. She'd tried it from her car in the parking lot. Once again, she crossed her fingers and moused over to the little yellow duck. She closed her eyes and pictured her corner office in *The World of Pondside*—the fabric swatches, the designer sketches, the interns taking her calls and running downstairs to pick up her latte, the big windows overlooking Forty-Seventh Street and Fifth Avenue—and then she opened one eye and used her crossed fingers to depress the mouse pad. A click, a breathless wait, the white window opening on the screen, and then—

*Page Not Found.*

That was different. Usually, it was *Server Not Responding.* Or, on the Mac in Stephanie's office, it was the more effusive *Safari can't open the page because the server where this page is located isn't responding.*

*The server where this page is located* had inspired Kitty to undertake a search of Robert Kallman's room that Thursday, after the police left. "Search" was overstating it. She'd had a look around. She didn't really know what to look for—what was a server, anyway?—but a distinctly undusty rectangle on the desk suggested that someone else had found it first, whatever *it* was. Someone who knew what to look for. She figured it was Foster Kresowik. She hadn't said anything to him about it because she didn't want to scare him off. That was why she kept trying the link. Why take the server if he wasn't going to start it up again? Maybe he was going to keep it for himself. People sold games like that for a lot of money. If anybody was going to make big money on Kitty's fashionista *World of Pondside* portal, she was going to get her share. All she *really* wanted, though, was to *go* there, to play. She had waited long enough. She was going to talk to Foster. She was going to find out what was going on.

On her way out, the profound silence of Pondside Manor finally made an impression on Kitty Landiss. The clock above the credenza said five after seven. That was too early for everybody to be in bed, even here. Where was everybody?

She turned down Boysenberry Boulevard. Across from Robert Kallman's room, she knocked lightly on Laverne Slatchek's partly open door, then poked her head in. Lights and TV off, bed made and armchair empty. Back in the hallway the silence was so complete that Kitty didn't really need to knock on Irma Hickerson's door or the Stevenses'—Pondside Manor's only cohabitating married couple. Around the corner, even Edith Cole's room was empty.

Not until she approached the nurses' station at the intersection of Boysenberry and Hawkeye Lane did Kitty hear something, at last. From behind the double doors that closed off a third corridor came a long and mournful wail, rising and falling, now a single voice, now a duet. The wailing meant that certain souls in Memory Lane were waiting for their meds to kick in. It was a relief to hear them. She was beginning to feel like a lost soul herself, or maybe somebody trapped in a *Twilight Zone* episode. She had just decided to go back and check the board to see who was on duty tonight when the big white meds cart came into view at the end of the hall on the far side of the nurses' station.

The nurse pushing it, Kitty could see as soon as it finished turning the corner, was Tori Mahoney—Kitty Landiss's second-least-favorite employee, after Foster Kresowik. Not that Tori wasn't a skillful, compassionate, intelligent, and apparently tireless nurse. The problem was that Tori knew she was all those things, and she knew that Kitty Landiss knew she was all those things, and they both knew that Kitty Landiss was lucky to have kept Tori at Pondside, where understaffing and the oversize building made working here even more grueling than it was at other long-term care facilities in the area, any of which would have been delighted to snatch Tori away. Of course, Tori knew *that*, too. And if all that weren't enough, she also had the kind of no-nonsense, wash-and-wear, inadvertently athletic body that looked ridiculously good in faded scrubs.

"Working late?" she asked Kitty in her husky, confident, you-can-trust-me-to-take-good-care-of-you voice. Tori maneuvered the meds cart into its parking spot alongside the counter of the nurses' station and reached for her charts.

Kitty almost launched into an explanation of her presence. She stopped herself just in time and asked, "Where is everybody?"

Tori stuck her pencil behind her ear and frowned up at the clock. "You know, I'm beginning to wonder the same thing."

"I beg your pardon?"

"I thought they'd be back by now. I'm going to have to give Dakota a call. Not that we have the staff for showers tonight, but I know Laverne will want—"

"Dakota?"

"Dakota Engelhart. He's one of the CNAs—the one with the commercial driver's license."

"I know who he is," Kitty said. "What I don't know is what's going on."

Tori appeared to gather herself before she spoke. "Some of the residents expressed a desire to go to Robert Kallman's funeral—the visitation part at the funeral home tonight—and Dakota was willing to take them. Almost everybody in Boysenberry and Hawkeye wanted to go. Twelve people—no. Eleven." Tori opened a chart, jotted something, closed it, and reached for the next one.

"A CNA drove eleven residents to a funeral?"

"It seemed pretty quick to me—Robert Kallman's funeral, I mean," Tori said, keeping her finger on the chart in front of her. "I suppose the arrangements were preplanned, so as soon as they released the body—" She shrugged. "Just one of the advantages of a terminal disease. You're always prepared for the worst."

The tone of these remarks reminded Kitty that there was a tragedy in Tori's past. Her husband was deceased—killed in the service, Kitty understood. Something odd about it, maybe friendly fire. Kitty didn't know the details. She noticed that the call light had come on above a door about halfway down the hallway called Iowa Avenue. With her head bent over the charts, Tori hadn't seen it yet. Kitty asked, "Who authorized this outing?"

"*Hmm?*" Tori kept writing on the chart. Her blond fountain of a ponytail bobbed perkily as she said, "I guess I did."

"You *guess*," Kitty said.

"All right, *I* did," said Tori. "As ranking officer on duty. So to speak. There was no DON to call, and I couldn't reach you. Maybe your phone is off?"

Kitty Landiss took a deep breath and exhaled. This is what she got, she supposed, for not offering the director of nursing position to Tori— except temporarily and with no increase in pay—back in August, when the former DON had to be let go rather suddenly. What Kitty wanted to say right now was: "Well, then I *guess* you're fired!" Even Tori Mahoney might flinch at that. Kitty took a few more deep breaths, started counting silently to ten, and at five, asked to see the paperwork documenting this "outing."

She had it right here, Tori said, shuffling papers on the counter, although she hadn't had a chance, being alone on shift, to fill in all the names—

Kitty took the form that Tori handed her and when she saw that it was mostly blank, she crumpled it into a ball. Tori had fallen silent. She appeared to listen as Kitty explained a few things, starting with proper procedure and respect for the chain of command—*so to speak.* She moved on to insurance and liability, the need for certain signatures to make a form like this one something other than a worthless piece of—Kitty paused—scrap paper. She mentioned specific instructions from Edith Cole's family that expressly forbade taking her anywhere without an accompanying family member and no, she was not interested in how long it had been since Edith had had a family visitor or even a telephone call. Kitty thought it might be about time for an all-employee meeting, she said, to remind everyone that just because Pondside was short-staffed, that didn't mean that current employees were immune to the consequences of their actions; that she, in fact, as administrator, was required to abide by corporate as well as legal guidelines when it came to both hiring and firing; and that *no one* on the current staff was so indispensable as to preclude dismissal in the face of flagrant disregard for procedure.

"Hold that thought," Tori said suddenly. She had spotted the call light down the hall. "I'd better go see what Mr. Palmer wants—oh. Wait. Is that the door alarm I hear? That's probably Dakota right now. Here's your chance to fill him in on how indispensable he isn't. I'd wait till he unloads the bus, though, if I were you."

With that, Tori turned her back and strode down the hall toward Mr. Palmer's door. Kitty took a few more deep, calming breaths and wondered, when the door alarm stopped buzzing, if she had enough CNAs to fire this Dakota on the spot. But it wasn't the offending CNA who came around the corner. It was Amelia Ramirez, a coat thrown over her scrubs and a scarf tied around her head. She was arm in arm with a frail-looking, wispy-haired woman. Wild Mary McIntyre didn't look very wild at the moment, shuffling along beside the nurse, an opened single-serving pudding cup in one hand and a plastic spoon in the other. Every few steps they both stopped so that the old lady could get another spoonful into her mouth. They had almost reached the nurses' station before Amelia saw Kitty behind the counter. If Amelia was surprised, she didn't show it. She bestowed a bright smile on her boss as she pulled off the scarf, setting free her glorious cascade of curls.

"Look who I found in the dining room, sitting all by her lonesome," Amelia said cheerily.

Beside her, the old lady rattled her spoon in the pudding cup, which sounded empty now. She closed one eye and seemed to aim the other one right at Kitty Landiss. "I had to look in three different places to find one of these that wasn't chocolate," Mary McIntyre said with a scowl. "Somebody should speak to the management."

Dakota Engelhart's phone had been buzzing in his pocket at regular intervals all the way back to Pondside. By the time he pulled the Senior-Mobile into the circle drive and parked it under the portico, he'd counted seventeen separate calls and texts. All of them, he had assumed, were from Erika, but when he had a couple of seconds free—right after calling out to his passengers, "Honey, we're home!" and before opening the door to disembark—he pulled out his phone and saw at a glance that the last text was from Amelia Ramirez, who had helped him load the bus before she left the funeral home. Her purple Saturn was already parked in the first row of spots off the circle drive.

She had beaten them here—no surprise, given the lumbering nature of the SeniorMobile, a former Blue Bird school bus with single wheelchair docks replacing the double seats in the front two-thirds of the bus. The surprising thing was the message. He'd had a few texts from Tori, usually when he was late and staff was short and she needed to leave to pick up a kid from soccer, but he'd never had one from Amelia Ramirez. Dakota distinctly remembered the day she asked him for his number. She was putting contact info from the CNAs into her phone for emergency staffing purposes, she explained, but not before his face had flamed red. When she looked up at him and saw it, she couldn't hide her smile. She assured him that he didn't *have* to give her his number; it was on a strictly voluntary basis. In a pinch, she could reach him through the office directory.

He tapped his phone now and read: "Landiss here!"

"Are we bedding down on the bus or are we getting out?" came a crotchety voice from behind him.

Dakota turned around and saw ten faces looking at him expectantly.

Edith Cole was still fast asleep in the first wheelchair behind the driver's seat, her stuffed rabbit tucked under her jaw like a travel pillow.

"The door," Duane Lotspeich prompted. "Open it."

Dakota was about to say that they needed to wait for assistance when Tori appeared outside the bus. Dakota pulled the lever and the door folded open. "You're still here?" he said to Tori and immediately regretted having stated the obvious. She stepped aboard without a word and set to work unlocking the first wheelchair. They had everybody inside the building—Amelia and another CNA named Jo-lyn relaying everybody from vestibule to room—before Tori laid a hand on Dakota's arm and said, "Lucky for you, Amelia got here first and worked her winning ways on Landiss. Next time you come up with a last-minute idea for an excursion, try telling me about it *before* you start making promises to people."

Dakota hoped he didn't look as stupid as he felt. "I'm sorry—"

Tori held up a hand to stop him. She seemed to hesitate then, glancing around before she asked, "How was it? The—service, I mean."

"I don't know. I guess it was fine."

"Did somebody talk? Was there a speech, a eulogy?"

"Yes." Dakota was ready to leave it at that, but Tori seemed to be waiting for more. "They talked about his military service and his travels and all the stuff he's done for the ALS community—and the game! It occurred to me later—that's what Laverne Slatchek was talking about when she asked me about her condo the other day. I thought she'd lost her marbles, but she was talking about that game they play."

"Who talked?"

"It was a military guy, an officer. I think they said he was Robert Kallman's CO or something. I can't remember his name. I'm sorry. He was in a lot of the photos in the slideshow."

"There was a slideshow?" Tori said. She seemed taken aback by the idea.

"Yeah. They do that a lot now at funerals," Dakota said, right before he remembered that Tori probably knew all too well what they do at funerals. It hadn't been all that many years since she lost her husband, had it? "Are you all right?" he asked her.

"I'm fine," she said, although she looked—Dakota wasn't sure how she looked, what the expression meant, but it was one he hadn't seen before, not on Tori's face. She moved her shoulders, hitched up her purse. "I guess I wish I could have seen the pictures."

"I know. It was really something to see what Robert was like—before. Maybe they'll show them tomorrow at the church service. I've got the card here somewhere that says when and where it will be." He dug into his jacket pocket.

Tori took the card but didn't look at it. "You'd better get in there," she said. "I can see three call lights on from here."

"Oh geez," Dakota said, turning away from her to look down the hall. "That's Lotspeich down at the end. Everybody's going to want something now." He turned around to say goodbye, but Tori was already halfway to her minivan.

# CHAPTER 7

One of the things Foster liked about his apartment above Panera was the choice he had between using the back door off the alley or the front door, which was next to the commercial entrance. Usually, he slipped in the back, hoisted his bike, and climbed the stairs to the landing where he stowed it for the night. He wasn't supposed to leave it up there on the landing, where, in the words of a notice at the top of the stairs, it might "obstruct emergency egress" for himself or the hypothetical resident of the unoccupied apartment behind his, but he couldn't fit a bicycle inside his apartment, not if he wanted to use the stove or refrigerator, and he had lost too many front wheels—plus one whole bike—to lock it up outside.

Other times, like tonight, coming home from Robert's funeral visitation, he preferred to use the front entrance, which required him to carry his bike up a longer flight of stairs and roll it down the hallway past both apartment doors to the landing in the back. Using the front entrance took him past the plateglass windows and doorway of Panera. Sometimes, the scene inside the coffee shop cheered him—people talking, laughing, eating, or just staring at a phone or a laptop with a cup of coffee on the side. He took consolation in the fact that there was light and life going on someplace—just downstairs, in fact. For the same reason, he enjoyed the smell of the bakery and the coffee (although he didn't drink coffee himself) and even the sound of the espresso machine or whatever it was that hissed and squealed loud enough to make itself heard upstairs. When he went inside the coffee shop—not often, for it was pricey—he liked to sit in the corner over there, where a guy in a wheelchair had just looked up at the window. His face was unusual, sort of Asian, sort of not. He caught Foster's eye. Foster dropped his gaze, embarrassed, and coasted past the rest of the windows.

Upstairs, he stowed his bike and let himself into his apartment, which was totally dark—thanks to the lined black drapes that were necessary to shut out the klieg-light brightness of the parking lot—and which smelled delicious. They must be baking cinnamon buns downstairs.

Foster pulled the ball and chain to turn on his Goodwill floor lamp with one hand and with the other dug into his pants pocket to see if he could find two seventy-five for a pastry item. He had a rule against using plastic at Panera, knowing from his early days in the place how easy it was to blow a whole month's food budget in a week by giving in to the aroma of a cinnamon bun that was likely to lead to a caramel cappuccino (the kind that tasted nothing like coffee but could keep you up half the night) or a smoothie or a bread bowl of French onion soup. The cash-only policy kept impulse buys under control. Robert used to insist sometimes that Foster take a fiver from the roll in Robert's shirt pocket—on the condition that he use it at Panera when he got home. "Eat a Danish for me," Robert would say. "Something with pecans. *Mmmmm.*"

Foster pulled two quarters and smaller change out of one pocket and a crumpled dollar bill out of the other. He spread them out on the desk next to his computer, pushed the power button, and sank into a chair. He closed his eyes while his computer whirred cheerily to life. With his eyes closed, he could have been anywhere—at least, anywhere that smelled like cinnamon.

It was possible, Foster thought, that he had never before felt *this* alone.

He opened his eyes. Files and icons littered the computer desktop, almost obliterating the scene behind them, a screenshot from his *World of Pondside* portal: wicker chairs and a wooden card table on a broad wooden porch, all of it awash in summer light and leafy shadow. On the card table—an ancient-looking one with the faded squares of a chess-board inlaid in the middle—sat a smiling yellow duck.

Foster's portal, which he had researched and coded all on his own, took him to what had been his favorite place in the world when he was a kid: his grandparents' screened porch. "It was like sitting in a tree house," he told Robert once. Foster had put in the giant trees surrounding the second-story porch, their great leafy branches brushing against the screens; he had the ceiling fan, the crown of tiny white Christmas lights along the tops of the screened windows, and the shelf that ran along the bottom, where he used to set up the train his grandfather bought him at a yard sale. His grandparents were big on yard sales and second-hand stores, which is where the wicker chairs and the ancient wooden card table came from. The only thing missing was his grandparents. He didn't have a single JPEG or video to construct them with (or remember them by), having failed to convince his grandmother at more than one yard sale that she ought to lay out the money for a digital camera instead of picking up another old Kodak number.

The truth was, except for playing chess or checkers with Gramps after supper, Foster had spent most of his porch time alone during the summer he spent in Wisconsin while his parents failed to work things out. On his grandparents' porch, Foster had set up the train to run over hill and dale and cushion and chair. He read on the porch—something his teachers weren't sure he knew how to do—cruising through books his grandfather had given to Foster's dad, who "never cracked the binding on a single one," Gramps said. Kurt Vonnegut became Foster's favorite. It was only years later, when he started working at Pondside, that he realized just how brilliant the man was. Like that bit in *Slaughterhouse-Five,* where it says Billy Pilgrim was "unstuck in time"? If that didn't describe certain gee-zers—especially the ones in Memory Lane—Foster didn't know what did.

Sometimes Robert showed up on the screened porch in Foster's *World of Pondside,* sitting across from Foster at the card table, sufficiently animated to give him a thumbs-up or a high five. More often, Robert left messages for him there. Some of the messages referred to the world outside the game, perhaps asking Foster to order a fish sandwich from Culver's for actual delivery to Robert's room on Boysenberry Boulevard. Or he might want Foster to try something within the program, to mouse over some object Robert had put on the table—a box or a dog—to test it out. (Did the box open? Did the dog bark?)

Robert had already lasted longer than he was supposed to. Foster knew that. Most people suffering from ALS were dead within five years of their diagnosis, many even sooner. Then again there were people with ALS, just a very few of them, who went on and on. Robert was diagnosed in November 2005 (not 2006, like the girl cop said), which was a pretty long time ago. He had lost a lot of function in his arms and legs right away—went from dropping things and stumbling over a dragging foot, to a cane, to a walker, to a wheelchair in the first year, he said.

Being Robert, he had gone to the internet after his diagnosis to look for information on ALS, which he found, a lot of it in blogs and community forums, where Persons with ALS reported their hopes and losses, their anger and despair. Some of those posts were pretty terrifying, Robert told Foster, glimpses of your own future. PALS also posted anything and everything they had tried by way of treatment—whether self-prescribed or advised by their doctors—from diet (steel cut oats were recommended, pomegranate juice, coconut water) and exercise regimens (swimming, weights, tai chi, etc.), to do-it-yourself medication (vitamin cocktails, food supplements, traditional remedies, and for a while, a certain kind of cough syrup).

One online forum alerted members to clinical research studies that began to open up here and there around the country and the world— if you could get there and if you qualified, which depended on things like onset of symptoms and date of diagnosis. Before long, Robert got himself signed up for one of these studies. It had been recommended by a woman Robert had gotten to know pretty well on the PALS forum. Sarah was a biochemist, which probably gave her extra insight, Robert had thought, into what might work.

"ALS is differrrent for everrrybody," Robert told Foster. For Sarah, speech and swallowing had been the first things affected; her limbs were still fully functional when she and Robert had their first face-to-face meeting in Chicago, where they both had gone to take part in the study. For Robert, it had worked the opposite way; his arms and legs were the first to go. That was part of the problem with the research. What looked like improvement from a drug might just be a difference in the progression of the disease from one person to the next.

Robert was supposed to meet Sarah at the hotel near the hospital. She'd already had her first infusion the day before Robert arrived. When he got there, it took him a while to locate her and even longer to find out why she appeared to be hiding in her room, not answering her phone. At first, he thought she was resting—one of the common side effects of the drug they were testing was fatigue—but it turned out Sarah wasn't feeling fatigued at all. She was sure that she was getting the placebo, and she was devastated. It was a double-blind study, and Robert couldn't help thinking that if Sarah was on the placebo, then it was a little bit more likely that Robert would get the drug. He was afraid that Sarah knew what he was thinking, partly because Sarah would have been thinking the same thing. Robert talked her into coming down to the dining room where they kept the coffee going all day, but neither of them really had much to say until someone came over to the table and asked them if they wanted refills. Sarah looked into the empty mug on the table in front of her and then back up at Robert.

"What happened to my coffee?" she said.

"You drank it," Robert told her.

Sarah said, "No." And then, "I did?" And then, as if someone had flipped a switch, her face lit up. Two days ago, it would have taken her forty-five minutes of concentrated effort to drink a cup of coffee, she told Robert. She had sipped and swallowed this one without even thinking about it. Her eyes filled up with tears, right there at the table. She wasn't getting the placebo. She was getting the drug—and it was already working!

When Robert got his first infusion the following day, the side effect fatigue knocked him so flat that he could hardly get out of bed. He was too tired to do anything for the first few days, but one afternoon—on the fourth day in the first round of infusions—he was sitting up in the hotel bed, hunting for the remote with his good hand, his left, when he noticed that he had the top sheet clutched in his right fist. He opened his right hand and held it out over the bed, fingers splayed wide, and then, slowly and deliberately, he closed it again, watching the fingers curl inward and the thumb fold down on top of them. He hadn't been able to keep his right hand closed tight since he came home from Iraq.

"When I told my motherrrr, she was so excited. She gave the woman who was cleaning ourrr suite two fifties forrr a tip."

"*Two fifty-dollar bills?*" Foster said.

One side of Robert's mouth lifted in a smile. "We had the cleannnest hotel rrrrooms in Chicago."

It was a five-month trial, five days on the infusions, sixteen days off. Robert kept in close touch with Sarah and many of the others the whole time. They compared notes on the PALS online forum, keeping track of any and every single thing they could do that they couldn't do before: drink a cup of coffee, use a fork, make themselves understood on the telephone, open an envelope, button a shirt—all kinds of things that had been taken from them and now they could do them again. Or some of them could.

Everyone knew that many people in the study had seen little, if any, improvement, but they told themselves that those people were getting the placebo. That's what everybody wanted to believe. Even the people who saw no improvement at all eagerly followed the progress of others because in the next phase of the study—Phase III—nobody would get the placebo. Everybody would get the drug. At the end of the five months, everyone on the forum was waiting to hear about Phase III: when it would begin, where they would have to go. One fellow used to email Robert every day, wanting to know how he was doing, wanting to know every detail. The guy lived in Davenport, Iowa. He told Robert he used to be a firefighter. He used to run marathons. One time he wrote, "I hope I don't lose my arms and legs completely before the drug kicks in!"

At this point in the story, Robert paused and leaned back against the headrest on his wheelchair. This was before he needed the brace and Velcro straps to keep him from falling to one side. Foster waited. He was accustomed to Robert needing long breaks in the telling of a story. They had been working all that afternoon on the game—Foster used to come in on his days off to do it—and they were taking a break outside, on the hill overlooking the pond. Robert had parked his wheelchair next to the bench. Foster pulled his cigarettes out of his pocket. When he exhaled, he was careful to aim his cloud of secondhand smoke downwind, away from Robert.

"When the letterrr finally came, *I* wanted to opennn it," Robert said. He could make a fist and slide the envelope between two fingers, he said, then use his good hand to slice it open. "It was a big deal, my being able to do that."

The letter thanked Robert for participating in the study and instructed him to complete the enclosed form in order to be reimbursed for travel expenses. It said nothing about Phase III. "I rrrread it twice beforrre I told my motherrr," Robert enunciated slowly. It took some phone calls to find out what was going on. "There was nnnno Phase III planned at this time, they said."

"Why not?" Foster said.

"The study didn't make its ennnd points."

"What do you mean?

"The drrrug wasn't effective ennnough to funnnd Phase III."

"I thought you said you could make a fist again."

One side of Robert's mouth curled up a little. "I was one subject."

"What about what's-her-name—Sarah—drinking the coffee?"

"Two subjects—nnnot ennnough."

"So they just cut you off? Cold turkey?"

Robert raised his eyebrows affirmatively.

"Even though it was helping you?"

Robert added a barely perceptible nod. He could still nod at that time.

"Couldn't they give you some samples?" Foster said. For years, that was the only way Foster ever got any prescription drugs. Not that he went to the doctor much anyway. He had a six-month supply of expired nicotine patches somewhere from one time when he had an ear infection. Luckily, they gave him some antibiotics, too.

Robert was getting tired, you could tell. He swallowed hard once, twice. Even two years ago, Robert had to gather himself to speak. He said, "We trrried to find out what was in it."

"Couldn't they just tell you?"

Robert raised one eyebrow. He did the neck stretch that meant a shrug.

Foster tossed his cigarette butt to the asphalt. "No wonder the world is so fucked up," he said.

They had gone back inside then and ordered pizza so they could work through dinner. Foster told the delivery guy which entrance to use and met him there to open the door and reprogram the lock. Back in Robert's room, Foster cut half of the pizza into bite-size pieces that Robert could spear with his fat-handled fork. (Later that year, Foster would have to slide the toppings—cheese and sauce and onions and mushrooms and sausage—off Robert's pieces and cut them up without the crust.) They put their heads together over the sample code in the software development kit Robert had ordered, chewing steadily, looking for a way to animate a JPEG of Laverne Slatchek's husband Bill so that he, too, could raise his eyebrows affirmatively in *The World of Pondside* whenever she suggested a Pecan Mudslide from Dairy Queen.

Alone now, in the glow of his Goodwill lamp, Foster watched his cursor circle the yellow duck in the center of the screen. Maybe it was time to try the link again, see if it would take him anywhere. He glanced at the time: nine forty-five p.m. He had fifteen minutes before Panera closed and cut off his internet access. He was still thinking about it when a loud and obnoxious buzzing sound nearly knocked him off his chair. It seemed to come from everywhere at once, an assault of noise competing with the pounding of his heart. Foster didn't have a lot of visitors—in fact, he had none—so it took a moment for him to understand that the noise was the doorbell. There was someone at the door downstairs.

Foster thought at once of the guy he'd seen through the window in Panera. The guy in the wheelchair. He tried to remember. Was the guy alone? Or had someone been sitting across from him? Foster had been so quick to look away after their eyes met that he couldn't be sure. For that matter, there could have been someone with him who was waiting in line or picking up their order at the counter. Someone in a military uniform? Foster closed his eyes to picture the scene—and thought, *yes!* There was a man in uniform standing at the pick-up counter. Of course, that could have been a coincidence, too. He might not have been with the guy in the wheelchair at all. And why would the guy in the wheelchair take an interest in Foster anyway? Nobody took an interest in Foster. He had been surprised that Mrs. Kallman knew his name. Thinking about her "Bless you, Foster Kresowik!" made him feel a little weird, and it also made him remember the guy in the honor guard who had given him a look when she said his name. An astonishing thought occurred to Foster, a thought that made his throat go dry. It was this: any one of those people at the funeral could have been the one who rolled Robert into the pond.

The doorbell buzzed again.

Foster carried his bike down the back stairs as quietly as he could. He made sure he'd turned off his brand-new headlight, even though he couldn't afford another ticket for riding without one. At the bottom of the stairs, he pushed the door open and pedaled away toward the dark outer reaches of the mall parking lot. When he reached the street, he stopped under a tree, out of the light, and looked back. There was a car pulled up in front of Panera. With the building in his way, all he could see of the car was one rear fender. It was a sedan of some kind. Not a police car. He took off again down the side street, glancing over his shoulder a couple of times. Nobody was following him, as far as he could tell.

Back in her room at Pondside after the funeral visitation, Laverne Slatchek had already decided that she was never going to speak to Duane Lotspeich ever again. Him and his big ideas. All they'd accomplished by cornering the kitchen boy at the funeral was to make him mad or scare him off, Laverne couldn't quite tell which. It was no secret that the kitchen boy—*Foster!* she remembered—spent a lot of time in Robert Kallman's room, helping the poor man. They had special attachments and things so that he could use his computers, but there were limits to what machines could make up for, and that was where Foster came in. If anybody knew how to fix the ducklink, it was that young man, and now they'd scared him off. They all should have stayed home.

One good thing about never speaking to Duane Lotspeich again, Laverne thought as she got ready for bed, was that she would never again have to hear him say that he, for one, could understand why that poor man—Duane, of course, said "poor bastard"—had committed suicide. A lot of them seemed to think that Robert Kallman had killed himself. But it could have been an accident, couldn't it? Or even murder! Didn't any of them ever read a book or watch *CSI*? She lowered herself to sit on the bed, pushed her walker to the side (within reach), and made sure she had the remote in hand before she swung her legs up off the floor, letting her slippers fall where they would. Then she leaned back against the pillows and took aim.

Foster coasted down a curved sidewalk in the subdivision adjacent to the mall parking lot, his headlight off and his mind busily second-guessing his decision to flee down the back stairs instead of answering his door. It wasn't that late—only a little before ten—a not totally unreasonable hour to ring somebody's doorbell. The question was, who could it possibly have been?

Another question was, where could he go now?

There was a Walmart out on Highway 9 that Foster usually avoided, having been told one time by an HR employee there that he would have to cut his hair before he could even *apply* to work part-time for America's largest retailer. That was at least three years ago, when, incidentally, his hair was considerably longer than what he had to stuff into his paper kitchen cap these days. Foster was pretty sure that, given the turnover rate, nobody at the Walmart on Highway 9 would remember him. He locked his bike in the rack and strode past the security cameras toward the food market area. Luckily, he had thought to shove the bills and change back into his pocket before exiting his apartment—he flipped open his phone—only twenty-some minutes ago. Walking through produce to the border with baked goods reminded him that he was hungry. Plastic bags of day-old dinner rolls and croissants beckoned. On the other side of baked goods, the all-you-can-eat salad bar and deli were shut down, the cashier station unstaffed, but a guy was sitting in the dining area beyond it, looking at his phone, a bottle of soda and a bag of chips on the table in front of him. It looked like it was okay to sit down, even if food service was closed for the night.

Foster went back and picked up a price-declined bag of croissants. On his way to the dining area, he stopped by a cooler and reached under the plastic cover for a pint of chocolate milk that cost more than the six croissants did. He considered trucking back to the regular dairy department to buy a whole quart for only pennies more. He was standing there by the self-serve cooler, gazing out a nearby window—unlike the rest of the store, the dining area had windows—thinking, too, about whether he could get away with consuming the food here and taking the empty packaging to checkout afterward, when a car pulled up outside the window right in front of Foster. The driver hopped out, as if he were just running inside to grab something, while the person sitting tall and straight in the passenger seat waited in the car. Foster didn't get a good look at the back seat or at the driver, who appeared to be wearing a uniform, because all of his attention was on the familiar-looking person in the passenger seat.

He could see right away that it was an older woman with her white hair swept up from the fur collar of her coat—more coat than she needed, temperature-wise, this mild October night. Foster knew from long experience that old people were quick to feel cold when the temperature dropped below, say, eighty degrees. At Pondside the poor geezers walked around in multiple layers of sweats and socks. Robert used to say it was the chill of the grave creeping up on them. Jenny said all the extra padding was good protection when somebody fell.

When the woman in the passenger seat turned toward the window, Foster felt a jolt of surprise that made him drop the chocolate milk back into the cooler. It was Robert's mother. Mrs. Kallman. She was looking him straight in the eye—a measuring look, cold and calculating, no hint of surprise in her blank expression—as if she had expected to find him here, as if she and her driver had followed him to Walmart from his apartment, where one of them had been watching the back stairs while the other rang the buzzer in the front. Foster stepped to the side, away from the window. When Mrs. Kallman's expression didn't change, he realized that she wasn't seeing *him* through the glass; she was seeing her own reflection. Still, it was electrifying while it lasted—the thought that she and her uniformed escort, or anyone else for that matter, might be out there looking for *him*.

After ten p.m. there was only one way out of Walmart. The garden center was closed and so were the pharmacy and the liquor store, each of which had their separate entrances. Foster had almost reached the sliding glass array of IN and OUT doors when he saw that he still had a stranglehold on the bag of croissants. Did Walmart put antitheft codes on every bag of day-old croissants? He didn't know. And why was his heart pounding? He didn't know that either.

Sure, it was kind of a pretty big coincidence for Robert's mother to show up out here at the Walmart on Highway 9, but did he really think that she—they—had followed him here? On the night of her only son's funeral? Let's say that Robert told her Foster was going to give her the *Pondside* laptop. Wouldn't she have asked him about it at the funeral—instead of following him home? (In which case, he would have had to tell her, *No, Mrs. Kallman, I blew it. I let the* Pondside *server disappear.*) This was Robert Kallman's eighty-something-year-old mother. How much would she care about the *Pondside* server anyway? Maybe she just needed to pick up a little something—aspirin, sleeping pills. So what if this edge-of-town Walmart was not exactly on her way between the funeral home and the wonderful big house on Summit Street? It was open twenty-four hours, even on Sunday.

"I can get that for you," somebody said. Foster stopped—just this side of the electric eye that would have opened the OUT door and turned him into a shoplifter of croissants. A pale young woman wearing a blue

Walmart shirt beckoned from the end of her checkout station, saving Foster's ass, as it turned out, from the security guy Foster hadn't noticed following him. As he dug his dollar bill and change out of his pocket, he watched the security guy wander off, trying to look aimless, in an Iowa sweatshirt that didn't go with his creased pants and shined shoes. Foster wondered if the cashier had saved him on purpose or if she had just seen a customer and done her thing. He appreciated the way she mustered up a smile to go with the mindless, "Have a great day!" they always gave you, even though it was after ten p.m.—almost eleven now. Instead of muttering, "Yeah, sure," Foster said, "Thanks."

Outside, suddenly ravenous, he twisted open the plastic bag and stuffed the end of one croissant into his mouth like a bulbous and buttery cigar. He bent to unlock his bike and nearly choked, finding himself eye to glassy blue eye with an unexpected passenger. Someone had tied a doll in a pink dress and baby bonnet to the back of his bicycle seat. He didn't wait around to find out who.

Laverne sat up in bed. She had heard something this time, she was pretty sure. Out in the brightly lit hall. There was the distant squealing of a bed alarm, and also voices, rising and falling—arguing, it sounded like, back and forth—but trying to be quiet about it. Laverne couldn't tell what they were saying, not even when she held her breath and listened. She threw back the covers, found her slippers on the floor, slid her feet into them, and then, holding onto first the bed and then the chair, she kind of skated over the vinyl tile to the door. The last thing she wanted was to trip and fall in the middle of the night. As soon as she pulled the door open just a crack, before she got a look at who was out in the hall, Laverne realized that it was only one voice talking, someone speaking animatedly to herself. Mary McIntyre was already past Laverne's door. She was pushing a wheelchair down the hall, shuffling along, wearing a nightgown, socks, loafers, and a windbreaker type of jacket. She hunched her shoulders and waved her hand in the air from time to time, like somebody in deep and lively conversation with someone else who just happened to be invisible. There was no one in the wheelchair. At the end of the hall she stopped, looked both ways, and then turned right, toward the nurses' station.

Laverne pulled her head back, retreating from the crack of light in the doorway, intending to return to bed. She was about to kick off her slippers when it occurred to her that she hadn't tried the ducklink since yesterday. She glanced at the clock on the wall above her TV. It was almost midnight. Chances were better than good that there would be no one using the computer at this hour. Laverne reached for her walker.

In the library, all was quiet, the computer screens dark. Luckily, Laverne knew she had to push the button on the big tower under the table *and* on the regular part up top to turn it on. She waited for the little pictures to line up on the screen. The word *Pondside* appeared below the yellow duck whenever the arrow passed over it, but her single click had no effect. Laverne counted to ten and clicked again. *Zilch.* She tried double-clicking. *Zilch again.* She sat, sweeping the mouse in circles around the computer desktop and pretending that the view outside the nearest library windows was not the stretch of stockade fence that hid a pair of dumpsters, but the orange peaks of the Golden Gate Bridge, which she could see from the wall of floor-to-ceiling windows in her *World of Pondside* condo. She noticed something glittering in the corner of the window. Was it the blue waters of the Bay glinting in the moonlight? She reached for her walker and followed it across the room to the windows.

The glittering thing was not outside but inside—a bottle of colored sand on the windowsill. Laverne was pleased to recognize it as a souvenir from the Buddhist monks that Stephanie, the activities director, had taken them all to see down at the community college library some time ago. Dressed in their orange sheets, the monks were pouring all of their energy and concentration into putting the finishing touches on one of those gorgeous pictures made out of colored sand, knowing that when they were done (Stephanie had explained), they were going to sweep it all off the table, just like that. "Nut jobs," Duane Lotspeich had called them. All that work and nothing to show for it. Laverne couldn't help thinking the same thing, but she took the small vial of colored sand the monks offered her, and she gave them two dollar bills to help them free Tibet.

The bottle on the windowsill in the library was bigger than the one the monks had given Laverne. She was admiring the way the light from the courtyard made the stripes and layers of sand sparkle, when something outside the window caught her eye, something moving on the far side of the courtyard. She craned her neck and squinted, as close to the glass as she could get without leaving a nose print on it, and was surprised, to say the least, by what she saw. The kitchen boy—Foster—was out there, rolling his bicycle into the fenced-in area that hid the dumpsters. He was still wearing the suit from the funeral, which was really a sport coat and pants, Laverne had noticed earlier. These clothes gave him a furtive, clandestine look. Like somebody in a movie. Although he did work odd shifts, Laverne had never seen him arrive in the middle of the night like this. But neither the sport coat nor the late hour was as surprising as the bedraggled object that he took out from under his arm for a moment, as if to have a look at it himself, on his way to the service door.

It was a doll, a baby doll in a pink dress and bonnet, and although it was smeared with dirt, Laverne had seen enough to feel quite sure that it was the same doll that Mrs. Kallman had brought to Pondside Manor for Mary McIntyre—either that, or one just like it.

Laverne had gone to some trouble to put that baby doll out of her mind at least twice and now here it was *again,* under the kitchen boy's arm.

# CHAPTER 8

Foster woke up in what he could see by the night-lights, exit signs, and blinking timers was Pondside Manor's industrial-size kitchen. His first thought was that he'd spent the night in worse places than on the stainless steel shelf under a steam table. There was, for example, the summer after he dropped out of high school, when his father changed the locks on the house and he'd spent almost a month sleeping in the back seat of the Nova in the driveway. That in itself wasn't so weird, but what about the night he drank two whole six-packs in the back seat of the Nova, one after the other, and woke up in the trunk? To this day, Foster didn't know if he had crawled in there himself or if someone—his father? one of the neighbors? a passerby with a twisted sense of humor?—had relocated him after he passed out. At least they hadn't closed the trunk down tight.

The trouble was, after sleeping on the shelf under the steam table, he eventually had to sit up. The hip and shoulder on which Foster had been curled in a loose fetal position protested sharply as he shifted his weight. He persisted despite the pain, using one arm to push himself up and the other to pull on the nearest stainless steel leg until he was sitting, hunched, with the top of his head barely clearing the underside of the table and his knees right under his chin. He knew before he slid his hand into his jacket pocket that he had slept on the last two cigarettes in the pack, crushing them both into unsmokable shreds.

Everything hurt at least a little—his head, his neck, his shoulders, and oh, his legs, he discovered, as he attempted to straighten them out in front of him. Not only stiff from the sleeping conditions, they still ached from the last long uphill stretch to the Pondside parking lot. Foster had hopped on his bike at Walmart with the doll still tied to the fender and ridden as hard and as fast as his burning calves would let him, right up until the doll flipped around and got stuck in the spokes of his rear wheel, almost sending him over the handlebars. It was a good thing he was going uphill at the time.

Foster straightened his legs, wincing. Both still appeared to be attached—ankle to stiff knee to aching thigh.

The doll had not fared as well as he did. Foster reached into the darkness under the shelf on which he sat. His hand found the leg first, and then, several inches away, the hem of the doll's dress. Feeling a little bit like a pervert with the doll and its leg in his lap, he pulled off the prepinned diaper and peered into the oval-shaped opening that the leg had obviously popped out of. The molded plastic body of the doll was hollow. Feeling more like a pervert, he stuck a couple of fingers into the leg opening and found the plastic knob at the top of the leg that was still attached. From the look of it, he thought he might be able to pop the other leg back in place. He was still working on it—surprised at how hard it was to reinsert—when he heard the squeak of hinges immediately followed by soft-soled footsteps. He straightened up. The resounding metal gong of his head hitting the underside of the steam table silenced the footsteps.

The clock on the nearest stove said 5:21. Foster held his head and took a chance. "Jenny?" he called in a loud whisper. There was no answer—but who else could it be? He took another chance. "It's me. Foster."

"Where you at?" came from the vicinity of the wall switches next to the door, and then light flooded the room.

Foster covered his eyes. "Over here."

When he could open them again, he was looking up at her. She had one hand on her hip; the other gripped the handle of a mop that had its head buried in a rolling bucket.

"You're early," she said, squinting down at him. "Or else you spent the night."

Foster wasn't sure what to tell Jenny. Should he say that somebody rang his doorbell last night, but he ran away instead of answering the door? Or that he saw Mrs. Kallman through the window at Walmart? Neither of those sounded like a reason to be waking up in the kitchen at Pondside. And what should he say about the doll he had stashed behind his back?

"What d'you got there behind you?" Jenny said.

"Nothing."

"It's a doll," she said.

He neither confirmed nor denied this.

"Let me see," she said.

He handed it over. First the leg, then the rest.

"And come on out from under there."

He did as he was told, slowly and carefully. Jenny let go of the mop handle—which remained standing in the bucket like a skinny sidekick—while she reattached the doll's leg. It took her all of three seconds to do it. Then she held the doll at arm's length, examining it. "This looks like that doll Mrs. Kallman brought along to give that crazy lady."

"Which crazy lady?"

"The one pulled the shower out the wall."

"Her? Why would Robert's mother bring a doll for her?"

"That I don't know. I came out of the kitchen the other morning and Mrs. Kallman was there, setting up their table, and she had this doll—looked like this one—in a basket. She told me it was for the new lady."

"Was this before Robert—?"

"Couple days before." Jenny licked her thumb and used it to rub dirt off the doll's face. Then she looked at Foster. "Where'd you get it from?"

"I found it," Foster said.

She set the doll on the steam table, arranging its chubby legs in a sitting position. As she smoothed its dirty pink dress over its lap, Foster realized he was still holding the diaper. He shoved it down into his pocket just in time. Jenny turned and looked him up and down. "*Were* you here all night?"

"It's a long story," Foster said. When Jenny kept looking at him, he added, "I needed a place to crash."

"*Hmph*," she said. She reached for the mop. "Don't suppose you care to help me clean up this mess I got to clean up. Waiting for me when I came in the door."

Foster took the handle of the mop from Jenny and pushed the rolling bucket ahead of them toward one of the big stainless steel refrigerators. On the floor in front of it, small white plastic containers were scattered like buoys in a shiny lake. They were pudding cups, the individual serving kind, some intact, some squashed, in a lake of brown pudding. Foster was glad he hadn't walked this way in the dark. "What happened?" he asked Jenny.

"That crazy woman was in here last night, they told me."

"Which—?"

"Mary. Mary's her name. Same one as pulled out the shower. Lord forgive me, I shouldn't call her crazy."

"What was she doing in here?"

"Hungry, I guess."

"Looks like she stomped on some of them."

"I heard she don't like chocolate."

Foster looked at the puddle of pudding. Smears and spatters were drying along the edges, like mud on a shore. "Wish I'd seen her do it," he said.

"Same here."

They cleaned it up, and Foster rolled the mop and bucket back to maintenance while Jenny washed her hands. They were already late starting breakfast, so he was surprised when Jenny said, "If you want, I could clean that doll up real quick so you could give her back."

Steam rose from the sink as she squeezed dish suds through the doll's dress and then held it under the stream to rinse. Foster didn't know how she could put her hands in water that hot. The doll waited, wet and naked but unperturbed, on the counter, a bit of clear tape, Foster noticed, stuck to its chest. He still had the diaper in his pocket.

"There you go." Jenny shook out the dress and the bonnet and hung them on the door of the oven she was heating up to bake biscuits. "Should be dry enough after breakfast. You can give it back to that poor woman then."

Foster almost pointed out that Mrs. Kallman wouldn't be at breakfast, and then he realized that she meant Mary McIntyre.

Breakfast was the liveliest meal of the day at Pondside Manor. No sooner had Foster finished helping Jenny roll the carts of hot biscuits, scrambled egg plates, and bowls of oatmeal around the dining room, than he heard somebody call, "Foster!"

He turned and saw it was Tori Mahoney. She was sitting at a nearby table with Dan the trembling man and three other residents—all of them pretty tough customers when it came to getting food down their gullets instead of on their clothing protectors. Tori sat down a spoon and stood. "Can you take over for me here?" she said. "I'm sorry to ask, I know you're swamped, but I've got meds to line up." She gave him a look—long and thoughtful enough to make Foster's mouth go dry. "You look like you had a rough night. Out late?"

Foster pulled back the chair, sat down, and picked up the spoon, mostly to avoid eye contact with Tori Mahoney. He wasn't about to tell her that he'd spent the night in the kitchen. "I guess I didn't sleep too good."

"You went to the funeral home," she said, as if she'd just remembered. "Amelia said she saw you." To his great surprise, Tori put her hand on his shoulder. He had to meet her eye then, if only for a second. She gave his shoulder a squeeze before she moved on. This froze Foster in place long enough to make Dan the trembling man say in his slow, deliberate drawl, "Let's eat, huh?"

"Sure," said Foster. "Sorry." He delivered a first mouthful of scrambled egg to everyone around the table, then a second. While they chewed,

Foster scanned the dining room. It looked like a skeleton crew of three CNAs, each one somehow handling two tables of four. He spotted Duane Lotspeich sitting by the windows where the Kallmans should have been. Duane was chowing down all by himself, right where Robert would have parked his wheelchair, as if the old man had been waiting for a chance to enjoy the view—except Duane wasn't looking out the window. He was looking straight at Foster, giving him a nod now that they'd made eye contact, possibly even *smiling* at Foster, although that might have been a grimace as he swallowed. Foster made a point of returning Duane Lotspeich's smile or grimace with a scowl before he looked away and found Dan the trembling man waiting with his eyes closed, apparently focused on keeping his head still and his mouth open, for another scoop of scrambled eggs. "Sorry, man," he said, as he shoveled in a heaping spoonful. Jenny gave him the evil eye from a neighboring table. She was busy with a trio of stroke survivors, all of whom could feed themselves but needed reminding to take another bite.

Foster didn't see Mary McIntyre anywhere in the dining room. He was relieved at first—until it occurred to him that a visit to Wild Mary's room might now be required to return the doll. His only prior encounter with Mary McIntyre—aside from leaving a food tray in her room while she slept—was on the previous Wednesday, when she had swept her full bowl of pureed spaghetti off the table, splattering herself and two geezers. One of them was the late James Witkowski, come to think of it. Foster had stuck his head out of the kitchen when he heard the cussing. Witkowski was wearing a white T-shirt and khaki old-man trousers. He looked like he'd been riddled with bullets. Foster was still cleaning up the wide expanse of pureed spaghetti that night when a CNA brought Mary McIntyre *back* to the dining room in clean clothes and a wheelchair to "finish dinner." The dining room cleared out pretty fast after her arrival, except, of course, for Robert, whose table looked like it might be within splattering distance this time. The CNA had seated her and then split, looking delighted to find Foster still on duty, since that meant *he* could microwave another serving of pureed spaghetti and offer it to Wild Mary. Mary McIntyre didn't look at Foster when he set the bowl in front of her. He backed away from the table as fast as he could. Just following orders, he wanted to say. While he was clearing tables, Mary sat quietly, the bowl untouched in front of her. Robert appeared to be keeping an eye on her as he chewed, although his wheelchair was angled discreetly away from her table.

"I wonder if my daughter knows I'm here," she said suddenly, in a loud, clear voice.

Robert turned his wheels in her direction. He said, "Your daughterrr comes to seeee you everrry day."

Mary McIntyre said, "I beg your pardon?"

Foster heard this exchange from the doorway between the kitchen and the dining room, where he was waiting to clear the last two tables and do the after-dinner vacuuming. He often stuck around after his shift to work on the game, and if he was still here at dinnertime, Foster would inevitably help with cleanup. From the kitchen doorway, he could see Robert gather himself in order to repeat what he'd said, with a tiny pause to regroup after each word. Foster hadn't heard Robert say this many words at one time for many months. So much effort to get the lips and tongue in the proper sequence of positions, one after another: "She. Comes. To. See. You. Everrry. Day."

"She does?" Mary McIntyre said. "Really?"

"Yes!"

"Are you okay?" she asked him.

"ALS," he said.

"Pardon?"

He took a breath. "Lou Gehrrrig disease."

"I've heard of that." She looked down at the bowl in front of her as if she'd never seen it before and asked, "What is this?"

"Spaghetti," Robert said, ruefully.

From the doorway, Foster saw her lips moving, as if she were trying out the same sounds Robert had just made. Then she said, "No, it's not."

Robert tilted his head back and looked around. Although Foster could have taken evasive action, he stayed where he was, and when Robert caught his eye, Foster came to the table. "What's up?" he said.

Robert said, "She can't eeeat this."

Mary McIntyre looked at her lap.

"It's her orders," Foster said. "Pureed. I looked at the chart. Due to level of consciousness, it says. I guess she was still out of it when they evaluated her."

"Can't you get herrr toast?"

"I can get pureed toast."

"Come on," Robert said. "Look at herrr. She can eat! Get herrr a jel-ly sandwich. Want a jel-ly sandwich?" he asked Mary.

She nodded.

"I can help you eat your spaghetti," Foster offered.

She pressed her lips tight together.

"Aren't you hungry?" Foster asked, and to his dismay, he saw her watery brown eyes fill up and almost spill over.

Robert growled.

Foster had lowered his voice then and glanced back at the swinging doors that led to the kitchen. "If I get you a jelly sandwich, will you eat it? I hate to risk my job if you're not going to eat it."

She kept her eyes lowered and her hands in her lap.

"I'll see what I can do," Foster said.

He had made the sandwich himself, and after delivering it, he took a well-timed and somewhat lengthy cigarette break. When he came back, Mary McIntyre was gone. Robert was still working on his garlic bread, chewing and chewing. Foster sat down across from him. Finally, Robert swallowed. He pointed to a small plate streaked with jelly on the next table. "Shhheee ate the whole thing," he said.

Only now, days later, at breakfast, as he carefully pulled the spoon out from between the clenched teeth of Dan the trembling man, did Foster realize that those five words were the last ones he ever heard Robert say.

# CHAPTER 9

After breakfast and cleanup and a lecture from Jenny about making hungry people wait for their next mouthful "while your mind wanders around the dining room," Foster watched her put the baby doll—again in its pink dress and bonnet—into a white bakery box he'd found in recycling. (Foster felt weird carrying the doll in his arms.) Mixed in with her lecture, Jenny reported that she'd heard a CNA saying that they couldn't rouse Mary in time for breakfast this morning after her late-night wanderings—"Plus, she must have been full of pudding," Jenny said—and that one of them was going to have to get her ready and take her to physical therapy.

"If you hurry," Jenny told Foster, "you can put the doll on her bed before she gets back to her room." She handed him the box. "Good luck."

Foster carried the box to the men's room at the end of Hawkeye Lane and locked the door. He took the doll's diaper out of his pants pocket. It was weird, lifting the doll out and then struggling to get its bare feet through the leg holes in the prepinned diaper. When he picked it up to put it back in the box, the eyes opened, the glassy blue eyes, and *that* sent a jolt through him like the one he felt when he found the doll on his bike outside Walmart, only minutes after seeing *Mrs. Kallman* outside Walmart—*Mrs. Kallman* who brought this very doll to Pondside, according to Jenny. Okay, this could be a different doll that happened to be *like* the other one, but either way, Mrs. Kallman had shown up in its—or their—vicinity twice.

The big question was: Why would Mrs. Kallman want *Foster* to have the doll? If it had anything to do with the laptop, if Robert *had* told her what he'd asked Foster to do, why didn't she just ask Foster about it at the funeral last night? What had she said to him? Something like: *You know better than anyone how many people depend on Robert to give them hope.* When she said it, Foster couldn't think of anything in the world that he knew better than anyone—except maybe how messed up the world was—but riding home, it had struck him that she was talking about the game. *The World of Pondside.* Which made her comment pretty ironic, he thought. Apparently, she didn't know that the game was down, and the server was missing.

Or did she? Foster looked the doll in the eye. "Wait a minute," he said out loud.

"Oh!" said a voice from the other side of the men's room door, and at that moment the door handle, which was in the closed-and-locked position, jiggled. "Sorry," the voice added.

Foster somehow managed to stash the doll in the box and close the flaps and—on second or third thought—flush the toilet. Then he ran water in the sink, stuck the box under his arm, and opened the door.

It was Dakota, the brown-nosing CNA, looking wholesome and apologetic but also a tiny bit amused. "Sorry," he said again, his eyes darting oh so quickly from Foster's face to the box and back to his face again. "I didn't know anyone was in there."

Foster would have liked to remind him that staff weren't supposed to use this particular men's room. It was for visitors only. Recognizing, of course, that he was in no position to do that, he mumbled, "It's all yours."

Under other circumstances, Foster might have kicked himself all the way down Boysenberry Boulevard for saying something so stupid—"It's all yours!"—instead of saying nothing at all, but all he cared about at the moment was getting another look at every inch of the doll to see if he had missed something Mrs. Kallman was trying to tell him. Suddenly, it seemed not only possible but inevitable that she *did* know the where-abouts of the *World of Pondside* server and that she was trying to convey exactly that information to *Foster* so he could reboot the game that so many people depended upon to give them hope—or at least, to keep them busy with whatever fantasy made them want to get up in the morning. Right about then, a little voice in his head asked him *how* Mrs. Kallman would have gotten hold of the server, *who* could have taken it out of Robert's room, and *why*, if Mrs. Kallman wanted to give him the server, had she given him the doll instead? Foster answered himself, silently but with a touch of sarcasm: she couldn't very well tie a laptop to the fender of his bicycle, could she? The doll was only the messenger.

He slipped past the nurses' station at the head of Hawkeye Lane. Nobody in sight, as usual. It had to be illegal for this place to be so sparsely staffed, Foster thought.

Mary McIntyre's room was 2202A-B, a double with only one oc-cupant—like so many rooms at Pondside—kitty-corner across the hall from Duane Lotspeich's. Duane had already voiced his opinion that the new girl belonged with the lost souls in Memory Lane, based on the loud wailing that sometimes came from her room—and, of course, there was the broken shower. Duane Lotspeich's opinions were usually pretty worthless, but this one might have some merit, Foster thought, although a doctor would have to sign the orders to move her to a dif-ferent level of care.

Foster could see from the end of the hall that some jokester had stuck a streamer of yellow caution tape to Mary McIntyre's door. It oc-curred to him that he couldn't risk her showing up while he dismantled her baby doll, never mind that he intended to reassemble it. Instead of continuing down Hawkeye Lane, Foster ducked into the shower supply closet this time and pulled the door shut. If anybody opened it, he would stuff the doll behind a stack of towels and pretend to be doing some-thing else entirely. He figured he had a little time before the scheduled morning activities broke up and briefly populated the hallways with geezers and CNAs.

He wasted no time pulling off all four limbs and holding each one up to the overhead light, looking for words or signs—clues of any kind. He couldn't bring himself to remove the doll's head, not only because it was stuck on very firmly but also because he could see that pulling the head off would ruin the eyes' open-and-shut mechanism, probably for good. Foster thought that if he were Mary McIntyre and somebody left a baby doll on the bed with its eyes sunken in or popping out, he would be pretty freaked out. Mary McIntyre didn't need any help in the freaking-out department.

Having seen Jenny reattach a leg, Foster was able to reassemble the doll and set her up in the box as if nothing had ever happened. (It was easier to get the diaper back on before attaching the legs, he discovered.) For all his trouble, he had found only three little words imprinted in the doll's pink plastic surface, just above the realistically dimpled butt: *Made in China.* The bit of tape he'd noticed earlier on the doll's chest area was gone. If only he had examined the doll before he tore out of the parking lot on his bike, he might have found something attached with the tape. Disappointed again, Foster put his ear to the door and, hearing nothing out in the hall, he pulled the door open and almost fell into the lap of Duane Lotspeich.

"Shit," Foster said as he danced back from the wheelchair.

"Not in your drawers, I hope," Duane said cheerfully. He sniffed a couple of times. "What's in the box?"

"I have to go, Duane. I've gotta put this—away." Lifting the box, Foster used it to gesture toward the door across the hall. He tried to step around the old man.

Duane Lotspeich gave one wheel a tug and his chair turned sharply into Foster's path. He could turn that wheelchair on a dime, Foster thought.

"In the new girl's room?" Duane said. "You're pretty brave."

Foster stopped trying to step around the wheelchair. "Is she in there?"

"I don't think so. It's pretty quiet right now. But she'll be coming around the corner when she comes." Duane nodded toward his room. The door was only a few feet away. "C'mon in here, kid. I got something I wanna show you."

"*Whoa,*" Foster said.

"For Christ's sake. What do you think I'm talking about? It's something you wanna see. It's what you're looking for."

"Yeah, I don't think so." This time Foster dodged the wheelchair. He dashed past Duane and across the hall.

Foster would have known this room was Mary McIntyre's even without the blurry photo above her name next to the door. The litter of pudding cups and plastic spoons on top of the regulation blond Pondside dresser gave her away. Except for the pudding, her room looked like any other room up and down the halls of Pondside Manor. Mary McIntyre's bed was already made, or hadn't been slept in. The fake leather lounge chair was draped with a towel and a few items of clothing, the bedside table littered with the usual—tissue box, plastic drinking cup with straw, etc. He was trying to decide where to put the doll and whether to take it out of the box when he froze at the sound of voices in the hall. He listened as they got closer, one voice murmuring in a professionally firm but soothing way and the other—the one that was saying, "I don't *need* a little rest, I just got up an hour ago!"—getting louder and shriller. Foster opened the top dresser drawer—it was filled with unopened pudding packs, no-chill, he hoped—and shut it again. He didn't try the other drawers. He left the doll in the box on the leatherette chair and stuck his head out the door to see if the coast was still clear.

On the other side of the hall, Duane Lotspeich was inside his doorway, waving Foster over. *What the heck?* Foster thought and sprang across Hawkeye Lane. The old guy was in a wheelchair, after all.

Once he was inside the room, Foster discovered that the old man had somehow gotten behind him to shut the door.

"Well, what do you think?" Duane asked, gleefully.

Foster had a theory that the Dirty Old Man (and Woman) behavior you sometimes saw among the geezers had to do with having spent their formative years in the ironclad sexual repression of the 1950s and so forth. In principle, there was something refreshing about their finally saying to hell with the puritanical bullshit and letting it all hang out—but that was only in principle, not in living color a few feet away.

Foster braced himself as he turned around, half-expecting to see more of Duane Lotspeich than he ever wanted to see.

But Lotspeich was merely pointing (with his finger) at the dresser in the corner of his room. Occupying what looked like a hastily cleared space on top of it was a laptop computer. Foster needed to go one step farther into the room to see the PALS sticker on the cover, with the little yellow duck standing in for the *S*.

Duane was chuckling in his wheelchair. "Didn't I say I had something you wanted to see?"

Foster tried not to sound astonished. "Where did you get this?"

"From the guy's room."

"Robert's, you mean?"

"It's the *World of Pondside* computer. Isn't it?" Duane sounded suddenly uncertain.

"You took it from Robert's room—*you* did? When?"

"Same day he went into the pond. That morning."

"It wasn't *in* his room that morning."

"*Ha!*" Duane said, the smirk returning to his voice. "You mean it wasn't in there when *you* went looking for it. I guess we know which one of us is the early bird, eh, kid?"

Foster approached the dresser where Robert's laptop displaced Duane Lotspeich's eyeglass case, nail clippers, foot powder, hair dressing, and other geezer shit—all of that stuff now pushed to the back and the sides—leaving a framed 5×7 of a young man in a tuxedo and a girl in a long dress, dancing, perilously close to the edge of the dresser. Foster moved the photo to a safer spot. He laid a hand flat on the silver cover of the laptop. It felt cool to his palm. He wondered if Duane had been smart enough to take the power cord. Foster couldn't remember if he had seen the cord in Robert's room Thursday morning. They could get one, no problem, if Duane didn't have it. But he wasn't going to let the old man off so easily.

"You *stole* this laptop," Foster said. "You could go to jail."

"Wait—you mean they could put me away in some little room where I didn't want to be?" Duane Lotspeich looked around. "I wonder what *that* would be like." He wheeled himself half a turn closer to Foster and the laptop. "I was thinking that you might be able to start this thing up again. Am I right?"

Foster made a further adjustment to the position of the dancing couple on the dresser. "Maybe."

"What do you mean, maybe? You've got a password, don't you?"

"So do you."

"Mine doesn't work," Duane complained. "I mean, I can't even get to the log in place where you put it."

"You've tried?"

"Yeah, I tried. I don't how many times. It just says, 'Not Found' or 'Not Responding.'" The old man tapped the laptop. "I figured the ducklink didn't work in the library because *this* thing was turned off. So I turned it on. The ducklink still didn't work. So I turned it off again."

"You mean the laptop was turned off when you found it? Are you sure?" Robert Kallman knew that people logged into *The World of Pondside* at all hours—geezers napped like cats. So why did he turn off the server? "It wasn't just in sleep mode?" he asked Duane. "Or the battery— it wasn't the battery that died?"

"Nope. It was plugged in, turned off. Maybe he didn't want just anybody messing with it after he was gone."

Foster had nothing to say about that.

Duane waited about five seconds—was he actually giving Foster a little space?—before he asked, "So did he give you a new password or not?"

Foster hesitated. Then he said, "Not."

"Well, that's the end then!" For the first time the old man sounded aggrieved. "Who else would he give it to? What else can we do?"

"We can try my log-in. Where's the power cord? I hope the modem's still on."

"You haven't even *tried* to get in yet?"

Foster himself wasn't sure how he had mustered the willpower to stay away from the ducklink this long. For five days, he'd made no attempt to log in. That was the longest he'd gone without in the two years since the game's creation. He had been telling himself that he was worried about what might happen with the *Pondside* server in unknown hands. He didn't want to click on the ducklink and download malware or give away his IP address to persons unknown. That's what he'd been telling himself. Now that he had the server in front of him, he knew *that* wasn't what he was worried about, not at all. Foster was afraid that Robert might be waiting for him on his grandparents' screened porch, and that all he had to say to Foster was "Goodbye."

# CHAPTER 10

Given the circumstances—which included James Witkowski's precarious cardiac health and the excessive weight of his tackle box (even with wheels), not to mention the stress of having (possibly) found a body in the pond—it didn't take long for the medical examiner to determine the cause and probable manner of the old man's death. The story that appeared in the local paper on Monday reported that Witkowski, eighty-seven, had died of a heart attack in the early morning hours on Thursday, October 10. The story was accompanied by a thumb-size photo of Witkowski and a larger shot of some police officers and paramedics maneuvering an inflatable Zodiac raft at the edge of the pond.

At Pondside Manor, someone had cut the story out of the paper and pinned it to the bulletin board over the handwashing station in the kitchen. Dakota Engelhart spotted it there when he came in at eleven a.m. He washed his hands thoroughly enough to read the whole thing. Robert Kallman's death by drowning, which occurred that same late night or early morning, was "still under investigation," the story said.

That explained the government plates on the unmarked Ford in the parking lot, Dakota thought.

At the nurses' station, he found the usually cheerful and optimistic Amelia Ramirez looking flushed and agitated. Amelia confirmed that the investigators had returned.

"They asked me the same questions they asked before!" she told Dakota. "I try to tell them that Robert's interest in eating was the *opposite* of suicidal and they turn it around as if I'm agreeing that the diet thing was a reason for him to kill himself. Too bad I couldn't tell them that half the CNAs would have brought him tacos from La Casita, if he wanted them—no matter what kind of diet he was supposed to be on." Her eyes flashed in Dakota's direction. "Don't you think that's true?"

Dakota did think it was true. He himself had occasionally been the beneficiary of the roll of five-dollar bills that Robert Kallman kept in his shirt pocket for tipping purposes, but he wasn't sure he should say so, even to Amelia Ramirez. While he was deciding whether or not to mention that he had (more than once) brought the man a Culver's ButterBurger and fries, one half of the double door that led to Memory Lane glided open and the meds cart appeared with Tori behind it.

"I really didn't know Robert Kallman all that well," Dakota decided to say. He hastened to add that, while he wouldn't go as far as the kitchen guy, who took every opportunity to declare the whole *investigation* "a pile of crap," Kallman did not seem to Dakota like the suicidal type.

"Not the 'suicidal type,' eh?" said Tori, who overheard. "Well, that's a professional opinion if ever I heard one. Wish I could have come up with something like *that* when the cops talked to me. All I could tell them was that nutrition wasn't Robert Kallman's only problem. We'd been upping his pain meds pretty steadily for months. And his blood gases haven't been great lately either. Next stop: tracheostomy and a ventilator."

Tori banged the cart into its spot against the counter and looked over it toward the window that faced the visitor's lot. "My God," she said, "look what just pulled in. Who the hell drives a yellow Hummer?"

Dakota couldn't see out the window from where he stood but he glanced up at the clock and said, "Shoot. It's Erika."

Both nurses' heads turned in his direction.

"She's my girlfriend," Dakota said. *I think,* he thought. He added, "It's her brother's car."

"Are you always this glad to see her?" Amelia teased.

"We're going to lunch," Dakota said. Lunch, in the middle of today's shift, was at 3:30 p.m., Erika had decided. It was now 3:29.

"Sounds grim," said Tori, and she turned back to sign off on her charts.

*Grim* was not a word that Dakota would have used to describe meeting Erika for lunch. Tense, yes, but not grim. Nothing about Erika was grim. She was like a ray of sunshine—literally, like one. Sitting across from him in a wooden booth at the Blue Bird Café, she glowed: her skin, her hair, her golden hazel eyes. Even now, in a less than excellent mood and thus without the added brilliance of an orthodontist's daughter's smile, she lit up the place. Once, when all the pledges in her sorority had to come up with a single adjective to describe themselves that started with the same letter as their first name, Erika had called Dakota for his opinion: Was she *enthusiastic, energetic, empathetic,* or *effervescent?* "The last two are kind of weird," she admitted, but unfortunately, neither *friendly* nor *bubbly* started with *E*.

"All of the above!" Dakota had diplomatically declared, and he suggested adding *excellent, endearing,* and *erotic,* each of which Erika rejected out of hand. If he remembered correctly, she had gone with *enthusiastic,* which was accurate but would have been his last choice.

The Blue Bird Café was nearly empty in the late afternoon, the perfect setting for a Make-Up-or-Break-Up lunch. Despite the silly name, this was the mechanism—neutral territory, cards on the table—whereby they had weathered several minor crises during the two and a half years they'd been together. Dakota assumed that she'd gotten the idea from her sorority, but it turned out this one came from her mother. "My parents have been married twenty-nine years," she'd told Dakota the first time she suggested the idea, "and they *still* do a Make-Up-or-Break-Up at least once a year." Dakota thought that added up to a lot of marital crises, but he decided not to mention it.

Erika worked at her salad, poking and picking at it without ever taking a bite.

"So now you want to be a *teacher*?" she said suddenly. Her expressive eyebrows, in concert with all the rest of her, conveyed disbelief, disappointment, disapproval, out-and-out disdain. Not an *E* word in the bunch, Dakota noticed. "Why don't you just switch to hotel management?"

*Too close to what I do already*, Dakota thought. "I like kids," he said.

"I like kids, too," Erika said, "but that doesn't mean I want to be a *teacher*."

*Upgrade from disdain to scorn*, Dakota thought. Or maybe that was a downgrade. Erika, who must have noticed it herself, changed her tone.

"Okay. So you like kids," she said, sounding brighter all of a sudden, as if this were a problem for which there might be a solution, a disease for which they could find a cure. "Be a pediatrician!"

"I could never give a kid a shot," Dakota said.

This was something to which he'd actually given some thought. Erika's sorority had brought in a speaker last semester, a "Personal Trainer for Success," who'd made a big impression on Erika and her sorority sisters, most of whom—like Erika—were prenursing. All you had to do to get where you wanted to go in life, she reported to Dakota with *enthusiasm*, was to "Visualize Yourself in the Future YOU Want!" It hadn't seemed like a particularly new or revolutionary idea to Dakota, but in his recent state of doubt about the future, he had tried it on a number of medical fields, including pediatrics. He had closed his eyes and pictured an examination room with Disney critters on the wall. He pictured himself in nice pants and a shirt with a *SpongeBob SquarePants* tie, his white coat hanging open, stethoscope on his neck, *Dr. D. Engelhart* embroidered on the pocket (that part of it was nice), and here, standing on the exam table, a little kid with his butt bared and his chubby arms around his mother's neck and both their chins a-tremble.

Visualization was shockingly effective, Dakota found.

The waitress came to their table then and asked if there was anything else they wanted. She had a tattoo on her chest, a fancy arrow that pointed into the plunging hand-cut neckline of her snug tie-dyed T-shirt. Erika had nicknamed her "Arrowhead." She had waited on them before. Dakota struggled to avoid dropping his gaze to her name tag, which was pretty deep in tie-dyed territory.

"Just the check, thanks," Dakota said. "Amber."

Erika waited until the waitress was out of earshot. Then she said: "*Those who can, do. Those who can't, teach.* Ever hear that expression?"

"Sure I've heard it, but I don't believe it. Do you?" Dakota said this more *emphatically* than he meant to. He expected an argument, but instead, Erika's shoulders slumped. "I don't know," she said, her head bowed over her barely touched salad. She sounded genuinely sad, very un-Erika. Dakota suddenly remembered that this was a Make-Up-or-Break-Up occasion.

She looked up at him, her eyes more gray than hazel, and said, "The nurses give the shots."

Hunched over the *Pondside* laptop on Duane Lotspeich's dresser, Foster took a deep breath and typed in his username. When the password to his portal didn't work, he tried every former password he could think of. No dice. He inserted numbers and asterisks and exclamation points, moving them around among the letters. Although he knew how foolish, not to say useless, it was to proceed randomly, now that he had his fingers on the keyboard, Foster couldn't seem to stop himself from trying anything and everything to get in. He typed in Robert's username, pairing it with a long list of possible passwords—including RobertKallman, RobertK, robokallman, roboman, and more. Eventually, he resorted to the names of other *World of Pondside* players variously spelled out and abbreviated, and all of *their* passwords—Kittyland, Playball!—at least the ones he knew by heart.

He waited until Duane was busy in the bathroom before he entered the site administrator's password. Robert had shared it with Foster to give him working access to the resources of the game. The admin password took Foster to a page littered with folders that had names like *Game Development, In Progress, Assets/Laverne,* and *Assets/Lotspeich,* etc. Foster should have been able to get to his portal from here, but the only live item on the screen was the administrator email account, which he and Robert never used, not wanting to slog through a daily deluge of ads and updates from the software development company. The subject lines of the first ten or fifteen messages, visible on the screen, were the usual junk. Ignoring them, Foster ran down through the menu of links that should have allowed him to log in to any player's portal, including his own. Not one of the links lit up when the cursor passed over them—no *World of Pondside* log in boxes appeared—until he reached the end of the list. Here was something new: an additional link, it appeared to be. The letters *N* and *L* with a hyphen between them. He moved the cursor and the link turned blue. He double-clicked. A dialog box appeared on the screen!

Foster could feel his pulse pounding in his fingertips as he typed in the admin password—but it was no good. The screen invited him to "Try again." At that moment, he heard the toilet flush, and suspecting that Duane was not the kind of guy you could count on to give you a minute while he washed his hands thoroughly, Foster closed the window before the old man rolled out of the bathroom.

When the phone buzzed in Foster's pocket, he almost knocked the dancing couple off Duane Lotspeich's dresser. "Jenny?" he said. "Jenny who?"

"Jenny Williams, that's who!"

"Where are you?" he said.

"In the kitchen! Where are *you?*"

It did not seem like a particularly good idea to tell her he was in Duane Lotspeich's room, trying to break into *The World of Pondside.*

Jenny didn't have time to wait for Foster's answer anyway. "Salads ain't gonna toss themselves," she said. "You best get back to work."

On his way to the kitchen, Foster spotted Pondside Administrator Landiss near the glass door to the vestibule talking to the same pair of

cops who had grilled Foster on Saturday. He asked Jenny, who was setting out the cutting boards on the salad table, if she knew what the cops
were doing here today.

"I been working for two here," she said. "No time to keep track of
the police department's activities."

Foster got back to work, chopping lettuce and tomatoes before
lunch, clearing tables and washing dishes afterward. He clocked out at
his regular three p.m. quitting time, and then put in an extra forty-five
minutes cutting pies and wrapping flatware in napkins to make up for
the time he'd spent in Duane Lotspeich's room. By four p.m., after a
combined cigarette break and brisk walk around the parking lots, he
was once again hunched over the laptop, which the old man had moved
onto a desk-high shelf in his closet. "Anybody comes in," Duane said,
"you just push the chair back, dive into the closet, and slide the door
shut—*bam!*"

Duane Lotspeich made no effort to hide his disappointment that
Robert Kallman had not entrusted Foster with some kind of top-dog
webmaster-type administrator's password, just in case.

"He did, actually," Foster said.

"Well then? Put it in there."

"I already did."

"Well, did it work?" Duane asked eagerly. "Your top-dog password?"

Foster shrugged. "He must have changed it."

"Changed it? Why?"

"It's a security thing. That's how you keep hackers out. People change
passwords all the time."

"Not when they're about to take a long ride on a short pier."

"Yeah, well, I guess Robert wasn't expecting *that* to happen."

"He wasn't expecting it?" Duane looked scornful. "You think he
*accidentally* rolled himself all the way down to the pond and fell in?"

"Or was pushed." Foster didn't really believe that Robert was pushed
into the pond—at least, he didn't want to believe it—but Duane Lotspeich could really get on a guy's nerves.

"*Pushed?*" he echoed obnoxiously. "Who by? His mother maybe?

Somebody looking to collect his life insurance? You're as crazy as Laverne. What kind of moron murders somebody who's already practically dead?"

Robert had made a similar point himself once. He had declined some procedure his doctor recommended—it was a feeding tube, Foster remembered—by saying, among other things, "over my dead body." The frustrated doctor had threatened a suicide watch. "So I asked him," Robert told Foster, "why would I go to the trrrouble of killing myself? My body was doing it for me. I didn't have to lift a fingerrr."

At the time, the feeding tube didn't sound like such a bad idea to Foster, although he never said as much to Robert.

"What do you mean," Foster asked Duane Lotspeich, "crazy as Laverne?"

Pondside administrator Kitty Landiss stood at the windows in her office and watched the two detectives return to their unmarked police car in the employee parking lot, the jackets of their business suits flapping wildly in a wind that was swirling fallen leaves into whirling dervishes here and there in the emptier expanses of the lot. The woman detective stumbled when her heel caught on something in the asphalt. The man pulled his flying tie around to the front once, twice, and then he just kept hold of it, as if he had himself on a leash. To Kitty, they looked less like police officers and more like teenagers cast as detectives in the school play.

Over the weekend, Kitty had dared to hope that things might soon return to something like normal at Pondside Manor. She guessed that more than half of the eighty-four residents currently living in the facility were only dimly aware (or had already forgotten and thus were not overly concerned) that one of their number had drowned in the pond last Thursday and another had gone fishing and never come back. Pondside had lucked out with the local TV news, whose coverage of death at a nursing home had been edged right out of the lineup by the firing of a high school football coach, a missing coed at the university, and a presidential visit to area wind farms, all on the same Thursday that

Robert Kallman drowned in the pond. If it hadn't been for the *field trip* to his funeral visitation, the general level of awareness of the tragic events might be even lower, at least among the residents. Their families were a different story.

Not that the deaths had made big headlines, but the stories were out there if you looked for them, and sadly, the online news had a lot more room for pictures. Photos of Pondside Manor signage and a pair of white-haired ladies in their wheelchairs in the parking lot (taken from behind, of course) kept showing up on news site after news site. The most frequently appearing quote came from Laverne Slatchek: "He was a nice man, but only his mother could understand him." Two more Pondside families had begun arrangements to transfer their loved ones to another facility—four residents had already moved over the week-end—and CNAs appeared to be quitting at a rate of one per day, some of them claiming to be "freaked out" by the tragic events, while others seemed nervous about the police presence for reasons of their own.

Kitty had been the last person to meet with the investigators today, and after answering many of the same questions for the third time, it was clear to her that, regardless of Robert Kallman's disposition and the reasons he might have had to take his own life, a ruling would never be reached in the case as long as one piece of information remained missing. No one had been able to explain how the man got out of the building and onto the pier. Someone must have opened that door for him, and someone rolled him up over the bump where the path met the pier, but no one knew who. In three rounds of questioning, the only name that anyone (including Kitty Landiss) could suggest was James Witkowski's.

Unfortunately, the police had already determined, using what-ever unpleasant evidence they use to determine such things, that James Witkowski had exited the building at least two hours *after* Robert Kall-man drowned. So the investigation of what had seemed to her like an open-and-shut case—a non-case, really—was far from over. The two detectives who just exited the parking lot had informed her that the aquatic team would be back tomorrow with wet suits and other para-phernalia to take additional measurements and, possibly, to dredge the

muddy bottom of the pond. That meant the reporter would undoubtedly be back on the premises, too, pestering people.

Gazing out the window at the sparsely populated employee parking
lot, Kitty wasn't sure what to do about the two bona fide, pretrained,
ready-to-work CNAs she had coming in for job interviews tomorrow.
One of them was a college student—prenursing, no less. When the college student spoke with Kitty on the phone, she had asked quite a few
questions about the tragic events, wanting to know if any CNAs had
been involved in the discovery of the victims, and so forth. (The other
girl only asked what Pondside was paying and was overtime available.)
Kitty wondered if she should contact either or both of them to resched-
ule, rather than risk scaring them off with all the commotion of police
in the pond. She couldn't imagine that dredging a former farm pond
was going to uncover anything pleasant.

When Dakota Engelhart got back from lunch at four thirty on the dot,
he couldn't help but notice Tori and Amelia talking in a kind of huddle
inside the circle of the nurses' station. There was, he thought, a hint of
urgency in the way Tori's top-knot ponytail was quivering—*Why hadn't
she gone home by now?*—and an uncharacteristic shadow of dismay, even
alarm, in Amelia's furrowed brow. When they glanced up, he lifted his
hand in greeting, consulted the clipboard of CNA tasks on the counter,
and turned briskly down Hawkeye Lane, en route to the Shower Tower,
which was parked outside the shower room, about halfway down the
hall from the nurses' station.

Dakota plunged both arms into the hamper of clean towels beside
the shelves and brought up a bundle for folding. He liked folding. His
mother had shown him how to smooth and fold a T-shirt, how to line
up the seams on a pair of pants. That was back in junior high, during
the laundry unit in Life Skills, after which she decided that he would be
responsible for doing his own laundry. He had been amazed later, when
he lived in the dorms, to see how many people took their bag of dirty

laundry home on weekends. "You'll make somebody a nice little wife," guys goaded him about his stacks of neatly folded T-shirts and shorts and towels, but the fact was that Dakota met a lot of girls in the laundry room. *(Thank you, Mom.)* Some of the girls didn't know the dryers from the washing machines either—Erika included. It was after he'd helped her smooth and fold a load of *her* clothes, his fingers getting into every pocket and corner of her sweats and underwear, that they went up to her room that first time.

The memory made him feel (among other things) a little sad.

"Dakota!" He looked up. The nurses' station was empty, and Tori was nowhere in sight, but Amelia was striding down the hall toward him in her sea-green scrubs. Amelia Ramirez's hair was abundant and so black it was almost blue. It made her look like a Marvel superhero. Dakota gave himself a break from folding towels to watch her hair floating around her shoulders as she walked. When she stopped—less than a foot from him and the Shower Tower—she had a strangely determined look on her face.

"We need to talk, Dakota. Right now."

It wasn't every day that raven-haired Amelia Ramirez grabbed your arm and pulled you into the shower room. Dakota offered no resistance, even when Amelia pulled the door shut behind them.

# CHAPTER 11

On Tuesday, Foster's phone alarm went off at 5:25 a.m., nearly catapulting him out of the leatherette chair and into Duane Lotspeich's closet. He made a grab for the open laptop he had almost knocked off the shelf and stared for a moment at the pastel polo shirts swinging in front of his face. Then he looked over his shoulder. On the other side of the room, a thin vertical stripe of light widened, and Duane Lotspeich stuck his head out of the bathroom. "Thought I'd let you get some shut-eye," he said around his toothbrush. "Time to rise and shine!"

Without exactly meaning to, Foster had spent another night at Pondside Manor. He made himself as presentable as he could at the sink in Duane's bathroom and reported to the kitchen at five forty-five.

When he returned to Lotspeich's room after breakfast cleanup, the old man was at his window, which overlooked the visitor's parking lot and the pond below it. "Cops in the pond!" he said cheerfully. "They're rolling a wheelchair down to the pier!"

Foster had seen two cruisers and a panel truck drive past the dining room windows during breakfast. The kitchen, where he did most of his work, had no windows, leaving him torn between wanting to know what the police were doing out there—"Looks like they'll be playing in the water," Tori Mahoney said when she came into the kitchen to wash her hands—and feeling grateful that he didn't have to watch. Already the mere mention of "cops in the pond" and "wheelchair" and "pier" had him picturing Robert securely strapped and Velcroed into his motorized wheelchair, rolling down the asphalt path to the pond. Foster couldn't stop his brain from adding details: the look on Robert's face as the wheelchair somehow got over the bump where the path met the pier, the whine of the battery-powered motor punctuated by the *bump, bump, bump* of the wheels over the boards. These images would be stuck in his head for the rest of the morning, if not for the rest of his life.

Duane rolled away from the window. "You know, I wouldn't use one of those fancy auto-powered chairs if they gave me one for free." He had come back to the room to get his jacket, he said. "Everybody's out there," he told Foster as he stuffed his arms into his sleeves. When Foster made no move to join him, Duane said, "You're not coming? Well, suit yourself."

Laverne Slatchek was as eager as the next person to see what the police were doing down at the pond, but first, she thought she'd take advantage of the general exodus to do a little investigating of her own. Laverne had no problem looking as if she were merely loitering in Hawkeye Lane when she was, in fact, eavesdropping with the help of a hearing aid turned to the max. She had placed herself right outside Duane Lotspeich's door, which put her just a few steps away from the door to Mary McIntyre's room on the other side of the hallway.

*Breathe,* Laverne reminded herself, and then winced. The hearing aid made her every breath sound like a monsoon.

Laverne wasn't sure if anyone was in Duane's room or not. She also wasn't sure she believed Duane when he claimed that he and Foster, the kitchen boy, had made no progress in gaining entry to *The World of Pondside.* How could they be in there fiddling with that computer for so many hours and make no progress? "I'll tell you how," Duane had growled in her ear at breakfast this morning. "That guy doesn't know any more about it than we do. That's how." Laverne didn't believe that either. Young Foster had been working with poor Robert on the computer for years now, it seemed like. Any time you had a problem with your portal—you couldn't get in or when you did, the sound was off or the picture was wonky—all you had to do was get that young man to come down to the library and he would click and tap and scroll around for a minute and *Bingo!* You were back in business. Sometimes he would say something incomprehensible like, "Just had to sink everything up," or, "Lotsa users on this machine. Time to clean the catch." Incomprehensible or not, the kid always seemed to know what he was doing.

Whatever he was doing in there now, if he was in there, he and Duane didn't talk much. Or maybe Foster was in there alone. If that was the case, then he must be talking to himself now and again. Laverne had heard a cuss word or two—very quietly spoken—but she couldn't tell who was talking. The hearing aid made some white noise of its own when it was turned up all the way, and she kept forgetting and holding her breath, which only made her heart pound louder. She was lucky, really, given the way she was leaning over the front of the walker toward Duane Lotspeich's door, that she didn't fall right into his room when somebody behind her said, "WHAT'S UP, LAVERNE?"

Tori Mahoney grabbed Laverne's elbow to steady her while she struggled to adjust the volume on the hearing aid. "LOOKING FOR SOMEBODY?" Tori said.

Laverne gave up and pulled the device off her ear. "No," she said too loudly.

"That's good," the nurse said. "Because I don't think you're going to find anybody. They're all outside, watching the show."

Laverne caught the word *outside*. She hoped she hadn't damaged her hearing permanently. "Yes, yes," she said. "Just on my way out to see."

"Take it easy now." Tori patted Laverne's shoulder. "You seemed a tad wobbly there."

"I'm fine," Laverne said. She looked up and down Hawkeye Lane. *Where*, she wondered, *had Tori Mahoney come from?*

"Why don't I just walk with you down the hall?" Tori said.

She might have approached from the shady recesses in Laverne's right field of vision—or she might have come out of Mary McIntyre's room. Suddenly, Laverne had an idea. Not wanting to be too direct, she said, "Do you think Mary McIntyre would like to come, too?"

"She's probably out there already."

Encouraged, Laverne said, "I wonder if she ever got that doll Mrs. Kallman brought for her, what with everything that was going on."

Tori Mahoney's reaction was more than Laverne could have hoped for. The nurse actually stopped and gave Laverne an inscrutable look. Then, she shrugged. "I don't know," she said and resumed walking. "I don't know if she found it or not."

Well, Laverne thought, at least no one could accuse her of imagining the doll now. Tori Mahoney had used the word *found*. Did Mrs. Kallman just leave the doll in Mary's room for her to find? Or did Tori mean that Mary McIntyre *had* the doll but lost it?

Laverne said, "I haven't seen it anywhere since—you know." This *since—you know* was a little white lie, under the circumstances. Tori would not assume that Laverne meant, *since the kitchen boy had it under his arm when he was locking up his bike out by the dumpster the other night*. When Tori didn't respond, Laverne tried again. "Do you think maybe somebody else found it?"

But Tori had lost interest in the doll, it seemed, and in Laverne as well. "Here we are," Tori said. She tapped the four-button code on the keypad next to the door. "I'm glad to see you've got a sweater. It's chilly out there." Holding the door open, she flashed a quick, sad smile by way of goodbye. It occurred to Laverne that Tori Mahoney had mastered the quick, sad smile better than anyone Laverne had ever known except, of course, for her husband Bill. Toward the end, a quick, sad smile was the only kind Bill could muster.

"Out you go!"

After the police aquatic team parked their white panel truck in the visitor's lot overlooking the pond and a motorized wheelchair came rolling out the back of it, word spread quickly at Pondside Manor. By the time a cop in a wet suit settled himself in the wheelchair and set out on the curving asphalt path toward the water, residents in wheelchairs and porch furniture had formed a hedge thicker than the spirea along the edge of the parking lot.

Despite her late arrival, Laverne found a seat right in front. The fake-wicker wing chair had been vacated (Irma Hickerson told Laverne) by none other than Mary McIntyre, who left—a worried-looking CNA on her trail—when the motorized wheelchair began its descent toward the pond.

The cop in the wheelchair chugged along slowly. It looked as if he was getting himself used to the controls. A half-dozen colleagues accompanied him, two of them also in wet suits and the others toting cameras and notebooks and black duffel bags. The entourage stopped for many minutes at the spot where the asphalt path met the wooden pier. It seemed to take a long time for the officers to figure out that one of them needed to grip the motorized wheelchair by the handles and help it over the bump. Notes were made and photos taken before, during, and after the assist. Then there was another long wait while the cameras and other devices from the black duffel bags were made ready in their new locations.

Expectations rose sharply among the spectators when the cop in the wheelchair pulled a diver's hood over his head and tugged on a face mask. The other two wet suits hopped off the pier and stationed themselves thigh-deep in the water at the end of it. At this point, like most members of the audience, Laverne had a pretty good idea about what was going to happen next. Sure enough, the cop in the wheelchair—*a rookie, no doubt*, Laverne thought—rolled slowly down the length of the pier and off the end of it. The wheelchair landed in the water with a subdued but satisfying splash. Some of the residents at the edge of the parking lot forgot themselves and applauded.

The wheelchair disappeared completely under the water.

Laverne held her breath as the cops standing in the pond plunged down to pull the chair upright. While they struggled with it, the officer who had gone under popped up again, coated in mud, looking for all the world like the creature in *Creature from the Black Lagoon*, a movie that every single one of the residents gathered above the pond had seen in their youth.

Laverne had seen it twice, once with a troupe of gasping, giggling girlfriends and then with Bill. If she had closed her eyes, she could have been sitting not in a wicker wing chair dragged to the edge of a parking lot, but in a red velvet seat at a movie theater called the Avalon that had twinkling stars embedded in the painted blue ceiling. She would be wrapped in darkness and the smell of popcorn, her face pressed against Bill's shoulder, both hands gripping the hardened muscle of his upper arm—he used to tense it up on purpose to impress her, he admitted later. She had ruined her 3D spectacles that way, forgetting that she had them on when she buried her face in the thrilling comfort of Bill.

"It was a good movie for a date," she told two CNAs who had been sent outside to bring people in but stayed to watch instead. The two girls didn't believe Laverne when she said the movie was in 3D way back then. They thought she didn't know what "3D" meant, so Laverne said, "Where you wear those special eyeglasses so it looks like the creature is coming out of the lagoon right into your lap?" One of the girls looked the movie up on her phone and found (*lo and behold!* Laverne thought) that Laverne was right.

While most everyone else was outside watching the police in the pond, Foster was spending his morning break in Duane Lotspeich's room, keeping his back to the window. He had returned to the *World of Pondside* admin page—the one his "top-dog webmaster" password had opened yesterday—to see if any of the passwords he had already tried without success on the little yellow ducklink might work on the mysterious *N–L* link, which had its own separate log-in. Foster wasn't sure why he didn't want Duane Lotspeich to know about the admin page and the new link, but he was glad to have the old man occupied elsewhere for a while.

He took advantage of Duane's absence to open his email and hunt for the link to a password-cracking word list generator that Robert had sent him back when Foster first started helping him with the game. "Just in case," Robert had said. He didn't say, *Just in case I turn off the server and then go rolling off the end of the pier,* but Foster was beginning to realize that Robert's *just in case* meant, in fact, just such a calamity. The generator could come up with exponentially more passwords than a mere human brain like Foster's could—assuming that he ever found the email with the link to it. Robert hadn't sent Foster a lot of emails—in fact, no actual human being sent Foster a lot of emails—but two years' worth would still be plenty to search through. He had just typed Robert's name into the search box and hit return when he heard a thump at the door and a voice that was not Duane Lotspeich's saying, "Oh. Hey. Sorry."

Foster straightened up in the fake leather chair. Dakota Dinglebutt, CNA, was poking his head around the partly opened door. His eyes flickered to the laptop and away from it the same way they had when Foster came out of the men's room with the doll in a box. *Unbelievable,* Foster thought. Was this asshole following him?

"I was looking for Duane," he said.

Foster closed the laptop without looking at it. "He went outside to watch the cops."

"It's weird what they're doing out there," Dinglebutt said. He stretched his neck and looked past Foster to the window behind him. "Can you see it from here?"

"Yes," Foster said without turning toward the window.

"I mean, sometimes the wheelchair tips over and sometimes it doesn't. I don't see what that proves, do you?"

Foster wondered if he should just pick up the laptop nonchalantly and walk right out the door.

"Well, here's the funny thing," Dakota said next.

Foster waited. Dinglebutt seemed nervous.

"Actually, I kind of wanted to talk to you. Also, I mean. About something else."

That did it. Foster stood up. He tucked the laptop under his arm. "Go ahead."

Dakota half ducked out of the room to look up and down the

hallway, as if for Duane or anyone else who might be out there in Hawk-eye Lane. He leaned back into the room and said, lowering his voice: "Could we talk someplace else? It's, uh, kind of a private matter."

Foster couldn't have been any more surprised if he had said, "Will you marry me?"

"Usually I work till eight, but I've got an exam tonight so I'm leaving early. Would, like, four o'clock work for you?" Dakota's eyes darted again to the laptop, which was now under Foster's arm. "At Culver's? I could drive."

"I've got my bike," Foster said, automatically. He hated when people offered him a ride, as if he wanted one, especially people who drove a piece of crap like Dakota's. Only after the words came out of his mouth did he realize what he had done.

"Great!" Dakota said. "See you there." This time when he leaned out the doorway to see if anyone was coming down Hawkeye Lane, he took a step back into the hall and said, all hale and hearty-like, "Well, Miss Mary, how are you today? You're looking very mobile!"

Foster heard some mumbling in reply. Then Dakota again, standing in the doorway. "I don't think we're going to find any pudding in your room," he said oh-so-reasonably in his know-it-all voice, and he turned around to give Foster a conspiratorial wink.

"She's got plenty of pudding in her dresser," Foster informed him.

"I do not!" said Mary McIntyre, who had just reached the doorway.

"Pudding packs," Foster said. "They're in the dresser drawers."

Dakota looked at Mary McIntyre, who shrugged elaborately.

"Maybe we'd better have a look," he said. He made an *after you* sweep of his arm, and she strutted into her room.

From across the hall, Foster heard Dakota whistle and then Mary McIntyre saying, "This is not my room."

# CHAPTER 12

Laverne Slatchek waited until after the police were gone and the audience dispersed—walkers and wheelchairs rolling toward the building and CNAs balancing stacks of porch chairs on their heads—before she pushed her own walker back to the veranda and lowered herself into one of the specially designed Easy-Down, Easy-Up Adirondack-style chairs to sit and think for a while.

There were certain conclusions you couldn't help but draw from watching that wheelchair landing this way and that in the water. After the first plunge, Laverne had taken rather detailed notes on the back of the financial statement from her retirement account, which her son Joseph kept trying to change the address on so that it would come to him instead of to Laverne at Pondside. (To do that, he needed a copy of the address change form that came with the statement. "Anybody could open your mail over there, Mom," he said, trying to convince her to hand it over. *Anybody but you*, she refrained from saying in response.)

She pulled the folded piece of paper out of her pants pocket—where she had found the last page of the statement in the first place, softened by a trip through the laundry—unfolded it like an ancient map, and admired her notes. They were accompanied by numbered stick-figure drawings, lopsided and wobbly but clear enough to remind her which way the wheelchair landed each time it went into the pond. In six plunges off the end of the pier and six more from various positions off the side of it, the policeman had landed upright in the wheelchair—with his head above the water—a total of seven times. In one spot, the water and mud barely covered his lap. In *no* spot did the wheelchair land on its side with everything submerged except for the one wheel, which was the way Robert Kallman had landed, according to Duane. She wasn't sure how he knew.

Even including Robert Kallman's actual landing in the total calculations, if only six out of thirteen rides off the pier resulted in man and wheelchair going completely under, then the "success" rate for submersion was a tad less than 50 percent. As a former science teacher, Laverne knew that the sample size was too small to prove anything, but it was enough to suggest that rolling your wheelchair off the end of a pier into a muddy pond of unknown depth (or, more to the point, of unknown shallowness) left a lot to be desired—if what you desired was to drown yourself. Unless he was going for pneumonia or exposure, rather than drowning, attempting to end his life by rolling off the pier was not a smart way to go. And Robert Kallman was no dummy. That much, at least, was obvious.

Something didn't add up. Laverne had felt this all along. She was glad to know the police felt it, too. She refolded her notes, slid the paper back into her pants pocket, and patted it with satisfaction. Leaning back in the chair, which, she could tell, was going to be hard to get out of despite the Easy-Up label on the seat, Laverne closed her eyes for a minute.

Foster had no intention of meeting Dakota at Culver's after work. He had no intention of doing anything except getting back to his place and taking a long, hot shower. Since Sunday, he had pedaled back and forth across town twice, spent a night in the kitchen, stayed up all the next night in Duane's room, and worked four meals in a row. He had scrubs in his locker for working in the kitchen, but his socks, T-shirt, and underwear were the same ones he had worn to Robert's funeral visitation on Sunday night. By lunch prep time today, which was Tuesday already for God's sake, he was smelling noticeably rank. He didn't realize just how noticeably, until Duane came back to his room after watching the cops in the pond and said, "*Whew.* I got some cologne you can use."

If Duane Lotspeich weren't an old man living in a nursing home, Foster might have told him to drop dead.

Duane's takeaway from watching the morning's aquatic activities was that Robert Kallman should have given some thought to his likelihood of success before he went and rolled himself off the pier. Without giving Foster a detailed report—Foster having made it more than clear that he didn't want one—Duane concluded, "The guy was lucky he didn't just sit there in the mud all night."

*Real lucky*, Foster thought, and for the second time he refrained from telling Duane Lotspeich to drop dead.

Down in the kitchen, Jenny's nostrils flared when Foster leaned over her to move some bowls from the salad table to a lunch cart.

"I know, I know," he said. "Sorry."

She relieved him of feeder duty at lunch, taking his tables herself, which meant that he got a head start on cleanup and was unlocking his bike a little after two o'clock—an hour earlier than he usually got out of work. The bike was parked inside the stockade fence that hid the dumpster, on the pond side of the building, but that didn't matter because the police were gone now. Foster coasted halfway through the visitor's parking lot toward his back-road shortcut before he decided to permit himself a quick smoke and a look down the hill at the pond. He stopped at the edge of the parking lot, far enough from the building to light up. From there, he could see the muddy tracks and footprints the cops had left on the weathered boards of the pier, a trail that grew fainter as it came up the asphalt path toward the spot where Foster stood with one foot on either side of his bike. The only signs of the audience were a couple of porch chairs and some plastic cups in the grass.

Foster swung his leg off the bike and lowered it to the ground—no kickstand—leaving it there while he stacked the two chairs and carried them back across the parking lot to the building. He was clumping awkwardly across the fake wooden floorboards, trying to see where he was going, when he noticed the old lady sitting at the far end of the "veranda," which is what the brochures called the porch at Pondside Manor. He stopped and peered around the plastic wicker.

It was Laverne Slatchek, snoring heartily in one of the Adirondack chairs. Foster was tempted to cough a few loud coughs to wake her up and ask her what *she* thought about the police rolling into the pond, but she was sleeping so peacefully, if noisily, in her slack-jawed old-lady way that he didn't have the heart to do it. Besides, he stunk. Plus, he had a cigarette between his lips, which he didn't want to throw away only half smoked. He was lucky that the wind hadn't carried any whiff of it in her direction. Foster happened to know from his access to a lifetime of her photos and one Super 8 movie at Candlestick Park that Laverne Slatchek was a former smoker, and there was no nose like a former smoker's nose to catch a whiff, even if its owner was asleep. She could have nailed him for smoking within thirty feet of the building.

Biking home, Foster wished he had the nerve to ride over to Mrs. Kallman's Victorian mansion and ask her—just come out and ask her—if she had the *World of Pondside* server, or if she knew who did. The downside of not meeting Dakota at Culver's, Foster had to admit, was not finding out what Dinglebutt wanted to talk about. *A private matter*, he had said. Something important enough to take time away from studying for his exam. Foster wondered what qualified, in Dinglebutt's brain, as a private matter.

*Could we talk someplace else? Would that work for you?*

What a dweeb. Maybe the guy just wanted to have a heart-to-heart about employee use of the visitor's restroom. That was pretty private, Foster thought as he pedaled toward home.

It was the sound of voices speaking urgently nearby that awakened Laverne out on the veranda. She couldn't quite hear what they were saying. She opened her eyes to see who it was. Tori Mahoney was outside in the parking lot, two rows in, talking with a rather glamorous young woman whom Laverne had never seen before. The two of them were standing between a big yellow vehicle shaped like an oversize Jeep and a little purple car that Laverne recognized as Amelia Ramirez's. Laverne's first thought was that they were going to set off Amelia's crazy car alarm. Tori Mahoney was doing most of the talking—almost all of it, in fact. She appeared to have planted herself in the young woman's path. Clouds of confusion—or maybe it was anger—darkened the glamorous young woman's face as Tori went on speaking. The young woman appeared to be trying to open the door of her bulky vehicle, but the nurse wouldn't step aside. Tori's voice was getting louder as she went on, until Laverne could pick out a word here and there. Laverne heard "drive that effing *tank*" and "how many people *died*" and something that sounded, oddly, like "four lousy miles per gallon."

When Tori finally paused, the young woman responded loud enough for Laverne to hear her say quite clearly: "It's my brother's car. What's it to you, anyway?"

Tori came back like an angry echo. "What's it to me?" she said. "What's it to *me*?"

And that's when Amelia Ramirez's ridiculous car alarm went off.

If there was one thing Kitty Landiss couldn't stand, it was somebody who came to an interview at a long-term care facility with her face perfectly made-up—cheek-contouring blush, lash-lengthening mascara, eye shadow, lip liner, the works—and her perfectly oval fingernails professionally enhanced. Who, Kitty wondered, did such a person think she was kidding? Beautiful people didn't last long at places like Pondside—the current exception being Amelia Ramirez, who was inadvertently beautiful rather than carefully made-up, and besides, she was an RN, which was a whole different story. All it took to discourage a glamorous CNA was a couple of exceptionally messy asses to wipe, or maybe a friendly hello from the wagging penis of a dementia patient. (Pondside had a couple of Memory Lane residents who were always at the ready.) Kitty had two theories as to why the beautiful people didn't last. Some of them, she believed, could not get over their own deeply held sense of entitlement and superiority. Consciously or not, they felt themselves to be destined for better things. Others, she thought, were simply lacking in personal resources, having gotten undeserved attention throughout their lives just for being their beautiful selves.

Kitty wasn't sure which theory best applied to the lovely applicant who had left her office only moments ago, but in the long run, it didn't matter. Either way, when things got tough, Kitty suspected that Erika Peterson would head for the hills in her Hummer, which she had managed to mention in the course of the interview and which was, come to think of it, another strike against her. Not only was she perfectly groomed and excessively beautified, but she showed up in a flashier, more expensive ride than her potential boss could ever afford to own.

Kitty had already *almost* decided not to hire the girl, despite her prenursing major—she was, in fact, filling in the blanks in her standard rejection email—when an incredible racket erupted in the employee parking lot outside her office windows. Two-toned siren blasts alternated with an excited robotic voice crying, "I am being tampered with! I am being tampered with!" After a startled moment, Kitty recognized Amelia Ramirez's car alarm. She went to the window. Amelia's purple Saturn was parked right next to applicant Erika Peterson's bright-yellow Hummer. More interesting than the contrast between the vehicles, however, were the two women covering their ears in the deafening vicinity of the alarm: perfectly beautiful Erika and an angry-looking Tori Mahoney.

And now here came Amelia Ramirez running out of the building toward the other two. Soon she was struggling to get her car door open, presumably to turn off the alarm, while Tori—whose shift hadn't ended quite yet, had it? Kitty took note—marched off to her minivan a few rows away. The car alarm suddenly fell silent. Amelia turned to Erika Peterson and began speaking earnestly, following her around to the driver's side of the Hummer. Amelia stopped talking and stepped back only when the Hummer's engine roared. Both the minivan and the Hummer exited the parking lot (Tori going out the Enter Only drive while the Hummer took the Exit). Amelia Ramirez was left looking after them, with her hands on her hips and her extraordinary jet-black hair blowing around her head.

Kitty Landiss asked herself: *What just happened here?*

It was more than a matter of two women being startled by a car alarm. Anyone could see that. Based on the scowls they were aiming at each other, it appeared that there was no love lost between them. Kitty found herself feeling less certain about *not* hiring the perfectly groomed job applicant. She sat down to check her email and discovered that her other applicant had written to cancel her Pondside interview, having taken a job at Greenwood Care Center, where the pay for a Certified Nursing Assistant (spelled out in full in the cheery message) *started* at a dollar *over* minimum wage. Kitty Landiss decided then and there that Erika Peterson deserved a chance to show them all what she could do.

Just as she suspected, it took Laverne a while to hoist herself up out of the *not at all* Easy-Up Adirondack chair. What she wanted to do was to catch Amelia Ramirez off guard, you might say, while the shouting match in the parking lot was still fresh—which was to say, before the nurse had time to consider what she should or shouldn't say about it to Laverne. However, by the time Laverne extracted herself from the chair and steered her walker into the building, she knew she would have to stop in her room and use the facilities before she could set out down Boysenberry Boulevard toward the nurses' station. Hurrying was one of those things—like remembering recent events or filtering out white noise or deceiving yourself into thinking that you were in charge of your destiny—that got harder and harder to do as the years added up.

When Laverne finally reached her objective, Amelia Ramirez was standing inside the circular counter at the nurses' station, both hands occupied with the task of getting her wind-blown hair under control with nothing but a single scrunchie to help them. What she came up with made her look like somebody wearing a curly-headed dog hat with one big lopsided ear.

"What can I help you with, Laverne?" Amelia asked, dropping her hands and shaking them out as if to restore circulation to her fingers.

"Any trouble with your car?" Laverne said. "I heard the alarm."

"Oh, yes—sorry about that. Somebody just got a little too close to the car, I think." She smiled, and without exactly dismissing or pointedly ignoring Laverne—Amelia Ramirez was too nice a person to do that—she looked down and started moving papers around on the desk part of the nurses' station, as if she had things to take care of. Laverne decided to let the nurse know that she had seen everything so there was no point changing the story.

"That girl with the big yellow car, you mean?"

Amelia Ramirez raised her head—the lopsided dog ear flopped backward—and she gave Laverne the eye. "You saw us," she said.

"I was on the veranda."

"Ah."

"Who *was* that girl?"

Amelia sighed a big shoulder-raising sigh. She reached up with both hands and attempted to adjust her hair.

Laverne waited patiently. Waiting was one of the few things that got *easier* to do as you got older. Gone, after all, were the days when you could tell yourself that you had better things to do. These days, waiting had a positive value: it simultaneously slowed time down and gave the minutes a purpose. You had something to look forward to— namely, whatever you were waiting for—and that was a good in itself. Bill had pointed this out to her one time while they were waiting for a Pecan Mudslide they'd just ordered. What could be more pleasant, Bill had said, than anticipating something delicious that you *knew* was coming to you? You didn't have to fight for it or worry about it—all you had to do was sit and wait. Once, when she was supposedly hogging the computer in the library, Laverne had tried to explain Bill's point to Duane Lotspeich. He said it sounded like "the friggin' lilies in the field," and added, "Time is money." She said it wasn't about money.

Duane said everything was about money. "Somebody had to earn the money to buy the damn sundae, didn't they?" Then he had suggested that she log off and let him give *her* a chance to enjoy the exquisite pleasure of *waiting.*

"It was Dakota Engelhart's girlfriend," Amelia Ramirez finally said, startling Laverne out of her thoughts.

"Dakota," Laverne said.

"Have you seen him around anywhere?"

"Which one is he?"

"You don't know Dakota? Guy with freckles? Reddish hair? He drove you all to the funeral on Sunday."

"Oh, sure. Him. I haven't seen him *lately.* Maybe at lunch."

Amelia looked down at the desk again. "Huh," she said. "Look at this." She tapped something in front of her that Laverne, lacking X-ray vision, couldn't see. "Says here on the schedule that he left at two thirty today."

"Oh well," Laverne said. "He probably worked overtime yesterday."

"Yes, but what was his girlfriend doing here if he'd already left? I figured she'd come to pick him up, take him to lunch. Like she did before."

"Is that why the other one—the nurse, Tori—was angry? Because that young man left early?"

"What?" Amelia gave Laverne another sharp look. "No," she said, "no, it wasn't about Dakota." Amelia paused, as if deciding whether or not to continue. "Tori just hates those things—Hummers—the kind of car what's-her-name was driving. For one thing, they're gas-guzzlers."

"I've heard they get four lousy miles per gallon," Laverne said.

"Oh, you have, have you?" said Amelia, giving Laverne the eye again. Then she pulled the first folder from a stack of files on the counter. "Well, maybe Dakota's girlfriend didn't know he'd left early. He might not have told her. They don't seem to be terribly close."

Foster expected darkness on the stairs and in the hallway when he got to his place. It was, after all, a gray late afternoon in October, and the windows in the hall—one at the top of the stairs and one in the door at the bottom—were grimy. It was the strip of darkness under his apartment door that gave him pause. True, if the drapes were closed, his apartment *could* be totally dark even on a sunny day, but hadn't he left a light on when he rushed out the back way—geez, almost forty-eight hours ago? His Goodwill floor lamp. Yes, he was sure of it. He specifically remembered thinking about the electricity he was wasting by leaving the lamp on, but once he'd decided to flee, running back down the hall into his apartment to turn off the light just didn't seem like an option.

Foster stood in the hallway and listened for a long time, trying to shut out the whistles and bells from Panera downstairs. As far as he could tell, no sound came from inside his apartment. He leaned forward until his head was resting on his door, and still, he couldn't hear a thing—not even the grunts and gurgles of the refrigerator kicking in. Total silence. He considered the possibility that someone might be lying in wait for him on the other side of the door. Maybe the same someone who came ringing his doorbell on Sunday night. Maybe that someone had been camping out in Foster's apartment ever since, just waiting for him to return.

*Oh, get serious*, he said to himself.

Suddenly, he was dead tired—tired of invalid passwords and "Try again," tired of cops in wheelchairs rolling into the goddamn pond, tired of trying *not* to picture Robert's startled face under the water, tired of feeling as though he was being followed by these people—*what* people?—when hardly anybody even knew that he existed, much less where he lived. Whoever had been at his door the night before last was probably looking for somebody else and what did Foster do about it? *He ran away*—as if anybody gave a shit about him and his whereabouts. Some totally buzzed kids probably bought that doll in Walmart and tied it to the only bike in the rack. They probably watched him ride away, laughing their heads off.

He straightened up, dug his keys from the pocket of his thoroughly bedraggled sport coat, and opened the door about a hand's breadth. When nothing happened, he opened it wide enough to put his head and one shoulder inside. It was dark and it was quiet, from the eerily silent refrigerator on the kitchen side of the room, past the table that still bore the bowl and cereal box from his Sunday supper, past the quilt-covered couch and the computer and the small flat-screen TV, to the bathroom and closet doors at the other end of the room. He was annoyed to feel his heart pounding as he checked to see that there was no one hiding behind the door. He stepped inside and groped the wall for the light switch. He flipped it up. Down. And up again.

"Shit," he said. "Shit, shit, shit."

There was enough light leaking through a chink in one curtain for him to see the electric company's envelope stuck to the refrigerator door with a big round magnet, reminding him not to let the third and final due date pass. The date in question, which he had printed on the outside of the envelope when it first arrived, was Monday, October 14.

Which was yesterday.

# CHAPTER 13

The worst thing about Foster's power being out was not food spoiling or the oncoming darkness or even the lack of hot water for the shower he had been anticipating so deliciously. The worst thing was that he couldn't turn on his computer. If he had a laptop in need of juice, he could carry it downstairs to Panera and wait for a table near an electrical outlet, but the Dell was a full-size PC. The last time his power was out, he used an extension cord to plug it into the outlet in the hallway. The landlord had since covered that outlet with a steel plate that appeared to be welded in place. There was nothing he could do here, on the computer, until the power was restored.

Sometimes Foster thought he might be the last person left on the planet—or at least, on those parts of the planet where people had electricity—to pay his electric bill in person each month, usually in cash. He couldn't do an automatic bill-payer thing on his minuscule checking account because he seldom had enough money to pay all of his bills—electricity, phone, credit card, and rent—in any given month. He would choose which one to skip, just this month, so as to cover the others and not leave any one bill too far in arrears. (Rent was the hardest to skip since the property manager was also the manager at Panera downstairs.) You could get two months behind with

MidWestern Energy, but if you passed your third monthly due date with no payment or alternate payment plan in place, they could disconnect you.

A glance at his phone—which would also need a charge before long—told Foster that he had time to ride downtown to pay his electric bill and fill out the paperwork for reconnection before the MidWestern building closed at five o'clock. They were nice and prompt about reconnecting you as soon as you paid your bill.

He got there at 3:39 and took his bike up in the elevator. The lady behind the counter at the "Pay Bills Here" window clicked some things on her computer, typed in his address, swiped his credit card, and told him he would be up and running again sometime tomorrow. She was sorry she couldn't be any more specific than that. The lady didn't sniff or wrinkle her nose at Foster. She didn't give him and his hair, wilder than ever after the ride downtown, so much as a crooked glance. He figured that she probably had to go through some kind of training to learn how to handle wild-looking deadbeat-types like himself, but he tried not to hold that against her. Foster couldn't think of any public or private institution that treated its (after all) captive customers as kindly as MidWestern Energy did. Plus, they were building all those wind turbines to save the earth. He would have liked to put them permanently at the top of his bills-to-pay list every month, but the sad fact was that you had to pay the assholes first.

Foster knew—from days even less prosperous than the present—that the locker room and showers at the rec center downtown were accessible to all, free of charge. The city's homeless population (of which Foster had twice, though briefly, been a member) took full advantage of the situation, although they were careful to avoid peak times like six to seven a.m., when the place was full of hard-bodied Master Swimmers, and mid-morning, when the old folks were there for Aquacise and Senior Swim, as well as Saturday night, which was Family Swim.

The locker room was all his at 4:10 p.m. on a Tuesday. He used the shampoo-body wash from the dispenser in the shower and dried his hair by standing under the dryers that were positioned high on the wall. He did what he could with his fingers by way of a comb, but after getting blown around by the dryer, his hair looked even bigger than it usually did. It looked, in fact, like a 1970s afro. In high school, before he got smart enough to drop out, guys would get on him because of his hair. Some jocks cornered him one time when he was outside in the hidden spot between the main school building and the new gym, having a cigarette. The jocks must have been waiting around for practice, looking for a way to kill some time before they went inside to get screamed at by whatever coach, when they saw his wisp of smoke and crammed their oversize selves into the space where he was coatless and shivering and sucking on a cigarette, his hair springing out a good two inches or more from his head.

"Look here! If it ain't our resident moo-lotto!" They had recently learned terms for mixed-race in social studies. "So how come a white runt like yourself has such a nappy head of hair? Some black buck get hold of your momma?"

Instead of answering, Foster had put his cigarette out on the satiny sleeve of somebody's letter jacket. They beat him up pretty good before they let him go.

After he left the rec center, Foster thought he might as well ride straight back to Pondside, possibly thumbing his nose at Culver's—where Dakota might still be waiting for him to show up—as he passed by. Foster had been looking forward to a break from Duane Lotspeich's room, but with the power out at his apartment until tomorrow, there was no place else to go. He hadn't even tried to talk Lotspeich into letting him take the laptop back to his place, mainly because the Wi-Fi went out at ten p.m., with or without electricity. In the old man's closet, they could keep the Pondside server plugged in, turned on, and hidden behind the sliding door. Foster had reminded Duane to keep the door and the laptop closed. "You don't want some nosy CNA to hear something and find you in the closet with stolen goods."

Foster wondered if Mary McIntyre had ever found the doll he left in her room. She never did come out shrieking with joy or anything. He and Duane would have heard her for sure. He wondered, too, if Dakota had turned her in, regarding the pudding packs. Foster hoped not. If they were no-chill, they wouldn't spoil. What was the harm in letting her keep a supply of pudding packs in her room? Nobody else liked vanilla anyway. They were all she was eating, probably, if her pureed lunch plates were any indication. Foster wished he hadn't mentioned the pudding packs to Mr. Goody Two-Shoes, who no doubt played by the rules.

That's what he was thinking when he realized that he had taken the wrong turn if he wanted to ride past Culver's. It was just as well. Now that Foster had turned down the road toward the mall parking lot and his place, he could stop at home and have something to eat, maybe some dry Cheerios or a piece of bread, if he had any. He had just come within sight and delicious smell of Panera when a happy thought occurred to him: if ever there was a time when buying a nice sandwich—something with bacon and cheese on focaccia bread—was appropriate and justified, this was it.

Foster coasted past the rows of cars outside Panera—all lined up with their shiny hoods facing the big storefront windows like dogs waiting for their owners to return. You didn't see as many rust buckets as you used to. He thought there was something they did to cars now to prevent rust— besides making parts out of plastic. In all the patiently waiting rows there was only one rust bucket, gray-green and lacy-brown along the bottoms of the doors and the fenders. An old Nissan.

Foster squeezed his hand brakes hard and skidded to a stop just at the edge of Panera's plateglass windows.

Leaning over his handlebars to see inside the place, Foster spotted not only the wholesome, handsome CNA at a table against the wall, but also at the table, facing Dinglebutt, Foster recognized the springy blond ponytail and nubbly sweater of Tori Mahoney. She was the one doing the talking, using her hands, lifting her shoulders, while Dinglebutt gave her his complete and total attention. They must have been here for a while to have a pair of half-eaten bread bowls on the table between them. Foster's stomach growled. He felt his face heat up with humiliation at having been "stood up" by Dakota after spending half the day savoring the fact that he, Foster, was going to be the one who didn't show. Thinking this thought—articulating it even to himself—was so additionally humiliating that Foster turned his bike around and pedaled to the back of the building rather than risk being seen by them, although he was pretty sure he could have gone inside and sat down at the very next table without their noticing he was there.

For once, Foster was grateful for the klieg-bright lights that came on at the first hint of dusk in the mall parking lot. When he uncovered the window next to the refrigerator in his apartment, they cast their eerie yellow glow on the kitchen counter. From downstairs came the usual aroma of coffee brewing and something baking—something yeasty like bread, but with chocolate undertones.

He opened the tall white cabinet that the property management guy had called the pantry when he was showing Foster the apartment. A jumble of cereal boxes, ramen, and cans crowded against mugs and bowls and empty lunch-meat containers, their red lids stacked up crookedly under them. He seemed to have more of those containers than anything else. The so-called pantry door blocked the light from the window, but he didn't need to read any labels to close his fingers around the peanut butter jar and squeeze, as if he had it by the neck. It was a good thing the jar was made of plastic, not glass. Otherwise, given the force with which he placed it on the counter, Foster might have had himself a fistful of peanut butter, mixed with shards and blood.

For Christ's sake, what did it matter? He was acting like a teenager who caught his girlfriend talking to another guy—no. Not even that. More like a ten-year-old *girl* whose BFF was sitting with somebody else at lunch. God. Foster never even had a best fucking friend. Or any friend, really, unless you counted his grandfather. And Robert.

He opened the door of the fridge for the briefest possible moment to extract the bread and a can of closeout store–brand cola. There were few things more *wrong* than a refrigerator that didn't light up in welcome when you opened the door. After he closed it, he untwisted the tie on the bread bag and sniffed. It smelled the same refrigeratory way days-old bread always smelled. He slapped two pieces on the counter.

Tori Mahoney was not his friend. It was a stretch even to call her a coworker since she was a nurse and he was a nobody. She had three kids, for God's sake. The oldest one was in high school already. Foster had been so pleased last year when he helped the kid with a programming assignment and Tori called it a professional courtesy, like the time she cleaned the gravel out of his elbow when he fell off his bike in the parking lot. But could he imagine her, even for a moment, saying to somebody else, "my friend Foster"? No, he could not. She probably called him the kitchen boy when he wasn't around.

He ripped a hole in the bread, spreading the peanut butter.

And Dinglebutt. He probably thought Foster was going to meet him here, at Panera. Otherwise, he would hardly offer Foster a ride, if he had really meant Culver's, which was right over the hill, behind Costco. Either that or he just ran into her and lost track of time. The twerp was late for work at least once a week. Foster shook his head. He couldn't believe he was even *thinking* about Dinglebutt. It didn't *matter*, for Christ's sake! It didn't matter, didn't matter, didn't matter.

He smacked the two pieces of bread together into something like a sandwich, picked it up, and had actually sunk his teeth into it when he saw that the crust all around the top slice of bread was fuzzy green. He opened wide, gagged—might have brought something up if there'd been anything in his stomach—and threw the sandwich across the room. It hit the wall near the door, stuck for a second or two, and fell to the floor. Foster didn't see where it landed, partly due to the semidarkness and partly due to the tears he was furiously blinking back. Other people smashed heads or furniture when they got mad, but not him. This was why he'd had to walk away from a fight his whole life—not because he was scared, necessarily, but because he couldn't keep from bawling whenever his feelings ran high.

Between the sniffling and the pounding of his heart, he barely heard the knocking at his door.

"I don't fucking believe it!" Foster yelled, and the knocking stopped. All was silent, except for the squeal of the espresso machine—or whatever machine it was that squealed—in the coffee shop downstairs. The silence didn't change the fact that somebody was out in the hallway, right there on the other side of his door.

The knocking resumed: three timid taps. A pause, and then three more.

*Well, what the fuck,* Foster thought. He took the four steps required to get from the kitchen counter to the door and pulled it open. Dakota Dinglebutt was standing in the dim hallway, a Panera bag cradled in one arm and a cardboard holder with a pair of to-go cups in his other hand. How had he even managed to knock on the door carrying that? With his foot? His elbow? What the hell was he doing here?

"I guess I missed you at Culver's," he said.

"You were there?" Foster said. He could have kicked himself.

"No, actually, I got delayed—but I guess you weren't there either."

They both looked down at the paper bag and the cup holder.

"Tori bought this for you," Dakota said, handing the cup holder to Foster. "She had to leave to pick up her son from soccer." Dakota nodded toward one of the cups. "That one's hot chocolate. She said you don't like coffee." He helped himself to the other cup and held the bag out to Foster, who was too surprised to do anything but take it.

"How did she—how did you know I was home?" Foster was suddenly deeply aware of the mostly dark apartment behind him. He wondered where the peanut butter sandwich had landed. At least it wasn't stuck to the doorframe.

"We saw you through the window. Did you know that you can hear somebody on these stairs—from down in Panera, I mean?"

"No wonder the property manager always knows when I'm here," Foster said.

"He hangs out at the restaurant?"

"Works there."

"That kind of sucks," Dakota said. "Landlord breathing down your neck." He seemed to be trying to see past Foster into the apartment.

"Power's off," Foster felt compelled to say.

Dakota glanced up at the overhead light in the hall. Then he lifted his coffee cup in farewell and turned to go. "Well, *enjoy!* I hope your power comes back on soon."

"What about the—" Foster almost said *private matter.* "I mean, what did you want to talk to me about?"

Dakota stopped at the top of the stairs. "Tori said she wants to tell you herself. She said she would see you tomorrow."

"It's about Tori?"

"Listen. I've got an exam. I've gotta go." Holding his coffee high, like a torch, he thundered down the stairs.

Foster went back inside and sat down, the cup holder and Panera bag in his lap, on the couch he had purchased from a downsizing Pond-side resident. Inside the bag was a Turkey Frontega sandwich on focaccia bread—one of the two things he was most likely to order on those rare occasions that he ordered from Panera, and of the two, his favorite. He wondered how she knew—some overheard conversation, maybe, or just a good guess—and then he tucked into it. He knew from Jenny saying it all the time that "hunger is the best sauce," and he hadn't eaten anything since breakfast, but by God, this sandwich was far and away the single most delicious thing he had eaten in a long, long time. The hot chocolate was good, too, although maybe too sweet by the time it was cool enough to drink. When he finished it all, he leaned his head back, gazed up at the shadowy ceiling, and wondered what it could possibly be—what kind of *private matter* it could be—that Tori Mahoney wanted to tell him herself.

# CHAPTER 14

Kitty Landiss didn't recognize the number on the first of three voicemails waiting for her when she got back to the car and pulled her phone out from under the driver's seat.

Cellphone use was ABSOLUTELY forbidden in all areas at Fitness World. Any phones on the premises had to be not merely silenced but powered *off.* "First-time violators," the signs in the locker rooms continued in small but angry-red print, "will be fined in the amount of one month's membership fee. Repeat offenders will be stripped of membership." These draconian—and suggestively worded—policies were the result of certain photographs that had made it from the Fitness World locker room to the internet without the permission of the subject and also without her clothes. If the phone policy had been in effect before Kitty handed over her nonrefundable superspecial introductory annual membership fee, she would have gone elsewhere, despite the convenient location between Culver's and Costco, a veritable stone's throw from Pondside Manor. (Convenience was key, Kitty found, to maintaining a fitness regimen.) She had tried setting the phone on vibrate, wrapping it in a towel, and leaving it on the shelf in her locker, only to set the whole row of ultracheap metal lockers buzzing like a sawmill while she was on the racquetball court.

Since she was new to Fitness World—she had been a member for less than a week at the time—and since she hadn't been actually using the phone, the Austrian weightlifter who was second-shift manager had given her a break on the fine. He warned her, though, that her name *vas on der list*.

She tried to turn her phone off after that but found she just couldn't do it. Turned off, the phone was like a little dead thing you were carrying around. She felt uneasy every time she slid it under the seat in the Subaru, as if she were leaving a child unattended.

The number she didn't recognize was Tori Mahoney's, calling from someplace where children were screaming in the background—an elementary school sporting event, basketball by the bouncing, squeaking sound of it—with the incomparably terrible news that her youngest had broken out in a rash that *might* be chicken pox. "In which case, why are you at a basketball game?" Kitty said aloud. Tori's voicemail went on to say that she was terribly sorry for the short notice, but she wouldn't be in tomorrow—tiny pause here, as if Pondside's one and only weekday first-shift nurse were deciding what her next words would be—"or for the rest of the week."

"It's after eight!" Kitty said into the phone. "Where am I going to get someone for *tomorrow*?"

The Subaru's windows steamed up around her.

The other two calls were from the nurses' station at Pondside. She steeled herself and tapped the first one.

"This is Amelia at Pondside. I'm afraid I've got some bad news." Kitty had time to say, "Already heard the bad news! Tori's not coming in tomorrow," before Amelia's message continued: "Mary McIntyre is missing."

Kitty dropped the phone. She scrambled to find it in her lap and hit Call Back.

"Pondside Man—"

"What do you mean, Mary McIntyre is missing?"

"What? Oh! She's back. I mean, she's not missing. Didn't you get my second message?"

"The first one seemed to require a response. What is going on?"

"Well, we just couldn't find her for a while. I went in to give her meds and she wasn't in her room, which was okay, but then we couldn't find her anywhere. It was really only about ten minutes, but with what happened to Robert and how she was wandering around outside that morning—"

"So where did you find her?"

"In the hall outside Edith Cole's room."

"She was in the hallway, and you couldn't find her?"

"Well, she wasn't there the whole time we were looking, of course!"

"Is she all right?"

"Yes."

"But?"

"She's got this doll. In a box. I don't know where it came from."

"Maybe Edith's basket?"

"No. Edith's actions made it clear the doll does not belong to her, so I would say, no."

"Maybe the daughter gave it to her."

"Maybe. It's a baby doll. She's always looking for her baby."

"That's probably it then. I suppose her daughter expects the doll will help her adjust." By now the windows were so steamed up that Kitty couldn't tell if there was a world outside the Subaru. She put the key in and turned on the defrost fan.

"There's something wrong with her head."

"You're telling me," said Kitty. She couldn't think of anybody she was sorrier to have admitted to Pondside than Mary McIntyre—unless it was Robert Kallman.

"The doll's head, I mean," Amelia said. "It's loose, almost coming off, and the eyes are sunken in—it's kind of creepy—and one of the arms fell off, too. It was in the box with the doll."

"It sounds creepy, Amelia, but we have another problem. A big one."

"Yes, I know."

"Tori called you, too?"

"Yes, I talked to her."

A clear spot was growing on the windshield, giving Kitty a view of Culver's cheery blue awnings in the next parking lot over. What she wouldn't give for a ButterBurger right now. At least the new CNA was starting tomorrow. That was a blessing. Well, maybe more like a small favor, but Kitty would take it.

"Amelia, is there any chance you could fill in tomorrow morning?"

"You want me to come back here at seven a.m.? You know, I live kind of far. I don't get home till after midnight sometimes."

"Maybe you could leave early tonight? I'm right over at Fitness World—near Culver's? I can be at Pondside in a minute or two and then I can stay until Bert comes in at eleven."

"Uh—you're not a nurse."

"No. I'm not."

In the silence that followed, Kitty wondered why fitness centers were always located near fast-food restaurants. The defrost fan was pulling in outside air, and the car had filled with the smell of french fries. "You've done all the meds already, right?" she asked Amelia.

More silence.

"Maybe Bert can come in a little early," Kitty tried next. "I'll call him and call you back."

She found Bert in her contacts and tapped the number. The call went straight to voicemail. Kitty left her message. It looked as if she'd be spending the rest of the evening in her office, which meant she would need sustenance. The windshield was clear enough now to drive the hundred yards to Culver's. Not many people were aware that a Butter-Burger had just three hundred and forty-seven calories. Not a bad total for dinner, especially if you ignored the rest of its nutritional nonvalue (the fat, the carbs). She would skip the fries.

# CHAPTER 15

Dakota blew the exam. He blew it totally. It wasn't even Organic either—just plain Chemistry. He had barely made it down to campus before the exam started last night. In retrospect, it might have been better if the TA at the door to the auditorium had turned him away for being late. And now, he thought as he switched off the ignition and his Nissan coughed a last time before the engine stopped, he was late for work again. It was 11:09 on the dashboard; 11:14 on his phone. He squinted across the sunny parking lot, only half surprised, given his own preoccupations this morning, to see a young woman in baggy blue scrubs who (except for the baggy scrubs) looked a lot like Erika. She was pushing somebody in a wheelchair on the walkway in front of the building. Dakota watched her stop and fuss over the occupant of the wheelchair, tucking a blanket around the person's legs, zipping up the jacket. It was sunny but chilly—typical October, still looking like summer, feeling like fall. As Dakota got closer to the building, he could see that it was old Mr. Wallace from Memory Lane in the wheelchair, and that the young woman who looked like Erika was, in fact, Erika! When she spotted him approaching, she straightened up and waved.

He ran the last few yards and met her on the walkway, too shocked to say anything but, "What are you doing here?"

"Same thing you are. Except I got here on time."

She slipped her thumb behind the plastic-covered name tag above her breast pocket, tilting it up for Dakota to read, neatly typed on two lines, boldface:

**Erika Peterson**
**CNA**

"It's temporary. I'll get my regular badge next week," she said. She looked pleased at the thought.

"Is this some kind of joke, Erika?" Dakota regretted these words, of course, the instant they left his lips. Erika glanced at old Mr. Wallace, who appeared to be dozing in the wheelchair, and turned back to Dakota, her lovely eyebrows drawn together.

"I don't know why you would say such a thing, Dakota. I honestly don't." She turned Mr. Wallace toward the spirea and set out along the edge of the parking lot.

Dakota hurried after her. "I didn't—I mean—what I mean is, you have to take a course, to get certified—you can't just start working someplace."

"I guess I *know* that."

"Well, when did you—?"

"I did the course during winter break," she said. "And I did the clinical part—or the *hands-on*, as they call it here—this past summer."

"You took a CNA course *last* winter? While you were at home?"

"Yes!" she said. "Is that so surprising?"

"Yes," he said. "Yes, it is."

She had gone home right after her last exam that December. In two of the previous semester breaks, she had talked Dakota into letting her parents pay for his flight to West Palm so they could have a week on the beach together, but this past winter, she said there wouldn't be time. She had to help her mother, a professional event planner, with some obscenely elaborate wedding she had to pull off on an uninhabited island. "Basically, it's a sand bar," Erika had told him. "Mom has to build a *pavilion* out there for the dinner. On stilts." After break, Dakota had picked Erika up at the airport. It was five below zero outside. She emerged from the concourse like a golden goddess in a sundress and flip-flops. He had to wrap her in a blanket and carry her out to the car. She did not mention any CNA training courses she had taken—not in the car, not in her room at the Gamma Pi house that night, and not in the many months since.

"Well, I'm sorry," she said, "but there is a lot of CNA training available in South Florida, which shouldn't be surprising with all the assisted living and LTC on practically every block down there."

It wasn't the *availability* of training courses that surprised Dakota, but he decided he had better not say so. "You just never mentioned it," he said.

"I wanted it to be a surprise for you. A nice surprise," she added sadly. "You don't look very happy about it, but I can tell you my prenursing advisor thinks it's a great idea. They encourage you to work in the field so you can see if you like it or not. Who knows? Maybe I'll decide *I'd* rather be a teacher, too. Or a biomedical engineer!"

Erika was working on a second major in computer science.

"Here?" he said, finally catching up with what Erika was saying. "You're working here?"

"Didn't I just show you my name tag? Am I not pushing this wheel-chair?" She gave Wallace another worried glance and lowered her voice. "I can see why this place is understaffed, by the way. They don't even have a director of nursing. When I told my advisor, she was shocked."

"But where's your car?" He made a visor of his hand and looked out over the parking lot. The Hummer was hard to miss. He didn't see it anywhere in the employees' lot. What he did see was Foster coming out of the building, tapping what appeared to be a pack of cigarettes against his hand.

"I'm not in the Hummer," Erika said. When Dakota turned to look at her, she was gazing across the parking lot, too.

"What are you driving then?" He was sorry to see that Foster was aimed in their direction, probably coming to use the bench above the pond as a smoking lounge.

"I'm in that Hyundai. The silver one." Foster was close enough to them now that Dakota had to nod and say, "Hey." Foster nodded back, assiduously avoiding eye contact, it seemed, and careful not to even look at Erika. After he disappeared around the spirea, Erika made her what-a-weirdo face. Dakota shrugged. They heard the bench creak. Dakota took Erika by the elbow—surprised at how familiar and right that felt—and together they rolled Mr. Wallace a few steps farther from the bench.

"Where did you get a Hyundai?" Dakota asked, keeping his voice down.

"I traded cars with Lisa. One of the pledges. You've met her."

"You traded the Hummer for a Hyundai? Does your brother know?"

Now Erika lowered her voice. "It's not a permanent trade. I'll just use her car when I'm coming here." Her voice got quieter still. "It's because of that nurse. Her husband was killed in a Hummer. I mean, a Humvee. Did you know that?"

Behind the spirea, Foster coughed—a long, complicated smoker's cough.

"Yes, well, I guess I don't want to be *reminding* her every time I come to work," Erika said.

All of a sudden, Dakota felt as if he were standing here with someone that he didn't know as well as he thought he knew Erika. It was disorienting, but, like the feeling of his hand when he took her elbow, it was not unpleasant. The opportunity to say anything else was lost when Foster stood up suddenly from the bench behind the spirea. He walked away from them along the edge of the parking lot, his face like a thunderstorm.

"Anyway," Erika said, "you're always complaining about how short-handed they are. I figured I could get hired"—she squared her shoulders, took hold of the handles on the wheelchair, aimed it toward the building—"and I did!" She and old Mr. Wallace set off across the parking lot on a path that was clearly chosen to discourage Dakota from following.

Foster's day had not started well. He woke up sitting on his couch, with the ceiling light shining on his upturned face and a terrible crick in his neck. The clock on the microwave was blinking 3:04 and the refrigerator was humming in a way that felt threatening. The clock was wrong, of course. He had just enough time to take a tepid shower, eat two spoons full of peanut butter, and pedal down to Pondside in the predawn darkness. When he got there, Jenny was waiting for him in the kitchen with her arms folded across her chest and her eyebrows lowered and her head shaking slowly.

"Boy," she said to him, "what is the matter with you? How could you do that poor woman like that?"

"What poor woman?"

"*Oooooh*," Jenny said. "Don't you pretend like you don't know what I'm talking about."

"I don't have to pretend. I don't know what you're talking about."

"Why didn't you do like you said you would and just give her the doll?"

"Give who—? You mean Wild Mary?"

"Show some respect, boy."

"I did give her the doll. Day before yesterday. When you washed the dress, I found a box—"

"I heard about that part. A box like a coffin and the head all twisted and the arms pulled off!"

"I put the arms and legs back on," Foster protested. "And I never took the head off."

Jenny turned her back on him in disgust.

He didn't find out until after breakfast that Tori had not come to work this morning. "What do you think that's about?" he asked Jenny back in the kitchen. She just pressed her lips together and raised one eyebrow. By the time he had finished his cigarette break and stationed himself by the employee lockers, Foster wanted some answers, and he didn't care who knew it. Dakota Engelhart came around the corner, looking shell-shocked from his encounter with the girl in the parking lot. He stopped when he saw Foster and made as if to turn around and go the other way, but Foster wasn't about to let him retreat.

"Hey—Dinglebutt!" This came out louder than Foster intended. He resisted the impulse to look around and see if any curious heads were poking out the doors that led to the laundry and the break room.

Dakota scurried over. "What's the matter with you?" he asked Foster in the same low, confidential tone he had used in Duane's room, when he first mentioned the *private matter* they needed to discuss. "What are you yelling about?"

"You said Tori was going to tell me something."

"Yeah?"

"Yeah, well, she's not here today!"

Dakota glanced around again and then opened his locker. He shrugged off his jacket—from some high school in Bumblefuck, Iowa—and hung it up as if he didn't get it, what Foster just said.

"To be clear," Foster said, "she took the day *off*."

Dakota shut his locker. "I thought that might happen."

"What the fuck does that mean?" Foster said.

"It *means* that I thought she might take some time off. Look, I have to punch in."

"Do you know how long I've been working here?" Foster said.

"No."

"Long enough to know that Tori Mahoney has not taken a day off in all that time—years, it's been. *Years*."

"I guess she's due then."

"I want to know what she was going to tell me."

Dakota turned away from Foster. "If she decided *she* wanted to tell you, then I can't—"

That's when Foster grabbed hold of Dakota's arm. They both stood still for a second and looked at Foster's fingers, the tips of which did not come close to meeting around Dakota's bicep. Dakota lifted his arm and used it to push Foster backward into the lockers. This time, the noise did cause a couple of heads to poke out into the hallway from the door to the laundry. Dakota waited for the metallic echoes to die and the heads to retreat and then he growled into Foster's face, "Tori's husband was in Iraq with Robert Kallman."

Foster sucked in a breath and held it. He hadn't realized what a big guy Dakota was—not tall, but muscular. The reddish hair and freckles, the fresh-faced look, fooled you. Even whispering, he seemed surprisingly dangerous.

"They were in the same—" Dakota hesitated, giving Foster an opening, a chance to reestablish his position, not that he knew, exactly, what his position was.

"The same unit?" Foster said. He tried to sneer. "The same squad? The same volleyball team?"

"The same *Humvee,*" Dakota whispered fiercely. "Kallman was supposed to be the driver. It was more dangerous to be the driver."

Foster's heart was pounding so hard he could feel it in his throat. An image flashed up in his brain: two men hopping out of the Humvee and running around the front of it to hop back in on the other side. "Let me guess," he said. "They switched places one day and—the other guy—*he* got it instead of Robert."

Dakota looked surprised, but only for a moment. He dropped his arm, letting Foster go, and said, "That was Tori's husband, the other guy, who *got it.* Mahoney. He was Tori's husband."

Of course, the matching names had occurred to Foster—not when Robert told him the story but later. He thought about asking Robert, but it seemed so dumb. Wouldn't he have said it was Tori's husband, unless he was trying to hide it, and if he was trying to hide it, wouldn't he have changed the name? It was a common last name anyway. Not Smith or Jones, but pretty damn close, especially in the Midwest. Foster had known two Mahoneys in high school, and they weren't related at all, not even distant cousins (as they made sure everybody knew). Besides, what kind of stupid coincidence would it be for Robert Kallman to wind up in the same nursing home where Tori supposedly-*that*-Mahoney just happened to work?

"The gunner guy contacted her," Dakota said, just as if Foster had said this out loud. "The gunner told her how it happened, how they switched places."

"Keith?"

"She didn't say his name. And Kallman contacted her, too. He came to see Mahoney at the VA, and Tori was there."

"Mahoney *died*," Foster said.

"Not right away. She said they stabilized him and did some surgery in Germany, saved one eye, before they sent him back to the States."

"The guy's face was gone," Foster said. Robert had told him how the other men couldn't even tell that it was Mahoney, not Robert, in the driver's seat.

"I know," Dakota said, "but he could *see.* It must have been a real horror show, for both of them. She was at the VA when Robert came to see Mahoney. When he told them about the ALS, she said it was a judgment on him, that she was glad, that now she wouldn't have to kill him herself—all crazy things like that."

"No," Foster said.

"*That's* why you can't keep saying it wasn't suicide—"

"Shut up," Foster said.

"Because it *was,* it *was* suicide."

"Shut up," Foster said again. "Leave me alone!"

"With *pleasure,*" Dakota said, packing a surprising amount of venom in the word. He shook out his arm—the one he'd used to push Foster against the lockers—and strode away, his shoes squeaking on the vinyl tile. Foster rubbed the back of his head and watched him go.

# CHAPTER 16

Night nurse Bert (with an *e*) Reynolds, RN, was a big muscular man in his midforties, so most people didn't give him a hard time about anything, including his name. Of course, he once told Kitty, he still had to put up with the double takes, the misspellings, the raised eyebrows when he gave his name to the police investigators, and the swiveled heads and titters that used to erupt when they called his name at places like the DMV. Kitty Landiss admired the way he didn't blame any of this awkwardness on his parents, who thought they were naming him Norbert, and she was glad he refused to take the easy, if uncool, route of being Norb. She also admired his muscles, which were evident even under his relatively baggy cotton scrubs.

Bert Reynolds didn't know what a thrilling chord he had struck in the heart of Kitty Landiss when he asked her one time, over a year ago now, what kind of workout she was doing lately—it was obviously getting good results. She had interpreted this as his way of telling her that he'd noticed she was looking good—something he couldn't come right out and say because that would be sexual harassment in the workplace—and although he had never followed up on it in any way, she refused to believe that it was merely the professional observation of a guy who worked part time as a personal trainer. She would be forever in his debt, she tried to imply on the phone last night, for agreeing to come in two hours early so that Amelia Ramirez could be home by ten o'clock to get her beauty sleep before she came back to work this morning for Tori Mahoney. (Kitty didn't say "beauty sleep" to Bert Reynolds, of course, nor to Amelia Ramirez.) Come to think of it, Kitty would be forever in Amelia's debt, too, but that didn't seem as positive a development.

Thinking further, Kitty knew very well that Bert Reynolds wasn't really doing her any favors. For one thing, being a nurse, he would collect overtime for those two extra hours. For another, Kitty had supported his sworn statement that he had *not* dozed off at the nurses' station in the wee hours last Thursday morning and thus allowed Robert Kallman to somehow exit the building without notice. It wasn't too hard for Kitty to give Bert the benefit of the doubt about that. The alarm system had been armed and ready to wake the dead between nine p.m. and six a.m.; even if he *had* dozed off, she was pretty sure he would have heard an unauthorized exit or entry.

It had taken Kitty only two phone calls to line up a temp for this afternoon, plus Thursday and Friday, which, she hoped, would cover Tori's need for "a little time off." (She had left a message for Tori—and why wasn't she answering the phone if she was at home with a sick kid?—asking for more specifics, like how much time off was "a little"?) Kitty could have found the temp in one phone call if the first agency hadn't been concerned about tarnishing their reputation by sending one of their nurse-clients into a questionable situation. Kitty had bitten her tongue and hung up. She hired the temp without waiting for the okay from corporate because what other choice did she have? You couldn't get away with no RN on first shift. There was too much going on, even when you didn't have a guy who just drowned in the pond and another guy who dropped dead in the parking lot less than a week ago.

The only things left to worry about right now were Mary McIntyre and her daughters, who had made an appointment to meet with Kitty Landiss this afternoon.

"Daughters?" Kitty asked Carol in the office. "I think I've only met one daughter."

"Well, two are coming to see you," Carol said.

Kitty checked the visitor's log entries since Mary McIntyre's arrival last Monday—only a week and a half ago? It seemed as if the woman had been here for decades already. Come to think of it, the Monday before last—or any day before the advent of tragedies and police and that one reporter-photographer who seemed to think there was a Pulitzer to be found in a drowning at a long-term care center—seemed like decades ago. During that week and a half, four signed-in visitors had written Mary McIntyre's name in the "I'm coming to see" column. They were "Daughter" (signed in namelessly nine times), Father Pete from St. Wenceslaus parish (signed in once), and two names squeezed together into one space (on two successive days) to see "Grandma McIntyre."

Unless Mary McIntyre's two daughters had identical handwriting, one of them had never been here before. That meant one of the two hadn't seen what the first week and a half at a long-term care center could do to a person, the kind of change that a difficult transition—and Kitty had never seen anyone have a more difficult time than Wild Mary McIntyre—could bring about. You talked to a first-time visitor differently from the way you talked to someone who was familiar with the place or, for that matter, from the way you talked to a *prospective* family member—someone who was still shopping around. It was no good pointing out the big arched windows in the spacious sunlit atrium to the daughter visiting for the first time, when all she was going to see was how small her mother had become.

"Um, excuse me?"

Kitty spun around in her chair. It was the new CNA—Glamour Girl, no, wait, Erika—wringing her manicured hands in the doorway. For God's sake, Kitty thought, a crisis on her very first day? What was it—a wagging penis? A messy poop? Exercising the greatest restraint, Kitty said simply, "Yes?"

"There's a phone call for you?" the girl said.

"And why are *you* answering the phone?"

"The lady in the office asked me to? Carol? So she could take a quick break?"

At least, in scrubs, the new CNA looked more like a regular person. She might have lightened up on the makeup, too. "Did you get a name?"

"Lieutenant Steinhafel," the girl said. "From Homicide?"

Foster didn't so much knock on Duane Lotspeich's door as slap it with the palm of his hand and stand there, waiting, until it opened. He went to the window without a glance at the laptop or a word to Duane, who, miraculously, seemed to sense that he needed some space. Foster stayed at the window, his hands in his pockets, longing for a smoke, bouncing a little on his heels, wondering if he could get away with lighting up in Duane's room—just a puff or two before the smoke alarm caught him—looking out at the all-brown cornstalks in the field that began where the Pondside grounds and parking lot ended, a last vestige of the farmland that used to be. Without turning around, he said, "Duane, how long have you been here?"

"I don't know. Maybe half an hour."

"No, I mean how long have you *lived* here—at Pondside?" Outside, a mostly black cat appeared to be walking the cornfield's perimeter, white-tipped tail in the air.

"That's a depressing question."

Foster glanced over his shoulder. The old man was squinting at the large-faced clock on the wall next to his bed, as if that would help him figure out the answer. Apparently, not much figuring was required. "I've been here one year, eleven months, and six days," Duane said.

"Shit," said Foster.

"My feelings exactly." Duane pulled his wheelchair into a sharp little turn toward Foster and the window. "Why do you ask?"

Foster looked out just as the cat's tail disappeared between two rows of corn. He wondered if cats—or squirrels or field mice—ever got chopped up by combines and dumped into those big blue wagons with the corn. Duane would know.

"Who do you know that's been here longer than, say, two years?"

"Not that many. Edith Cole. And that snooty broad, Eleanor." He shrugged. "And Robert Kallman. He was here already when I first came. Why do you ask?"

Foster knew he should shut up now, but he felt words rising in his throat. "I'm trying to find out—some information," he said. "From somebody who's been here a while." He looked over his shoulder at Duane.

"Does it have to be a patient, a resident? Could you ask a staff member? Not that many of *them* have been around for more than a year or two. I'm sure you don't want to talk to your friend Landiss, and apart from her and you—you were here when the place first opened, weren't you?"

"Yeah, but I left and came back." Plus, Foster thought but didn't say, he had never talked to anybody outside the kitchen before Robert came to Pondside and they started working on the game together.

"The only other person I can think of is the nurse, Tori Mahoney."

Foster turned back to the window. The cat had reappeared from between the rows. She crouched suddenly, as if she'd spotted her prey. Behind him, Duane kept talking.

"I've heard Laverne say how anybody who could stick around that long, they ought to promote her. Why all this interest in who's been here the longest?"

*What the hell*, Foster thought. "Did you ever hear anything about Tori Mahoney and Robert Kallman—about them knowing each other before they came here?"

"Oh, sure," Duane said.

Foster turned around. "'Oh, sure'?"

"Yeah," Duane said. He swung his wheelchair over to the laptop on the shelf in the closet, the door of which he had opened against Foster's advice. "Her husband was in Iraq with Kallman. You knew that, right?"

"Well, yeah."

"Also, she used to be Kallman's visiting nurse or something."

"His *visiting nurse*?"

"Yeah, before, when he was still at home, living with his mother." Duane sighed. "I guess we won't be seeing her around here anymore."

"Why not?" Foster snapped.

"Why not? Because her son doesn't live here anymore. Not to mention, he drowned here. Thanks for the memories."

"You mean Mrs. Kallman," Foster said.

"Who did you think—the nurse, Mahoney? She didn't quit, did she?" Duane actually looked concerned. "What makes you think *she'd* quit?"

"I *don't* think that! She wouldn't quit," Foster protested—too much. He could hear it.

"I hope not," Duane said. He looked thoughtful. "She must've been pretty upset, finding him in the pond like that."

"We both found him," Foster said and immediately wished he hadn't.

"Well, sure. Everybody could tell how upset *you* were."

*Great*, Foster thought. It was hard to sink lower than geezers feeling sorry for you. He looked out the window again and was startled to see the cat sitting there, gazing back at him in the calm and dignified and somehow calculating way cats had.

"I suppose she had to be professional about it," Duane said. "But it makes you think."

"About what?" Foster scowled over his shoulder at Duane.

"Kallman comes back from the war. Her husband doesn't. Grief does funny things to people. You wonder why, of all the guys, your guy is the one who didn't come back. You probably think about the other guys saving their own skins, you think about friendly fire—"

"It wasn't friendly fire!" Foster said. "It was a piece-of-crap armored vehicle with no armor on it. They hit an IED. Robert didn't know Mahoney was going to get it when they switched. They took turns driving all the time."

"Oh," said Lotspeich.

A surprised silence followed. Apparently, there were some things Foster knew that Duane did not—at least until Foster saw fit to blurt them out. "Oh, for Chrissake," Foster said. He turned back to the window. The cat was gone. The sound of furniture moving behind him made him turn around again. Duane had pushed the fake leather chair back into position near the laptop in the closet. "So!" he said briskly, rubbing his palms together. "Did you find that log-a-rhythm you were looking for on your computer?" Duane actually leaned over and patted the seat of the fake leather chair.

For the first time since finding out that Tori *that*-Mahoney hadn't come in this morning, Foster remembered the password-generating algorithm. He'd found it in his email when Panera's Wi-Fi came on this morning, minutes before he left for work. He had intended to run it on the server in Duane's closet as soon as he got a chance. Now, suddenly, the thought of actually finding the password made him feel light-headed. What if it worked? And what if it nailed the right password while Foster was occupied elsewhere? He sure as hell didn't want Duane Lotspeich opening the door to *The World of Pondside* while he, Foster, was squirting whipped topping on pie slices in the kitchen.

"I gotta set tables for lunch," he told Duane, although the tables were already set. "I'll be back."

"What? Wait! Sit down! Just for a minute."

But Foster was already out the door.

It seemed to Laverne that Duane looked smug as he rolled into the dining room for lunch, and when he steered his wheelchair over to the table she was sharing with Nick and Noreen Stevens, she knew that something was up. Usually, Duane avoided the Stevenses. They were like that nursery rhyme where the man could eat no fat while his wife could eat no lean, although Noreen Stevens didn't so much lick the platter clean as hound the hell out of her husband if he attempted to consume so much as a milligram of cholesterol, thus ruining the enjoyment of anybody trying to eat a strip of bacon or a slice of cheese in their vicinity.

The Stevenses had been talking nonstop at lunch about Tori Mahoney, who had gotten everyone's attention by not showing up at work today. Laverne was only half listening to them, busy as she was trying to catch Duane's eye while he craned his neck and twisted in his chair and made multiple attempts to get the attention of the young woman wheeling the salad cart around the dining room. Laverne turned to Nick Stevens, who had just called Tori Mahoney an *interesting* person in a tone of voice that invested the word with some kind of weird innuendo. It was time to change the subject, Laverne thought.

"Of course, Tori is an interesting person," she said. "She's an animal lover, too. The other day she told me something I didn't know about raccoons. Did you know they—"

"Not an *interesting* person, Laverne," said Noreen Stevens, coming to the aid of her husband as she snatched a packet of ranch dressing from his hand. "He said a *person* of *interest*. I thought you watched *CSI*."

While Duane took his time choosing one of the identical bowls of iceberg lettuce so as to give himself an extended opportunity to ogle the salad-cart girl, Laverne reconsidered tall, bald Nick and plump Noreen. She looked from one to the other of them. "Are you suggesting that the *police* are interested in Tori Mahoney? For what?"

"As a possible suspect, I suppose," Nick said. "Isn't that what a 'person of interest' is?"

"What are you talking about?" said Laverne. The young woman with the salad cart had finally escaped and moved on to the next table. Suddenly, Laverne recognized her. She was the Hummer driver from yesterday, her glamorous appearance altered, though not entirely disguised, by scrubs and a hairnet.

"He's talking about poor Robert Kallman," said Noreen. She glanced at Duane (who was drizzling ranch dressing on his salad from four packets at once, two in each hand) and lowered her voice. "They're thinking he *didn't* commit suicide."

"I said that all along!" Laverne exclaimed. Then she darkened. "What does that have to do with Tori Mahoney?"

"I expect the police are wondering if *she* is the one who opened the door for him," Nick said. He, too, was watching Duane wield the four salad dressing packets.

"How do you know what the police are wondering?" Laverne said. The Stevenses merely exchanged what were obviously supposed to be knowing glances. Laverne couldn't keep herself from adding, "She doesn't even work at night."

"Maybe she made a special trip *that* night," Noreen said.

"That would be quite a coincidence, her just happening to come here *that* night," Laverne said. She didn't like the way this conversation was going. Again, she tried to catch Duane's eye. He reached for the salt and pepper in the middle of the table without looking at her.

"Not if it was planned in advance," Noreen leaned forward to say.

Laverne tried to picture it. Tori meeting Robert Kallman at the door, punching the numbers on the keypad for him, her ponytail bouncing, him grunting something that meant "Thanks." It was easy to picture— so easy, it was as though Laverne had actually seen the nurse open the door. To Laverne's dismay, it was equally easy to picture Tori guiding his wheelchair across the parking lot, to the far corner where the path to the pond began, following him down the path and giving him the little boost the wheelchair would need to get over the bump and onto the pier.

"Why would she do it?" Laverne asked. "You've got to have a motive. I'm sure she felt sorry for him in his condition, but everybody felt sorry for him. If that's the thing, we would all be persons of interest."

"Not because she felt sorry for him." Duane said this with his mouth full. They all looked at him. He went on chewing, one cheek bulging, ranch dressing white in the corners of his mouth.

"Then why?" Nick asked hungrily.

Duane paused to swallow before he said, "A different motive."

"*Pffff*," Laverne said. It was just like him, like all of them, Laverne thought, to make mountains out of molehills. Person of interest, for heaven's sake. A different motive. "What *motive?*"

Duane waited—*no doubt for maximum drama*, Laverne thought. He dabbed his mouth with a napkin. When he spoke, it took her another moment to comprehend the word he had spoken, which had no connection, she thought, to anything they had been talking about so far.

"Revenge!" is what he said.

Both Stevenses' faces lit up. They leaned closer for details.

# CHAPTER 17

Mary McIntyre's daughters showed up at Pondside Manor inconveniently close to noon—about two hours before Kitty Landiss expected them—when the dining room was clamorous with residents variously eating, refusing to eat, or demanding to be fed. Mary McIntyre, Kitty noticed when she came out of her office, was not among them. It was too bad the lack of CNAs had made it impossible to keep up the kind of supervision the woman obviously needed. They were doing the best they could, but that's not what the daughters wanted to hear.

They arrived in separate cars, a Volvo wagon and a Toyota sedan making the turn into the circle drive one right after the other. Kitty just happened to be standing at the windows in the dining room—she had come to have a word with Foster Kresowik, who should have been working in the kitchen but was nowhere to be found—when the two cars snaked through the visitor's lot. They pulled right up to the building and parked side by side. She didn't know they were Mary McIntyre's daughters until the one who'd visited before, whom Kitty recognized by her electric-blue pullover fleece, got out of the Volvo station wagon. She walked around to where a woman who could have been her twin, as far as their faces were concerned, was getting out of the Toyota. Daughter #2 was a little taller and somewhat slimmer and her hair—long, and darker than her sister's—was pulled back into a ponytail. They were both wearing jeans, but Daughter #2 had, overall, a more polished look in her short trench coat and boots. Both cars, Kitty noticed, had Iowa plates, although the second daughter was from a different county, farther west.

Mary McIntyre's daughters did not come right into the building. Daughter #1 pointed across the visitor's lot toward the pond, and the two of them set off in that direction. They walked slowly through the clear October light, Daughter #1 pointing at this and that—the pond, the pier, the SeniorMobile, the head of the asphalt path where James Witkowski's fishing gear was found—while Daughter #2 turned herself all the way around, getting the lay of the land. They stopped to look over the spirea hedge and down the hill to the water. Daughter #2 shrugged out of her trench coat and draped it over her arm. Underneath, she had on a long, lean turtleneck and short cardigan sweater—definitely smarter than her sister's fleece.

Kitty met them at the door in the vestibule. "Beautiful day, isn't it?" she said. Handshakes, introductions—up close, Daughter #2 looked younger than her sister, considerably less like a twin. Kitty pressed the buttons on the keypad to open the interior door. The alarm buzzed until she hit the same four numbers on the keypad inside.

"So you have to push the right buttons to get in or out," Daughter #2 observed.

"Or you can ring the doorbell and someone will come let you in," her sister said.

"We used to change the code weekly, but we've been doing it more often since"—Kitty paused. Nothing like starting things off with a mention of—"the events."

She led them not to her office but to the sunny conference room and seated them at one end of the long table, Daughter #1 at the head, Daughter #2 in the first chair on her sister's left, and Kitty on the other side, across from Daughter #2. They made an intimate little triangle at one end of the expanse of polished oak—a little too intimate, Kitty found, when she tried to shuffle through the papers she'd brought from her office. She had deliberately asked Carol to look up Daughter #1's name and write it on a bright pink Post-It. It was not possible to be unobtrusive about looking for it with the stack of papers right under all of their noses.

"The police talked to Mom," Daughter #1 said. She hadn't offered her own name when she introduced her sister, no doubt thinking that Kitty knew all the names of all the family members who came to visit their loved ones. And in her efforts to find or remember Daughter #1's name, Kitty had already forgotten the just-mentioned name of Daughter #2. Was it Mary? Like her mother?

"The police talked to everyone," Kitty quickly assured both daughters. She knew, having checked the visitor's log, that Daughter #1 had been here every day since Mary McIntyre's arrival last Monday. If only she had signed her *name,* instead of writing "Daughter."

"They said she was wandering around outside that morning, when they found the dead guy," Daughter #2 said.

"There were two dead guys," her sister pointed out.

"What I don't understand," said Daughter #2, "is how did she get out? With the code and the alarm? How did nobody hear her?"

"We don't know," Kitty admitted.

"They said the guy who drowned couldn't have opened the door for her—before he drowned, I mean."

"That's right. Robert was incapacitated."

"But there were two dead guys," the first daughter pointed out again.

"They said Mom was wandering around, looking for 'her baby,'" said the second daughter. She added, with what seemed like more than a hint of bitterness, "It's always babies with Mom."

"Yes!" Kitty said. "We've noticed that, and we wanted to talk with you about it. You'd think that the doll would be a comfort to her, but I'm afraid it hasn't worked out that way."

"What doll?" the second daughter said.

Kitty looked from one daughter to the other. They regarded each other suspiciously. She could see that they were not a united front.

"I understand completely why you'd want her to have it," Kitty said.

"Somebody gave Mom a doll?" Daughter #2 turned to her sister. "Did you do this? Because I sure didn't."

"Oh!" Kitty said. "I just assumed—"

"It wasn't us," said Daughter #1.

"Oh for heaven's sake," the other daughter said, as if she'd heard quite enough. "Can we see her now?"

Kitty glanced at the wall clock. "She might be at lunch."

"I doubt it," said Daughter #1, obviously glad for a chance to re-assert her authority as the one who had been here for Mom all along. "The only meal Mom will eat here is breakfast, because they give her Cream of Wheat. For lunch and dinner, it's pureed goop, which she won't touch with a ten-foot pole."

Summoning the gently dispassionate tone she used with distraught family members, Kitty explained. "All of our residents are observed at meals at least weekly. If a resident shows signs of difficulty swallowing, or if they appear less than fully alert, then our speech therapist orders a pureed diet for that resident. For the most part, it's the same menu that's served with the regular diet—"

"Mom has difficulty swallowing?" Daughter #2 interrupted. "Is that because of the stroke?"

"Your mother's problem is her fluctuating level of consciousness. She's alert at times, but at other times her medication makes her—less alert."

"They drug her up to calm her down," Daughter #1 said.

"So the pureed thing is to keep her from choking?" Daughter #2 frowned at her sister. "We can't give her that fish sandwich then."

Kitty sniffed. She thought she'd detected a whiff of Culver's on them. She added, "We're especially concerned about the dangers of aspiration, which can lead to pneumonia. For a person whose physical health is already precarious, pneumonia is usually fatal."

"So is starvation," said Daughter #1.

*I had no idea you were such a pain in the ass*, Kitty thought. *What a pair.* She offered first one daughter and then the other a smile of sympathy for their mother's plight. "Why don't we see if she's in the dining room?"

"She *won't* be," Daughter #1 said.

"Let's try her room then," Kitty said, her sympathetic smile still in place.

Mary, meanwhile, was sitting in a chair in her living room. She was waiting for George to come home from work and take her to the hospital because she'd already had two contractions—big ones—and they knew how fast it went the last time. Their first daughter was almost born in the back seat of Uncle Charlie's 1960 Oldsmobile. That was a time, wasn't it? Stuck in traffic on Oklahoma Avenue and heading toward the railroad tracks, afraid that if the barricades came down before the Olds had inched its way up there, then there was no chance that Mary could keep that baby from coming out onto Uncle Charlie's tweed upholstery. She had already leaked a little onto the seat, and she could feel the weight of the baby pressing down—at least, she figured it had to be the baby, although the truth was that it felt like the biggest and most urgent movement that her bowels had ever had to make. "George! George!" she couldn't help but shriek from the back, and poor George, his butt hopping up and down on the seat and his hands squeezing the fancy leather cover Uncle Charlie had on his steering wheel, begged her, "Don't!" and "Wait!" and "Here comes a cop—hold on!" He'd seen the motorcycle weaving between the lines of cars in the rearview mirror, and only now, after it squeaked past them, did he think to roll down the window and stick his head out and holler, "Help!" which made the cop put a foot down on either side of the motorcycle and look back over his shoulder.

The Olds was in the right-hand lane, so it was just a bump over the curb to follow the policeman's motorcycle down the sidewalk and over the tracks and beyond them to the corner, where a squad car he had summoned with his radio was waiting, lights flashing, to lead them all the way to the hospital. The baby was born twelve and a half minutes after they whisked Mary out of the car at the ambulance entrance. George, who barely had time to park the Olds and run on shaky legs to the obstetrics floor, was so grateful to and inspired by the cop who helped them that within a year he had sold his service station and set out to become a policeman himself.

That baby—their first daughter—was six years old now. Mary had the little girl stationed out on the front porch to watch for George's car. As soon as she saw it turn the corner, she was to come and tell her mother, so Mary, who already had her coat on and her purse in her lap and her little suitcase on the floor next to her feet, could come outside and start the long descent to the curb.

A police car and an ambulance came around the corner. The little girl stood there at the top of the porch steps as a policeman emerged from the squad car and signaled, "Wait," to the two men who had already hopped out the back of the ambulance. The policeman was bounding up the steps toward the girl before she jumped into motion again and flung open the front door to race in just ahead of him, calling, "Mama!"

In the living room, Mary listened to the policeman explain that he and the ambulance had been sent by George to come and take her to the hospital. "I'd rather wait for George, thank you," she told the policeman. He took off his hat and tucked it under his arm before he reminded her, as delicately as possible, that she barely made it to the hospital on a previous occasion—here he glanced at the little girl—and that George had sent the ambulance for that very reason.

Mary closed her eyes and pressed her lips together. She gripped her purse with both hands. Suddenly, she let out a long breath and said, "I'm not riding in that ambulance. I'm going to wait for George."

"Mom?" said Daughter #1.

The other daughter, the one who hadn't visited before, was hanging back just a little.

Mary McIntyre lifted her head, slowly, her face expressionless. The doll, wearing only a pink baby bonnet, lay in her lap, its plastic arms and legs akimbo and its head askew. She looked at Kitty, then at her daughters, first the one and then the other. At the sight of Daughter #2, Mary McIntyre's eyes opened wide. A transformation occurred in her face. It was the most dramatic transformation Kitty Landiss had ever seen in any human face. It was as though a light had come on, not just in the old woman's eyes but under her skin, a light that slowly brightened until she looked lit up from within, Kitty thought, like the glow-in-the-dark statues that teachers used to give kids for good behavior in grade school—the Virgin Mary, the Angel Gabriel, or, if you were *really* good, a crucifix, Jesus stretched out all aglow on a brown plastic cross. Mary McIntyre's eyebrows rose, and as the down-turned corners of her mouth also lifted, years seemed to fall away from her face. It became by degrees as hopeful and open as a girl's.

*This is what people meant*, Kitty thought, *by a beatific smile.*

Thus illuminated, Mary McIntyre clasped her hands together, the broken doll obviously forgotten in her lap, and said to her daughter, sounding breathless with joy, "Molly! I thought I'd lost you!"

At that, Daughter #2 turned without a word and fled the room.

It was her fault, Mary knew that. She almost lost that baby from all her stubbornness. They scolded her, didn't they? You should have ridden in the ambulance, they said. They said the cord was around the baby's neck, they couldn't hear a heartbeat, they thought the baby was dead—but they were wrong! The baby came out and she grew up, and now here she was, her daughter Molly, sitting in a little room, both arms wrapped around her own big round belly, rocking it back and forth. They could be wrong, is all Mary meant to say. They were wrong then, and they could be wrong now! "You can't be sure," Mary had cried. "Don't believe them! Pray! Ask God to save the baby. He can do it, He saved you, and He raised Lazarus, but you have to pray. You have to believe! He can tell if you don't mean it. What happened, Molly? Did you fall? What did you do?"

# CHAPTER 18

In the kitchen, Jenny was still giving Foster the silent treatment. That was fine with him, he told himself, especially if it meant he could get back to Duane Lotspeich's room before the old guy finished his lunch. With the new CNA helping Jenny wield the salad and entrée carts, Foster was free to tackle the tower of pots and pans that needed to be leveled before the lunch dishes came back from the dining room. He finished them in record time, rearranged the racks to accommodate the dishes, stocked the dessert carts with pieces of pie they had cut after breakfast (half of them flagged sugar-free and four in bowls, pureed), and made his escape.

Back in Duane Lotspeich's room, Foster shut the door. If there had been a lock, he would have locked it. His knees collided with the shelf in the closet when he sat down in the fake leather chair. The whole shelf assembly rocked back and forth, and he had to grab the laptop to keep it steady on a stack of three coffee-table books Duane had borrowed from the library to adjust the height: *The Ultimate Baseball Book, The Arts of China*, and *Hammond's International Atlas of the World*. Foster had, at one point or another in the past day and a half, tried using all of these titles in various scrambled ways as passwords to *The World of Pondside*, knowing full well how stupid that was, what a waste of time. You could get into a kind of fever, he'd discovered, where something caught your eye and you couldn't *not* try it.

As far as Foster was concerned, their inability to access the game continued to prove that, whatever weird and tragic thing had befallen Robert Kallman, he had *not* committed suicide. Taking the *World of Pondside* to the grave with him was the last thing that Robert wanted. Foster was one hundred percent sure of that. Robert would have told *somebody* that he changed the password—and what he'd changed it to— before he did anything else. It was impossible for Foster to believe that Robert would even go out on the pier to make a phone call or see the stars, for God's sake, without first sending a message to Foster—or to someone, although Foster couldn't think who else it would be—to let him know that he had changed the password.

The problem was that there was no message from Robert, not on Foster's dumb phone and not in his email. It was true that Robert didn't usually contact Foster by phone or email. Usually, he left a note in the middle of the ancient card table on the screened porch in Foster's *World of Pondside*. But what good would that do if Robert also changed the password so Foster couldn't get into the game? If all he had was the password for the *admin* page, and no live links there to use it on, nothing but the equally inaccessible *N–L* and the crap-ass company email account? Robert wouldn't use the software company email account to say goodbye. Foster was 99 percent sure of that. At *least* 99 percent sure.

But he was not 100 percent sure of it.

Foster's heart was not exactly pounding, but it was picking up the pace as he clicked on the ducklink. The admin page looked the same way it did before: a scattering of folders, a list of player portal links that still didn't light up when he skimmed over them with the cursor, the *N–L* link that did, and the company email account. He groaned. The email icon reported 7,382 unopened messages. He clicked on it anyway. He started scrolling past messages about special offers, upgrades, new software, security advisories. He told himself that all he wanted to do now was to get *in,* preferably without Duane Lotspeich breathing down his neck. He was ready to learn *anything* that would help him figure out what Robert was up to when he changed the password, when he turned off the server, when he rolled out onto the pier. Surely there was something more to it than just *Goodbye*.

Foster stopped scrolling.

Here it was. Dear God. A message from Robokall.

Foster blinked, squeezing his eyes shut for a moment before he opened them. The message was still there. Sent last Wednesday, the date stamp said, at 8:39 p.m. Robert had sent him a message—here it was—just hours before he went into the pond. On Robert's last night on earth, he had sent Foster this message.

Foster folded his hands in his lap. He was not in a fever now. More like a cold sweat. The message from Robokall had no subject line. Only that date and time: 8:39 p.m. For Robert, 8:39 would be not long after dinner on spaghetti night, not long after Wild Mary splattered a bowl full of the pureed stuff all over herself and James Witkowski. Robert had been there the whole time, at his regular table, chewing and chewing. When Foster came in with the mop and bucket, he'd caught Robert's eye. He remembered thinking that Robert looked amused—not that he smiled, exactly, because he couldn't exactly smile, but the eyebrow went up. Did he know then? Was there, like, a plan in place? Did he already know this would be his last meal, complete with live entertainment, a little comedy act, compliments of Wild Mary? Is that what Robert was thinking about while he chewed and chewed? While he grunted, "Yes," to an offer of extra garlic bread? While he talked Foster into making the jelly sandwich for Mary McIntyre? Did Robert go back to his room after that and compose this message, figuring that Foster would get it eventually? That there was no big rush, after all, to say goodbye?

Suddenly, it was obvious why Robert would change the password before rolling into the pond. *The World of Pondside* was *Robert's* game, *his* invention. What made Foster think that Robert would hand the game over to them in the end, no matter how the end happened to come? Maybe Robert had a buyer lined up. Maybe he'd had one lined up all along. Sony. Epic. Microsoft, for God's sake! What was Foster *thinking*? What did he imagine Robert's farewell message was going to say? Of *course* Robert didn't want to take *The World of Pondside* to the grave with him, but that didn't mean he was going to entrust the game to the kitchen boy, did it? What kind of fool would do that? Well, shit, Foster didn't have to open the message at all, did he? He could let Robert take whatever last words he had to offer right into the pond. He could delete the damn message! He could drag it straight to the trash. Let the stupid cops keep investigating, let them drain the fucking pond for clues! Let them arrest somebody for *murder*—shit, they could arrest Foster if they wanted to—what did he care? He could delete everything—empty the whole damn inbox right now!

Or he could just open the fucking message.

It was short. One sentence. A question. Foster's heart stopped, then it started again. It was a question that only he, of all the people living on the face of the earth, was sure to understand:

*Who ate the whole thing?*

Foster closed the email account. He was about to close the admin page, but he changed his mind and clicked instead on the only other live item on the page: the *N–L* at the bottom of the list of player portals. A log-in box popped up, inviting him to enter his password. He hunted and pecked, slowly and carefully, typing into the log in box two words he had never thought to try. In retrospect, of course, he couldn't believe that he'd never tried them. He didn't know he was holding his breath until he hit Enter.

*Invalid password.* The dialog box suggested that he *Try again.*

He took out the word space after Mary.

*Invalid password.*

He removed the caps on *M*, *M*, and *I*, even though Robert had decided long ago that *World of Pondside* passwords would never be case sensitive, so as not to give the geezers trouble logging in.

*Invalid password.*

He and Robert had also decided not to limit the number of mistakes a person could make while typing the password, because that, too, would discourage the geezers. Foster put back the caps on *M*, *M*, and *I*, variously. No dice.

He restored the word space, with and without caps, and tried again, and again. When the letters blurred on the screen, he blinked furiously. He could see it: the small white plate with a few smears of purple jelly on it. Who *else* ate the whole thing, for God's sake? The door to Duane's room opened behind him. He didn't turn around.

"Kid! Glad you came right in and made yourself at home. I was just talking to the new CNA—have you *seen* her?"

"Maybe."

"Oh, there's no maybe about it," Duane said. "If you'd seen her, you'd know. She's a knockout. And get this. That redheaded clown—Idaho or something—"

Foster hadn't tried "Dakota." If that turned out to be the password, or any part of the password, he thought he might just take the server and throw it in the pond.

"He's her boyfriend—*her* boyfriend." Duane rolled farther into the room, having pushed the door mostly shut behind him. "There's no justice—no logic to it. What could she possibly see in a guy like that? I mean a girl like her. You have to see her to believe it—that's she's here, I mean, working *here*." He shook his head. "Her name is Erika. She's got a name tag. Are you okay, kid? You look a little strange."

"I've got a name tag, too," Foster growled. "It doesn't say *kid*."

"Okay, okay," Duane said. "I know your name." He rolled up next to Foster and said, cheerily, "Just don't ask me how to spell it."

Foster sat up straight. "How do you *spell* it?" he said.

"I just told you not to ask me that."

"Mary Mc-In-tire," Foster said, picturing it.

"What are you talking about?"

"I'm talking about her *name*. How do you spell her name? Do you know?"

"M-A-R-Y?"

"Yeah, thanks. The *last* name." Foster arched his fingers over the keyboard.

"M-C-capital—"

"Caps don't matter!"

"Okay, okay. I think it's M-C-I-N-T-Y-R-E."

"*Y?*"

"What do you mean, why? Because that's how you spell McIntyre. But why—"

"We're in," Foster said.

"Say what?"

"We're *in*."

Together they stared at the screen. The background was still that noncommittal blue, but the log-in box had disappeared, replaced by giant yellow letters that said:

## WORLD OF PONDSIDE

Riding the *I* was a yellow duck, this one wearing a white skipper's hat. Foster moused over it and sure enough, the arrow became a hand. The ducklink was live.

"Mary McIntyre?" Duane Lotspeich said. "*That's* the password? I don't believe it."

Foster found he couldn't say anything at all. He lifted his finger from the touch pad and lowered it again, slowly, lining up the arrow. He double-clicked the yellow duck in the skipper's hat. The screen went dark—only for an instant—and then it filled with row after glowing row of letters and numbers and brackets and slashes, an apparently infinite supply of them shimmering and trembling like a beaded curtain in a doorway, scrolling and scrolling up from the bottom to the top of the screen.

Duane Lotspeich rolled forward again to see. The light from the scrolling rows of code flickered on his face.

"Shit," he whispered. "It's like in *The Matrix*."

# CHAPTER 19

Laverne was alone in the dining room after lunch, with her cold cup of coffee and an uneaten piece of peach pie. Duane Lotspeich had wolfed down his overdressed salad and his grilled cheese sandwich and gone back to his room, skipping the pie and leaving Laverne and the Stevenses to ponder what he had told them about Tori Mahoney's so-called motive with regard to poor Robert Kallman. "Did you know about him and her husband being in the same what-do-you-call-it?" Noreen had asked Laverne after Duane left. "No," Laverne said. She wasn't sure she believed it either.

"Do you think that she really might have—?"

"No!" said Laverne. "It's a ridiculous idea," she told Noreen, and repeated, disdainfully, "*Revenge.*"

The Stevenses had left the table much more interested in Duane Lotspeich's dramatic version of things than in anything Laverne had to say, and now it was her turn to ponder. She had been so busy worrying about *The World of Pondside* that she hadn't given a single thought to what kind of grief poor Robert's death must be causing for Tori Mahoney, who had known him longer than anyone else at Pondside. Laverne fervently hoped that this "person of interest" idea was the product of bored old folks' overactive imaginations—and not something someone had overheard from the office or the police. Laverne winced at a bitter sip of cold coffee, tossed her clothing protector onto the table, and reached for the walker she was, sadly, getting more and more attached to.

That's when the commotion started.

It started slowly. First, there was the woman who came running from the end of Hawkeye Lane, past the dining room, through the atrium, and apparently out the door, which set the alarm to buzzing. The woman reappeared outside the dining room windows and got into a car in the short row that was right up against the building. Through the windshield Laverne could see the woman sitting in the driver's seat, leaning forward, resting her head on the upper curve of the steering wheel. She thought at first that it was Mary McIntyre's daughter, who had been coming here every day, but when the woman lifted her face, Laverne could see that it was someone who only looked like the daughter who had been coming every day—this must be a different daughter, also weeping, of course. Speaking of the other daughter, the one who had been coming every day, here she came, too, scooting past the dining room in her sister's footsteps, as if in pursuit, though slowing down as she went. She must have paused in the vestibule to punch the numbers on the keypad because the buzzing finally stopped, but she didn't appear in the parking lot outside. Meanwhile, through the dining room windows, Laverne watched the car containing the other woman, the first one to come running, as it backed out of its parking spot and lumbered away.

For a few moments after that, everything was quiet again. Then a distant *tap-tapping* grew into a louder *clip-clopping*, and the social worker—an impossibly young woman who wore high heels every day— peeked into the dining room. She said, "Hi," to Laverne, who was still seated at the table, one hand on the walker, and then spoke to someone in the atrium. Laverne couldn't see who it was—there was a useless freestanding wall with fake plants growing out of it between the atrium and the dining room that blocked her line of sight—but she thought it must be Mary McIntyre's daughter, who had followed her sister to the vestibule but not, apparently, out the door.

"Are you all right?" the impossibly young social worker said.

Mary McIntyre's daughter replied, in a warbly voice, the kind that made you know she was lying, "I'm fine."

The social worker didn't pursue it. She gave a cheery but nameless "And how are *you*?" to someone else who must have been in the atrium—whoever it was didn't say anything in response—and then she *clip-clopped* away, back toward her office.

Laverne waited a moment in the dining room to see if anyone else would come running past, and when nobody did, she pushed herself away from the table and got to her feet. She had just aimed her walker to exit the dining room when the shouting began in the atrium, on the other side of the wall. Well, shouting was an overstatement. It was more like growling, loud enough and angry sounding but low in pitch and consequently hard to understand, a voice that Laverne did not recognize. She pushed her walker to the wall that separated the dining room from the atrium, at which point she left the walker behind and slid her hand along the railing until she reached the end of the wall. Peeking around it, she saw an astonishing sight.

Mary McIntyre's daughter—the one who had been coming every day—was sitting in the middle of a sofa, weeping. That was not the astonishing part. That was business as usual. What Laverne could hardly believe, despite the evidence of her eyes, was Edith Cole, standing knees to knees with Mary McIntyre's daughter, the front legs of her walker pressed into the padded skirt of the sofa on either side of the other woman's feet as if to prevent her from getting away. The gruff and rusty growling sound was Edith! Little S-shaped Edith, her question-mark back curling her forward over her built-in basket full of stuffed animals, her arthritic hands gripping the walker like a preacher holding the sides of a podium. Edith was exhorting Mary McIntyre's daughter—and this was the first whole sentence that Laverne could understand—to "Get your mother out of here, for God's sake!"

Mary McIntyre's daughter replied, as if to any frail and angry but ordinary person, "I can't take her out of here. She needs twenty-four-hour supervision."

"So supervise her!" Edith growled.

"Twenty-four hours a day? I can't! I have a job."

"You had babies, didn't you? Who supervised *them*?"

*My goodness*, Laverne thought. This was *Edith*? Laverne looked around. The glamorous new CNA, who appeared to be rolling Dan the trembling man's semireclining wheelchair toward a sunny spot by the windows, had also stopped to stare. Laverne couldn't quite tell where Dan was looking. It occurred to her that the new CNA, like Mary McIntyre's daughter, probably didn't know what Laverne and Dan the trembling man knew, namely, that Edith Cole spoke only to her stuffed animals. No one at Pondside had ever seen her look directly at, much less speak to, another human being.

"Babies are different," Mary McIntyre's daughter was saying. "They can't wander out and get hit by a car."

"Let her get hit by a car then!" Edith cried, causing both Laverne and the daughter to flinch. "Is that any worse than the slow torture here—not only that she's starving to death, and not only that her legs have swollen up to twice their size—have you looked at her legs? Is the skin splitting open yet? That's what happens when you spend most of your day sitting with your chin on your chest like she does."

"They're supposed to exercise—they're supposed to walk her around," Mary McIntyre's daughter protested.

"They're *supposed* to." Edith spat out the word. "Have you *seen* how empty the hallways are? Did they tell you she's lost control of her bladder and bowels yet? They love checking that off on your records because it means they don't even have to *try* and get you to the toilet if they're too busy. You remember that from when you had your babies, don't you? Lots quicker to change a diaper than wait around while the kid sits on the toilet. Well, if they take away your ability to walk across a room—for your own safety, of course, so you won't *fall*—then how are you supposed to get to the toilet? Put your call light on? *Ha*. Somebody'll come eventually, sure. To clean up the mess in your pants. You can only hold it so long, honey. Try it yourself and see. For just one day—oh, and overnight. No getting up overnight—you might fall! You can wet or even shit your bed and lie in it, but try to get up to the bathroom and *that* sets off the alarm.

They'll come then—not right away, there's not enough staff for that, but they'll come. Of course, you waited too long by now. Besides, if you keep setting off that alarm, they'll write that in their records, too. They'll write they found you crawling on the floor. And they'll add out-and-out restraints—tie you to the bed, if necessary—for your safety! You might crawl down the hallway—unless maybe you can still walk—and get out the door and crawl to the highway and get hit by a car!"

Mary McIntyre's daughter shrank into the sofa as if she'd been struck, repeatedly, and Edith, who had been leaning toward her—*dangerously*, Laverne thought—straightened up, at least as far as her curved spine would allow.

"It's the sadness that kills you," Edith growled more quietly, but with no less fervor. "It's the terrible, terrible sadness of knowing that nobody cares enough to come and take you out of here. Nobody cares enough about you to inconvenience themselves that much. That's the real suffering." Edith's voice appeared to be giving out on her. "It's a death sentence, putting her away in here. Do you hear me?" She finished in a hoarse whisper. "It's a death sentence."

With that, Edith turned her back on Mary McIntyre's daughter, and if she saw Laverne clinging to the safety rail on the wall across the room, she gave no sign of it. Hunched protectively over the stuffed animals in her basket, Edith steered her walker toward the edge of the atrium carpet. Trembling Dan and the new CNA were in full retreat and already half-way down the hall. For a moment, Edith appeared to be following them. The girl, who was having some trouble keeping Dan's unwieldy chair on course, looked anxiously over her shoulder, but when Edith reached her room, only a few doors from the atrium, she turned and went in.

Laverne was tempted to make her own escape—she was pretty sure that Mary McIntyre's daughter hadn't noticed her—but the poor woman looked so small and lost sitting there in the middle of the sofa, her head bowed low, chin to chest, just like her mother's, that Laverne cleared her throat and said, "Don't pay too much attention to Edith. Nobody ever comes to see her. It makes her bitter. I believe she's forgotten how to talk to people. In fact, I've never heard her talk to anyone before."

Mary McIntyre's daughter looked up, understandably wary.

Laverne approached the sofa cautiously, *sans* walker. "Besides," she said, "Edith must be thinking about somebody else. Your mother's legs aren't that bad. She gets around okay." *When she's not zonked out*, Laverne could have added but didn't. She had previously avoided the floral sofas and matching armchairs in the atrium, all of which looked like the pillowy kind that could swallow a person and never let her up again. Seating herself as close as she could get to the upholstered arm of the sofa, Laverne was pleasantly surprised to find the cushions firmer than they looked.

Mary McIntyre's daughter whispered, "Do *you* think it's a death sentence?"

For some it was, Laverne thought, but she only shrugged and said, "Life is a death sentence."

Mary McIntyre's daughter looked down at her hands, which were folded in her lap. "All she eats is pudding."

"Two food groups in pudding," Laverne pointed out. "If you make it with eggs. Was that your sister—the one who ran out ahead of you?"

"Yes," she said. "I was supposed to stop her. I told Mom I would. But what's the use?"

"I don't believe I've seen your sister here before."

"You haven't. Molly keeps her distance from Mom. She always has— at least, ever since she lost the baby, and that was twenty-five years ago, so it's as good as always."

"Your *sister* lost a baby," Laverne said.

"You can't blame her. Here Molly had all that trauma to deal with and instead of helping her, Mom goes off the deep end herself. She went crazier than Molly did. Molly didn't speak to Mom for—well, I don't know, but for a long time. For years, Christmas was terrible." Mary McIntyre's daughter gave Laverne a pleading look. "I *know* Mom would do better at home. I took twelve weeks of leave when she first had the stroke, and she ate everything. But it was twelve weeks! I had to go back to work."

"Well, what about"—Laverne hesitated, she despised the phrase— "adult day care?"

'They won't take her. She's too out of control."

"You're probably right," Laverne said, thinking about the shower-head Mary McIntyre had pulled out of the wall. "It's too late for that."

"Too *late?* It was always too late for that. You don't know my mother. She won't do *anything* she doesn't want to do. She never has. My sister almost *died* before she was born because my mother didn't want to ride in an ambulance. The cord was wrapped around my sister's neck. They almost lost her."

Laverne could identify. In the end, Bill had also insisted on no ambulance. No emergency nonsense. He made Laverne promise. When she went ahead and called 911 anyway, Bill made sure he was all but gone before anybody got there. Laverne had wasted precious last minutes directing the police and paramedics to their hidden driveway. This was one of those memories Laverne had to drive from her mind any way she could or else be plunged into a forty-year-old abyss of guilt and regret and—if she was honest—a lingering whiff of anger at Bill, as if it were so important for him to prove her wrong, to have it his way, that he was willing to shave a few minutes off the end of his life to do it.

"What about when you were a baby, though?" Laverne said. "What about all the nights your mother must have gotten up every few hours and fed you—and your sister—did she want to do *that*, do you think?" These questions came out sounding crabbier than she intended, that old whiff of anger swirling faintly around the words. Like the one at lunch, this conversation had taken a turn that Laverne had not expected; it was going somewhere other than where she wanted it to go.

"*Yes!*" Mary McIntyre's daughter exclaimed. "Yes, she did. If she could have stayed up 24-7 and sat there and looked at us, watched us breathe around the clock, she would have done it. It's all she wanted in the world. It's all she cared about. Keeping us alive, keeping us safe, never letting us out of her sight, for God's sake."

Laverne felt a little surge of something—guilt? defensiveness? Whatever the feeling was, it quickly turned surly. She had been the same way with her son Joseph, or so she'd been told. No one seemed to understand how difficult it was to let go of a child's hand, to let him run down a hill or climb the stairs or let him cross the street without her, to close the door to his bedroom and trust that he would still be breathing when she opened it in the morning! Bill used to tell her she couldn't keep the boy in a velvet box. Bill, in his infinitely maddening wisdom, had warned her that Joseph would not thank her for protecting him from every last danger, real or imagined (but mostly imagined, Bill would sometimes go so far as to say), and oh, hadn't Bill been right about that. Was there ever a son less grateful to his mother for all the attention she had lavished on him? To look at them now, who would think that Joseph had ever been the weaker one, the one in need of care? A word from the lunchtime conversation with Duane and the Stevenses came to Laverne then. It came with the force of discovery, and to her own surprise, she said it aloud: "So this is revenge."

"*What?*" said Mary McIntyre's daughter.

Here was a chance for Laverne to take back what she said, but she didn't take it back. Instead, she repeated it. "Are you getting revenge on your mother? Is that what all you people are doing? Getting revenge?"

"Oh, God!" Mary McIntyre's daughter cried. She stood, swooping up a reusable grocery bag from the sofa behind her. Laverne spotted a little arm sticking up out of the bag. Mary McIntyre's daughter followed Laverne's gaze. She pulled the doll up by a loosely attached arm and shook it, making the eyes rattle in its head. "Some stupid person here gave this *baby* doll to my mother! Look at it!" Laverne could see that it was the same kind of doll Mrs. Kallman had shown her days ago, which meant it was the same kind that Foster was carrying under his arm when he got off his bike by the dumpster. But this doll was looking considerably worse than either of those. For one thing, except for the pink bonnet, it was naked. The head was on crooked, and one slightly sunken eye appeared to be stuck open, the other shut. "My mother was sitting in her room with *this* in her lap. Who would give her such a thing? A baby doll all messed up like this! Why? What do you think, huh? Maybe someone else wanted *revenge?*"

Mary McIntyre's daughter stuffed the doll back into the bag. She stood up and exited the atrium with as much righteous indignation as anyone clutching a doll in a grocery bag could. It seemed that only seconds passed before the station wagon bobbed into view outside the atrium windows.

Laverne ventured without her walker to the edge of the atrium carpet and stopped there. Her own indignation was fading into embarrassment over what she had said to Mary McIntyre's daughter—*revenge, for heaven's sake!*—which gave way, in turn, to puzzling over the torn-up doll. *Was* it the same one she'd seen under Foster's arm? Except for one leg that seemed to be missing, that doll had looked all right. It wasn't naked either. It had a little pink dress on. Why on earth would Foster tear that doll—or any doll—apart and then give it to Mary McIntyre like that? Laverne couldn't think of a reason why, nor could she picture Foster Kresowik—*ha!* his whole name had come to her just like that—doing any such thing. It just didn't seem like the sort of thing that young man would do. She looked back across the atrium to where her walker appeared to be waiting for her near the half wall that marked the border with the dining room. After all the noise and drama, the silence felt especially profound.

Kitty Landiss had expected Mary McIntyre to rise up in furious confusion and fly down the hallway after her daughters. Instead, Mary McIntyre remained sitting next to the bed with her chin on her chest and her bony arms limp over the arms of the chair, as if she had expended all of her resources on the beatific transformation of a few moments ago. Sitting there, she looked harmless, even helpless, but Kitty wasn't fooled. She knew from experience that Mary McIntyre possessed a kind of life force fueled by fury that had no respect for fragile bones or aging organs but pursued its ends with implacable determination. Kitty had seen it in her on the day she'd arrived at Pondside in the transport van, strapped into a wheelchair that was chained to the floor, thrashing from side to side and roaring like a rogue elephant. Kitty had half expected the old woman to break an arm, if that's what it took to escape. Then, too, there was the broken shower.

Even if Mary McIntyre was not going to rise up in fury, it seemed unwise to leave her alone here after her daughters had run off so abruptly. Kitty's gaze traveled to the pull cord for the call light. She was reaching for it when Mary McIntyre lifted her head, slowly and with obvious effort. Kitty felt an absurd desire to hide—to duck into the closet or behind the door—any place that would keep that wounded and bewildered gaze from landing on her. The old woman's eyebrows drew together, as if she were trying to focus on Kitty's face, trying to place her. Kitty edged closer to the cord that hung between the bed and the chair. It was almost within her reach when Mary McIntyre's hand shot out toward her. Her fingers closed around Kitty's wrist.

"My poor baby," she said.

"No!" Kitty said, "I'm not your—"

"Tell Molly I'm sorry," Mary McIntyre pleaded. "I know it wasn't her fault. Tell her I'm sorry."

"I will," Kitty promised, although she had already heard the distant buzz of the door alarm that probably meant one or both daughters had gone.

"I didn't mean to hurt her," Mary McIntyre said. There was not a trace of fear or confusion in her voice now, only sadness. "I know these things happen. We just have to accept them. It's nobody's fault."

"I'll go after her right now," Kitty said.

Mary McIntyre's fingers opened like a sprung lock, and Kitty snatched her arm away. As she backed toward the door she heard, or thought she heard, someone out in the hallway calling "Hey!" or maybe "Wait!" She poked her head out into the hallway, hoping that help had arrived, but there was no one in sight. Almost directly across the hall, Kitty could see a border of light flickering around the door to Duane Lotspeich's room. He must be watching something lively on television. She looked down Hawkeye Lane—no sign of Mary McIntyre's daughters. A voice was rising and falling emphatically somewhere, toward the front of the building, maybe in the dining room, but it was too far away, around too many corners, for Kitty to make out anything but a kind of insistent growl—probably a resident expressing some wordless grief as she (or he, but usually she) waited for a ride back down the hall after lunch. With a glance over her shoulder—Mary McIntyre remained sitting in the chair next to her bed, head bowed once again—Kitty stepped out into the hall.

The light was still flickering around Duane Lotspeich's door. Most residents watched television at top volume. Many of them were hard of hearing, of course, but the volume seemed more like a matter of principle: *your* TV was not going to drown out *my* TV. Duane's was silent, or else very quiet. She stepped closer until she was standing with her toes nearly touching the bottom of the door—no sills to bump a walker or a wheelchair over at Pondside Manor—and anyone seeing her there would assume, correctly, that she was trying to hear whatever there was to hear on the other side of it. This close to his door, she detected the sibilant sounds of whispering. It could have been the old man talking to himself, arguing with the silent television, narrating his lonely day—but then she heard mumbling in response to the whisper. Unless old Lotspeich was a ventriloquist, there was somebody in there with him.

# CHAPTER 20

The scrolling had stopped, the screen had gone dark—causing a catch in Foster's throat—and then it bloomed with an image that made his stomach feel suddenly hollow: wicker chairs and the ancient wooden card table, big screened windows with great leafy trees crowding them from the outside, the leaves swishing and trembling. The porch looked just the same as he'd left it before the game went down—except for Mrs. Kallman sitting at the table and the baby doll on the table in front of her, its chubby arms outstretched.

That was new.

"What the H is this?" Duane said, sounding more perplexed than crabby.

Mrs. Kallman looked pretty much the way she had at Robert's funeral visitation. A little smoother maybe, especially around the edges—a little simpler and more colorful. Robert liked to put the same effects on all the video images they used in *The World of Pondside* so they would "match up" and look real in their surroundings. Mrs. Kallman's hands, clasped in front of the doll as if to keep it safely on the tabletop, had no age spots or wrinkles. The doll itself looked exactly the same as Mary McIntyre's doll—not that Foster was likely to know one baby doll from another. It was dressed the same. Pink dress and baby bonnet. The only difference that he could see was the folded note attached with an oversize safety pin to the front of its pink dress.

"So what the hell *is* this?" Duane asked again. "Do you know?"

"It's my grandparents' porch," Foster said. The real question was, what were Mrs. Kallman and the doll doing here? Assuming that Robert had added them—because, who else?—when and why had he done it?

Duane had other issues. "How do we get to our stuff?" There was no *World of Pondside* menu on the screen, no toolbar across the top. "Click on something!" he said. "The note—on the doll—click on that!"

Foster hesitated. There were folded notes in all the *World of Pondside* portals: "Back soon," "I love you," "Third door on the left," "Meet me at the corner of 12th Street & Vine!" Recipes, directions, secrets, all kinds of "in-world readables," as Robert called them. A note looked simple on the screen, but making it unfold convincingly required a heap of code, and there was plenty of room for trouble in all that code. Unfolding a note always made something happen—it was supposed to—but it didn't always work as planned. Foster remembered unfolding a note one time that opened up a whole portal, totally replacing the one he was working on. It had taken him days to find his way out of it.

He tried clicking other objects on the screen—the doll, of course, and Mrs. Kallman, the table, chairs, the train on the shelf below the windows—but nothing happened. Finally, holding his breath, he clicked on the note. It flashed open instantly to fill the screen with columns and rows of pink letters scrolling like a slot machine. When they stopped, all the rows of letters read *Phone Home*, which was what Robert used to say—actually, ET said it for him—when he needed help with the Bluetooth to call his mother. Foster's throat tightened a little. Then the screen went black.

"Now what?" Duane cried.

Foster tapped the keyboard, and the screen lit up again, but Mrs. Kallman and the doll were gone. The scene had changed to what looked like a park, a fancy pavilion in the middle of lush, low trees and blue sky, a surprising backdrop of skyscrapers.

Duane scowled. "Is this another one of your—*what-d'ya-call-it*—portals?"

"No," Foster said. He leaned closer to the screen to be sure he was seeing what he thought he was seeing. "It's Robert's."

In the foreground, cedar trees balanced on short trunks, holding their branches up like arms delivering trays of greenery. A white stone bridge led across a perfectly rectangular pool fed by the heads of dragons, streams of water spewing from their mouths. Lotus plants floated on the surface of the pool, a pink flower here and there among the round pads of the leaves. On the other side of the bridge, the paving stones turned into steps. They climbed to a pair of great green copper doors at the front of a wooden building that branched out, long and low, on either side of the doors, enclosing the park in a polished wooden arcade. The whole park was like a garden growing in a wooden box set down in the middle of a city. Skyscrapers in the background looked photoshopped in place.

"Pretty fancy," Duane said. "You've seen this before?"

"Robert showed it to me back when I first started working with him on the game. As an example, you know, of what a portal could be."

It was modeled on photos Robert had taken of a Buddhist monastery he visited when he was in China. He had gone all the way there for a drug trial that got shut down almost before it started, and he'd done a lot of sightseeing, he told Foster, waiting around to see if the study would resume. Foster had admired the monastery portal—he knew enough to be impressed by the level of detail: the grain of the wood, the way the cedar branches quivered. Now it looked even better than he remembered. He moused over to one of the pillars. It felt as if someone had upgraded the interface: instead of lurching forward, you took three steps on-screen and you were there. Close up, you could see how the wooden pillars grew into curving braces and brackets at the top that held up roofs and cornices, all of it fitting together like elaborately carved Lincoln Logs.

"I don't see a menu here either!" Duane said, sounding crabbier than before. "Wait! When you put the mouse over the—over there, there's a whole list—there's Black Ops!"

"But it's not a live link. See? It doesn't light up."

"Click on it!"

"Just keep your shirt on, will you?" Foster said.

On-screen, a man was approaching from the far end of the white stone bridge. He was walking toward the viewer. He had dark hair, but he was not an Asian man. He was taller than the other people milling around the scene, including a few who came over the bridge and walked past him. He had a fairly ordinary face, just this side of good-looking, neither old nor young. His arms swung at his sides as he walked, long strides, back straight. He was wearing a white shirt tucked loosely into gray pants. His collar was open, his sleeves rolled back almost to his elbows. His right hand was curled in a fist. He looked familiar to Foster. Very familiar.

Duane leaned forward then. He said, "Is that who I think it is?"

It was Robert Kallman striding toward them, looking whole and healthy.

"It's from before," Duane said softly. "Before he got sick."

In *The World of Pondside*, Robert had always put himself in action using a generic figure—created by the same kind of software other game designers used—but customized to make it look at least a little like the photographs of Robert from his pre-ALS days. He and Foster employed the same method to put the rest of the players—including Foster—in action most of the time, making use of video clips or footage digitized from home movies when they had any for the non-player characters that existed only in the game, like Laverne Slatchek's husband Bill. The scene they were watching now was different. This almost looked as if a cameraman had shot it in a real place somewhere, with Robert Kallman walking toward the camera.

Robert stopped in the middle of the bridge, as if he'd spotted someone he was looking for. His hand shot up, effortlessly, to wave to someone out of the viewer's sight, on the nearer end of the bridge. Sitting at the laptop in Duane Lotspeich's room, Foster suddenly knew that *he,* Foster, was the person across the bridge from Robert Kallman, the person Robert was waving to. All the time that Foster had been trying to get into *The World of Pondside*, Robert had been here, on this bridge, waiting for Foster to show up.

Robert opened his mouth to speak. At the same instant, a phone began to ring, loud and insistent, an old-fashioned telephone ringtone.

A white rectangle popped up on the screen, blocking Robert and the scene behind him. In the middle of the rectangle was a green button labeled *Accept Call*.

"For Christ's sake!" Duane Lotspeich said. "What now?"

Foster tapped the green button. The screen filled immediately and completely with the parchment-pale face of Robert's mother, Mrs. Kallman. She appeared to be leaning down toward the camera at her end, as if she were using a laptop that was open in her lap. It was not, to say the least, a flattering angle. She looked terrible, her face drawn and her hair sticking out over her ears. There were beeping sounds in the background, very little of which could be seen with Mrs. Kallman's giant wrinkled countenance taking up all the space. "Is that Foster Kresowik?" she said, bringing her head even closer to the camera. "Finally!"

Foster recognized the nature of the beeping sounds in the background at the same moment he saw the clear plastic tube pressing down on Mrs. Kallman's upper lip, an oxygen cannula, aimed into her nostrils.

"Mrs. Kallman?" he said. "Are you in the hospital?"

"I'm afraid so. You must come and see me at once." She sounded breathless. "Bring Laverne with you."

"Laverne?" Foster repeated stupidly.

"Laverne Slatchek. Bring her with you."

"What if she won't—"

"Who is that behind you?"

Foster didn't bother to turn around. "It's Duane Lotspeich," he said.

"No, it's not."

"Yes, it is!" Foster said. "We're in his—"

"Room," said a woman's voice. "At Pondside Manor."

Foster looked over his shoulder. Kitty Landiss stood behind him, arms folded across her businesslike blazer, well inside the slightly opened door that she must have slipped through—just now? moments ago?

"You've got the *World of Pondside* on that computer, don't you, Foster?" she said. "You stole it from Robert Kallman's room."

Foster tried to catch Duane Lotspeich's eye, but the old guy hunkered down in his wheelchair, as if he thought maybe he could disappear.

From the laptop came Mrs. Kallman's thin voice, crying, "Close the computer, Foster! Shut it down!" Foster reached blindly for the laptop, almost knocking it off its plateau of coffee-table books. To save it, he snatched it in both hands, which put him face-to-face with Mrs. Kallman on the screen. He felt as if he were holding her head on a tray.

Carol, the office lady, appeared in Duane Lotspeich's doorway just then and announced: "They're here! Two officers. From Homicide."

Mrs. Kallman's tiny voice said, "Oh dear!" and Foster almost dropped the laptop. By the time he righted it, the screen said, *Call Ended.*

Kitty Landiss told Carol, "Put them in the conference room." Then she turned back to Foster. "If you remove that computer from these premises, I will see to it that you are charged, at the very least, with felony theft. Do you understand?"

Foster nodded. Landiss scowled at him (*with all her might*, he found himself thinking) and then she slipped back out the door. Foster waited until the sound of her boot heels clomping down Hawkeye Lane had all but faded before he told Duane, "Go get Laverne."

"What about Landiss? She said—"

"*Go.*"

Duane did one of his twirl-on-a-dime turnarounds and rolled out the door. Cradling the laptop in one arm, Foster closed the video call window. The screen filled again with Robert standing on the white stone bridge over the lotus pond, his hands in his pockets and his lips parted, about to speak. Foster tapped *Play*. In a deep and resonant voice, like a TV or radio newscaster doing a commercial spot, Robert said: "Welcome back to *The World of Pondside*! It's time, my friends, to leave your private comfort zone behind and step up to the *Next Level*. A whole new adventure awaits as you work together—" Foster tapped *Pause* and Robert froze. In *The World of Pondside*, even with the most careful editing of sound, Robert's voice had always had a stilted quality—words bitten off oddly, their intonation not quite right, the result of stitching together words spoken in other real times and real-life places—most of them words that Robert had recorded himself while he still had the chance. Foster had never heard Robert's speech like this, completely unaffected by ALS. He set the laptop down on the bedside table and then, hands trembling, he did three of the hardest things he'd ever done: he closed the window on Robert, logged out of *The World of Pondside* program, and shut down the machine.

Foster was pretty sure that Landiss was bluffing—she wouldn't tell the police that he had the server; she wanted to get back to *The World of Pondside* as much as they did—but that didn't stop him from pulling a T-shirt out of Duane Lotspeich's closet and sliding the laptop into it. He stepped out into Hawkeye Lane without a plan and froze when he spotted Mary McIntyre wringing her hands at the end of the hall. She glanced warily over her shoulder at him. Then he heard Amelia Ramirez, just out of sight around the corner, saying, "Mary! You're missing the ice-cream social." The nurse came into view for a moment. She put her arm around Mary McIntyre's shoulders and gave Foster—still frozen outside Duane's room—an awkward little wave. "It's in the library," she said to Mary. "Come on." Foster heard Mary McIntyre say, "Is my daughter there?" and then, more faintly, "She knows I don't like chocolate," as she let herself be led away.

As soon as they were out of sight, Foster scooted across the hall to Mary McIntyre's room. Apparently, old Dakota Dingleheart had not ratted her out regarding the pudding cups. Foster pushed aside a couple of empties on her dresser to make room for the T-shirt-covered laptop. He checked all four drawers, one after the other, and decided on the second from the top. By borrowing some pudding cups from the top drawer, he was able to arrange three solid layers of them, stacked close together, in the second drawer, with the laptop underneath, looking like nothing but a folded T-shirt.

Back in Hawkeye Lane, outside Mary McIntyre's door, he stopped to consider the mysterious new link that had taken them to Robert on the white stone bridge: *N–L*.

It stood for *Next Level*.

# CHAPTER 21

When Stephanie, the activities director, asked Dakota if he would drive her and a half-dozen residents downtown to the Senior Center for the opening reception of the annual Alzheimer's Art Show—"They were supposed to come and pick us up," she told him, "but their Bionic Bus broke down"—Dakota jumped at the chance. His argument with Erika, followed by finding out that Tori Mahoney hadn't come in, and *then* slamming Foster Kresowik against a locker, had pretty much ruined Dakota's day before it started. Piloting the SeniorMobile was a chance to salvage some shred of dignity, some sense of duty fulfilled.

Pondside Manor had a blue-ribbon winner and four honorable mentions in the Alzheimer's Art Show this year. Mrs. Abigail Yoder, eighty-four, was to receive first prize for the heartbreaking series of self-portraits she had painted in art therapy. Mrs. Yoder did not remember painting any of the watercolors displayed in the Senior Center gallery downtown. From the first one she had painted not quite three years ago—a rosy-cheeked, crinkly-eyed face framed by wisps of gray hair—to the last in the series—a pink-and-gray smudge whose most distinctive features were not blank black eyes, as Dakota thought at first, but a pair of oversize nostrils—Mrs. Yoder had forgotten every one of them. She was delighted, however, to accept her prize—a showy box of chocolates wrapped in gold foil—and opened it immediately. When the adjunct art professor who was judging the contest leaned over to pin the blue-and-gold first prize ribbon on Mrs. Yoder's sweater, she gave him a chocolaty kiss on the cheek.

It was well after two o'clock when Dakota pulled the Senior-Mobile up the circle drive and under the portico to Pondside Manor's main entrance, all hands onboard—except for him and Stephanie—chocolate-stained and dozing. Dakota used to enjoy really getting into the bus driver's role on the SeniorMobile, calling out stops and telling people to stay behind the white line while the bus was in motion, until one time, at the end of a multistop excursion that included the public library, lunch at Peking Buffet, and—the real draw—shopping at Target, Dakota had pulled up under the Pondside portico and announced, "Pondside Manor! End of the line!"

The late James Witkowski had broken the awkward silence that followed Dakota's announcement. "No kidding," the old man said.

Dakota pulled the lever that opened the door. He turned off the engine and set to work disengaging the guest of honor's wheelchair from its dock at the front of the bus. Leaving Stephanie to handle the remaining passengers, all ambulatory, Dakota rolled Mrs. Yoder onto the lift platform, secured the wheelchair, and slowly lowered her and her blue ribbon and her half-demolished box of chocolates to the pavement just outside the building. As he punched the numbers on the keypad next to the glass door, taking care to keep one hand on Mrs. Yoder's wheelchair, he was surprised to see Laverne Slatchek standing in the vestibule, as if she were waiting for someone. She was wearing a full-length red coat—a stylish wool coat that Dakota couldn't remember seeing her wear before—and a dark-blue fedora. Clearly, she was on her way somewhere, with her cane hooked over one arm and a large black purse on the other. What was most notable about her, however, was the undisguised annoyance on her face. She did not look happy to see the SeniorMobile unloading passengers out front, not happy at all. When the outside door clicked open, she hurried toward it and appeared to wait, none too patiently, for Dakota to get Mrs. Yoder and her wheelchair out of the way.

"What's up, Laverne?" Dakota greeted her as cheerfully as possible, despite her sour expression.

"I'm going out," she snapped. "I *can* go out, you know. I don't need anybody's permission."

Dakota heard the *least of all yours* that went unspoken at the end of this sentence. Meaning only to show Laverne that he had no intention of getting in her way, he asked, "Is your son coming to pick you up?"

"What? No! No, he is not. I am going somewhere with someone else who is picking me up outside this door, and I don't need *anyone's* permission. Will that bus be out of the way any time soon?"

"As soon as I get Mrs. Yoder inside," Dakota said.

Mrs. Yoder, who had perked up considerably since exiting the bus, gave Laverne a bright and friendly look. "Chocolate?" she said, holding up her slightly flattened golden box.

Foster was feeling less and less optimistic about getting himself and Laverne Slatchek to Mercy Hospital to see Mrs. Kallman. He sat sweating in Amelia Ramirez's purple Saturn, one hand on the steering wheel and the other on the sporty gearshift knob that stuck up from the floor. An unlit cigarette bounced between his lips. The car itself was half in and half out of the parking space, having leaped backward to an engine-killing stop as soon as he turned the key. On his second try, he pushed the clutch pedal to the floor first, then turned the key. When he lifted his left foot off the clutch, the car took another backward leap and died. It was now out of the parking space. All Amelia had said about the car as she slid her key across the nurses' station counter was that the fob didn't work and that it was already in reverse, so be careful. He must have looked hesitant—*how could she leave it in reverse*, he was wondering—because she'd stopped, key halfway across the counter, and said, "You do have a valid driver's license, don't you?"

"Yes!" he said. *For crying out loud*, he was thinking. Just because he didn't have a car—

"Okay, okay. Sorry." She slid the key the rest of the way. "Please don't smoke in my car." Then she trundled away, emphatically, with the meds cart, her mass of black curls bouncing. Conversation over.

Foster pushed the clutch pedal in again. He wiped his sweaty hand on his pants to get a firmer grip on the gearshift and poked around for a forward gear. When he thought he'd found one, he turned the key and the engine rumbled, then screeched—he guessed that wasn't first gear after all. With a little more poking, he finally got the gearshift in position, and mercilessly riding the clutch, he aimed the car toward the portico, where Laverne Slatchek was supposed to be waiting for him. He couldn't see if she was there or not because the SeniorMobile was parked in front of the building, in the way. He was grateful for that small favor, the bus blocking Laverne's view. He could only hope that no one else was watching the car as it leaped and bucked across the parking lot, revving up to a high whine whenever he stepped on the clutch and coming to a final lunging stop behind the SeniorMobile. He released the clutch and the engine died again.

"My goodness," Laverne said as she peeked around the back end of the bus. Foster got out of the car and stood, shamefaced, looking across the hood at her. Laverne sniffed a few times and raised her eyebrows. A burning smell—that would be the overheated clutch plate, she told him later—hung heavily in the air. "Is there something wrong with the car?" she asked.

"It's me," Foster confessed. "I've never driven a stick before."

"Are you talking about a standard transmission?"

"It's Amelia's car," he said.

"I know," said Laverne.

"She didn't *say* it was a stick. I can't drive this thing in traffic. All the way to Mercy Hospital? I'll kill us!"

Laverne looked the car up and down, back and forth. She reached up to straighten her hat, her cane swinging rakishly from the crook of her arm. "Want me to drive?"

Foster didn't know what to say. Without her walker, Laverne looked, well, "younger" was going too far, but certainly she looked less frail, more capable. The red coat and the jazzy hat helped, too. They had to get to Mercy Hospital and talk to Mrs. Kallman. Whatever she had to tell them, it sounded pretty urgent. She hadn't looked too good on-screen, Foster thought. Maybe they didn't have much time.

"It's like riding a bicycle," Laverne said. "One of those skills you never forget." She paused. "Or so I assume."

Foster handed her the key. In the car, he glanced at her profile, the way she had her neck stretched to see over the wheel. She was barely tall enough for her toes to push the clutch pedal to the floor. "People shrink," she told him. "Which hospital did you say she was at?"

"Mercy!" he said, and to his surprise, she laughed.

Laverne revved up the engine, and the car pulled away from the SeniorMobile. She took a practice spin around the parking lot and backed up for a Y-turn with no trouble at all. At the stop sign at the end of the service road, about to turn left onto the highway, she asked Foster to keep an eye out for traffic to the right.

"All clear," he said.

"That'll be your job," she said as she pulled onto the two-lane, shifting from first to second to third without a hitch.

"Watching for traffic?" Foster said. He was more than glad to do his part.

"Just to the right. Since the stroke, I can't see much on that side."

As luck would have it, the first person Dakota saw after he delivered Mrs. Yoder and her box of chocolates to her room in Memory Lane was Erika. He came out the double doors, heard them close with a pneumatic hiss behind him, and there she was on the far side of the deserted nurses' station. She was standing at the bulletin board outside the library, studying the calendar of Upcoming Events & Activities—the whole last week of October was marked H-A-LL-O-W-EEEE!-N—her shoulders drooping more than she usually allowed them to droop, and her mouth open a little, as if she were too tired to keep it shut. She seemed

dazed, in fact, as she turned his way. Dakota was surprised at how ordinary she looked in plain blue scrubs that were a little too big for her,
and yet how endearing. "So," he said, casting about for something that
wouldn't sound too friendly or presumptuous after their argument—if
that's what it was, this morning—but just friendly enough. He settled
on the obvious. "How's your first day going?"

"It's about over," she exclaimed, "and I never even got any lunch!"

This morning was a long time ago for Erika, he realized. She hadn't
been brooding all day, the way he had, spending half the time going
over what he should and shouldn't have said to Erika about her being
a CNA, and the other half wondering if he should try to get in touch
with Tori Mahoney, who had seemed pretty worried yesterday about the
way the police investigation kept going on and on. Erika had been too
busy standing up to the sensory and psychological assault of her first
day at Pondside to do any brooding.

"You didn't eat?" he said, as if that were unheard of. "Did you bring
something?"

They stopped at the lockers for jackets and then in the staff room
to get her yogurt and his ham sandwich out of the refrigerator. Now,
Erika seemed to be brimming with things to say. She didn't wait until
they found a bench in the courtyard before she started with the most
remarkable thing she had witnessed: a tirade delivered by an old lady
in the atrium.

"You should have heard her, Dakota! 'It's a *death sentence*,' she kept
saying."

"Who was it, do you know?"

"I don't know her name. It was the lady with the stuffed animals.
She's got pretty severe osteoporosis—her spine is like an *S*."

"Edith? Edith Cole?"

"Is that her name?"

"It must have been somebody else. Edith doesn't talk to people."

Erika raised her expressive eyebrows. "Can you think of any other
S-shaped ladies who have a bicycle basket full of stuffed animals attached to their walkers?"

"No," he admitted.

"Then it must have been her," Erika said.

"Did anyone else witness this—speech?"

Erika's eyebrows lowered. "Are you saying I don't know what I saw and heard?"

"No! No," he said. (Maybe she hadn't forgotten about this morning.) "I just thought—"

"Well," she said, "Dan was there. I was taking him from the dining room to the atrium so he could look out the windows. He heard her."

"Dan the trembling man?"

"His name is Howard, actually. Dan Howard. We can ask *him* who it was. And there was a lady in the dining room, too. She must have heard it all. Plus, there was the woman that—what's her name? Edith?—was yelling at. Some poor woman just sitting on the couch. *She* witnessed the whole thing."

"It's not that I don't believe you," Dakota said.

"Oh no, of course not. It's just that it must have been somebody else."

"I shouldn't have said it like that. I'm sorry, but—Edith Cole!" Dakota shook his head. He tried to picture it. "I have never heard her say a *word*, except for mumbling to her critters." He watched Erika stir her yogurt, find a blueberry, spoon it into her mouth, all without meeting his eye. He said, "Then again, it's like that with me and Mary McIntyre."

Erika licked her plastic spoon clean. "The one that pulled the shower out of the wall?"

"Yep. Everybody else calls her Wild Mary, but when I talk to her, she's always perfectly nice. I mean, not just rational, but polite!" He shrugged. "Nobody believes me either, half the time."

"Well," Erika said, "she's probably got a crush on you. It's your boyish charm."

Dakota was surprised at the effect these words, accompanied by Erika's mere hint of a smile, had on him. His face heated up, too. Feeling a little pathetic, he took a bite of his sandwich.

"Actually," Erika said, "Mary likes me, too. I helped her take a shower this morning, no problem, and the nurse—Amelia?—was, like, stunned. That's how I found out about the showerhead." She stuck her spoon into her yogurt, stirred it up again, then finished it quickly and set it aside. "Are people really starving here, Dakota? Like, they'd rather starve than eat pureed food?"

"I don't know. I don't think so. When people get close to the end, they don't eat much, even if they aren't on pureed. They'll say they're hungry, so you get something for them, and then they only take two bites and they're done."

"Maybe their stomachs shrink," Erika said. "Like anorexics."

"I don't know," Dakota said. "The pureed stuff looks bad, some of it, and maybe people with dementia can't understand why they should eat it, but if you were really starving, wouldn't you eat whatever was there? Wouldn't you eat *anything*?"

"Not necessarily. Remember Kirsten Simmons? Dance major? Went out with that guy Jared Something? After they put her in the hospital, they came to the house and gave us all these talks about eating disorders. It was kind of a drag since everybody was on some kind of diet, but they said anorexia was different because it's mostly about feeling helpless and needing control of *something*, and it turns out the one thing you can absolutely control is what you eat, or don't eat. Maybe that's what these people here are doing—staking out the one thing they can control. Maybe they're all on kind of a hunger strike!"

"But if you don't *eat* . . ." Dakota said. "I mean, that girl, Kirsten, died. Didn't she?"

"She did. People would go visit her—we'd drive all the way to Illinois when she was in rehab—and she would try to get us to help her escape. She pulled her feeding tube out, I don't know how many times."

"She sounds like Mary McIntyre," Dakota said.

"Our housemother kept saying, 'You can lead a horse to water, but *blah, blah*.'"

"Or Robert Kallman," Dakota said. "A lot of people think he rolled himself off the pier when they put him on a pureed diet because he knew what that meant. It was all downhill from there. Plus, he loved to eat."

"But anorexics aren't *trying* to kill themselves. Right up to the end, Kirsten thought she was going to make it as a dancer." Erika shook her head. "She was like sticks tied together." She looked at Dakota, and he saw no lingering signs of annoyance with him on her face. Nothing but *E* for *empathy*. "They just want to have control over something in their lives. Maybe that's what the lady with the stuffed animals was saying about people here."

"Edith Cole, you mean?"

"Yeah." Erika smiled a faint smile, which Dakota felt himself returning. "Her."

From a window in her office, where she'd stopped to collect herself on her way to the conference room to meet Lieutenant Steinhafel, Kitty Landiss had been surprised to see Foster Kresowik walk across the employee parking lot to Amelia Ramirez's car. He was empty-handed—she noted—no bag or backpack in which to stow the *Pondside* laptop. Kitty had cringed, waiting for Amelia's outlandish car alarm, but there was no incredibly loud burst of "I am being tampered with." Foster pulled keys from his pocket. She watched him open the door and get in. A moment later, the car jumped backward out of the parking space and stopped dead. It looked as if he didn't know how to drive a car.

Kitty would have liked to watch Foster's halting progress across the parking lot, but the police were waiting for her in the conference room. She straightened her shoulders and tugged at her skirt to smooth out the wrinkles across her lap.

She was finding it difficult to look Lieutenant Steinhafel from Homicide in the eye—not out of fear or any attempt at deception on her part, but because he had the bluest eyes she had ever seen on anyone other than the young priest who used to teach religion classes at St. Mary's Academy, her long-defunct all-girls high school alma mater. Father What-a-Waste, the girls used to call him—referring to the sad fact that his genes stopped here, prevented by a vow of celibacy from ever doing anybody any good. Kitty Landiss did wonder briefly—with eyes *that* blue, you had to wonder—if Lieutenant Steinhafel was wearing tinted contacts. She thought it would be quite disappointing to learn that he was. He didn't seem like the kind of man who would go out of his way to make his eyes a few shades bluer. No, Kitty suspected that Lieutenant Steinhafel had no idea how blue his eyes were unless someone—his wife?—had told him. If he was married. He didn't wear a ring, but, as Kitty knew all too well, that didn't *necessarily* mean anything.

"Ms. Landiss?"

"What? Oh, I'm sorry, Lieutenant. Could you repeat the question?"

"I asked at what point you were aware of Ms. Mahoney's prior relationship with Mr. Kallman."

"If you're asking did I know when Tori applied for a job here that she had worked as Robert Kallman's private nurse when he was still living with his mother, the answer is yes, I did know. Robert's mother was one of her references."

"And that's when you learned of the prior relationship? At the time of Ms. Mahoney's application?"

Kitty wished he wouldn't put it that way. "Relationship" suggested something—it made her picture Tori Mahoney *doing* things with poor Robert Kallman.

"Yes," she said. "It was right on Tori's application form, under previous work experience. Private nurse. Home health care."

"And what is your understanding as to why Mr. Kallman moved from his home to Pondside Manor?"

"His condition had deteriorated. He'd become a two-person assist."

"A two-person assist," Lieutenant Steinhafel repeated, giving his junior officer—a chubby fellow who looked at least a decade older than Steinhafel, Kitty thought—time to write it down.

"That means two people are needed to transfer the person safely from his wheelchair to the bed and so forth," Kitty explained. "It's an official classification. Staff members know that if a resident is a two-person assist, then one person should *never* attempt to transfer the patient without help."

"And yet you didn't mention Ms. Mahoney's prior relationship with Robert Kallman in either of your previous interviews."

Lieutenant Steinhafel's eyes had taken on a steely glint, more hard than blue. That used to happen with Father What-a-Waste, too, when he caught somebody passing notes about him in religion class.

"No one asked me about any 'prior relationship,'" she said. "I mean, I never even thought of it." That was the truth. Kitty would not have hesitated to make Tori Mahoney sweat a bit. "Didn't Tori mention it when she was questioned?"

"I'm not at liberty to reveal what Ms. Mahoney did or didn't say."

"Of course you aren't. Sorry," Kitty said. "But can I ask—are you at liberty to say—why the homicide department is involved in this case? Robert Kallman had every reason to want to end his life. His disease had progressed to the point where he didn't have much to look forward to. I mean, do you know anyone who—are you familiar with ALS?"

"My brother-in-law," Lieutenant Steinhafel said.

"Your wife's brother?"

"My sister's husband."

"Oh. I'm so sorry."

"Personally," Lieutenant Steinhafel said, "I understand completely how Mr. Kallman's situation might have made him want to end his life. But the scene re-creations complicate that story."

"Rolling the wheelchair into the pond, you mean, making sure it—went under."

"Yes, ma'am."

"Because," she said hesitantly, "if he intended to end his life but he needed help—"

"Then we could be talking about a homicide."

"In this state."

"Under the circumstances, in any state."

"Okay. Of course. But this stuff about Tori Mahoney—I hope you're not saying that she is a *suspect?* I know, you're not at liberty to say. But I have to tell you. She didn't do it. There is no way. And I don't even like Tori Mahoney."

Lieutenant Steinhafel looked at her. His eyes were blue again.

"Ms. Landiss," he said.

"One of the reasons I don't like her is exactly the reason I know that she did not do this thing. You see—and I don't know why I'm telling you this—what bothers me most about Tori Mahoney, well, maybe what bothers me second most, is that I know she's a good person. I know that pretty much everything she does around here, she does it to relieve somebody's suffering, to make somebody's dreadful, dismal day a little less dreadful."

"Ms. Landiss?"

A sudden impulse to confess had taken hold of Kitty. Back in the days when she was a chunky innocent in Father What-a-Waste's religion class, it would not have occurred to Kitty to resent someone like Tori Mahoney—worse, to wish her harm—just because she was smarter or kinder or better looking. Back then, when Kitty believed that she herself was good enough just the way she was, when she believed that happiness was everyone's birthright and that she would get her share, back then, she would have admired a person like Tori Mahoney, simply admired her, instead of resenting her.

"You shouldn't be fooled by her tough-as-nails exterior, Lieutenant. I know Tori's not your typical ray of sunshine," Kitty said, "but you should, what do you call it, *shadow* her for a day and see the way she talks to these people. Some of them, their own children don't show them as much love and respect in a year as Tori Mahoney packs into the three or four minutes that she can spend on each resident per shift. She's like Florence Nightingale. And what do I do about it? I resent her for it. That's God's truth, Lieutenant Steinhafel. I resent how unselfish she is, and how unselfconscious, and how good—" Kitty stopped herself in time. "And I know what kind of person that makes me, to resent someone for being good, and yet"—she raised her hand to stop him from interrupting her—"I am telling you, that she would not, could not—"

"Ma'am?"

"*What?*"

"We haven't identified any suspects. We only want to talk with Ms. Mahoney."

"Well, you *can't*," Kitty cried, "because she's not here, and I wish you'd stop calling me *ma'am*!"

"Are you saying that Ms. Mahoney took the day off?"

"Yes," Kitty said, calming herself with an effort. "She did."

Lieutenant Steinhafel made a mark on his index card. "We'd also like to talk to Foster Kresowik."

*Of course, you do*, Kitty thought. "He's not here either," she said.

The lieutenant's blue eyes were steady, unblinking. "Another day off?"

"No. He worked today. Until three thirty. Or so."

The lieutenant consulted his watch. (*How quaint of him*, Kitty thought.)

"Do you think we can catch him?" the lieutenant said.

*Maybe with lights and sirens*, she thought. "He already left," she said.

"You're not obstructing this investigation, are you, Ms. Landiss?"

"Of course not."

"In that case, you are probably willing to come down to the station to sign a statement."

"Are you arresting me?"

"Far from it," Lieutenant Steinhafel said. "Ma'am."

Dakota had left the SeniorMobile parked out front for so long that he had to let the diesel engine warm up for a few minutes before he could drive it around to its spot behind the building. Back inside, after he had watched Erika drive away in her friend's Hyundai, the day turned into one of those late afternoons that are so busy you really can't think about anything outside of the unsavory task of the moment, which happened to be loading the plastic sack of soiled bedding he had recently collected into a laundry cart parked at the intersection of Hawkeye Lane and Iowa Avenue. He was already deeply regretting his decision to collect a little "overtime"— not that Pondside actually paid time and a half for anything—by working through the dinner hour. The temp who came in for Tori Mahoney had left at three o'clock in what looked like a huff, without doing any of the shift-changing tasks that Tori normally did, and Dakota now had the feeling he would not be getting out of here until long after the dinner hour. He closed the lid on the laundry cart and let out the breath he'd been holding.

"Is that man gone?" an anxious voice asked.

Dakota looked up. Mary McIntyre had come around the corner. She was gripping the safety rail with both hands so she could lean back, away from the wall, the better to peer down Hawkeye Lane behind her. From here you could see all the way to where the wheelchairs were lined up near the main entrance. "I didn't care for that man," she added. "You all ought to be more careful who you let in here."

Aside from visitors, the only strangers Dakota had seen inside the building lately were the wheelchair guy picking up a rental and the police. "Do you mean the police?" he asked her.

"I didn't care for that policeman either," Mary said. She quit craning her neck to see down the hall and turned back to Dakota, scowling for all she was worth. "If you think I'm going to get in that ambulance and ride with the siren and all, you've got another think coming."

*Let's not change the subject*, Dakota thought. "I guess I haven't seen that man," he said experimentally as he pushed the laundry cart away. "Where did you see him? Was he asking about Robert?"

"She doesn't know anything about Robert." Duane Lotspeich made this announcement from the doorway to his room, where he and his wheelchair had just appeared.

"Maybe not," Dakota began, "but—"

"No *but* about it, Idaho. This woman has advanced dementia. She can't remember where she is, much less anything about Robert."

"Robert's dead," Mary pointed out.

Both men turned to look at her. Dakota held back the moderately triumphant glance he could have shot at Duane Lotspeich, who was doing his best to look more annoyed than surprised.

"She's just repeating what she heard," Duane said.

Mary let go of the safety rail. Her arms hung at her sides. "Robert's dead," she said again, uttering the words with resignation, like a truth she had finally accepted.

"I know," Dakota said to Mary. "It's very sad, what happened to Robert."

Mary seemed not to have heard him.

"I miss Robert," he tried again. "Do you?"

"It almost killed his mama, when he died," Mary said sadly. "I know I said the wrong thing. It's been a long time. But she never forgets."

"Or else she's remembering something from her own past," Duane Lotspeich put in. He, of course, did not hesitate to shoot a triumphant glance at Dakota. "Something from a *long* time ago."

Mary McIntyre appeared to be finished with both of them. They watched her move stealthily down the hall, one hand sliding lightly along the safety rail although she didn't seem to need it much, until she reached the dark rectangle that was the doorway to her room and disappeared. Dakota took the cart by the handles and made a U-turn toward the laundry. He was trundling away with it when Duane Lotspeich said something else.

"I've been talking to your girl."

The cart nearly got away from Dakota. "I beg your pardon?" he said.

"We had a little chat at lunch. A charming girl. Appears to be a bit distressed where you're concerned."

Dakota looked at Duane Lotspeich. He was a scrappy-looking guy, long and lean, with just enough hair to say he wasn't bald. His long, drawn, pale, and craggy face was probably handsome once. Always reeked of Old Spice.

"She says you want to be a teacher all of a sudden, instead of a doctor. What's wrong with being a doctor?"

"Erika told you that?"

"Doctor makes a lot of money—hell of a lot more than a teacher, for God's sake." Duane Lotspeich rolled himself a foot or two closer to Dakota and leaned forward in his chair. "I suppose you're one of those touchy-feely community-minded losers who don't care about money."

Dakota was busy processing the apparent fact that Erika had been talking to this old man about him, about *them*.

"She says you always wanted to be a doctor. If you change your mind about something like that, how does she know you won't change your mind about other things—about her, for example?"

"No," Dakota managed to say then. "That's not—I mean, I'm—"

"I'll tell you what you are," the old man said. "You're a fool." He used a pair of well-developed arms to turn the wheelchair sharply, and as he rolled away, he announced, loud enough for anyone in Hawkeye Lane to hear, "I'd work in a salt mine if it meant I could come home to someone like *her*."

# CHAPTER 22

It occurred to Laverne Slatchek, as she handed Amelia Ramirez's car keys to the parking valet, that she had not set foot in a hospital since she had that stroke. Come to think of it, she probably hadn't *set foot* in the hospital that time either, the way they rolled you in and out and everywhere in a wheelchair, whether you needed it or not. It seemed entirely possible that the last time she had *visited* anyone in the hospital, it had been Bill. She used to go every day after school to spend the evening with him when he was recovering from his first and, as it turned out, his only surgery. He would have his dinner on a tray, and she would bring a sandwich from Subway. She had to stop and get a coffee in the hospital cafeteria on the way to his room because they didn't sell coffee at Subway. It was nice, they both agreed, to be *recovering*—getting a little stronger every day, needing less and less pain medication, eating more, taking longer and longer walks around the hospital—even though the news had not been good, the cancer had spread, they couldn't "get it all," not without taking all of Bill's liver and then some. The news, after all, was abstract—at least for now—the cancer invisible, while recovering from surgery was a matter of daily progress they could see, progress no amount of bad news could take away. An IV port removed. A breakfast heartily consumed. A ball game watched from first pitch to final out.

Laverne didn't realize that she was nervous about visiting Mrs. Kallman until she was actually in the hospital elevator with Foster.

At first, they couldn't find Mrs. Kallman. They had quite a scare when the ICU room number they were given at Patient Information was for an empty cubicle, the narrow bed stripped to its plastic-covered mattress, all monitors quiet and dark. While they were still on their way to the hospital—with Foster serving as Laverne's right field of vision and Laverne at the wheel, wishing Bill could see her now—Mrs. Kallman had been moved out of the ICU into the Progressive Care Unit. The PCU was a step in the right direction, they were told. They took the elevator to third and followed the colored tape on the floor to a setup that looked like the ICU—the nurses' station was a central island surrounded by little rooms—but with more of a party atmosphere. Young people in colorful scrubs were putting their heads together over monitor screens. The laughter bubbling up quietly here and there made Laverne wonder just what they were watching. When she and Foster reached the counter, a young man whose name tag identified him as Tyler (unreadable last name), RN, asked who they wanted to see. Laverne told him, and just to be on the safe side when it came to visitor policies in the PCU, she added, "I'm her sister. And this is her grandson."

To his credit, Foster didn't blink an eye at this news.

Neither did Tyler the RN. He consulted a clipboard and said to Laverne, "Susan would like to see *you* first, she said."

"Who?" Laverne said.

"Your *sister*," said Tyler. "Susan Kallman." He turned to Foster. "There's a lounge at the end of the hall. I think one of your cousins is having a coffee down there right now."

Mrs. Kallman's room was in the corner of the PCU. There was a window in the middle of the door so that passing staff could peek in on a person. Laverne had found the lack of privacy distressing when Bill was in the hospital—nurses asking about his last bowel movement and telling him to pee "in the hat" instead of the toilet so they could keep track of his output, the hospital gown swinging open when they got him out of bed, and so forth—but the one time she mentioned it, Bill had said privacy was the least of his worries. Of course, Laverne had been a hospital patient herself when Joseph was born and again, less happily, in the years since, so she knew what Bill meant. Personal questions and the touch of strangers might be problems for the loved ones, but the patient had bigger fish to fry.

When the nurse's aide leading her to Mrs. Kallman's room pushed the door open and announced, "Your sister's here," Laverne had no choice but to square her shoulders and go in.

She recognized the IV trees and the EKG-type heart monitor, but the rest of the equipment on various rolling carts and stands and hanging from the ceiling around the head of Mrs. Kallman's bed was strange to her. (Medical science had made some advances, apparently, in the years since it failed to save Bill.) Strangest of all was Mrs. Kallman herself, in an off-the-bony-shoulder hospital gown with her white hair sticking out over her ear on one side and flatter than a pancake on the other. She was almost as pale as the sheets and, despite the plastic tube blowing oxygen into her nose, she was breathing as if she had just carried two bags of groceries up the stairs. She waved Laverne into the vinyl armchair next to the bed. Laverne sat down and, as Bill would have said, Mrs. Kallman cut straight to the chase.

"Laverne," she breathed, "I'm going to ask you a favor."

"Okay," said Laverne, momentarily distracted by the silvery laptop computer she'd just noticed on the rolling tray table at the foot of Mrs. Kallman's hospital bed. It was mostly hidden by tissue boxes.

"A big favor."

Laverne returned her attention to Mrs. Kallman. "Okay," she said again.

"But first, I want you to know why."

"Okay."

"It's kind of a long story," Mrs. Kallman warned.

"Listen, Mrs. Kallman," Laverne said. "You don't seem like you are in any condition to tell me a long story. You don't have to tell me a story. I'll do you whatever favor you want me to do. No story is required."

Mrs. Kallman appeared to think about that for a moment. She took a deeper breath and held it—which caused one of the machines to beep—then let it out and took another, like a swimmer about to go under, Laverne thought. When she did this a third time, the pause between her inhalations reminded Laverne, suddenly and against her will, of Bill's last breaths. The way they'd come farther and farther apart. (Why, oh why did she remember things like this as if they'd happened yesterday or maybe just this morning?) With his Do-Not-Resuscitate card sticking out of his shirt pocket at all times, they couldn't really do anything for him in the ambulance anyway, apart from slapping on an oxygen mask. That was another reason not to call 911, Bill kept telling her, but that was easy for him to say. He wasn't the one being left behind, all alone at a time like this, their son sitting in an airport somewhere. In the ambulance, Laverne had taken to holding her own breath, waiting for Bill's next one. *How could it be that a person's lungs forgot how to breathe?* she remembered thinking. *How did a heart know it was time to stop?* She had understood for the first time that this was it, *this was it*, and in the end, she had held her breath until she couldn't hold it any longer, knowing that when she took another, it would be her first breath in the world without Bill.

In the vinyl chair next to Mrs. Kallman's hospital bed, awash in a sea of chiming, hissing, and quietly beeping machines, Laverne suddenly felt untethered, like a balloon, light and floating. She recognized this feeling. She'd felt it sitting beside Bill in the ambulance, and she had felt it again as she walked into the funeral chapel with her son, and again the first time she took herself to Dairy Queen and ordered a Pecan Mudslide and ate the whole damn thing herself. She had felt it as she watched Joseph and his wife walk across the Pondside Manor parking lot to their car on the day she told them she was not going to live in their remodeled garage.

"Laverne?" Mrs. Kallman said. "Are you all right?"

"Yes!" Laverne said, rousing herself. "Of course, I'm all right." Who, after all, was the patient here? "You were going to ask me something," she said. "What were you going to ask me?"

Mrs. Kallman didn't answer right away, although Laverne thought she seemed to be breathing easier now. Those long, deep breaths had put a tinge of color in her skin. She gave Laverne what felt like an appraising look, her head tilted and her brow furrowed and her oxygen hissing—a look that went on for so long that Laverne began to wonder if she needed to remind Mrs. Kallman that she, Laverne Slatchek, had come here at Mrs. Kallman's specific request for an unknown reason that Laverne was hoping had something to do with *The World of Pondside*, a hope that had begun to fade, despite the laptop on the tray table, the longer Mrs. Kallman looked at her. When Mrs. Kallman finally spoke, Laverne was pretty sure that she must have misheard what she said. It sounded like: "Have you ever been to China?"

The lounge at the end of the hall was really nothing more than three armchairs and a watercooler on a strip of carpet next to some windows. Foster almost didn't recognize Tori Mahoney in jeans and a sweater, her hair unleashed from her fountain of a ponytail. She was sitting in one of the armchairs, reading a magazine—*Sports Illustrated*, it looked like—one foot bouncing on the other knee. He stood at the edge of the carpet and watched her for two seconds? five? ten? Finally, she looked up. When she saw him, she leaped to her feet—she really did—and let the magazine fall to the carpet. "You're here!" she said. Which was funny, Foster thought, because he had been thinking those same two words about her, only with more of a question mark at the end. Next, she asked, "Where's Laverne?"

Grateful for an easy question to answer, Foster said, "She's in with Mrs. Kallman." He hesitated before he asked, "What are you doing here?"

"The same thing *you're* doing here," she said.

"Really?" he said. "You got a call from Mrs. Kallman telling you to get down here pronto and bring Laverne?"

This came out snippier than he intended, but the ride to the hospital in Amelia's car—telling Laverne Slatchek when to stop and when the coast was clear—had pretty much exhausted Foster's limited supply of interpersonal resources. He didn't realize how used up he was until just this moment.

"Not exactly," Tori said. "In fact, I was here when she called you."

"So, what *are* you doing here?"

"Well," she said, "that's kind of a long story. It's—"

"Don't tell me—it's *complicated*. Right?"

Tori answered warily. "It *is* complicated, Foster—more than you know."

A strong feeling gripped Foster in the chest and stomach. It took him a moment to recognize the feeling as anger, plain and simple and directed at Tori Mahoney. "Oh, I don't know about that," was all he could come up with to say.

"You talked to Dakota."

"Sure did." The moment when Dakota shoved him against those lockers flashed in Foster's mind, the pressure of the guy's arm across his chest. "What *he* said, I already knew."

This was not exactly true, of course, but Foster felt no need to tell Tori Mahoney exactly what he did and didn't know, and when he came to know it. After all, the Mahoney "connection"—or at least the coincidence of the guy's name being the same as hers—had occurred to him before. The part about Mahoney living long enough for Robert to go and see him in the hospital—that had been a surprise, but the real shock was what Duane Lotspeich told him about Tori. It still didn't seem possible: She had been Robert's nurse? Before he even came to Pondside? Against his will, Foster's brain kept lining this fact up, if fact it was, with the nasty scene Dinglebutt told him about, the one at the VA hospital where, supposedly, Tori told Robert that she was glad he had ALS, that it was a judgment on him, that now she wouldn't have to—well, that was as far as Foster would let the scene run.

Tori sat down again on the arm of the easy chair in front of the window. Late afternoon sunlight bouncing off the watercooler moved like little waves across her face and her sweater, as if she were sitting on the porch of a cottage on a lake, or maybe in a rowboat. Or on a wooden pier. She said, "You know at the end of that old *Indiana Jones* movie—I'm sure you've seen it—where the guy looks into the Ark and his face starts melting off? Can you picture that?" She didn't wait for

Foster to answer. "Scott looked like *that*—only not so symmetrical. Almost half the bone structure of his face was gone, too. He could still swallow, you could see his tongue move, although he couldn't swallow *something*, because he didn't really have a mouth to hold it in. And he had the eye they had saved for him, so he could see my stupid weepy face, and he could catch a glimpse of himself, every now and again, in the bed rail, or a pitcher, or the window. You can imagine how nice that was for him."

She had been facing the windows, which overlooked the emergency entrance and parking lot, but now she turned and looked Foster straight in the eye. It was the first time he had ever experienced unwavering eye contact with Tori Mahoney. It just about burned a hole right through him.

As if she knew exactly what kind of thoughts had been roiling in Foster's head, she said, "I'll tell you something, Foster. At first, I really did want to hurt somebody. I wanted to hurt somebody the way Scott was hurt, which wasn't possible anyway because even if there was, say, a fire or an explosion, and somebody else's face got blown off, it wouldn't be the face *my* little boys were waiting to see, the one they were holding in their heads while their father was away, the face that went with the voice of their daddy the last time he talked to them." Here, finally, she released Foster by looking away again, out the window. "I knew it wasn't going to help my boys—getting revenge, I mean—but that didn't keep me from imagining it, from fantasizing, down to the last detail."

Only now did Foster realize how much he had wanted to hear her scoff at the very idea. *Revenge?* he had wanted her to say. *Are you kidding? Revenge?* Could it be true—this terrible thing that had occurred to him—that she had taken the job of being Robert's private nurse just so she could watch him suffer? Foster couldn't ask her such a thing. He didn't have the words for it. He didn't even know how to tell her that he *knew*, that Duane Lotspeich told him she used to be Robert's nurse. It would be easier to ask her if she had pushed Robert into the pond, Foster thought, than to ask her if she had followed him to Pondside so she wouldn't miss out on what she knew ALS would do to him.

"But Scott was a different story," Tori was saying. "Scott wasn't thinking about revenge. He was thinking about *us*. About me and the boys—and the baby. It's funny how things turn out. When I found out I was pregnant, right after Scott redeployed, I couldn't help wishing that we had been more careful, but, I'll tell you, that baby saved us. Scott was still at the VA when Henry was born. Mrs. Kallman said if I took Henry over there so Scott could hold him and feed him, they would bond no matter what Scott looked like. The baby wouldn't care. And she was right. They did. Scott only had the one good arm at the time, but we fixed up a way for him to hold the baby and the bottle."

The sun had dropped behind the buildings across the street from the emergency entrance. In the lounge, the watercooler no longer sent its trembling reflections like waves around the room. Foster didn't remember sitting down on the ottoman in front of the armchair, but here he was. He noticed that his fingers were doing the little dance they did sometimes when he went too long without a cigarette. He slid his hands under his thighs. There was a long silence—at least, it felt long to Foster.

"Scott couldn't come home when he got out of the VA," Tori said finally. "He looked like a horror movie. The boys were six and four. They would have been terrified. We hated the idea of a nursing home— excuse me, a long-term care and rehabilitation facility—so Robert said, bring him here."

"Bring him where?" Foster said.

Tori looked at him.

"You mean Robert's house? He stayed at Robert's house?"

"They had plenty of room," she said, and Foster could tell that his sounding so surprised had surprised her. "Have you ever been there?"

"Yes," Foster said. He had ridden past it many times. She didn't have to know that he'd never been inside.

"I was opposed to the idea at first—I guess I was still angry at Robert—but Scott was all for it. They have this apartment on the third floor. I don't know if you've seen it." She waited a second or two before she went on. "It's very nice. There's even a tiny elevator. The lift, they call it. They sweetened the deal by offering me the job, which I needed desperately, and which I took, even though Robert didn't need a nurse at the time, not yet. I'd go to 'work' every day—take the baby with me—and after school, I had the bus drop the boys off there so Scott could see them. There was a curved window that looked out over the backyard. We'd crank up the bed and put it by the window with the blinds angled just the right way so he could see the whole backyard, but if the boys looked up, all they saw was sunlight reflecting off the glass."

The sunset flaring in the windows behind Tori Mahoney had cast her face into shadow at that very moment, which made it possible for Foster to ask her, "Did they know he was up there?"

Another silence. Tori stood up. Two steps took her to the window, where her profile cut a sharp silhouette against the remaining light. "We told the boys he was missing in action," she said finally. "I don't know if that was a good idea or not, but that's what Scott wanted them to think. He said that it was true, in a way. He *was* missing. He said all we had left was a monster in the attic." Then, as if it had just occurred to her that Foster would be interested in this, she turned to look at him and added, "That's when he started working on the game."

*The game*, Foster thought. He said, "What game?"

"The one you all play."

"*World of Pondside?*"

"They didn't call it that. They both worked on it. I think it was based on something Robert designed when he worked for DARPA—what is it? Defense Advanced Research something?" She glanced at Foster. "You know he worked for DARPA."

"Yes," Foster lied, surprised at how easy it was.

"Maybe it wasn't the same game, I don't know. Scott had a lot of time on his hands. He made a—what do you call it, a portal?—for the boys, some quest they went on, and oh, Foster, they loved it. It was like they had their dad back to play with them. Which they did, but they didn't know it." Her voice, which had gotten wobbly, petered out.

"What about you?" Foster said after a moment. "Did you play the game?"

"I couldn't even look at it," Tori said. "I know it was a mistake, not telling them the whole truth, letting them think he was missing. I think I knew it even then. We did it to buy time. The team at the VA had closed up Scott's throat and they said they could take a little out of each hip and build a jaw for him. Scott started talking about a face transplant."

She exhaled, a long and audible breath that made Foster picture her on the bench at Pondside, blowing out a cloud of smoke. To his surprise, he found himself thinking that she might be making this up as she went along. But why would she do that?

"A face transplant," he said.

"It became Scott's favorite search term on the internet. This was in 2006. No one had done it in the US yet, but there was this woman in France he read about and a man in China. They had before and after pictures. Scott pored over them, especially pictures of the man in China, who'd been mauled by a bear. His new face didn't look like a million bucks, but he didn't look like a monster either. And they both were still alive a year or more after the surgery—taking boatloads of immuno-suppressants, which you have to do for the rest of your life—but still alive. Scott wanted to sign right up. Either it would work or it wouldn't, he said. He wanted to come out of hiding and rejoin the human race. France? China? He didn't care where he had to go. He was ready to go to Timbuktu, if necessary."

An ambulance pulled into the emergency entrance below the window, silent but flashing its blue and red lights, animating Tori's face the weird way flashing lights do, so that she seemed to smile and wink and scowl. Foster figured he must look the same to her. He said, "Did he go?"

Tori looked at him sharply. "Go where?"

"To Timbuktu."

She took a deep breath, the kind that usually keeps people from saying something they'll wish they hadn't. "No, Foster, he didn't go to Timbuktu." She took another breath. "He went to China with Robert. In 2007." The ambulance lights stopped flashing and her face was still. "Only Robert came back."

Why would she lie about something like this? Foster couldn't think of a reason.

"The Kallmans paid for everything," she said. "They took out mortgages and sold stocks. If Scott had waited a few years, the Department of Defense would have paid for it and he wouldn't have had to go to China, but we didn't know that in 2007." She shrugged. "Even if we had known, how can you ask a person to wait a few more years?"

He also couldn't think of anything to say.

"I'm sure you can imagine how many things can go wrong with a procedure like that," she said. "Rejection, infection, just surviving the surgery itself. Plus all the waiting for a donor, the right tissue type. Scott figured it was a long shot. Before they left, he made Robert his medical power of attorney because he knew Robert would be able to pull the plug. That's how Scott put it. 'I need somebody who can pull the plug.'" For a moment, Tori looked far away. "I wasn't even there," she said. Then she seemed to bring herself around. She looked at Foster. "You can see why I promised to help Robert, can't you? When the time came?"

"You promised to help," Foster said. They were back to Robert now. She was talking about helping *Robert*. He wanted to be sure he understood.

"I had to, Foster. If it hadn't been for him—both of them, really. Robert and his mother, I mean. I can't even tell you all the ways they saved us."

"But you're not—you weren't—Robert's medical power of attorney," Foster said. "Are you?"

"No."

"So that's not what you mean when you say you promised to help him."

"No."

Foster tried hard not to picture it: Tori Mahoney in her teddy bear scrubs, with her ponytail bouncing, walking down to the pond in the dark with Robert.

"I promised to do anything Robert asked me to do," she said.

Then, when the path runs out, she falls behind and takes the handles of the wheelchair—even those fancy ones have handles, just in case— and she tips first the front wheels and then the back ones, up, gently, over the bump, onto the pier. And then what? Does she wait while he powers himself over the edge? To make sure, oh God, that his head goes under? Foster closed his eyes. As if he could shut out a scene like that.

"But here's the thing, Foster. He never asked me."

Foster opened his eyes. "Are you saying you *didn't* help him?"

"I never set foot on that pier."

Foster drew a long, ragged breath. He felt as if he had just come up from underwater himself. He said, "I *knew* it wasn't suicide. Something happened. Somebody must have—"

"Oh, Foster," Tori said. "Of course it was."

"Then why didn't he ask you to help? You promised him, you said."

"I don't know. Maybe he didn't want to get me in trouble."

"Who else could he ask?"

"I don't know. Maybe he didn't ask anyone."

"Then how did he get onto the pier?"

"All right, somebody helped him," she admitted. "Somebody must have."

"Who?"

"I don't know."

"Somebody he *wanted* to get into trouble?"

Tori stood up and said, "Foster, I don't know."

He sagged on the ottoman. He could picture various people punching the keypad code for Robert—that was easy. Anyone could have done that part. Robert could have figured a way to do it himself, for that matter. But rolling him onto the pier? Into the water? Was there anyone at Pondside capable of doing that? And even if someone *were* capable, who could Robert ask? He wasn't that close to anyone—except, apparently, for Tori Mahoney. And his mother.

And Foster himself. Not that they were *close* exactly. But what if Robert had asked him to do this thing? To roll him onto the pier. That's all it would take. Once you got him over the bump, you could leave him there and go inside and tell yourself he was going to make one of his phone calls. He did that sometimes—for privacy and reception, he said. Foster had taken him down to the pier more than once to make a phone call. He wouldn't need any help coming back because the pier sloped up gently like a little ramp from the pond side. He could have put the chair in reverse and backed up the ramp. It was only from the shore that the bump was too high to power over, even in a state-of-the-art chair like Robert's. So you could take him out there and leave him and never know when—or if.

"Maybe he tricked someone into taking him out on the pier," Foster said to Tori's back.

"Robert wouldn't do that," she said firmly. "Think of what a terrible thing that would be to do to somebody." She turned around, frowning; he could see she was thinking about it. "And they would still be in trouble if anyone found out—it could be gross negligence or conduct regardless of life or something." She shook her head. "He wouldn't do it."

"Maybe he paid somebody to take that chance."

"No."

"Maybe it was an accident."

"*No,*" she said.

Foster stood up. "How can you be so sure? You weren't there, remember?"

Although he'd barely more than whispered this, she raised her eyebrows and pointed her chin as if to say, *Behind you!* He looked over his shoulder, expecting trouble, but it was only Laverne, coming around the corner with her aluminum cane and her large black purse, red coat draped over her free arm and the fedora still jaunty on her head. Foster noticed that Laverne didn't seem the least bit surprised to see Tori Mahoney.

"Next!" Laverne said. She looked at Foster. "Better hurry."

Foster felt his chest tighten. "Why? Is she—?"

"Visiting hours end at five."

# CHAPTER 23

"Come in!" Mrs. Kallman wheezed when Foster poked his head in the door. She didn't look any better in person than she had in the video call. He must have looked alarmed. "I had a little heart attack," she admitted. "I'm feeling much better now. The oxygen helps a lot." She nodded toward the vinyl armchair next to the bed, clearly the one that Laverne had just vacated. He could see the indentation she'd left in the seat. "Sit," Mrs. Kallman said.

Foster sat. The seat was still warm. He hated that. On the tray table pulled halfway across the bed was a laptop that looked like Robert's, but without the yellow duck sticker on the lid.

"His backup," she said.

Foster stared. *His backup.* Of course there was a backup. A backup *Pondside* server. And here it was! Robert's mother had it all along.

"I'm so glad you came, Foster." She said this a bit louder, as if making an effort to sound brisk and normal. "I can't tell you how disappointed I was. After the visitation. When we couldn't find you."

She paused, just to breathe, he thought at first, but then she seemed to be waiting for him to say something. All he could think of was to ask, "Who's *we*?"

"Well, me, for one. And Keith—I don't think you've met Keith. And Tori Mahoney. Have you spoken to her?"

"Yes."

"Tori was quite sure, in the car that night, that Robert had told you everything."

Foster needed a moment to process *in the car that night*. At Walmart, he thought. Mrs. Kallman meant the car he saw her in, through the window, at Walmart. Tori was in that car? She could have been. It was possible. He couldn't see into the back seat from the window. Foster hesitated to ask the big obvious questions, like why were they looking for him, and what did she mean by "told you *everything*." He aimed for the particular and, really, the most pressing thing.

"Did *you*—I mean, one of you—put that doll on my bike?"

"Oh, Foster, the doll was my fault. Tori found it in the Pondside parking lot right before we picked her up. Robert thought that doll would be a comfort to Mary McIntyre, but I don't think she cares very much about it. Tori said she's left it outside more than once."

"But why did you put it on my bike?"

"I thought you would recognize it."

"*Recognize* it?" Foster said. "Why would I recognize it?"

"Because it's in the game, isn't it? Robert put it in the game. He showed it to me. On the porch in your—what do you call it, your—?"

"Portal," Foster said.

"The doll is there, isn't it?" she said. "Sitting on a table?"

"Yes, but I didn't—"

"You *didn't* recognize it, I know," Mrs. Kallman said. "You did just what Tori and Keith said you would do. No, no, I told them. Even after you rode off, I thought when you read the note, you'd call."

"There was a note?" Foster said.

"Of course—just like in the game." When Mrs. Kallman shrugged, her hospital gown moved up and down on her shoulders like clothes on a hanger. "I didn't know baby dolls were so scary. I guess I haven't seen enough horror movies. Perhaps I should have listened to Tori. She wanted to go back to your place and try again."

After saying all that, Mrs. Kallman took what the yoga instructor who taught occasional classes at Pondside Manor would have called a cleansing breath, which gave Foster a chance to consider what she meant by "go *back* to your place." One of the machines next to the bed beeped.

"Wait," he said. "That was Tori Mahoney at the door?"

"I thought you said you talked to her."

"Hold on a minute," Foster said. Mrs. Kallman seemed happy to oblige. She leaned back and let her head rest against the pillows propped up behind her while Foster considered the amazing fact that he had been right about the doll on his bike. It *was* a message. He said, "You thought I had the server all along!"

"Yes," she breathed. "I had just about given up on you, Foster, when you called."

"When *I* called?" Foster said. He looked at Mrs. Kallman. Her color wasn't bad, and she wasn't panting, just breathing a little faster than you would expect somebody in bed to breathe, but she was hooked up to an awful lot of stuff. For the first time, it occurred to him to wonder if Mrs. Kallman's thinking might be affected by reduced oxygen to her brain, or something.

"I couldn't answer," she said, "because the doctor was in here. I had to call you back."

Foster pictured the letters scrolling into *Phone Home* after he clicked on the folded note, and a few minutes later, Mrs. Kallman's face filling the screen. "When I clicked on the note, I called you!" he said.

"At first, Robert had a Chinese figurine standing on the card table, instead of the doll," Mrs. Kallman said. "Smoke came out of its mouth when you tapped it. I guess baby dolls are scarier than Chinese warriors." She shrugged and a monitor beeped. "The moment Robert saw that doll, he *had* to get it into the game. I took photos of it for him before we gave it to Mary."

"But why would Robert want me to call *you*?" Only after Foster said this did he realize how it sounded.

Mrs. Kallman smiled, sort of—or maybe it was just the oxygen cannula pressing on her upper lip. "I think he wanted us to keep in touch."

"I was supposed to give you the laptop."

"Yes."

"You must have thought I was holding out on you."

"I wasn't thinking anything about it, Foster. Not at first. Tori was a little worried, though."

"She knew about the laptop?"

"Of course." Mrs. Kallman took hold of the side rail on the bed and drew herself closer to him. Foster resisted the urged to lean back. Off to the right, something started beeping insistently. Mrs. Kallman said, "I know Robert didn't want to burden you—that's the word he often used—or put you in a difficult position." Another monitor started beeping. Mrs. Kallman ignored it. "I have always respected Robert's privacy, but now I need to know how much he told you, Foster, how much you know."

"How much I know about *what*?" Foster said. This came out louder and more forcefully than he intended, perhaps because of the beeping monitors, which had set his heart to racing. "About what happened to Robert? Because I *don't*—"

Robert's mother put a finger to her lips. She fell back against the pillows. Seconds later, a guy in a white lab coat came striding through the door. He tapped something on the machine, and it stopped beeping. He stepped over to the bed and took Mrs. Kallman's hand, very gallantly, as if he were about to kiss it. Instead, he fiddled with the sensor clamped on her middle finger and squinted at the monitor again. "Enough with the calisthenics!" he told her. Then he winked at Foster and left as quickly as he'd come.

Mrs. Kallman waited until the door closed again before she turned back to Foster. "How much you know about *The World of Pondside*," she said in a whispery voice, "and what it's really for."

Foster sat back. What *The World of Pondside* was really for? Wasn't it for giving selected geezers—not to mention losers like himself—a reason to get up in the morning? He opened his mouth to ask what the hell she was talking about and then closed it again. Mrs. Kallman had closed her eyes and pressed her lips together. Her nostrils flared. Foster was relieved to see the door move inward again, more hesitantly this time, suggesting that help was nearby. Mrs. Kallman sighed loudly.

She opened her eyes and said, "What *now?*" but it turned out to be Laverne and Tori slipping into the room. Foster stood up.

"They had a code down at the other end of the unit," Tori whispered. "We took advantage." She listened for a moment, bedside. "They're remarkably quiet about it."

"Probably don't want to alarm the survivors," said Laverne. "Do you mind?" she asked Foster as she lowered herself into the vinyl chair.

Tori, meanwhile, had taken Mrs. Kallman's hand and laid two fingers on the inside of her frail-looking wrist. "Tori, dear," Mrs. Kallman said, "I'm afraid we've been chasing a wild goose."

Tori glanced at Foster before she said, "What do you mean?"

"I don't think Foster knows what the game is for."

"Of course he does," Tori said. She turned to Foster. "Robert used it to communicate with his contact at the drug company. You knew that, right?"

Foster looked from Tori to Laverne to Mrs. Kallman. Nobody looked surprised. "The drug company," he said, doing his best to sound matter-of-fact.

"In China," Tori said. She was watching him closely. "Robert must have told you about the drug trial he was in over there." Now she sounded impatient. "You know Robert went to China. We just talked about it."

Sure, Foster knew Robert had been to China—he knew it even before Tori told him the face transplant story—and he also knew that Robert had been in several drug trials, none of which went anywhere, at least for Robert. The one in China got shut down temporarily. Robert had stayed there, waiting around for it to start up again, until his visa ran out. That's why he had so many pictures of places in China. ("Couldn't you go back?" Foster had asked him, and Robert had blinked the long blink that meant *no.*) Now Foster wondered if the drug trial was the real reason Robert stayed so long in China. Maybe it had more to do with Mahoney and his face transplant—assuming that Tori had told Foster the truth about that. Just to show them that Robert had told him a thing or two, Foster said, "That trial—the one in China—had some kind of problem. They had to shut it down."

"They hadn't reported their animal studies," Mrs. Kallman said. "There were firings, I suppose. Long delays. Robert had to leave the country before the trial resumed."

Foster was reminded that Robert's mother was a doctor herself.

"Yes," Tori said, "but Robert had a friend in the research department—someone directly involved in the clinical trials." She glanced at the door that she and Laverne had closed behind them. There was no one peeking in the window. Tori continued more quietly. "For years, Robert's friend has been providing him with medications that are not approved for ALS in this country, including the drug in that first study. Those medications may be the reason he survived as long as he did."

In the silence that followed, they all looked at Foster. He tried to arrange his face in neutral, but he was pretty sure they could tell he didn't know what Tori Mahoney was talking about. He'd never heard of anyone sending Robert drugs from China, for God's sake. What was he supposed to say? He thought about reminding them all that Robert was dead and no longer in need of medications that were not approved for ALS in this country.

As if she knew what he was thinking, Tori said, "There are other PALS here who use the medication."

That, at least, was something Foster knew about. Do-it-yourself treatment. Persons with ALS were very organized about it, Robert told him once. They shared information, tried treatments, and reported their results. Robert had shown Foster some websites. There was one where you could get a team of actual researchers to study a do-it-yourself treatment and report on how, and if, it worked. Robert said that particular site—it was *ALS Untangled* or *Unbound* or something—was especially amazing to him: doctors letting patients tell them what to do! He never said anything about smuggling drugs from China, though. Never mentioned "his friend at the drug company."

"So now you're in touch with this person?" Foster said. "At the drug company?"

After an exchange of glances with Robert's mother, Tori said, "Not exactly."

"What does that mean?"

"No one but Robert knows—knew—who the contact is."

Foster looked from one of them to the other. "Well, then—"

"A pickup has been scheduled," Mrs. Kallman said.

"A pickup," Foster repeated. "Of the drug—or drugs—you mean?"

"That's right," she said briskly.

"But you just said you don't know who the contact is. How do you know—"

"We know," Mrs. Kallman told Foster, "because I received my ticket from the travel agency, the same as always. The contact always books my flights. Round trip to Beijing."

Foster looked around. Tori was biting her lip. Laverne was sitting on the edge of the visitor's chair. "You go to *China* to pick up the drugs?"

Mrs. Kallman looked regretful. "Not this time, I'm afraid. Laverne will go in my place." Then she smiled. "I've provided Laverne with the name of the doctor I see at the traditional Chinese medicine hospital in Beijing. His English is quite good. She'll come back with an assortment of teas to address every ailment."

"It's too bad I didn't stick with tai chi," Laverne said. "They do it in all the parks. Mrs. Kallman says anybody can join in."

Neither Laverne nor Mrs. Kallman sounded as if they were kidding. Tori was inspecting the drip on Mrs. Kallman's IV. Okay, Foster thought, he could play along. "Beijing is a big place," he said. "How do you know where to go when you get there?"

"That's where *you* come in!" Laverne said. She sounded as if she'd been holding herself back with an effort. "Where to go is in the game! Can you believe it? In *The World of Pondside*! Mrs. Kallman says there's an Easter egg somewhere *in the game* that reveals the secret location and what the actual physical package looks like and everything. Robert's friend in China puts the information in the game."

"An Easter egg," Foster said.

"Yes! It's hidden in the game."

"There are no Easter eggs in *The World of Pondside*."

"Oh, well, it's not really an *egg*. An Easter egg is just what they call it because you have to hunt for it. It's like a secret passage or a hidden room or an extra adventure, something like that, right?" Laverne looked at Mrs. Kallman. "Something you don't expect. A surprise!"

"I know what an Easter egg is," Foster said. "I'm telling you there aren't any in *The World of Pondside*. It's not that kind of game."

"But there must be!" Laverne said. "Mrs. Kallman said there was. It's in the *Next Level*."

"Yeah, well, I don't know anything about the *Next Level*. I never even heard of it until today."

Tori gave Foster a different sort of look then. He thought it was the kind you might give a person if you were seeing him for the first time and he looked very different from what you expected. After a pause, she said, tentatively, "You mean you didn't help Robert build it—or develop it—whatever you call it?"

"No, I didn't," Foster said.

"You never even *talked* about it?"

"Well, if what you mean by the *Next Level* is expanding the game, adding maps and portals, making it so multiple people could play to-gether, that kind of stuff—sure, those are things we talked about." In his head, Foster heard the rich radio voice inviting them to step up to the *Next Level*. "We talked about a lot of things," he said.

"Are you saying that you don't know how to find the Easter egg?" Laverne asked in her point-blank way.

"I already said I didn't."

"That can't be true," Tori said.

For a moment Foster just looked at her. Then he said, "What?"

"That can't be true. You're supposed to know about the *Next Level*. Robert must have told you."

"I'm telling you he didn't. He didn't tell me anything about it." Foster looked from one of them to the other. He could tell that the same wheels were turning in all of their heads now. They could see what a mistake they'd made, thinking that Foster knew anything. What the hell did they expect? Tori, especially. Foster had seen her and Robert every day practically, for at least two years, and neither one of them had ever mentioned the small fact that she was Tori *that* Mahoney. Robert never said it, she never said it, they never *hinted* at it. Foster had to learn it all from the likes of Dinglebutt and Duane Lotspeich! *Foster* was the one who should be pissed. "Yeah, well," he said, "maybe I wasn't as good a friend of Robert's as all of you thought. But at least *he* didn't go and tell *Dinglebutt* every last thing about—"

"Dinglebutt?" said Laverne.

Mrs. Kallman held her hand up to say, *Stop.* Judging by the tangle of IV and monitor wires trailing from her raised arm and the beeps from multiple machines, Foster thought they might have half a minute at most before the guy who didn't like calisthenics—or some other enforcer of hospital rules—was upon them. Mrs. Kallman lowered her arm, and some of the beeping subsided.

"It seems we've come to a dead end," she said solemnly. She looked at Tori and Laverne, and they looked back at her, all of them careful, Foster thought, to avoid looking at him. Well, two—or four—could play at that game. He aimed his scowl at the laptop on the bed table. "It's nobody's fault," Mrs. Kallman added, in a way that made it painfully clear, at least to Foster, whose fault it was. "We've done everything we could to carry out Robert's wishes"—here she paused—"but without the information only he, apparently, could provide, we simply cannot make this pickup."

Everyone continued not looking at everyone else. Suddenly, Foster thought he knew what they were doing, what they were after, what they—Laverne especially, he thought—wanted from him. *Sure,* he was supposed to say, *we could find the Easter egg—if we went in and played the game.* He didn't have to say it, though. He didn't even know if it was true. He didn't have to give them what they wanted. It was crazy anyway—going to China to pick up drugs? All he had to do to get himself off the hook was just let the silence go on. He started a mental count to ten. He got as far as eight, and then, inexplicably, he found himself saying, "Unless—"

Three faces turned to him like time-lapsed flowers to the sun.

"Unless what?" Tori said.

"Unless maybe we could find your Easter egg—if we went in and played the game."

Laverne lit up. "*The World of Pondside*, you mean?"

"There's no guarantee we'd stumble on the right thing," Foster hastened to add, "but maybe with three or four of us looking?" He shrugged.

"How long would that take?" asked Mrs. Kallman.

"Depends on how hard Robert made it," Foster said. He was thinking, *Who the hell knows?* Robert hadn't told him the truth about Mahoney, or about Tori being his private nurse and her boys playing in the backyard of the big fancy house on Summit Street. He surely wouldn't want to put Foster in touch with his contact in China.

"Looks like there's a party going on in here," somebody else said, and they all turned to the door. It was young Tyler, RN. "I'm sorry to break this up, but Susan has an echocardiogram scheduled for"—he looked at his watch—"right now."

Mrs. Kallman sat up straighter. "Young man, I don't have much time left. Can't I spend it with my friends?"

"And family?" Laverne put in.

Tyler the RN offered a shrug of apology as a technician who looked about sixteen pushed her cart full of electronics into the room, forcing friends and family out into the hall.

They were halfway to the elevator when Foster heard someone say his name. He turned around. Tyler the RN was leaning out the doorway of Mrs. Kallman's room. He was holding up a pink-and-purple paisley thing that Foster recognized (after a moment) as a laptop sleeve. "You forgot your computer," Nurse Tyler said.

# CHAPTER 24

Working the dinner hour at Pondside meant that Dakota Engelhart was too busy to go outside and make a phone call or send a text. This was just as well. The sooner he talked to Erika, the more likely he was to say something he would regret. For the past forty-five minutes, ever since he'd heard that Duane Lotspeich would be willing to work in a salt mine if it meant he could go home to someone like Erika, Dakota had been resisting the urge to call her and demand to know why she was discussing his—or still, possibly, their—future with the likes of Lotspeich!

True, Dakota pretty much thought it was over between them after their lunch the other day, but when they were talking in the courtyard a while ago, everything had felt normal. Better than normal, in fact. He had to admit—although he had not yet admitted to Erika—that he was pretty impressed by the way she had shown up here at Pondside, already certified in two states and apparently capable of taking on some pretty challenging characters. And who would have thought that Erika would trade the use of her brother's Hummer—which she had been so delighted to "inherit"—for a Hyundai, even temporarily, just to avoid making Tori Mahoney feel bad? And that brought him back to what Duane Lotspeich said: Did Erika really think that changing his mind about med school meant that Dakota would change his mind about her?

*Had* he changed his mind about her, about them?

For the next two hours, he wouldn't have time to think about it. The dinner hour was upon them—the sundown hour—the darkest, craziest hour of the day. He had three one-person assists to the bathroom to handle (always important to address before dinner), and the first four non-ambulatory residents listed on the dry-erase board at the nurses' station to retrieve and deliver, one by one, to the dining room. In between assists and retrievals, he cleaned up a hazardous puddle of what looked like chocolate pudding on the floor outside Mary McIntyre's room and helped Mrs. Hickerson decide what to wear at dinner in case her son showed up immediately afterward to take her home. He was on his way to retrieve the last non-ambulatory left on the list—embarrassed that it had taken him a moment to recognize "Jean Piotrowski" as a reference to Screamin' Jeannie—when a bout of giggly laughter stopped him cold in the middle of Library Lane.

It was coming from the library, and it was not an old person's laughter—*that* Dakota knew without a doubt. He thought he recognized the breathless giggle but told himself it couldn't be Erika, who had driven away in the Hyundai over an hour ago. Then, he heard her speak. Though muffled by the door—and why were the doors closed anyway?—and by music that was playing in the background, the words came through surprisingly loud and clear.

"I feel kind of silly with you watching me," Erika said.

And then it was—Duane Lotspeich?—saying, "Not bad for an old coot with one leg, eh?"

Whatever else they might have said was lost on Dakota when the music came up louder—something that sounded like Glenn Miller, maybe "A-Train," Dakota thought, although he always got that one mixed up with "In the Mood," neither of which he would ever have heard of if Erika hadn't been on the sorority's swing dance team. Just then, Edith Cole appeared from around the corner, pushing her walker down the hallway toward him, hunched, as usual, over her basket full of critters. She was about to pass him by when Erika's voice rose again above the music, from the other side of the library doors, saying, "That's the coolest thing I've ever seen!"

Dakota was trying to put it all together when he realized that Edith Cole had, uncharacteristically, stopped there in the hallway beside him and that, even more uncharacteristically, she had raised her bowed head and was looking him right in the eye. Dakota had never seen Edith Cole's eyes before. They were dark and deep, and they seemed to demand something from him—an explanation, perhaps, for why he was standing there, looking stricken, outside the closed library doors. Just to say something, he said, "Erika went home an hour ago. I saw her drive away."

"Guess she came back," Edith growled.

Dakota stared.

Edith Cole returned her gaze to the stuffed animals in the basket on her walker, taking a moment to adjust the position of a fluffy white rabbit. Dakota watched the rabbit lean this way and that way before it stood up straight, and for the smallest instant, it seemed possible to him that the *bunny* had spoken, rather than Edith, who was already shuffling away from him, her S-shaped back and brittle-looking shoulders hiding all her little friends from view. Before she turned the corner, either Edith or the bunny spoke again.

"For God's sake, don't just stand there," one of them said. "Open the door."

Dakota waited until Edith was out of sight. Then he reached for the handle.

Under ordinary circumstances, Laverne would have gloated—inwardly, of course—as she passed the dining room half full of residents who had *not* recently enjoyed a Pecan Mudslide from Dairy Queen and who appeared to be spooning red Jell-O—instead of soft serve, hot fudge, caramel, and pecans—into their mouths. At the moment, however, she was swept up in more pressing issues, not least of which was getting to her room to use the facilities. She had spent more time in Tori Mahoney's minivan than she had anticipated. It was really very nice of Tori to stop when Laverne pointed out a Dairy Queen on the way back to Pondside Manor, but if she had known that they weren't going inside—just getting takeout— Laverne might not have mentioned it. She should have visited the ladies' before they left the hospital.

And what about poor Foster, who missed out on DQ entirely? He had been climbing into Tori's minivan for the ride back to Pondside when Laverne rediscovered the valet ticket for Amelia's car in her coat pocket. Tori passed it back to Foster without even turning around. He didn't say anything to Tori about his lack of experience operating a manual transmission. Well, he would get the hang of it, Laverne thought, by the time he got back here, assuming he didn't burn out the clutch first. She couldn't help but notice, when Tori drove around to the back of the building, that Amelia's purple car had not yet returned to the employee lot.

Tori Mahoney hadn't wanted to make this stop at Pondside Manor at all. She thought it would be "safer" for Laverne to go straight to the airport—not because they were pressed for time, but because the fewer items of her own that Laverne carried with her, the less likely she was to blow her cover, as Tori put it. "We'll get all your medications relabeled for you," Tori had said before they left the hospital, and Mrs. Kallman's luggage contained every possible health and beauty aid, from eyedrops to flushable wipes (not to be used in flight). "You're all set."

"I'll need my toothbrush," Laverne had said.

Mrs. Kallman's bag had a brand-new toothbrush in a brand-new toothbrush holder, Tori assured her, along with toothpaste, mouthwash, dental floss, and—

"I'll need *my* toothbrush," Laverne insisted, and Tori had given in without further protest, even though Laverne suspected that Tori suspected that Laverne was feeling the need to bring along something more personally significant than her toothbrush. When they pulled up to the employee entrance at Pondside, Tori reminded Laverne that whatever she put in her big black purse, there should be nothing—not a note or a bill or a membership card—that identified her as anyone other than Susan Alice Kallman. For the same reason, Laverne had changed her clothes at the hospital, trading her perfectly nice black knit pants and autumn-themed embroidered sweatshirt for Mrs. Kallman's admittedly classier travel outfit. When Tori first handed her the shopping bag in the visitor's lounge, Laverne had sorted through it and said, "My goodness! Can't I keep my own underpants?"

"Are they marked *LS*?" Tori had asked, knowing very well that all items of clothing were labeled for laundry purposes at Pondside Manor.

At least she still had her fedora and long red coat, both of which were labeled "Dry-clean only."

Passing the dining room, now in Mrs. Kallman's linen-blend travel pants and tunic, the coat over her arm, Laverne spotted the CNA whose name Foster had permanently dislodged in her brain by calling him something else—Dinglebutt? Dangleheart?—at one of the tables. He was trying to get a spoonful of something into Screamin' Jeannie's mouth. Poor Mrs. Hickerson was at the same table, and so was Edith, looking a bit fiery, though nothing like the way she'd been in the atrium after lunch. Laverne would have liked to stop and see if something was going on—was Edith still talking?—but the call of nature prevailed.

When she came out of the bathroom, Laverne found, to her surprise, that her legs felt a little wobbly, and she was glad to have the walker handy, even though she seldom used it in the confines of her room. "Too much excitement in one day," Bill would have said. Laverne sat gratefully on the bed, sinking into the floral comforter that her son Joseph and his wife had given her last Christmas to "add color to the room," the wife had said. On the bed beside her, leaning against her hip, was the big black purse she had dragged around all day. There wasn't much left in it, aside from the medications Tori was going to relabel—just a comb and some tissues and some loose change, a pressed powder compact without a powder puff (she used the mirror to check for food stuck between her teeth), a ziplock bag of dried apricots, a salted nut roll, and the 9×12 envelope with the airline itinerary—final destination PEK—and Mrs. Kallman's passport inside.

"PEK is for Beijing, China," Laverne had whispered to Foster earlier in the hospital lobby while they waited for Tori to bring the minivan around. "It used to be called Peking."

"Are you really going to do this?" Foster had asked her.

"It's the opportunity of a lifetime," Laverne had replied.

The opportunity of a lifetime. Mrs. Kallman had said that at the hospital, after Laverne admitted she had never been to China. When Laverne pointed out that what Mrs. Kallman was proposing sounded like it might be illegal, she said, "Smuggling drugs? Oh, yes." And when Laverne also supposed that it was possible to get caught by the authorities, if not for drug smuggling then for whatever kind of crime it was to use somebody else's passport, Mrs. Kallman said that criminal trials tend to drag on for years before anybody actually goes to prison. She had winked at Laverne and said, over the faint whistling of oxygen from the cannula that was slightly askew under her nose, "Even if we did live long enough to be convicted, I believe we could count on pretty short sentences. One way or another."

Laverne rummaged in the big black purse until she found the compact, and after squinting at her own face in the little round mirror for half a minute, she pulled Mrs. Kallman's passport out of the brown envelope and opened it to the photograph. She experimented with the mirror, holding it closer and then farther away, until her reflection was about the same size as the passport photo. She tried to match her expression to Mrs. Kallman's unsmiling face. Aside from their blue eyes, white hair, and general agedness, she and Mrs. Kallman looked nothing alike. You could see that they didn't, if you really looked, but the sad (though in this case, useful) fact was that no one really looked at an old woman. Laverne knew from experience—in grocery stores, at the doctor's office, and even with the CNAs in the Pondside dining room—that white hair and wrinkles were enough to make the differences between herself and any other old woman, including Mrs. Kallman, pretty much invisible to anyone under fifty. Laverne was not entirely confident that this general rule would hold true for airport security and passport-checking people, but Mrs. Kallman told Laverne she had nothing to worry about. "Just get in the line that leads to the youngest-looking agent," she'd advised.

Laverne reached for the hinged photo frame on her bedside table. It was a triptych: a wedding photo of her and Bill on the left; a Sears family portrait of the two of them with Joseph in her lap on the right; and in the middle, a just slightly blurry 5×7 of Bill in his Giants cap and minor league jersey, posing at home plate in Candlestick Park with Willie Mays. Laverne had already asked herself, back in Mrs. Kallman's hospital room, what Bill would do. She suspected that he would agree with Mrs. Kallman that this adventure was the opportunity of a lifetime. On the other hand, he might have some qualms about the criminal aspects of the trip—which covered pretty much everything about it. *You could find yourself in a heap of trouble, Laverne,* he might say. Or maybe getting his advice regarding the trip would be like the many times she tried to get him to tell her if he thought it was time for her to stop coloring her hair. (She'd started going gray at a very young age.) All he would say was, "It's your call, Laverne. Your hair, your call." She knew what he was really thinking, though, which was that it didn't matter: *Brown hair, gray hair. Six to one, half a dozen to the other.* That's what he was thinking. She finally stopped coloring it not long after they got the bad news about his liver. He'd lasted long enough after that to see her hair grow out silvery-gray and to whisper one time, "It suits you, Laverne," without her even asking.

Laverne returned the compact to the big black purse and the passport to the envelope. She laid the triptych frame facedown in her lap, carefully removed the middle picture, and slid it into the envelope behind the many pages of flight itinerary. It occurred to her that she had in her possession—specifically, in this big black bag—everything she needed to get on an airplane tomorrow morning and fly to China! What a thought.

Suddenly, she sat up straight. Didn't Mrs. Kallman say that she had called Foster on the laptop computer in her room only moments after he logged in? Did that mean—? Yes, it must! Foster had gotten into *The World of Pondside*! Could that possibly mean that if Laverne went to the computer in the library and clicked on the ducklink, she, too, could get back into the game at last? Her heart fluttered at the prospect. She grabbed the walker and hauled herself to her feet with surprising ease. What she thought at first was a ringing in her ears brought on by the sudden change in her position resolved itself, when she reached her door, into actual music coming from somewhere. She stepped out into the hall, pushing the walker ahead of her, and hoped the music wasn't coming from the library—a hope that faded as she got closer and the music got louder. Glenn Miller it sounded like, or Benny Goodman, lots of horns, something jazzy. She turned the corner into Library Lane and put on the brakes when she saw Mary McIntyre swaying to the music in the hallway outside the library door.

Foster probably could have driven Amelia Ramirez's car three slow and jerky miles from the hospital to Pondside Manor, killing the engine at every stop. Or he could have admitted to Tori Mahoney that he didn't know how to drive a stick. He had watched in stoic silence as Tori's minivan pulled away from the hospital entrance, Laverne waving goodbye and good luck from the passenger-side window.

Luckily, other people were waiting to retrieve their cars at the valet parking station in front of the hospital. It soon became clear to Foster, watching the owners get in their cars and drive off one by one, that there was no way he could take Amelia's purple Saturn stopping and starting and leaping and bucking up that long driveway to the street while five or six guys in valet jackets, hands in their pockets and smirks on their faces, watched him go. Amelia would have no trouble getting a ride here later to pick up her car. Foster would pay for the all-day parking. He put the valet ticket in his pocket and slunk away.

He figured he'd have sidewalks through neighborhoods for the first mile or two. After that, the houses would thin out until he was walking along the gravel shoulder of the blacktop that led out to Pondside. It would probably take an hour to get there on foot. The last of the daylight would be gone. He tucked Robert's backup server more snugly under his arm, trying to cover as much of the pink-and-purple paisley laptop sleeve as he could.

The downside of walking—apart from the fact that he wasn't dressed for it—was that it gave him time to think. He was already regretting his offer to "find the Easter egg," as Laverne must have put it a half-dozen times while they were waiting in the hospital lobby for Tori to bring the minivan around. On the most practical level, there was the problem of personnel. With Laverne gone—to actual *China*, for God's sake—where was he going to find three people he could trust to play the *Next Level* in search of whatever they would be searching for? For that matter, they only had two computers—no, three, he thought, with the backup server. To come up with four of the "three or four of us" he had so casually suggested to Mrs. Kallman, Foster would either have to play from his place (until the Wi-Fi went out at ten)—or he would have to bring the Dell out to Pondside. Nobody else on the Pondside premises had a computer of their own with *The World of Pondside* loaded and the processing speed to play, except for Kitty Landiss, and she, needless to say, was not an option. So let's say Foster lined up Duane Lotspeich and one or two others. Who knew how long it would take them to navigate the *Next Level*? And if they did manage to stumble across whatever the hell they were looking for, how would they know that they'd found it? Thinking it through, Foster could hardly believe that he had even suggested that he might be able to find the information in time for Laverne Slatchek to use it on the other side of the world.

The scary part was that they all seemed to believe he *could* do it, no sweat.

The walk back to Pondside was colder than Foster expected it to be. His T-shirt and hoodie were plenty warm enough in the car when he was sweating it out with Laverne at the wheel, but they were no match for the wind, which had picked up as the sun went down. Foster pulled up his hood, shoved his hands in his pockets, and pinned his arms— and the laptop—against his sides. He was walking through an older part of town, not far from the university—block after block of student apartments in formerly grand old houses, here and there the occasional hold-out: a well-maintained Victorian with a fancy paint job on the gingerbread trim and no couches on the porch, a couple of soon-to-be geezers no doubt peering out at him as he slunk by in his hoodie.

It occurred to Foster that he wasn't all that far from the Kallmans' nicely painted gingerbread trim and the tower with the rounded glass windows. The house was on this side of town anyway, on a block of better-kept places. He stopped at the next corner, checked the street signs and took a right, walked five blocks, took a left on Summit, and there it was: the third house from the corner on the other side of the street. He had to get past the next-door neighbor's head-high hedge before he could see that there was a car parked in the long driveway that led to the bungalow-size garage behind the house—a silver sedan that could very well be the car that he'd seen at Walmart that night. Looking up, he could see the curved glass window in a dormer jutting out from the roof. He couldn't help thinking about faceless, legless Scott Mahoney looking down through that attic window with his one good eye at his little boys playing in Robert's backyard. Foster pictured the guy in a wheelchair, from the back, like the corpse in the rocking chair in *Psycho*, a movie that had scared the shit out of him when he watched it as a kid at his grandparents' house. *The monster in the attic.*

When a light came on in the dormer, Foster's knees almost buckled. He had to stagger back a step to stay on his feet, and by the time he regained his equilibrium, there was no way for him to tell whether or not he had really seen someone or something move away from the window up there.

Then he saw that lights had come on in other parts of the house, too: a couple on the first floor, one window on the second, and a yard light on the side of the garage, plus the one up there under the eaves. He held his breath, his pulse pounding in his ears, but there was no movement in any of the windows. "Timers," he told himself as he backed up two steps to the sidewalk again. The lights must be on timers. Even so, he needed all of his resolve to walk, not run, to the end of the block, where he turned the corner without looking back.

All right, so Robert never mentioned that Tori was *that* Mahoney— heck, maybe Robert thought Foster already knew. What was harder to understand was why Robert also never said a word about Scott Mahoney surviving the blast in the Humvee. Foster was still trying to get over that. On the other hand, Robert had never actually lied about it either, had he? Did Robert ever *say* that Mahoney died *in the Humvee*? Probably not. That was something Foster had assumed. Of course, it was something any reasonable person would assume if they hadn't been told otherwise. Robert would have known that. Didn't he say that was what bothered him the most? That Mahoney gave his life "for nothing"?

And Tori! What the hell was with *her* all of a sudden? The way she kept saying, *That can't be true.* Well, it *was* true. If there were any Easter eggs or "next levels" in *The World of Pondside*, he had never seen or heard anything about them before today. *They* were the ones who made a mistake, thinking that he knew—that Robert had told him—what they were looking for. And there was something about the way Tori said it. She didn't say, "That's not true." It was, "That *can't* be true." Why *should* he know where the Easter eggs were, assuming there were any, for God's sake? Why should he know anything about the *Next Level*? He hadn't helped build it, and whatever Robert might have planned to tell him about it—like all of Robert's intentions, as well as his hopes and schemes and his vast knowledge—had gone with him into the pond.

Foster felt suddenly, immeasurably sad. This must be what people meant when they said they felt the rug pulled out from under them. Except it was more than a rug. It was like the earth itself dropping out from under him, a sinkhole opening under his feet.

Foster was never Robert's *friend*, any more than he was Tori Mahoney's. No matter if Jenny called him that when she was talking to the cops or not. Just because somebody gives you a computer and shows you how to line code and lets you use their Netflix account—plus, shares an incredible DVD collection of vintage sci-fi with you—that doesn't mean you're *friends*. Shit, Robert was practically old enough to be Foster's father, wasn't he? For Robert, Foster had been a way to get things done. Half the time, Foster didn't really know what he was doing, sitting at the keyboard pasting libraries of code into the game engine that drove *The World of Pondside*, while Robert looked over his shoulder, grunting his approval, or making it clear with a sharper intake of breath or even a groan, that Foster needed to stop and undo whatever he had just done.

Things hadn't always gone well either. Foster could make a list of failures and frustrations a mile long, of Robert trying to get him to do some damn thing—some new code to type in, a script Robert had come up with to customize something, some step so simple that it shouldn't have been necessary for Robert to explain. But sometimes Foster just couldn't get it, he couldn't understand what Robert wanted him to do. They would be in the middle of something, and he would be messing it up, and Robert couldn't explain fast enough to fix it.

There were times when Robert got so frustrated that all he could do was back his wheelchair away from the desk and leave the room. It really killed Foster when Robert did that. Not to mention the terrible time when he meant to roll sharply *away* from whatever frustrating thing they were failing to do, but the wheelchair had lurched forward instead, *into* the desk, lifting the door part of it up off the filing cabinets on impact, turning the top of the desk into a ramp aimed downward at the wall. Things had tipped over and slid away—some all the way to the floor—and then, when Robert did manage to put the chair in reverse, the desktop door had come back down on the filing cabinets with a bump. More things fell over, and Robert said, "Damn it to hell!" (Foster understood *those* words all right.) Later, when he cooled off, Robert had cranked up the digital voice to make it clear to Foster that he was disgusted with *himself.* "Not with you. Foster. Not with you. Foster. Not with you."

By the time Foster reached the highway, it was dark—as dark as it got out here among the strip malls and box stores—and it was rush hour, which meant a stream of headlights blinding him as he walked on the shoulder of the four-lane. First chance he got, he abandoned the highway for the lighted bicycle path, which came into view at about the same time as the more distant lights of Pondside Manor. Getting to the bicycle path from the highway required climbing two fences and walking blind through a lumpy pasture littered with cow pies. The bicycle path curved away from Pondside for a bit and came up on the far side of the pond. When it reached the pond, the path split in two, the lighted branch running along the top of what looked, in the moonless dark, like a deep hole, while the other branch, which was unlighted but not entirely dark, dropped down into it. The hole had been carved out by the retreat of the glacier that once covered Iowa, Robert told Foster one time. Now, at the top of the path leading down to the pond, Foster enjoyed picturing Pondside Manor and its parking lots, along with the highway and the box stores, all buried under the ice.

He could see the little waves glinting below, except where the dark, narrow rectangle of the wooden pier extended over them. He felt warmer as he descended the asphalt path, out of the wind. When he reached the pier, he stepped over the gap between the path's edge and the sloping, snaggletooth planks. This was the spot where Robert's wheelchair would have needed an assist from somebody. Foster walked out onto the pier, testing every board before he put his weight on it. The waves moving in his peripheral vision made him a little dizzy. At the end of it, he edged the toes of his shoes out over the water. He wondered, not for the first time, if Robert had come out here to make a phone call. He did that sometimes. Cellphone reception sucked inside the building. He would have had his Bluetooth in his ear. Somebody would have had to help him with it. Probably his mother, before she left. Foster hadn't seen any Bluetooth on Robert, but it might have fallen out when he went into the water. Or maybe Foster just didn't notice it. Either way, the police would have found it. Maybe they did. It's not like anybody would be keeping Foster posted about what was going on. He made himself look down into the water at the end of the pier, even though he knew what he would see: Robert in his wheelchair, strapped in, his arms floating in a way that had made Foster's heart constrict at first, at the sight of Robert *moving*.

Mary heard the music from the bottom of the stairs, where she'd stopped, nervously, to look up and down the street. Usually, she went with her sisters or her friend Gladys to the USO, which took up the whole second floor above the hardware store. The other girls would serve punch and shoot the breeze with the servicemen while Mary, who was too shy for small talk, stood at the edge of the dance floor—a cleared space adjacent to the jukebox in the corner of the room—and waited for someone to ask her to dance. Her average wait time was forty-five seconds. (Her sister Mildred had worked this out one afternoon, using a stopwatch she borrowed from a young man—only a PFC but very nice-looking—from Austin, Texas.) If somebody played "String of Pearls" or "Chattanooga Choo Choo," the wait time dropped to fifteen seconds or four bars, whichever came first.

At the bottom of the stairs, Mary listened. It was "A-Train"—not a favorite, but at least you could dance to it. She climbed a few steps in her slippery black dancing shoes, scooting her hand up the railing, and tried to hear if it was crowded up there on this Sunday afternoon. There were some Baptists who didn't dance on Sundays, including her own sister, which tended to thin out the crowd considerably. Mary climbed a few more steps and thanked the Lord she was a Methodist like her mother. She had spent all day Saturday working the grill at the officers' club on the base, where there was seldom any dancing, due, she'd been told, to the presence of a lot of old farts who preferred to drink their whiskey and smoke their cigars in peace and quiet. Officers who cared to dance could go and mingle with the enlisted men above the hardware store. One of Mary's two favorite partners was an officer, a young lieutenant from Atlanta who was a pilot in the Army Air Corps.

Her second favorite dance partner was a fellow named Frank. Frank was the best friend of another fellow that Mary sometimes thought she might have feelings for. His name was George. He (like Frank) was from *up north*—somewhere in Iowa, they said, or maybe it was Idaho. George had dark eyes and even, white teeth and a pretty nice singing voice—this Mary had discovered one day when he and his friends came over to the USO after consuming a bottle of brandy that came in someone's Christmas package from home—but he couldn't jitterbug, not to save his life, he said. And so he paid Frank to dance with her. "It's good work when you can get it!" Frank said when she coaxed a confession out of him on the dance floor. Frank's job was to keep her away from the other guys—especially that flyboy from Atlanta. She had decided to be flattered instead of offended. "Good call," Frank said as he dipped her down thrillingly, almost to the floor. "Georgie's crazy aboutcha."

Mary reached the top of the stairs. She took several deep breaths, hoping against hope that George and Frank had guard duty or something today because she knew for a fact that the flyboy was waiting to dance with her on the other side of that door. Sure enough, it swung open, and somebody tall, dark, and handsome said, "Honey, come on in!"

# CHAPTER 25

The worst thing about driving downtown from Pondside Manor at the end of the day, Kitty Landiss thought as she waited at the service road stop sign, was having to turn left onto the two-lane highway that led into town, when everybody else on the highway seemed to be zipping past her front bumper on their way *out* of town and into freedom.

She parked in the lot behind city hall and had no trouble finding the double doors in the lobby that had "Police Department" stenciled on their frosted glass windows. Lieutenant Steinhafel greeted her at the counter and promptly handed her over to a clerk, or maybe she was a detective, in one of six cubicles identified by a sign suspended from the ceiling as "Homicide." That was the last Kitty saw of Lieutenant Blue Eyes. She was expecting the third degree, but the clerk/detective just offered her some undrinkable "cappuccino" from a vending machine and then asked her all the same questions she had answered on two different occasions at Pondside Manor, plus a few additional ones about Tori Mahoney and Foster Kresowik—what their attendance records were like, whether Kitty had ever had trouble contacting them in the past, etc. She finished by asking if Kitty had any pictures of the "missing employees," by which she seemed to mean Tori and Foster.

"What, in my wallet?" Kitty said.

"In your employment files. Something you could email?"

"I'll have to scan them first," Kitty said. She didn't bother to point out that neither of her missing employees was actually "missing."

*Or were they?*

This question popped into Kitty's consciousness like the sprouting of a noxious weed while the clerk/detective printed out a copy of the statement for her to sign. Every one of Kitty's recent calls to Tori's cellphone had rung and rung and then gone to voicemail. Kitty had imagined Tori scowling at the phone number on the screen while she let it ring. But what if the phone was in airplane mode? What if she was getting the heck out of town? No wonder Lieutenant Steinhafel was suspicious about Kitty's insistence that Tori Mahoney wouldn't hurt a fly. As she dug through her purse for her car key, Kitty remembered Foster Kresowik's attempts to back Amelia Ramirez's car out of her parking space. Were *all three of them* involved somehow? And what, exactly, were they involved in?

Her Subaru appeared to be the last citizen's car in the parking lot behind city hall. She ran to it—actually ran—and had to call on all her powers of self-control *not* to peel out like somebody in an action movie. It had struck her with the force of a thousand speeding tickets that she had made a terrible mistake by leaving *The World of Pondside* laptop in the hands of Duane Lotspeich and Foster Kresowik instead of taking it back to her office with her when she had the chance. She hadn't wanted Lieutenant Steinhafel to see her with it, for fear he might collect it as evidence or something. Kitty knew now that no such precaution was necessary. Of all the officers who had been prowling the premises since last Thursday—including Lieutenant Steinhafel—not one had asked her a single question about Robert's array of computer equipment. Ditto for the clerk/detective who just took her statement. To Kitty's knowledge, the police had shown no interest in Robert's computers beyond locking them up with everything else in his room. They seemed totally unaware that they had locked the barn after the horse was gone. One of the horses, anyway. She shouldn't have let that laptop out of her sight.

Back at Pondside, Kitty was dismayed to see no sign of Amelia Ramirez's purple Saturn in the employee parking lot. She told herself that its absence did not *necessarily* mean that Foster Kresowik had absconded with the *World of Pondside* server after all. She reminded herself that she had seen him get into the car empty-handed. Of course, he'd had plenty of time to come back from wherever he went, pick up the server, and disappear forever while Kitty was at the police station. And what about Amelia herself? Had she also disappeared?

Inside the building, Kitty dashed down the short hall to her office and unlocked the desk drawer where she'd put her own laptop. It was still there. Closing the drawer, she felt calmer. Music was coming from somewhere—something Glenn Millerish, which was a little surprising, since the big band fans at Pondside Manor had mostly died off by now. As she came back out to the entryway, she caught a reassuring glimpse of Amelia Ramirez turning the corner down at the end of the hall and reminded herself that you couldn't always go by the cars in the employee parking lot. Kitty hadn't seen the yellow Hummer out there yesterday or today, and yet Erika Peterson had been here both days, hadn't she?

At least Peterson was working out surprisingly well. She had worked a full shift on her first day without a single crisis, and when Kitty stopped at the nurses' station earlier today, she learned from Amelia Ramirez that Mary McIntyre had taken such a shine to the new CNA that she'd agreed quite cheerfully to a shower with young Erika's assistance. Peterson, who had to leave for class in the afternoon, had even promised to come back this evening with some music she thought would help Mary McIntyre at bedtime—perhaps the very tune that Kitty could hear coming from somewhere right now. "Who would have thought?" Kitty had said, and yet that happened sometimes, where a resident would get attached to someone on the staff (probably thinking that the staff member, usually a CNA, was somebody else—a daughter or a grandchild). All of a sudden, the troublesome resident would be cleaning her plate at every meal and cheerfully going to PT and attending social events and so forth—at least until the CNA found a better job, and the poor resident was abandoned by yet another loved one. Kitty wished she had known about the bond between Mary McIntyre and Erika Peterson when the McIntyre daughters were here.

Due to the open layout of the common areas, Kitty could not avoid the atrium and the dining room on the way to her destination: Duane Lotspeich's room in Hawkeye Lane. The atrium was deserted, more or less as usual, and the dining room more empty than not, only a few tables still occupied, the smell of roast chicken hanging in the air. Before last Thursday, Robert Kallman would have been one of the stragglers, his big, complicated wheelchair pushed up to that empty table over by the window. Foster Kresowik might be keeping him company long after the end of his shift. The very laptop Kitty was now looking for would often be right there, open on the table between them, Foster fiddling with it while Robert chewed and chewed.

Kitty had not intended to poke her head into Mary McIntyre's room in Hawkeye Lane. It was reasonably tidy earlier this afternoon when the daughters were here. Now it looked, alarmingly, like a crime scene. Bedding pulled off the bed, chair tipped over, closet open and clothes strewn, dresser drawers half dumped, and most mysteriously, pudding cups everywhere. Many of them were squashed and splattered on the floor, including the one that the heel of Kitty's ankle boot landed on when she stepped into the room. At least there wasn't a body—although, of course, as soon as Kitty had that thought, she had to tiptoe stickily toward the bathroom and peer inside.

She crossed the hall to Duane Lotspeich's room and stopped to listen outside the door. She heard nothing from the other side of it, knocked lightly—still nothing—and pushed the door open. The room was empty, that is to say, both the old man and Foster Kresowik were gone. So, of course, was the laptop—she'd expected that—closet door open and shelf cleared to mark the space where it had been. She understood, suddenly and with certainty, that she wouldn't find the *Pondside* laptop here, in Duane Lotspeich's room, because *he* was the one who had ransacked Mary's room across the hall, looking for it.

Back in the hallway, Kitty could see that her smeary white footprints weren't the only tracks that crossed from Mary's room to Duane's. A wheelchair had come out of Mary McIntyre's room and painted the faintest of lines down Hawkeye Lane toward the music, which was coming from the library.

She hesitated for a moment outside the library door to see if she could hear what was going on inside. There was the music, and some giggling, and a "Take it easy, you two!" followed by "Not bad for an old coot!" in a voice she recognized as Duane Lotspeich's.

No one even looked up at her when she finally opened the door.

Foster wasn't sure how much time he spent out there on the wooden pier, gazing pointlessly into the pond, before he climbed back up the asphalt path to the parking lot. When he first spotted Tori Mahoney's minivan back near the employee entrance, a cloud of white exhaust rising behind it, he felt a jolt of *she followed me!* Then he realized that Tori must have brought Laverne back to Pondside to pack or something, and now she was waiting to drive her to Chicago. (Laverne's flight left from O'Hare.) He fingered the valet ticket in his pocket. They were both going to wonder what happened to Amelia Ramirez's car. In fact, Tori was probably wondering already. He would have to stick to the hedge here and go around to the front of the building if he wanted to get inside and give the valet ticket to Amelia without being seen. He was so intent on staying lower than the top of the spirea as he skirted the parking lot that he didn't hear any of the sounds—a car door opening, footsteps—that must have preceded what he did hear: "Foster? What are you doing?"

Tori Mahoney peered down at him over the top of the hedge. He stood up slowly, hugging the laptop and trying to come up with some kind of explanation for his behavior. Tori did not appear to be interested in explanations. She had a rolling suitcase with her, a hard-shell carry-on that he could tell must be empty or nearly so by the way she swung it toward him, one-handed, over the hedge.

"Give this to Laverne," she said. "Tell her to put some things in it from her black bag. And send her out here! I think she forgot I'm waiting for her." Tori paused then, as if she had just remembered that Foster might not be too eager to follow orders, especially if they were coming from her. "Will you do that?" she added. "Please?"

Now that he was standing up, Foster could see the main entrance to the building. Kitty Landiss's Subaru was parked haphazardly under the portico. No wonder Tori Mahoney wanted *him* to take the suitcase inside. It was oddly shaped and a tortoise-shell color. It looked like a turtle lodged crookedly in the top of the hedge. Because they were pretty close to one of the halogen lights that turned night into day around Pondside Manor, Foster could read the luggage tag on the extended handle: Susan Alice Kallman.

"It's for the pickup," Tori explained.

"Okay," Foster said. He lifted the carry-on down to the ground. "I'll send her out."

"Thank you." Tori said this as if she meant it. Foster was trying to avoid eye contact, hoping to escape before she thought to ask him about Amelia's car, but when Tori said, "I'm sorry I was sort of an ass at the hospital," he couldn't help but look at her in surprise.

"It was just so hard for me to believe that Robert would"—she stopped and drew a long breath—"that he would do anything without telling *you* first."

The way she said "without telling *you* first" made Foster's nose prickle. He blinked hard and cleared his throat before he spoke. "Like I said, maybe I wasn't as good a friend of Robert as you thought."

Tori smiled, surprising him again. "*That* can't be true," she said.

Foster watched her walk back toward the darker corner of the lot where the minivan was parked. He half rolled, half swung the carry-on to the front entrance.

He heard the music as soon as he opened the vestibule door. It sounded like one of the vintage tunes they'd used for the dance hall part of Duane Lotspeich's portal in *The World of Pondside*, and it probably meant that Duane had found the server in Mary McIntyre's room. Foster was sure that he shut down the laptop before he hid it under the pudding packs in Mary McIntyre's dresser drawer—but did he *log out* before he shut the server down? He thought he did, but if he hadn't, then it was possible that Duane Lotspeich had figured out how to access all kinds of things— maybe even found his way back into the game. Logged in, all Duane had to do was click on this and click on that until he got lucky and something familiar opened up for him.

Foster attracted a few curious looks from a handful of residents as he passed the dining room. Mrs. Hickerson, sitting on a chair opposite the vestibule in one of her nicest going-home outfits, had looked disappointed when she saw that it was Foster coming through the glass door, but she gave him a little wave anyway. He nodded and waved back. The Stevens couple turned away from the bulletin board where this week's activity schedule was posted and stared at him. Mrs. Stevens actually elbowed her old man's bony rib cage, making him wince, as Foster went by.

In Hawkeye Lane, Foster didn't bother to stop and poke his head in the doorway to Duane Lotspeich's room. He did take a peek into Mary McIntyre's across the hall. ("Did you have to tear the whole room apart?" he asked Duane later. Lotspeich said, "It's always in the last place you look.") Foster rolled the carry-on right through the mostly dried streaks and footprints of vanilla pudding from Wild Mary's stash and set a course for the library. Turning the corner into Library Lane, he almost ran head-on into Dakota Engelhart, who had a goofy smile on his face. Foster stopped. Dakota kept going but turned around and said, walking backward, "They're in the library." He raised an eyebrow at the pink-and-purple paisley-covered laptop under Foster's arm, but he didn't say anything about it, just turned around again and moved away down the hall.

The sound of saxophones swelled when Foster opened the library door on a surprising scene. In a cleared space in the middle of the room, the new CNA—the one who was possibly, well, probably, Dinglebutt's girlfriend— was dancing with Mary McIntyre. They were not just holding hands and stepping around either. They were all-out *dancing*—pulling close, then twirling away, the works. Mary McIntyre appeared to be a much younger person when she was dancing, Foster thought; her old lady wrinkles and knobby joints looked like a costume she was wearing. Her feet matched the new CNA's step for step, and her face was flushed with happiness. At least, Foster hoped it was happiness.

On the far side of the room, Kitty Landiss and Laverne Slatchek were leaning together like old friends, shoulder to shoulder, over the back of Lotspeich's wheelchair, the three of them huddled over the *Pondside* server on the table in front of them. Foster could see the yellow duck on the lid. They were watching the screen with obvious delight.

Foster had a pretty good idea of what they were looking at. Off to the side of the dancers, a device about the size of a cereal box was set up—much too precariously—on a tall wooden stool made taller by a stack of fat encyclopedia volumes. The black cereal box was the Natural User Interface module that Robert called the Nooey. It was tracking the moves of Mary McIntyre and the new CNA, sending data from differ-ent points on their all-out dancing figures to a program on the *Pondside* server that turned the data back into a pair of figures dancing. On the screen, the dancers would look like a guy in a tuxedo ("What do you mean, 'a guy'?" Duane Lotspeich said to Foster the first time they ran the program. "Are you blind? That's me!") and a perky-looking blond that Lotspeich had named Ginger Rogers. They hadn't used the Nooey for *The World of Pondside* yet. They hadn't done anything with it except for the demo they put together featuring debonair "Duane" and Ginger Rogers. The hardware was usually stowed in a locked library closet—not just the sensor array currently balanced on the stool, but all the cords and adapters that were creating a serious trip hazard on the library floor. Landiss could have unlocked the closet. But who the hell had set it all up?

When the music stopped, Mary McIntyre and the new CNA col-lapsed against each other, laughing. On the other side of the dance floor, the trio huddling over the laptop straightened up. Laverne said, "Oh, dear!" as if the sight of Foster in the doorway had reminded her of something she'd forgotten. Lotspeich grinned at Foster over the top of the screen. "It's about time you showed up," he said. "If it hadn't been for Erika here, we wouldn't've had a thing to do but sit here twiddling our thumbs. Come and get a load of this."

Foster left the turtle-like carry-on in the doorway. He kept the paisley-covered laptop lodged securely under his arm.

"Nice purse," Kitty Landiss said.

Foster looked at the dancers frozen on the screen and said, "*Who* set this up?"

Erika, the new CNA, raised her hand like a kid in school. "Double major," she confessed. "Prenursing and computer science." She and Mary McIntyre strolled over to the library table, arm in arm. Erika peered over Foster's shoulder at the screen. "I'm doing my senior project using *this very* interface to motivate people to exercise. Isn't that a kick? I couldn't believe it when I saw the same software on the laptop here. There's all *kinds* of cool stuff on this machine!"

"We couldn't get into *The World of Pondside*, though," Laverne complained. "Even though *Duane* said he knew the password."

"Your game sounds amazing, by the way," Erika told Foster, "from what I've heard about it."

He looked at Duane, who said, "Don't look at me."

"Laverne claims there's some kind of 'next level,'" Kitty Landiss said narrowly, as if she thought Foster might deny it.

"I already knew about that," said Duane.

"And there's this certain Easter egg you're looking for?" Erika said.

Foster looked at Laverne.

"You said you needed people to play," she reminded him. "Who else are you going to get?"

"Erika here is going to be Laverne," Duane said, with enthusiasm.

"*Temporarily,*" Laverne added.

Mary McIntyre, meanwhile, had settled herself in the library chair in front of the laptop. "Aren't they going to dance?" she asked, leaning forward until her nose almost touched the screen.

Erika looked at Foster, her eyebrows raised. When he realized that she was asking his permission to run the program, he blushed and made a move that was supposed to mean, *Be my guest.* She leaned over Duane—who *could* have moved out of the way, Foster thought—to reach the keyboard. After a couple of taps and clicks, debonair Duane and his partner cut loose again on the otherwise blank blue screen. Mary McIntyre tapped Ginger Rogers with the tip of her finger. "That one there is me," she told Foster. "I know I don't look like her but this TV changes you up some."

# CHAPTER 26

After hastily considering other locations—including the Kallman place, Kitty Landiss's condo, and Erika Peterson's room at the Gamma Pi house (which was, Duane Lotspeich pointed out, the least likely and thus most secure location of all)—they decided that hiding in plain sight was the best plan. With the boss on board—thanks to Laverne—there was no reason not to access the *Next Level* right here in the library at Pondside Manor. Considering the drive to Chicago, a long wait at O'Hare, and the actual fourteen-hour flight to Beijing, Foster estimated that they had about twenty-four hours to look for the pickup location in *The World of Pondside* before the real Laverne Slatchek beat them to actual China. There was no way to know if this was plenty of time to find it, or not enough. It was Erika's idea to prepare themselves for a marathon game session—something she apparently had experience with—by taking some time to lay in supplies and snacks before they started to play.

"Can't we just get started?" Duane groused, but when Mary McIntyre grabbed the handles on his wheelchair, he let her wheel him away to where they both knew they could find pudding snacks. Before she had the stroke, Mary McIntyre had a hospital volunteer job wheeling discharged patients to the entrance. This was something Erika had learned about her, and it explained several things, including a tug-of-war Wild

Mary once had with a wheelchair repairman, as well as the time she had gotten up from her untouched meal to grab the handles of a tablemate's wheelchair and roll him, with fork in hand and clothing protector tucked under his chin, to the vestibule door.

Erika stuck around long enough to help Foster dismantle the tower of books and put the Nooey and cables and whatnot in the boxes they'd come in. He did his best to hide his surprise when she pulled the key to the library closet out of her pocket. She caught his eye—which almost made him drop the box he was carrying—and explained, "Duane found it in the activity director's desk. I told him we had to put it back." Hands on hips, she surveyed the storage closet. "I think your box goes right there," she said, pointing to a spot on the bottom shelf.

It took Foster a few seconds to figure out what she meant by *your box*—the one he was carrying, of course! He was pretty sure she didn't notice his hesitation. When he straightened up again, she handed him the key and he said, "Thanks," in what was, he hoped, a slightly offhand and perfectly normal tone of voice.

Kitty Landiss took the opportunity to go back to her office to retrieve her laptop, and, with luck, to find someone who could cover Foster's shift in the kitchen tomorrow morning. Unfortunately, the latter task required opening her work email. Normally, she prided herself on emptying the inbox each time she opened her Pondside email account, which was devoted *almost* exclusively to Pondside business. An empty inbox was not only a thing of beauty, as far as Kitty was concerned; it was evidence—concrete, incontrovertible evidence—that she was in the driver's seat on the ride that was her life. Normally, when an email came in, she was compelled to open it, reply or forward it, and then move it to one of a dozen folders, the fattest and fullest of which was always the Trash. In today, out today; that was her motto. One of the difficult things about the past few days had been her inability to empty her inbox, to feel the glorious clean sweep of *delete, delete, delete.* Every time she thought she'd done it, she would turn around and find five or six new ones from Simply the Best Care corporate headquarters and a few more from the usual suspects: retail offers, fundraising campaigns, etc.

If she had time after the email, she thought she might also scoot over to Fitness World for a quick shower. The day had been stressful, to put it mildly, so far, and now she was looking at a possible twenty-four hours in the library with the likes of Duane Lotspeich and Foster Kresowik, not to mention the capable Erika Peterson.

The onslaught of emails from corporate was no surprise, of course, and since she half expected each one to say that Pondside Manor would be closing its doors effective yesterday, she read most of them with more relief than dismay. Four of the five new ones were of the "one size fits all of our nationally franchised nursing homes and senior-living facilities" variety. The fifth one informed her that the Department of Inspections and Appeals would be calling soon to set up interviews with each and every member of her staff. She forwarded it to Carol, adding, "Please schedule. Thanks." Then she deleted a special offer from SwimOutlet and heartfelt pleas from three of the ten environmental-nature outfits she had given money to in the last year, often mistaking one for the other (which is how she ended up donating to ten different orgs).

Having attended to—though, sadly, not emptied—her inbox, Kitty turned to the task of finding someone to take Foster Kresowik's place in the kitchen at six a.m. tomorrow (which was less than twelve hours from now). The temp RN on first shift—a woman named Virginia Pinckney—had agreed to return tomorrow, thank God, but that probably meant that Kitty couldn't get away with diverting a first-shift CNA to the kitchen, even if she could have gotten in touch with one so late in the game. Chronically late but flexible Dakota Engelhart was already taken, as he would be replacing Erika on first shift. He had better not be planning to get himself out of his regular second-shift spot tomorrow, Kitty thought, and that very thought gave her the idea of finding a second-shift CNA to come in and do the first shift in the kitchen instead. She might find some takers if she offered them double time. Corporate wouldn't like that, but she could face the music later. The considerate thing to do first would be to talk to Amelia Ramirez, who would be worried about having enough second-shift staff on hand tomorrow to get people squared away after dinner. However, there was no time to track Amelia down, not if Kitty expected one of these CNAs to actually see her email in time to switch shifts tomorrow. Copying Ramirez on this message to the (hopefully, up-to-date) email list of CNAs was the best Kitty could do.

She was about to hit Send when the contents of her inbox jumped and shifted to make room for new messages. There was one from SaveTheSeaSquirts (the second today—a double-your-donation deadline was approaching), one from Amelia Ramirez, and yet another from corporate HQ. Saving Amelia for last, she deleted the Sea Squirts (muttering, "Sorry!") and opened the email from corporate, which informed her that a letter of resignation was expected from her within twenty-four hours of receipt of this message if she wished to receive the severance package her contract specified. Her interim replacement had been appointed and would report in person to Pondside Manor on Monday. Kitty had to read the message three times before she got it.

"You're firing me by email?" she cried to the unfeeling screen of her laptop.

Ten minutes later, she was naked in her favorite shower at Fitness World, bearing the full brunt not only of the shower's hottest, hardest spray setting, but also of the second thoughts she was having about the two-word "letter of resignation" she had shot off to corporate. Toweling herself dry at the locker that she would not be able to afford for long, she decided, Scarlet O'Hara–like, that she would think about that tomorrow. In the meantime, she would soon be Katherine Landiss, fashionista, again—at last—in *The World of Pondside*! And if that thought was not enough to lift her spirits, minutes later she found herself depositing her towel in the hamper in the Fitness World lobby at the very moment night nurse and part-time personal trainer Bert Reynolds was doing the same. Their paths had crossed in this very spot (seven times) before, but never had he leaned closer, smelling like shampoo, and said, with a grin, "Tossing in the towel, eh?"

"Funny you should mention that," Kitty said.

Alone in the library, Foster positioned the laptops where he thought they would work best, avoiding the Wi-Fi dead zone in the northeast corner. At one point, when a visitor wheeled her dozing father into the library—"Look, Dad! There's a TV in here"—to watch the ball game, Foster convinced her that the picture was better on the widescreen in the atrium. He looked under tables for available outlets and plugged in the laptops. He checked their speakers and mics. In one of the drawers, he found two headsets with attached microphones. He tested them both on the PC in the corner and put the crackly one back in the drawer. He knew the geezers didn't always use the headphones, preferring to rely on the computer's speakers—and they never used the mics—but with four people in the library together, all logged in at the same time, they might need individual audio, especially if they ended up in different places in *The World of Pondside*.

When he was finished rearranging the furniture and equipment, Foster sat down at Robert's backup laptop and tapped a key to wake it up. He wished they hadn't taken a supply break, as Erika called it, because the clock was ticking away. Laverne might be halfway to O'Hare by now, if they got lucky with the traffic. Foster pictured her sitting in the gate area with her black purse and funny carry-on, waiting for her flight, or she might be in the slammer if the TSA had figured out that she wasn't Mrs. Kallman after all. Foster felt a sudden pang of guilt for letting Laverne Slatchek put herself in such a position, as if what *he* said would have mattered to anybody anyway. He stared at the screen for a moment, hardly seeing the happy duck with its jaunty white sailor cap, and then he surprised himself by tapping the browser's search box and typing in "face transplant."

The first ten of 57,983 reported results popped up on the screen, including a row of before and after images of people whose faces had been bitten, blasted, or burned off to varying degrees. One of the first ten links had the word *China* in the headline. It was about the man who got the second face transplant ever in 2006, the one who was attacked by a bear.

So Tori hadn't made that up. The story said the man stopped taking his antirejection drugs and died two years after the surgery. In the photo, you could see that the donor's skin didn't quite match the color of the guy's forehead, cheeks, and nose. He looked like he was wearing a *Phantom of the Opera* mask. Apart from that, though, he didn't look bad. Foster wondered why he stopped taking the drugs. Was he unhappy with his new face? Did he just get tired of it all? Or did he think, after two years, that they had to be kidding about taking the drugs for the rest of his life?

Before Foster could click on another link, Kitty Landiss showed up in the library with damp hair, a gym bag, and her laptop, along with the news that she had found someone to take Foster's place in the kitchen tomorrow morning. There seemed to be more to this news, but then Erika Peterson came in bearing two reusable bags full of groceries, and the focus promptly changed to the inventory of fruit and bite-size vegetables with hummus and gluten-free crackers that Erika had selected to sustain them. Duane Lotspeich rolled into the library a few minutes later with a dresser drawer full of pudding cups bridging the arms of his wheelchair. Beverages were lined up around the edges of the drawer: bottles of water, cans of soda, juice boxes, bottled coffee drinks. It looked like Duane had either vandalized a vending machine or raided the staff room refrigerator. Straws and plastic spoons stuck out of a foam cup in one corner of the drawer.

"What happened to Mary?" Erika asked him.

"Passed out and snoring when I left her room," Duane said. "All that dancing wore her out, I guess."

Kitty Landiss plucked a spoon from the drawer. "I didn't get any dinner," she explained, as she looked the pudding cups over. "Are they all vanilla?"

Then—all of a sudden, it seemed to Foster—they were ready, stationed around the room at their designated tables: Landiss licking her spoon and tilting the lid of her laptop to change the angle of the screen (then tilting it back again), Duane Lotspeich complaining about the headphones at the PC in the corner, and Erika Peterson looking eager to log in as Laverne. She had the laptop from Robert's room, the one with the yellow duck on the lid. Foster was surprised to find that his fingers were trembling as they hovered over the keyboard of the backup server that Mrs. Kallman had given him. He glanced around the library again. Everybody's hands were poised over their keyboards.

"Okay," he said. "Double-click the ducklink."

"For God's sake," Duane said, his voice extra loud and obnoxious due to the headphones he was wearing. "I double-clicked the ducklink a half hour ago."

Foster ignored Duane. "Does everybody have the log-in box?"

Everybody did. There was a burst of clicking as they typed in their *World of Pondside* usernames (Erika using Laverne's). Foster hoped this was going to work, that the one password would get all of them in, that they would all land in the *Next Level* at the same time, and that it wouldn't take them all night to find one another there.

"Okay," he said again. "Here's the password. *M—*"

"Wait!" cried Erika.

Duane Lotspeich groaned.

"Is it capital *M*?" Erika asked.

"Doesn't matter," Foster said. "Nothing in the log-in is case sensitive. I should have told you that. Sorry. Okay. Here we go. It's *M*—just the one *M*—*A, R, Y,* space, *M, C, I, N, T, Y, R, E.*" He typed it as he spelled it.

"Mary McIntyre?" Kitty Landiss said.

Erika exclaimed, "No kidding!"

"What are we *waiting* for?" Duane Lotspeich moaned.

Foster didn't know he was holding his breath until he said, "Enter!"

The laptop screen on the table in front of him went blue, then black—for one, two, three, four heart-stopping seconds—and then, suddenly, it was all leafy shade and sunlight shining on a wooden card table and four ice-cream parlor chairs.

Laverne Slatchek found that she didn't have much to say to Tori Mahoney, and vice versa, on the long drive to ORD (which somehow stood

for O'Hare International Airport) in the minivan. For one thing, Laverne was afraid she might slip up and mention the photo of Bill and
Willie Mays that she had slipped into the envelope with the airline itinerary. If she so much as mentioned having looked at the photo, Laverne
was pretty sure that Tori would insist on looking through Laverne's big
black purse one more time. They had already started off on the wrong
foot when Laverne came out of the building without the funny-looking
carry-on. Tori had to call Amelia Ramirez, who was on duty inside, and
ask her to send someone out to the car with it. The red-haired boy—
whose name was Wyoming? No. Who would name their child Wyoming?
It was Dakota!—he brought the carry-on out. He was all smiles and
good luck wishes and bon voyage, but Tori didn't seem all that happy
to see him either. Laverne assumed that Tori was anxious to get underway. Personally, Laverne welcomed the cheerful send-off.

Their first stop was the Kallman residence, where they picked up Laverne's travel escort, Keith. He was waiting for them on the front steps
of the grand wraparound porch when they pulled into the driveway, his
suitcase—a silver hard-sider—standing at attention on the step behind
him. If Laverne had seen him before—say, at Robert's funeral—she didn't
know it. He was of medium height, dark-haired, and—here was a nice
surprise—he was wearing a San Francisco Giants cap and T-shirt. When
he turned around to pick up his suitcase, she saw on the back of his shirt
the number fifty-five and the rather odd name *Lincecum*. Laverne, who
hadn't seen a real-life Giants game since Bill died in 1984, was not familiar with Lincecum, but she was glad to see a Giant's T-shirt on any young
man's back. Not that Keith was terribly young, but he wasn't old either.

He slid his suitcase into the back seat and climbed in beside it. Laverne
knew—because Mrs. Kallman had told her—that Keith had been in the
military with Robert, and that Keith's father, who served in the first Gulf
War, had suffered from a condition that looked like ALS but turned out to
be a more treatable and thus less terrible nerve disease caused by breathing
in harmful chemicals in the burning oil fields. Keith reached forward into
the space between the front seats to shake Laverne's hand.

"Nice to see you looking so well, Mrs. Kallman," he said with a raised eyebrow and a sly smile. Laverne found it mildly thrilling to reply in character, as it were, sounding as much like Mrs. Kallman as she could, "Keith, dear, the pleasure is all mine."

"You can use your own voice, Laverne," Tori said as she backed the minivan down the driveway. She sounded tired, Laverne thought.

Laverne was too wound up to be tired. She had never traveled outside the country before, except for a honeymoon trip to the Canadian side of Niagara Falls. (The whole time they were there, with the sound of the Falls roaring and sloshing and pounding all around them, Laverne had never stopped feeling like she needed to use the bathroom.) She had never stayed in an airport hotel either, the kind with views of the runways and soundproof windows to keep out the noise.

She was surprised and touched when Tori Mahoney announced her intention to spend the night with Laverne at the hotel—since Keith had his own room and Laverne's featured two queen-size beds—although it soon became clear that Tori had an agenda, which was to make Laverne run through everything Mrs. Kallman had told her about the pickup, and then to make her run through it again. If all had gone according to plan (which, of course, it hadn't), they (Keith and Mrs. Kallman, that is) would have known before they set out exactly where they were going. They would have had a location—a temple or a park or some such place— retrieved by Robert from the secret Easter egg in *The World of Pondside* where the contact had placed it. When they arrived at PEK, they would have gone by taxi to this temple or park or some such place, directly from the airport, arrival time permitting, and located the gift shop. ("There is always a gift shop," Mrs. Kallman had told Laverne.) In the gift shop, there would be a person toting the same kind of tortoise-shell hard-sided carry-on that Mrs. Kallman had. They would notice and laugh over this coincidence, and then go their separate ways, having subtly exchanged their identically odd bags. Later, Mrs. Kallman would transfer the contents of the carry-on—to all appearances, a supply of inexpensive souvenirs— to her checked bag for the return flight.

"That's all you need to do, Laverne," Mrs. Kallman had said. "Switch bags and then enjoy two days of sightseeing. Don't miss the Summer Palace."

The most obvious wrench in the works was not knowing where in
*The World of Pondside* the location of the gift shop would be revealed.
Foster, or one of the others, had to find that Easter egg! Only then
would Laverne's escort get a message on his Chinese cellphone that
told them where in the real world to go in order to make the exchange.
The uncertainty of the arrangement bothered Laverne, of course, despite assurances from Mrs. Kallman that (a) the message would come,
and (b) if it didn't, then all Laverne had to do was a little sightseeing,
followed three days later by the long journey home.

Lying in that enormous bed and looking out the soundproof hotel
window at the rows of twinkling lights on the runway, Laverne fully expected to be awake all night. She was quite surprised when she opened
her eyes to the chiming of Tori Mahoney's cellphone in the morning. At
breakfast, which was not complimentary, Tori selected a table as far from
Keith as possible, and although Laverne knew that this was all part of the
plan—"Loose lips sink ships," Mrs. Kallman had said, explaining why
she and Keith always kept their distance en route to Beijing—Laverne
could tell (or thought she could tell) that Tori Mahoney was perfectly
happy to sit down with her back to Keith and to the CNN newscast
blaring from the wall-mounted screen over his head.

They took the shuttle (which *was* complimentary) from the hotel to
the international terminal, where Tori Mahoney helped Laverne check
in for her flight, holding onto Mrs. Kallman's carry-on and cane while
Laverne boldly presented Mrs. Kallman's passport to the agent behind
the counter. From there, Tori escorted Laverne to airport security. Tori
got a little misty-eyed at that point and gave Laverne a surprise kiss on
the cheek, right there in front of the TSA officials and people waiting in
line, before she handed over Mrs. Kallman's cane. Laverne would have
preferred to use her own aluminum cane, which was currently collapsed
inside the checked bag, but Mrs. Kallman had said (and Tori agreed)
that her fancier wooden one would make it easier for Laverne to walk
through security without setting off alarms. Mrs. Kallman's cane was
made of solid hardwood with a veneer of ebony. Inlaid ivory leaves and
flowers traveled up and down the glossy black length of it, the initials

*SAK* following the curve of the handle. It wasn't collapsible, but Mrs. Kallman said that the flight attendant would put it in a closet. All Laverne had to do was ask.

At the security checkpoint, they gave Mrs. Kallman's fancy cane a nerve-rackingly long look—so long a look that Laverne wished Mrs. Kallman had just kept the darn thing, initials and all. When she was finally reunited with "her" belongings and seated again in the wheelchair that would carry her to the gate, Laverne made a point of lifting the cane to the brim of her fedora in a gallant salute, just in case Tori Mahoney was still watching from the other side of the security checkpoint.

# CHAPTER 27

His grandparents' porch was *not* where Foster expected to land in *The World of Pondside*. Where was the white stone bridge, the monastery, the *Next Level*? Where was Robert? Why was Foster back here in his portal (but with no Mrs. Kallman and no doll on the ancient card table)?

He used the mouse to move closer to the big screened windows enclosing the porch. When he looked out through the branches of the nearest tree, he had a shock. Instead of the generic landscape of hills and trees and a river—*Grant Wood digital*, Robert called it when Foster asked him for something to use as the view from the porch—Foster was looking down at a mix of city streets and countryside and other oddities that stretched to the horizon. It was a patchwork, from block to block, of brownstones, Victorians, high-rises, and little business districts; he could see the awnings like colorful flags. An island of skyscrapers shimmered in the middle distance, beyond them a stretch of sparkling blue. Foster recognized none of it until he saw the Golden Gate Bridge emerging from the mist, looking orange-red and familiar and a little too big in scale to go with the nearby skyscrapers. And there, beside the Golden Gate, an equally outsize and old-fashioned stadium—you could almost see the rivets from here—poked out from behind the skyscrapers. It was Laverne Slatchek's San Francisco. He was looking at portals! This was a landscape of individual portals side by side—many, many more than could be found in *The World of Pondside* as they knew it, portals as far as the eye could see, times and places mashed together with no regard for geography or scale.

"Holy coq," Foster typed in the chat line without taking his eyes from the screen.

"Holy cock, huh?" a snarky old man's voice said.

When he turned around on the screened porch, Foster had another shock. Three of the four chairs at his grandparents' card table were occupied by Laverne Slatchek (looking a little younger than the real Laverne but still with the silvery-gray hair "so Bill will recognize me," she'd explained when Foster was working on her avatar), Duane Lotspeich (two legs stretched out in front of him, crossed at the ankles), and the glamorous Katherine Landiss, wearing wickedly slim pants (a silk and rayon blend laced with spandex, Foster happened to know, having borrowed them from a designer website and optimized them himself). Their faces were smoother, less finely detailed, and thus a bit younger-looking than their real faces, but all of them were clearly recognizable as their *World of Pondside* selves.

"I think he meant to type 'Holy cow,'" Laverne Slatchek both typed and said in a young woman's voice quite unlike her own.

"Do we have to type what we want to say?" Duane complained from the corner of the library. "We're all in the same room. Can't we just talk?"

"Where are we, anyway?" Landiss wanted to know. The tone of her real voice was a perfect match for the arch of her carefully shaped eyebrow on-screen. Foster had picked the right default expression for Katherine Landiss, that was for sure.

"That's what I was going to ask," said Erika-as-Laverne.

Foster told them.

"You mean, this is your *World of Pondside* portal?" Landiss said.

"Looks like it."

She had moved herself over to the double doors that would have led into the house if there had been a full-fledged house attached to Foster's grandparents' porch. She jiggled the handles.

"Be careful there," Foster said.

Duane Lotspeich stood and walked on his two legs over to the screened-in wall of windows. "What the hell is all that?" he said, squinting out. "And what the hell are we doing back here, in *your* portal? I thought we were supposed to be in the *Next Level*. What happened to that place where we were, that park or whatever?"

Foster was about to remind them that he didn't know any more than they did about the *Next Level* when he spotted something on the shelf below the windows, where he used to run his trains. It was folded like a road map, the kind you pick up at a highway rest stop. He moused over, picked it up, and moved it to the card table. *World of Pondside* was printed in a script-like font across the top of the folded map, with a big bold *The Next Level* underneath it, all white letters against a plain blue background, a little yellow duck dotting the *i* in *Pondside*.

"It's a map!" Duane Lotspeich said. "Open it!"

"I'm thinking about it," Foster said.

"What is there to think about?" said Erika-as-Laverne.

"What might happen if I open it."

"Like what, for example?" asked Landiss.

"Oh, just open it," Erika-as-Laverne said.

Foster clicked on the map. It unfolded itself beautifully on the card table. It looked like the same jumbled business they could see from the screened windows, only flattened out and labeled. "It looks like a bunch of individual portals mashed together," Foster said. He bent over the map. "That's Manhattan over there, so maybe that's yours, uh—"

"Katherine." Landiss said it for him. She glanced around, her eyebrow arched, at the others on the porch. "You can all call me Katherine."

"And there"—he looked up, keeping one finger on the map and pointing with the other hand at the view beyond the porch—"you can see Golden Gate Bridge and Candlestick Park. That would be Laverne's portal."

"Candlestick Park?" Erika-as-Laverne said.

"It's an old baseball stadium," Foster said. "At least, it was in Laverne's day."

"Oh no. Not baseball."

"Don't let Laverne hear you say that."

"I *am* Laverne," she said.

"Then don't let anybody hear Laverne say that. Especially Bill."

"Who's Bill?"

"Who's Bill!" Duane Lotspeich and Foster said together.

"I thought Laverne briefed you," Duane added.

"Oh, is Bill her husband? I'm not sure she ever said his name. She always said, 'my husband.' I think she was feeling territorial." Erika-as-Laverne folded her arms across her chest on the screened porch. "She never mentioned baseball either."

"I don't see my Black Ops out there," Duane Lotspeich said. The *World of Pondside* version of him was still standing at the screened windows, hands on his hips, peering out, but his voice came from the corner of the library, where he sat in his wheelchair, squinting at the computer screen.

"It's here on the map, though," Foster said. "Maybe it's hard to see it down there where everything's crowded together. It looks like all our *Pondside* portals are on this map." *Plus a whole lot more,* he thought. Did each of the places laid out on this map of maps belong to a particular player? If so, there were a lot more people playing *World of Pondside*— or playing *something* that Robert had going—than Foster knew about. He supposed he shouldn't be surprised by that. He looked up from the map. How strange it was to see these characters on his grandparents' porch. "I'm guessing that we can go from one portal"—suddenly he felt a little self-conscious—"to another."

"Is that how the game works?" asked Erika-as-Laverne. "Is it like a race to the finish or something? Do we collect stuff? Earn points?"

Foster tried turning the map over, whereupon it went missing, the card table and bits of the floor along with it, just a green square of nothingness in its place. Apparently, the *Next Level* was not quite coded down to the last detail. Flipping it back to its incredibly detailed right side, Foster couldn't blame Robert, or whoever had made the map, for leaving the underside undone. "There are no instructions. I think we just—go."

"Go where?" Landiss was still standing by the French doors. "Can we go inside?" she said and gave the handles another tug.

"There is no inside," Foster said.

"What do you mean?"

"My portal is the porch. That's all."

"You mean it just drops off on the other side of this door?" She turned and pressed her nose against one of the glass panes, trying to see inside.

"It doesn't drop off. It's just not there."

"Then how do we get off this porch?"

Foster looked down over the edge of the shelf that ran along the bottom of the porch screens. "Looks like we jump."

"Fun!" said Laverne in her Erika voice.

"We can't *jump*," Landiss said in horror. "We'll all be killed."

"Who cares?" Erika-as-Laverne said. "It's a computer game."

"That's reassuring," said Landiss, peering down at the jumble of cityscapes and so forth below them.

"You always get extra lives in a computer game." Erika tapped her keyboard. On-screen, silver-haired Laverne had no trouble hopping up on the shelf where Foster used to run his trains. "Look at this!" she said in Erika's enthusiastic voice, and she held up a bungee cord attached to the harness that had appeared on her character. The screened window melted away in front of her and with a cheerful "Whoo-hoo!" she was gone.

# CHAPTER 28

Laverne had enjoyed the wheelchair ride through the airport—chatting with the young man in what Laverne would have called a skycap uniform who was going to school to become a pilot—but now that he had deposited her at Gate 37 in Concourse B, just in time to hurry up and wait for a few more hours, she found herself wallowing in regret. Here she was, it suddenly occurred to her as she observed everyone around her glued to their phones and other devices, sitting out the greatest *World of Pondside* adventure of all time. Sure, sure, she was having a *real* adventure, but from this end of it—at least since she had gotten through security without a hitch, despite the long look they gave the cane—a real trip to China was looking less like the opportunity of a lifetime and more like fourteen hours on a plane. Keith, her escort, told her she would fall asleep on the flight and wake up in China before she knew it. He looked like he was getting a head start over there, on the other side of the seating area.

She hoped she hadn't made a mistake by letting that girl, Erika, take her place in the game. Laverne couldn't help wondering what Bill was going to think when he came up to someone who looked like Laverne but actually had a twentysomething girl "inside," or at the helm, or whatever would be the right way to describe Erika controlling Laverne's character. Would Bill even notice the difference? Would there be any difference for him to notice? What if Bill liked Erika, disguised as Laverne, better than he liked Laverne? She was reminded of those Shakespeare plays, where the guy falls for somebody who is only disguised as his girl or vice versa. The phrase "wolf in sheep's clothing" came to mind. She knew very well that her questions and worries were absurd, that Bill wasn't really *there* in *The World of Pondside*, any more than they really watched the Giants play at Candlestick Park or went to Dairy Queen there. *In her head*, she knew these things. In her heart, she felt otherwise.

Oh well, like the kitchen boy said, *The World of Pondside* would be waiting for her when she got back. She couldn't believe she'd forgotten that boy's name again! He wasn't a boy either. He was a young man. A young man named—she held her breath, trying to trick herself into remembering—ah, never mind. The secret to remembering something was to forget about it, distract yourself, let whatever it was sneak up on you while you were occupied by something else entirely. Laverne decided it was time to visit the ladies'—always a good place to let your mind wander.

When the lights went out in the family restroom near Gate B37—a one-holer that Laverne had chosen because of the long line trailing out of the regular women's restroom upon the arrival at Gate B36 of a flight from Cozumel—Laverne was startled, but only for a moment. It didn't take her long to figure out what the problem was: she'd been sitting too long, thinking. The motion sensor that turned the lights on and off had forgotten she was in here and plunged the restroom into darkness. It was exceptionally deep darkness, the kind that was impossible to find back at Pondside Manor, between the exterior lights shining on the building, the bright fluorescent hall lights seeping under your door, and the multiple plug-in nightlights that were required by law in facilities that housed the trip-and-break-a-hip-prone elderly.

Here, when the lights went out, they went out. The darkness was like a black velvet bag dropped over Laverne's head. She looked around but there was *nothing* to see—ah, except for a bright seam of light that appeared quite suddenly from under the door when she turned her head to the right. As she grew more accustomed to the dark, she could also see the silver reflection on the stainless steel toilet paper dispenser near her knees and the grab bar gleaming above it on her left. She reached for the bar, missed, and reached again. Missed again. She tried closing her eyes and putting her hand where she knew the grab bar was supposed to be—and there it was. She had it! She opened her eyes and waved her other hand in the air, thinking, *Let there be light.* When the light came on, she was surprised to see that the grab bar appeared to have moved three or four feet away, toward the corner of the restroom, almost to the adjoining wall. And yet her fingers were still curled around it.

*Uh-oh,* she thought. This looked like trouble.

When she got herself to the mirror above the sink, her suspicions were confirmed. She looked as if someone had taken her by the chin and the forehead and given them a pull and a twist. Her face was stretched out like a piece of warm taffy, one eye missing—no, not missing, just misplaced. As she kept looking, the one eye would do its best to pull away from the other one and go back where it belonged. She blinked once, twice, turned her head this way and that, until the missing eye materialized in more or less the right spot, which is to say, next to the other one, although it remained cantilevered upward and, every now and then, would disappear.

Laverne recognized the look all too well. When she'd had the stroke that took out her right field of vision, the world had undergone similar distortions. For weeks, she had to wait for people to open the mouths in their weird faces and speak before she could recognize them. At the sink in the family restroom, she was just thinking, *Goodbye to Beijing,* when the face in the mirror suddenly returned to normal. Not that normal was any great shakes when it came to Laverne's face nowadays. Still, she could not remember ever feeling quite so relieved to see her wrinkled cheeks and saggy jawline and milky blue eyes looking back at her. She waited, blinked, looked away, and looked back at the mirror. It had gone away! She didn't have a stroke! Not a full-fledged one, anyway. It was, perhaps, one of those temporary reduced blood flow things with the initials TIA that did not stand for anything Laverne could remember. Of course, she should probably tell somebody that she'd had one of those. That's what anyone in their right mind would do. However, if she did that, she would almost certainly miss "her" flight.

She had to stop thinking about "her" flight and "her" passport in quotation marks, Laverne told herself sternly, not for the first time.

Just then the toilet flushed, which made her jump. After all this standing around and looking at herself in the mirror, she had better get cracking. Keith, her escort, was probably getting ready to send a rescue team into the family restroom. She washed her hands, waved three times at another motion sensor, thinking, *Let there be towels!* before it gave her one. Then she lifted the cane from where she'd hung it on the door handle. She waited a moment in the family restroom doorway (to make sure she wouldn't land in the path of someone hurrying to make a flight) and stepped out carefully, cane first, into Concourse B.

Back in her seat in the gate area, Laverne sat up straight and turned her head slowly to the left, casting much of the gate area into the dim fog that was her right field of vision. Then she turned her head, slowly, all the way to the right, as far as she could turn it, to bring the gate area back into view. She was relieved to find the faces and arms and legs of all the travelers in her field of vision appropriately located and looking normal in size and shape.

She would have to be very careful, she thought, from here on out.

# CHAPTER 29

In the silence that followed Erika-as-Laverne's leap off the porch, Foster joined Landiss and Lotspeich at the screened windows, and they all looked down. There was no sign of Erika-as-Laverne. The bungee cord appeared to have vanished as well.

"Where did she go?" Landiss asked in a small voice.

"She might have jumped off the grid," Foster said.

"What does that mean?"

"Usually, if you go beyond the borders of the grid, your guy—I mean, your character—disappears."

"Forever?"

"Nah." Erika Peterson's voice came at them from her table in the library. "I'll probably show up again when you get to the next map. I mean, *Laverne* will show up again."

"But first," Duane Lotspeich said without much enthusiasm, "we have to jump off the porch?"

"Or we could take the elevator," Katherine Landiss said. She had moved back to the doors she'd been fiddling with earlier.

"What elevator?" said Foster. "There isn't any—"

*Ding!* interrupted him. The pair of doors slid open, and Katherine Landiss stepped through the doorway, disappearing from view until she stuck her head back out and called, cheerily, "Going down?"

The doors closed and the elevator clicked so smoothly into motion that only the echoey hum, as of invisible cables overhead, suggested that Foster, Duane, and Katherine Landiss were moving—that and the changing red numbers in the LED display.

"For the record," Foster announced, "I had nothing to do with this elevator."

"Wait a minute." Duane Lotspeich pointed with his chin to the red numbers. "Aren't we going up?"

They were—if you could believe the numbers. Foster noticed that the floor buttons on the panel next to the elevator doors were unlabeled except for the one on the bottom, which was marked *Porch*, and the one for the twenty-fourth floor, which had a brass faceplate next to it that said in fancy script: *Katherine*.

Landiss shrieked. "This is my building!" she cried as the elevator came to a barely perceptible stop. "We're in my building! Look! This is my floor!"

The elevator doors opened, and Katherine Landiss stepped out, her digital Stuart Weitzman boots clicking realistically on the polished concrete floor.

"What do you mean, *your* floor?" Duane Lotspeich asked as he followed her out of the elevator. "What is all this?"

Foster recognized the Manhattan offices of Katherine Landiss by Design, which he had assembled and coded himself, right down to the art on the walls and the two red desks where two young women sat and vied for the privilege of delivering the boss's coffee and hanging up her coat. Obviously, Duane Lotspeich had never seen *The Devil Wears Prada*, or he, too, would have recognized the spacious and many-windowed suite as a total rip-off of Meryl Streep's office in the movie, which Foster had to watch twice—an ordeal he had gotten through by turning the volume to mute the second time around and listening instead to the *Star Wars* soundtrack playing in another window on the Dell—in order to reproduce all the underlings and objects (chiefly, clothes) that Landiss required in her portal.

The elevator door slid shut behind them. At the red desk that curved away to their left, a young woman who would have fit right into an ad in *Vogue* (which is where Foster had found her) changed her pout to a brilliant smile and said, "Good morning, Miss Landiss! Are you ready for your latte?"

Landiss clicked the Alberto Pinto coffee mug on the desk and a steaming mug promptly appeared in Katherine's hand on-screen. She sipped as she looked over the leather-bound calendar that lay open on the red desktop. "Thank you, Belle," she said in a cool but somehow still ecstatic voice. "What do we have on the schedule today?"

"Mr. Vuitton has some things to show you? In the sample room?"

"Tell him I'll be right in," Landiss said. She *clip-clopped* away across the gleaming concrete, leaving Foster and Duane with the assistant, who was still smiling brilliantly.

"Now what?" Duane said.

The young woman responded, "Good morning, Miss Landiss. Are you ready for a latte?"

"Tap the mug," Foster told Duane.

"Don't mind if I do," Duane said, "but I wish she wouldn't call me Miss Landiss."

Foster shrugged. "I didn't think anyone else would ever come through here."

"Through where?" Duane said. "Aren't we in the *Next Level*? I thought you didn't know anything about the *Next Level*."

"I don't," Foster said, "but my grandparents' porch and this office suite look pretty much the same as they were in"—he wasn't sure what to call it—"in the original *World of Pondside*. Except for the elevator and the map connecting everything."

Duane sniffed at the steaming mug in his hand. He raised it to his lips and scowled. "This stuff doesn't taste like anything. Must be low-cal."

"Maybe we have to go through all of our own portals before we even *reach* the *Next Level*," Foster said, thinking about it.

"That's not how it worked before," Duane complained. "We went straight from the porch—with Mrs. Kallman and that weird doll on the table—to the place where Robert Kallman was on that bridge."

"I think we should split up," Foster said. "We can cover more territory that way. You find Black Ops, and I'll try to get to Candlestick Park, see if I can locate Erika."

"Laverne, you mean," Erika called from her corner of the library.

"How am I supposed to find Black Ops?" said Duane. "And also, what the hell are we looking for?" He peered at Foster and then past him. "Well, well," he said in a different tone of voice. "What have we here?"

It was Katherine Landiss coming their way, back already from the sample room and wearing a different outfit. Foster recognized the sparkly Valentino gown featuring "fun fringe and a daring plunge neckline," one of several dresses he'd found on a website last spring in a story about the Golden Globe Awards. One of the features of the Katherine Landiss portal was that her character changed clothes every few minutes. This dress fit her like a glove—thus, Duane's ogling. Katherine Landiss had quite a nice figure in *The World of Pondside*, but Foster was more interested in what was rolling along on the floor behind her, partly hidden by the fringe that swung from her knees like a beaded curtain as she walked.

"Look what I found in the sample room!" she said. "Is this what we're looking for? The Easter egg?"

It was a hard-sided tortoise-shell carry-on that looked just like the one Tori Mahoney had brought for Laverne. Seeing it here in *The World of Pondside* gave Foster a sudden rise and fall of the stomach—like riding over a speed bump on his bike. It looked like this was it. They'd found it already! If the information they were looking for was inside—

"Does it open?" he asked.

"I don't know." Katherine Landiss looked down at the carry-on as if it were a dog—or a turtle—on a leash. At her laptop in the library, Kitty Landiss double-clicked it. Nothing happened. On the screen, Katherine crouched next to it in her glittering second skin of a dress, the better to tug on the pair of fasteners that appeared to hold the suitcase shut.

Duane Lotspeich edged closer to her on-screen. "Can *I* try?"

She shot him a look from under that arched eyebrow. As she stood up, her glittery Valentino morphed into a sunshine yellow off-the-shoulder gown from the Michael Kors Collection. "Please do."

"Wait a minute," Foster began, but he was too late. Duane double-clicked and the carry-on popped open. They all flinched. Inside was what appeared to be a piece of paper folded into a two-inch square. Foster was about to say, "Don't click on it!" when the paper began to unfold itself, opening into bigger and bigger squares until two words appeared in bold black letters.

"Black Ops!" Lotspeich read aloud from the corner of the library, and by the time his character could look up, puzzled, on the screen, the scene had changed. Darkness had fallen—sudden, impenetrable darkness from which Duane Lotspeich's voice seemed to come, sounding a little rueful. "Guess I found it."

"What's going on?" Katherine Landiss cried.

The sound of a nearby explosion answered her. The floor trembled under their feet. What looked like tracer fire erupted, red lines criss-crossing the dark screen.

"Oh my God," she said, "people are *shooting* at us!"

"What do you expect from something called *Black Ops?*" Duane shouted over the combat noises.

"This is Black Ops? I thought you said Black Ops was a dance studio!"

"It is!" Duane grabbed Katherine's hand, dropped into a half crouch, and said, "Follow me!" He looked back over his shoulder and shouted at Foster. "Come on!"

"Think I'll sit this one out," Foster yelled. He felt around on the ground for the carry-on. It seemed to have disappeared. Finally, he gave up and crawled off, under heavy fire, in the direction of the elevator.

At least, he hoped he was heading back toward the elevator. All he really knew, crawling under a low ceiling of black smoke, was that the sounds of gunfire and shouting and pounding footsteps (exactly like the ones Foster had sampled from a video on YouTube) were fading. If this was indeed the *Next Level*, then it had obviously been constructed using some of the portals Foster helped Robert put together, but the geography of it was new and had little to do with the layout on the map. On the map, the irregular gray patch labeled *Black Ops* was nowhere near the island of skyscrapers labeled

*Manhattan*, and his grandparents' screened porch was a long way from both. Obviously, geography was irrelevant when it came to finding your way from place to place. Instead, what you had to do was open the right carry-on or unfold a certain note. Or take the elevator. Or jump off the porch.

The map was in Foster's back pocket. He pulled it out and, throwing all caution to the wind, he flapped the map open by giving it one hard shake—which is to say, by clicking on it twice. It floated, magic-carpet style, for a moment before it sank slowly to the ground. He squatted to have a closer look at the haphazard arrangement of worlds on the map: a grove of oak trees sloping down toward a graying frame farmhouse took up about the same amount of space as what looked like most of Manhattan, which was right next to the farmhouse. On the other side of the oak grove, a warren of gray-walled alleys gave way to an old-fashioned drugstore with a sign out front—here Foster found out that he could point and hold to zoom—that said *Pearson's*. Above the store was a dance hall full of soldiers in shined shoes and uniforms. Candlestick Park was still out there in what would have been the northwest corner of the map if this had been a map with any respect for the compass.

"How did you do this?" Foster said aloud. "Where did all of this come from?"

"Who are you talking to?" somebody said.

In the library, Foster almost fell out of his chair.

Erika Peterson was looking at him over the upper edge of her laptop screen. "Sorry," she said. "I didn't mean to startle you."

He looked around the room. "Where did the other two go?"

"Bathroom break," said Erika.

"Together?"

"Separately, but at the same time."

"Oh," he said. "So where are you?"

"In the ballpark."

"That's where I thought you might be."

"The game seems to be stuck in the bottom of the first inning. I've seen this same strike out, like, nine times. Care to join me?"

"Soon as I figure out how to get there," Foster said.

"Have you tried double-clicking?"

In the library, Foster looked at Erika for another moment—and then he turned back to his screen. The map he'd spread out on the ground had changed. Candlestick Park was bigger and more central, as if he'd zoomed in on it. And maybe he had, since the yellow duck in the "You Are Here" cape appeared to have landed at Gate A, the one Laverne and Bill always entered when they went to the Giants game in *The World of Pondside*. (It was the gate closest to Dairy Queen.) Foster could see that the arrow of his cursor was hovering over the gate. He double-clicked and he was in the ballpark.

The concourse was deserted except for a silvery-haired woman sitting on a concrete bench opposite the concession stand. She was leaning back against the cement block wall.

"Laverne!" Foster said, and the woman straightened up. As he crossed the concourse, Foster saw the turtle-like suitcase at her feet. Another one! "Where did you get that?"

"I found it under a seat," Erika's voice responded.

"How did you know where to look?"

"I looked under every seat. Luckily, only the first row in each section is interactive. It was under seat sixteen in row one of section VR three-one-three," she said, and suddenly, they were in the stands. "Right here, actually. That's the seat. You're sitting in it. Pretty good seat, if you like watching baseball."

They heard the crack of a bat, the roar of the crowd—which they were suddenly surrounded by—and here comes a high foul ball that's heading straight for them. Although he knows the ball will sail over their heads, Foster ducks and so does Laverne. When they straighten up, she has a baseball glove in her lap. The carry-on is at their feet. Fans a few rows back are whooping and jumping because one of them caught the ball.

"You have to be careful when you open it," Foster said, nodding toward the little suitcase.

"It doesn't open." Erika-as-Laverne looked out over the field. "This stadium is really impressive."

Foster clicked on the suitcase once, twice, three times. On-screen, he appeared to be kicking it.

"It doesn't open," Erika pointed out again. "Hey!" she said. "Isn't that Bill pitching? It is. It's Bill!"

Foster looked up. The lanky guy on the mound did indeed look like Laverne's husband. Bill was not supposed to be pitching, was he? "How do you know it's Bill?"

"Because it says so right there." She pointed to the score sheet in Foster's hand, the lineup already filled in. "Bill Slatchek. Isn't that Laverne's name? Slatchek?"

Bill, the pitcher, releases the ball. The batter hits another high foul that's heading straight for them. Erika-as-Laverne struggles with the glove, trying to get it on in time. Foster ducks again, and when he straightens up, the fans a few rows back are whooping and jumping.

"It's the wrong kind of glove," Erika complained.

"What are you talking about?"

"It's a left-handed one."

"What does it matter?"

"What does it *matter*?" she said. "Have you ever caught a baseball?"

"No," he said. (Only then did it occur to Foster that this was the sort of thing you might not want to admit, especially to someone like Erika or, for that matter, Laverne.)

"Are you left-handed?" Erika said.

"I am." *This is crazy*, Foster thought. Bill was not supposed to be pitching. Bill was supposed to be sitting next to Laverne. *Bill* was supposed to catch the ball so the game could move on. He was supposed to be sitting right where Foster was sitting, and he was supposed to— *uh-oh*—catch the ball.

"Bill's left-handed, too," Erika said, shoving the glove at Foster.

"No!" he said, but it's already on his hand. His left fist is punching the pocket.

The ball comes at them again. Foster closes his eyes and holds the glove up over his head.

*Thwap!* He's got it. The crowd goes wild.

# CHAPTER 30

Laverne didn't know how long she had been waiting at Gate B37, trying to remain vigilant, stealing glances at people's faces and looking hard and long at anyone whose appearance seemed to waver, before she dozed off. The next thing she knew, someone was touching her shoulder and saying, "Mrs. Kallman? Mrs. Kallman?" Laverne was a split second away from telling the tired-looking woman in an airline skirt and blouse and little necktie that Mrs. Kallman was in the hospital when the woman said, "It's time to board," and the whole business—the opportunity of a lifetime!—came flooding into Laverne's brain just in time. Behind the airline lady, she saw that the waiting area was deserted. The airline lady glanced around, too, and signaled to a not-so-young man in airport-blue waiting nearby with a wheelchair. He looked as if he'd been running. "You were sleeping so nicely that I thought we'd wait before we rolled you down the jet bridge," the airline lady said as the man pushed the wheelchair closer to Laverne's knees. "It's a bit of a bumpy ride."

Although she suspected that it was the arrival of an available wheelchair they'd been waiting for, Laverne did her best to channel Mrs. Kallman's genteel manner. She told the airline lady and the wheelchair man, "That's very nice, thank you."

Laverne was rolling down the jet bridge with Mrs. Kallman's cane and her hard-shelled carry-on in her lap before she thought to wonder what happened to Keith. She hoped he had boarded ahead of her. The thought of going all the way to China by herself was, she had to admit, daunting. Tori Mahoney had given her a card with key phrases written in English and in Chinese characters—so intricate and lovely—but that wasn't much comfort.

When it was time to leave the wheelchair behind at the door to the aircraft, Laverne allowed the airline lady to take her by the elbow and guide her down the aisle, rolling her carry-on like a stroller in front of her. They had to stop and start a few times to let people squeeze past them or pop up to put something in the overhead bin and take it out again. It was the biggest airplane Laverne had ever been on—two aisles with three seats, and then three seats, and then three more across—and it was bustling with passengers and crew members. A flight attendant with an armful of plastic-wrapped blankets pointed Laverne and the airline lady to a row of three empty seats. Mrs. Kallman's was the one by the window.

"We might have a couple of no-shows here," the flight attendant said. She was a young Asian woman who had been speaking what Laverne assumed was Chinese to another passenger a moment ago. Behind the flight attendant, a few rows farther up the aisle, a familiar-looking man in a black T-shirt with orange lettering leaned out of his aisle seat. He gave Laverne a quick thumbs-up. It was what's-his-name. Keith.

"This could be your lucky day!" the flight attendant said before she moved on, handing out blankets in English and Chinese.

Laverne wasn't feeling particularly lucky. She was feeling strange. Part of the strangeness was undoubtedly coming from her own brain. If only she hadn't had that little Transatlantic Incident in the restroom, she thought, her head might be clearer.

The whole thing was pretty crazy. If she weren't actually sitting here, on this airplane, wearing Mrs. Kallman's linen travel outfit, she, Laverne, would probably think that she was going to wake up any moment in her own bed, having dreamed the whole "real-life adventure." That sort of thing used to happen to her all the time. She would dream a long, lovely afternoon with Bill—or even a not-so-lovely afternoon—and it would feel so real that when she woke up, it would take her a while to figure out which was the dream and which the waking. Maybe they were waiting for the streetcar, trying to make first pitch, and every car that came would be full, people hanging off the back and on the steps, and Bill just about tearing his hair out until she told him, "Go on, take the next one and I'll catch up with you at the ballpark," and only after he jumped up onto the streetcar and went on without her did she remember that the tickets for the game were in her purse. Bill had gone on without her—and he didn't have the tickets! They weren't going to let him in, she told Foster, who happened to hop off the next streetcar right in front of her. He said, "Don't worry, Laverne! It's only a game."

"*Foster*!" Laverne thought, her eyes opening wide. *That* was the kitchen boy's name. How could she have forgotten?

"Actually, I'm Eammon," said a voice on her left. She turned her head and looked down. The formerly empty seat was now occupied by a small boy. He had dark-brown hair and brown eyes and a space where one of his two front teeth should have been. Laverne felt vaguely that she knew him from somewhere. At any rate, he was giving her a friendly smile. He had one of those connect-the-dots coloring books on his tray table. It looked too complicated for a child his size, but he had succeeded in connecting enough dots for Laverne to see that the picture was of Mount Rushmore. Laverne was not particularly disappointed to find the little boy sitting next to her, despite her loss of the empty seat. The trouble was that she had absolutely no recollection of his arrival.

"We got here just in time," the little boy informed her. "You were sleeping. I thought maybe you were dead, but then I could see you breathing."

Laverne resisted the impulse to thank him for taking a closer look. A glance out the window told her that the plane, though rumbling, was still on the ground.

"We're fifth in line for takeoff," the little boy said. He leaned forward and stretched his neck, trying to see past Laverne to the window. Then he sat back. He lowered his voice to say, confidentially, "I'm not supposed to tell anybody what I just did." He paused for effect, then leaned closer and whispered, "I peed in a bottle!"

Laverne's eyes darted to a Coke bottle lodged in the seatback pocket next to what looked like a fourteen-hour supply of connect-the-dots books. The boy nodded. He looked quite pleased with himself. "I had to go, but the seat belt sign is on," he explained. He leaned toward her again and added, whispering pointedly, "Desperate measures, you know!"

The child was very well-spoken, Laverne thought. She would have guessed his age at six or seven, based on his size and missing tooth, but he sounded older. A man in the aisle seat a few rows up was looking back over his shoulder at them. Laverne felt she knew him, too. Was it the boy's father? No! Of course not. It was Keith.

"I like your cane," the little boy said. "Are those your initials?"

"What? Oh, yes." Laverne had stuck the cane between her seat and the next one, hoping the flight attendant wouldn't see it there. The beautifully etched *SAK* was only a few inches from the little boy's head. He said something else that she didn't quite catch.

"I beg your pardon?" she said.

"I'm like the son you never had," he repeated, still with the friendly smile.

"But I did—I do—have a son."

"Is he anything like me?"

"No, no, he's not."

The boy raised his eyebrows significantly, as if to say, *See what I mean?* He patted her hand on the armrest, which made Laverne pull her hands into her lap.

"Take it easy," said a familiar-sounding male voice.

Laverne looked up. The man sitting on the other side of the boy, in the previously empty seat on the aisle, was smiling at her. "This trip was your idea, after all."

"Bill?" She didn't mean to whisper, but that was all the breath she had. Even as she said it, a subtle change took place in the man's face. He looked younger all of a sudden. "My son's not bothering you, is he, ma'am?" He sounded younger, too. It wasn't Bill after all. No, of course it wasn't.

"Not at all," Laverne said automatically. She held out a shaky hand, first to the man and then to the boy, and did her best to smile in what she imagined to be a grandmotherly fashion. "Pleased to meet you," she said. "My name's Laverne."

The boy grasped her fingers with his small hand and gave them a boisterous shake. "I'm Eammon," he reminded her—and did he wink at her?—before he went back to his connect-the-dots book. She watched for a while, mostly to avoid glancing at the boy's father, as Teddy Roosevelt's head took shape in a staccato series of pencil moves. About mid-mustache, the pencil stopped. Eammon leaned toward her and whispered, without looking up from Mount Rushmore, "Laverne doesn't start with S." The pencil moved on.

# CHAPTER 31

"I can't believe we had to watch the whole game," Erika-as-Laverne said. They were back on the concourse, near the concession stand.

Foster shrugged. "Laverne wanted extra innings."

"Okay, but couldn't you throw in some home runs? Just to spice it up a little? I mean, no score till the bottom of the *twelfth*? And it wasn't even a no-hitter."

That was Foster's mistake. It was supposed to be a no-hitter. Laverne had been after him to fix the sixth inning, when the other team's leadoff hitter got a single up the middle. "Laverne hates home runs," he said. "She's always on the pitcher's side. Hey—look who's here."

Duane Lotspeich and Katherine Landiss were coming down the concourse, side by side. She was wearing a Versace gown that Foster recognized. Duane was in a tuxedo. He had two carry-on suitcases in tow, one trailing from each hand. Landiss had a large ice cream sundae in one hand and a long red plastic spoon in the other.

"I don't see why you call it Black Ops," she was saying to Lotspeich as they drew nearer. "It's totally misleading."

"That's the point of *black ops*—to be misleading."

They stopped when they spotted Foster and Laverne. Katherine's Versace gown became a sporty jumpsuit by Calvin Klein.

"Hey, Laverne! You survived your bungee jump!" Duane Lotspeich said. He pointed his chin at the carry-on leaning against the concrete bench. "You've got a suitcase, too?"

"Don't get excited," Foster told him. "This one is empty." It had been a great disappointment to him and Erika-as-Laverne, after the excitement of the ball landing in his glove and the suitcase popping open, to find there was nothing inside: no note, no darkness, no portal to another dimension, nothing. When it snapped shut, they were here, on the concourse again, near the concession stand. "Where'd you get yours?"

"We won a dance contest!" Katherine Landiss said. "Best Novelty Tango."

Duane lifted the carry-on in his left hand like a trophy. "Two free coupons for Dairy Queen in this one," he said.

"It was crazy," Landiss said. "The shooting stopped, the smoke cleared, and there we were on the dance floor!"

"They liked her costume changes-as-you-go," Duane said. "Some of those outfits—*whoa*." He called to Erika-as-Laverne, who was looking at the menu on the wall above the concession stand. "There's a DQ downstairs, right outside Gate A. Did you know that?"

Erika-as-Laverne turned to all of them and asked, "Who orders a *jelly* sandwich at the ballpark?"

Foster looked up at the menu. There it was, ballpark price and all: Grape Jelly Sandwich . . . nine dollars. A bowing, smiling Chinese-looking man appeared quite suddenly behind the counter, obviously ready to be of service.

"I'll have the jelly sandwich," Foster told him.

"You want hot pot?"

"No, I said the jelly sandwich."

The Chinese guy just looked at Foster. When Foster double-clicked him, he bowed. Erika-as-Laverne muttered pointedly, "Um—could we be any more racist in the depiction of an ethnic group other than our own?"

"I didn't depict this guy," Foster said. "I never saw him before."

"Except maybe in a hundred cartoons and movies," she grumbled.

"Excuse me?" Foster tried the guy behind the counter again. "The jelly sandwich, please? Make it four of them."

"*I* don't want a jelly sandwich!" Katherine Landiss said with disdain.

"They have other sandwich choices at Dairy Queen," Lotspeich pointed out. "Plus Pecan Mudslides. It's a kind of sundae."

"Hot pot!" the guy said. "Come this way," and he bowed again.

Erika had a point about the stereotype, Foster thought.

"What is hot pot?" Duane asked.

"It's good," said Erika-as-Laverne. "Like stir-fry except kind of boiled in oil."

"I don't think I like the sound of boiled in oil," Landiss said.

"Maybe it's broth, not oil," Erika-as-Laverne said. "Believe me, it beats a jelly sandwich."

The Chinese fellow had been standing by, but when Erika-as-Laverne said, "jelly sandwich" again, the words threw him into action.

"Hot pot!" he cried, more decisively than ever. "Come this way."

They didn't have to "come this way," or any way, as it turned out. The concession stand—indeed the whole concrete concourse of the stadium—suddenly flattened out and fell over, like a painted backdrop in a theater. Foster, Landiss, Lotspeich, and Erika-as-Laverne found themselves on a busy sidewalk, buffeted by generic-looking passersby, just outside the big storefront windows of a restaurant. Underneath large red Chinese characters on the windows were the words "Old Chang's Hot Pot," and standing in the doorway of the restaurant was the Chinese fellow from Candlestick Park, waving them in.

"Are we in China?" Duane Lotspeich and Landiss asked together.

"Look over there," Foster said. He pointed down the street to a distant skyline, where two orange-red peaks of the incorrectly located Golden Gate Bridge could be seen above the rooftops. "Laverne and Bill ate in Chinatown on their anniversary, at a place like this. If Laverne was here, she could tell you."

They all looked at Erika-as-Laverne. She shrugged. "Should we go inside?"

"I don't even know if there *is* an inside," Foster said.

"You're always saying that," Katherine Landiss said. She squinted and peered through the front windows. The man in the doorway continued to wave them in, tirelessly. "It looks like people in there. Lots of people, in fact. Why do you keep saying there's nothing inside?"

"I didn't help make it, that's all—the inside of the restaurant, I mean."

"But I thought you said Laverne and Bill ate here."

"In real life, I guess they did," Foster said, "but Laverne didn't give me any details about the inside. She just wanted to be able to walk down a street like this with Bill."

All the time they were talking, the Chinese fellow in the doorway— was it Old Chang himself?—continued to wave them in.

Inside—for there was an inside, which went on and on, repeating itself, like successive reflections in a series of mirrors—Old Chang seated them at a table with a large round hole cut in the middle of it to allow for the placement of an equally large round pot filled with murky bubbling liquid. Duane Lotspeich and Katherine Landiss looked at it doubtfully. Foster didn't blame them. Landiss sniffed once or twice. She was now wearing a white dress with a mandarin collar and a long jacket in a black-and-red bamboo print—an ensemble that Foster had never seen before. This was truly new territory, he thought.

"What next?" Katherine Landiss said, raising her skeptical eyebrow.

Erika-as-Laverne shrugged again. "They bring you stuff to put in the pot, and you let it cook and then you take it out and eat it. Be careful, though. It's hot!"

"What kind of stuff?" Duane asked.

"Meat and vegetables usually." She looked around. "There doesn't seem to be anyone else here all of a sudden, does there?" She had no sooner said this than every table was suddenly populated by duplicates of themselves.

"Not sure this is a positive development," Foster said.

"At least we can tell which ones are us," Katherine Landiss said. "We're the ones with the funny little suitcases. Except for you, Foster."

Foster saw that it was true. Leaning against the side of every chair but his was a carry-on suitcase like the one Tori had given Laverne. So far, the carry-ons seemed to be pulling them along through the game, or at least marking their trail. It seemed reasonable to conclude that Foster had to find one, too. Maybe Foster's would complete the set and then all four would pop open at once, and inside one or all of them would be the information they needed to give Laverne—Easter egg found.

"Or maybe I'm supposed to find something else," he said aloud.

Foster looked around the restaurant scene. When he scrolled up, he saw a shelf that ran along the walls a little below ceiling height. The shelf was crowded with decorative vases, ginger jars, smiling buddhas, and—he almost didn't believe his eyes—the doll! Nestled between two buddhas sat a baby doll in a pink dress and bonnet that looked like the one Mrs. Kallman was holding on his grandparents' porch, which, of course, looked like the one Foster had found tied to his bike, the one that found its way back, in sorry shape, to Mary McIntyre. The doll on the shelf held its chubby arms out as if it might be waiting for some-one to come along and carry it off. Foster stood up. He stepped on the seat of his chair and from there up onto the table, his foot mere inches from the boiling hot pot.

"What the hell are you doing?" Duane Lotspeich said.

"Oh, be careful!" said Katherine Landiss.

Foster reached up, and just as he got a good grip on the frilly pink dress and noticed, incidentally, that there was a folded note pinned to the doll's chest, here came Old Chang, yelling. Behind him was a woman bearing a tray of serving dishes. Mrs. Chang? She shrieked. Foster dropped the doll.

Straight into the hot pot.

They all looked down at the doll roiling and turning in the bottom of the pot. The note unfolded and they could see marks of some kind, maybe writing, unreadable through the murk. Foster had already jumped down from the table. He slid his sleeve up and was about to plunge his hand into the pot when Katherine Landiss grabbed his arm.

"Wait! You can't put your hand in there. It's boiling hot!"

Foster looked her in the eye, thinking, oddly, that this was the first time he had ever looked Administrator Landiss in the eye. It reminded him of making eye contact with Tori Mahoney in the hospital waiting room. He said, "This is a computer game. If my arm falls off, it falls off."

"You might lose health points," warned Erika-as-Laverne. "Does the game keep track of that?"

Landiss let go of his arm. "But won't it hurt?"

All four of them stared into the murky, oily, boiling liquid.

"I don't know," Foster said. "We'll find out."

He reaches in, yells, and the hot pot overturns. Bubbling liquid flows out in all directions, making everyone fall back from the table, yelling. Foster is twirling and turning through something like oil, like water, like nothing he's ever twirled through before, until he comes up from under the surface and people are still yelling. They're looking down over the rail of a white stone bridge, people he's never seen before, pointing at him and yelling. In Chinese, it sounds like. Someone extends a hand. He grabs it and lets himself be hauled up out of the water. In keeping with the laws of computer-game physics, he is dry by the time his feet gain the bridge, where he stands, toe to toe, with Robert Kallman.

# CHAPTER 32

Dakota was supposed to hold down the fort while Erika and the others were playing the game. Holding down the fort had become a kind of specialty for him, he noticed. This time, his particular job was to keep everybody else out of the library. Erika had given him this assignment earlier, when she came out of the library herself, purse on her shoulder and key fob in hand. She was off on a supply run for an all-nighter, she'd told him.

"You're going to be in there all night?" Dakota said.

"Actually, it could be longer. Can you stick around?"

"Till when?" His shift ended at eleven.

Erika didn't know, she admitted. It was hard for Dakota to make sense out of what she was saying. Something about Laverne Slatchek picking up a package for Mrs. Kallman. "The location of the actual package is revealed somewhere in *The World of Pondside*. We have to play the game and find out exactly where Laverne is supposed to go to get the package. Foster thinks we have about twenty-four hours to do it, tops, before she gets to China."

"Wait a minute," Dakota said. Laverne had left with Tori Mahoney. He had carried that weird little suitcase out to them. "Did you say, 'before she gets to *China*'?"

"*Shh!*" Erika looked around the deserted hallway.

"Laverne Slatchek is going to *China?*" Dakota whispered this. "China on the other side of the world? That China?"

"I thought you knew that," Erika whispered back. "Somebody has to pick up the package. Mrs. Kallman can't go."

"What's *in* this package she's picking up—in China?" he said.

"Drugs."

"*Drugs?*"

"A drug," she corrected herself. "Something Robert and a bunch of other people were taking. I guess it's not approved for ALS in this country."

Dakota hesitated. "Are you sure you should get mixed up in this?"

Erika frowned and shrugged.

*That didn't look like she was sure,* Dakota thought. "Maybe you should tell them to find somebody else, Erika."

"No!" she said. "I want to play the game." She had kissed him then, a quick one on the lips, and left in a hurry.

Holding down the fort had not been especially challenging thus far. No one had so much as approached the library door on Dakota's shift, much less attempted to gain entry, except for Amelia Ramirez, who peeked in a few times, and Dakota himself, who opened the door on the hour and always found the gamers glued to their screens and keyboards, headphones or earbuds in place, ignoring one another's presence but occasionally speaking with great animation to the screens in front of them.

Bert Reynolds, the third-shift nurse, who seemed to be in an exceptionally good mood when he came in at ten thirty, had gone to the library to see for himself what on earth Dakota was talking about. "Don't worry," Bert said. "I won't interrupt their little marathon." (That's how Dakota had described it—no mention of drugs or China.) "They won't even know I'm there." When he returned, looking a bit baffled but mostly amused, it was as if he hadn't heard a thing that Dakota had told him. "The boss is in there," he said. "Landiss! She's playing a *computer* game with the guy from the kitchen and what's-his-name with one leg—Duane—and a girl I never saw before." Dakota waited for the superlatives that usually accompanied sightings of Erika, but Bert

Reynolds only said, "What a hoot." He paused, like a man taking stock of something. Then he said, "What game did you say they were playing?"

"It's called *World of Pondside.*"

"What a hoot," Bert said again.

Dakota took one more peek into the library—there they were, the four of them, oblivious to his presence—before he pushed a reclining armchair into the conference room and found himself a blanket. It was surprisingly hard to think of leaving Erika in the library all night with Duane Lotspeich. He closed his eyes, expecting—or at least, hoping—that she would come looking for him before long, crazy mission accomplished (or abandoned) and ready to go home.

When he woke up, it was light outside, and someone was knocking sharply on the conference room door. He looked at the big toe sticking out of his left sock, down where the blanket fell short of his feet, and then at his phone. To his surprise, it was 7:43 a.m. The door opened and Kitty Landiss came in, very excited. She had a paper kitchen cap on her head. "You have to get out!" she said. "They'll want the conference room. Take that blanket and go!"

"Who—?" He struggled to right the recliner and get to his feet.

"It's the FBI!" she said. "Go get Foster." When Dakota only stared back at her, she cried, "Get him! Before they get to the library." She turned, apparently to go back out the door, then stopped. "Shit," she said and pulled the paper cap off her head.

Standing in the doorway, which led into the atrium and the dining room beyond, all Dakota saw and heard at first was the barely controlled chaos of breakfast in full swing. A few early visitors were signing in—a clergyman (by his collar), an old man with a bouquet of flowers, and a woman toting an oversized shoulder bag who was pushing a baby in a stroller. Then, through the glass doors of the vestibule, he saw the suits. Carol, the administrative assistant, was punching the keypad to let them in. There were four of them. Two looked familiar. They had been here before, asking questions. The other two he'd never seen before. *They must be the FBI*, he thought, although he wondered how Landiss knew that, since they hadn't even gotten in the building yet.

Dakota forced himself to walk, not run, through the atrium and down the hallway to Library Lane. The sounds of breakfast and other voices grew fainter behind him. When he reached the library and opened the door, he saw right away that things were different. Landiss was gone, of course, but that wasn't the main thing. It was the way both Erika and Duane were sitting back in their chairs, just watching their screens, Erika's hands folded in her lap, Duane's resting on the arms of his wheelchair. Only Foster was hunched forward over his laptop, his arms almost curled around it, as if he had just pulled it a little closer.

Dakota cleared his throat—he didn't want to come up from behind and startle anybody—and stepped through the doorway. That was as far as he got. Erika jumped up, her disconnected earbuds dangling. When she reached the door, she put her hands flat on Dakota's chest and pushed him back out into the hall.

"The police are here," Dakota managed to tell her. "And the FBI, Landiss said! They're looking for Foster!"

"He can't come now," Erika said, urgently. "He's talking to Robert!"

"He's talking to *whom*?"

"Wow," she said. "Maybe you *should* be a teacher."

"Oh, you mean in the game. He's talking to Robert in the game." Dakota looked over Erika's shoulder into the room. Foster hadn't budged. "But the police—"

"We have to stall them," she said, looking down Library Lane toward the atrium, which they couldn't see from here. "Create a diversion or something."

"What kind of diversion?"

"I don't know! We could start a fight?"

"Are you crazy? You want to get shot?"

"We have to do *something*," she said. Her hazel eyes were blazing. She looked back over her shoulder into the library, where they could see Foster gripping the sides of the laptop. Off to one side, out of sight, Duane Lotspeich suddenly said, "Well, shit. Lost my audio again." And then: "Goddamn it. Where'd he go?"

"On second thought, I'd better stay here," Erika whispered.

Against his better judgment, Dakota said, "I'll go see what I can do."

Foster wasn't exactly *talking* to Robert. Foster was still too stunned to speak to the man in gray pants and a white shirt who had pulled him up onto the bridge—for that's where they were, on the same white stone bridge he had first seen on the screen in Duane Lotspeich's room. Then, as now, Foster knew that the man was Robert Kallman. Or, more accurately, an electronic avatar of Robert Kallman. A new and digitally improved version, Foster thought, noting the raised eyebrows and almost feeling the warm grip of his hand, compared to the Robert who used to show up at the card table on Foster's grandparents' porch. The crowd of yelling people who had surrounded Foster when he first emerged from the water had dispersed or disappeared—he wasn't sure which. His brain was almost fully occupied by trying to decide if he could feel Robert's hand gripping his, or if just seeing it on the screen was enough to make the nerves in Foster's hand imagine firing.

He looked down at himself on-screen. There was no sign that he'd just come swirling through a pot of hot broth and no sign of the doll he had briefly but firmly grasped on the way, in the same hand that now grasped Robert's. When Foster looked up, Robert was smiling a broad and symmetrical smile. "Welcome to the *Next Level*!" he said in that wonderful broadcaster's voice. There was a beat here, a brief pause, an opportunity for Foster to reply. When he didn't, Robert continued, hearty and cheerful. "It's good to see you, Foster." With a final, friendly squeeze, he let go of Foster's hand. "I know I have some explaining to do," he said, "but first, I want to show you something."

In the library, Foster's head and heart were racing; his mouth was dry. He barely heard what Robert said next. Something about "the doors behind you." On-screen, Foster looked over his shoulder. A pair of great green copper doors led into a building that looked like a carved wooden box. Foster recognized the low cedar trees holding up their carefully trimmed branches in front of the building, and the glass-and-steel skyscrapers that looked so out of place above the roof. When he turned back to ask if this was the very same portal—based on some kind of monastery, wasn't it?—that Robert had shown him long ago, there was no one to ask. Foster was alone on the bridge.

In the atrium at Pondside Manor, four business-suited individuals were following Kitty Landiss—still in her apron but minus the paper hat— toward the door marked *Conference Room*, following her like ducklings, Dakota thought, or maybe more like ducks in a row. They walked right past the young woman who was leaning over the credenza, burdened by her large shoulder bag, trying to sign the visitor's log with one hand while her other hand pushed and pulled her fussing baby's stroller back and forth. A casual observer coming into the atrium at that particular moment would have had no reason to connect the young woman pushing the baby stroller with the old lady wringing her hands in a corner of the room, her eyebrows lowered in a way that made her look both worried and stern.

But Dakota was no casual observer. He was looking for trouble and, perhaps for that reason, he recognized it when he saw it. Even before Mary McIntyre stopped wringing her hands and took her first steps toward the baby in the stroller, Dakota had a pretty good idea of what was about to go down.

When Foster opened the copper doors, he was expecting something grander inside the building than a grassy field shaded by a couple of big trees. The field seemed to float in the otherwise undifferentiated space, and something like sunlight was everywhere, except for the center of the field, where the two trees made a generous patch of shade. The trees were the kind whose leaves sound exactly like rain when the wind rustles them. Foster couldn't think of what that kind of tree was called. As a matter of fact, he could hardly think at all.

"This is what I wanted to show you," said a voice behind him.

Foster spun around.

"Sorry about disappearing," Robert said, raising his hands—both hands, together—in a gesture of apology. "It's a glitch in the program. I've tried to fix it, but I can't quite find the right spot in the code."

"What is this . . . place?" Foster managed to say.

"This is my favorite portal," Robert said. He looked past Foster to the trees and smiled, as if he felt pretty good about it. "Does it ring a bell?"

Foster turned back to the field and the trees. There was something new in the scene now: two figures stretched out on the grass under one of the trees—each with his ankles crossed, his hands behind his head, looking up through the leaves. Now Foster recognized it. One time, more than a year ago, he and Robert had gone for a walk beyond the parking lot and the pond, and they had gotten to a pair of trees, tall ones, their leaves rustling like rain. It was Foster's idea to stretch out on the grass and look up at the sky through the branches. It was just something he liked to do, he'd explained to Robert. Foster had a heck of a time getting Robert out of his wheelchair and down on the ground, and after they got situated, neither one spoke for a while. Then Foster had said, "When I was a kid, I could ask my grandpa what kind of tree we were looking up at and he would always know."

"Cottonwoods," Robert had said, breathlessly.

Foster had turned his head and was surprised to see how normal Robert looked with his hands behind his head, his face and neck relaxed, gravity taking a different angle on him than when he was propped and Velcroed into his chair. Also surprising was the shining stream of tears that ran from the outer corner of Robert's eye down across his temple and into his ear. Foster was about to ask him if he was okay when Robert said, the words breathless but clear, "I neverrr want to get up again. I want to stay rrright here and look up at the sky."

The problem with that plan, as they soon discovered, was that lying on his back gave Robert's diaphragm extra work to do, making it harder for him to fill his lungs with air. After a few minutes, he was panting like a sprinter. Foster also learned that it was even harder to get Robert back into his wheelchair than to get him out of it. Just pulling him up into a sitting position on the grass was a challenge. They both had to rest after they got that far, sitting back-to-back under the tree. And then they had to call for help. Tori Mahoney, who was usually pretty relaxed about rules and things, had laid into Foster for putting Robert flat on his back like that. Come to think of it, she had laid into Robert, too. "You know better," she said to him. Foster remembered being surprised by Tori's sternness, the way she'd scolded Robert. He hadn't thought about that afternoon in a long time. It seemed like an odd choice for a *World of Pondside* portal.

"Close your eyes and hold down alt-POV," Robert suggested. "Then open your eyes."

Foster tried it. When he opened his eyes, he was flat on his back under the cottonwoods, looking through leaves flickering in a remarkably random pattern, at a digitally enhanced kaleidoscopic sky. "Oh!" he said. And for a good long while, he couldn't say anything else.

Dakota Engelhart could have prevented the standoff in the atrium. His mistake—he told Erika later—was not moving in as soon as he saw Mary McIntyre crouch down in front of the stroller. She was spry, that woman, for a person her age. Dakota was still half a room away when the baby, suddenly quiet, reached out with both chubby arms toward the apparently interesting face of Mary McIntyre, who must have undone the safety straps with one hand because she scooped that baby right up without any preliminary cooing or tickling. Dakota's cry of "Wait!" died in his throat. The last thing he wanted to do was startle Mary McIntyre and make her drop the baby, who was now gurgling and babbling, as if he was glad to be free. He didn't seem to care who had liberated him. The mother glanced first at the empty stroller, which was hardly an arm's reach away from her, and then, her eyes widening, at the old woman whose fluffy gray hair her baby had clutched in his fat fingers. Dakota could see the mother holding down her alarm. "Look who's got you, buddy boy," she cooed. Then she held out her arms and said to Mary McIntyre, with a phony supersweet smile exactly like the kind of smile that people give babies, "I'll take him now."

Mary McIntyre took a step back.

Now it was a standoff.

Mary McIntyre said, sternly, "You know that baby was not buckled in the way he ought to be."

"I was just—"

"He could fall right out of that stroller on his head before you had time to blink!"

The mother looked around for help.

Dakota moved in carefully. In the most casual voice he could manage, he asked, "Who've you got there, Miss Mary?"

Her eyes darted over to Dakota, to the baby, and back. "It's Robert," she said.

A hush fell in the atrium then. All eyes turned to Mary McIntyre and the baby in her bird-leg arms.

# CHAPTER 33

"So what do you think?" Robert said to Foster under the cottonwood trees.

Foster tried to think of a word other than *awesome*. He knew he was talking to a computer program that would not be impressed by his vocabulary or lack thereof, but that didn't matter somehow. Robert had obviously written the program to have a conversation with Foster, and Foster was going to hold up his end of it. Robert hadn't needed him as much as he seemed to, not if he could make something like this without help.

"It's awesome," Foster said.

Robert responded, "I haven't told you the whole story."

*That's putting it mildly*, Foster thought.

There was a pause, as if the program was deciding what to do with Foster's silence, and then Robert said, "You've learned that the game we call *The World of Pondside* is much bigger and more complex than you thought."

This time Foster said what he was thinking. "No kidding. And then there's the drug smuggling part. That was another surprise."

"You've spoken with my mother," Robert said.

"How did—?" Foster began, then stopped. Of course. Foster wouldn't be here in the *Next Level* if he hadn't clicked on the note pinned to the doll on the card table in front of Mrs. Kallman. "Were you ever going to tell me what the game was really for?"

"The game is for you, Foster."

"Oh, come on."

"I'm sorry," Robert said. "I didn't get that."

"Okay, fine," Foster said. "Let's hear the whole story then."

"You remember Sarah," Robert said.

"Who?"

"Sarah was in the drug study I told you about."

"I remember that one," Foster said. "They cut you off cold turkey, even though the drug was working."

Robert remained silent. The program was waiting for something about Sarah, Foster thought, so he said, "Sarah must be the one who suddenly noticed the drug was working. She drank her coffee right down."

"That's right," Robert said promptly.

"She was a scientist." *Was or is one*, Foster thought.

"That's right," Robert said again. "When the pharmaceutical company refused to release information about the drug, Sarah did some research of her own. One thing she learned was that a former student of hers, a young Chinese woman, had taken a job in Beijing with the company that produced the drug. It was not a Chinese company, but they had a research facility there. Sarah contacted the former student, who alerted us when another study of the same drug was about to get underway. As you know, Foster, that study in China was interrupted. Unlike me, Sarah was able to return when it resumed. The new director of the study was someone who had excellent training: Sarah's former student."

Robert stood up and pointed at something. For a moment, Foster remained stuck like a turtle on his back. "Alt-POV," Robert reminded him, and Foster was upright, standing next to Robert under the trees.

In the corner of the grassy field, a gray brick wall had appeared—or maybe it had been there all along, Foster wasn't sure. He remembered seeing something like it in the mash-up of portals below his grandparents' porch—gray walls flanking narrow alleys. Spilling out of a doorway in the wall was what looked like a tiny open-air restaurant, and there, sitting with three other people at one of the mismatched wooden tables, was Robert—another one! One of the other three appeared to be Chinese—a woman in a white lab coat who sat directly across from Robert. All were equipped with chopsticks. Foster watched the Robert at the table lift a stream of noodles from his bowl, twirl them expertly around his chopsticks, and then use the sticks and the side of the bowl to cut the bundle of noodles free before stuffing them into his mouth. No fat-handled forks needed in the *Next Level*. Sitting at the table on Robert's right was a broad-shouldered fellow in a T-shirt, maybe thirty-five or forty years old, tanned and good-looking in a rugged sort of way, his long legs sticking out from under the table in baggy fatigue-style pants. Across from the rugged guy sat a wiry, athletic-looking woman with a friendly face and curly gray-blond hair. She picked up a mug and drank from it. She peered into it, turned it upside down, and grinned.

"Must be Sarah," Foster said under the trees.

"That's right," Robert said. "In the course of the study, the drug continued to reverse her symptoms until you would hardly know she had ALS. Once in a great while, something like that happens. Nowadays they're studying these cases where something works for one person, trying to figure out why it works, the mechanism, but as you know, at the time, just one cure was nothing more than an anecdote."

"That drug worked for you, too," Foster pointed out. "You could make a fist."

Robert continued. "The drug never was developed or approved for ALS, but when Sarah's former student saw firsthand what was at stake for Sarah, what the drug seemed to be doing for her, she decided that she couldn't let Sarah's supply be cut off again. Eventually, the same drug was marketed in some Asian countries for multiple sclerosis. Sarah's former student takes the enormous risk of sharing it with us. We've passed along that medication to many PALS in the past several years. No one else in the group has responded quite like Sarah did, but some of us have been helped." Robert nodded his head toward the table and added, "We've kept in touch by meeting here, in the game."

Foster looked at Sarah again. The repeated action with the mug probably meant that she was a non-player character, like Laverne's Bill—at least in this portal, at this moment. All the characters at the table seemed to be repeating a cycle of actions. They were probably all NPCs: part of the game program, not player-controlled. The broad-shouldered guy was using his chopsticks to help himself to something from a platter. Foster thought he looked familiar, but that might have been because he resembled some handsome actor or other. Foster was about to ask Robert, "Who's the other guy?" when the fellow looked up from the table, right at Foster, appearing to give him—unless Foster was imagining it—the faintest of smiles. With an effort, Foster pulled himself away from the guy's steady gaze and turned back to the Robert Kallman who was standing beside him, only to find Robert locked in what they used to call the "listening attitude," his head tilted to one side. In *The World of Pondside*, it was a way to pause a character unobtrusively while something was loading. Foster waited for the program to resume. In the meantime, he heard an urgent stage whisper coming from somewhere in the library behind him.

"Foster!" It was Erika. "Ask him about *Laverne*."

He looked around. On the other side of the library, Erika was peering at him over the upper edge of her laptop screen.

"Aren't you going to ask him about Laverne?" she said.

Foster had totally forgotten about Laverne.

In the corner of the library, Duane Lotspeich pushed his wheelchair away from the table as if he'd given up on the desktop computer. "These damn headphones don't work worth shit," he said loudly, pulling them off. "I can't hear what anybody's saying."

"Where's Landiss?" Foster said. Duane and Erika gave him the same look.

"She's been gone for hours," Erika said.

"For *hours?*"

"A long time, anyway," said Duane.

Foster wondered how long they had spent under the cottonwoods, looking up through the leaves at the sky. Time passed differently when you were inside a computer game. He knew that all too well. You could play for hours and feel as if you'd logged in minutes ago. It was the exact opposite of the way time worked in a dream, where hours could go by in your dream world, and then you'd wake up ten seconds after you fell asleep. He looked at the time on the top of the screen and tried to do the math to figure out how close Laverne was to PEK. In the heat of the moment, the math was beyond him.

"You might not have much time left," Erika said. "To spend in the game, I mean. The police are here."

"And the FBI," Lotspeich specified, always ready to report the worst.

"The FBI!" Foster said. "Do you think they know about the pickup?"

"They must know about something," Erika said. "Has Robert told you anything about it?"

"You mean you can't hear him either?"

"No, we can't—Foster, we're still back in Old Chang's restaurant."

"Then how do you know I'm talking to Robert?"

"Well, we can hear *you*. And we can see what's on your screen."

"I can't," Lotspeich groused from the corner. "Not from here." He wheeled over to squint at Foster's screen. "Where the hell are you? Why don't you ask old Robert what the hell is going on?"

"Okay, okay," Foster said. "Give me a minute." He turned back to the laptop screen and found the scene had changed. That must have been what Robert's "listening attitude" was about: loading the new scene. He and Robert were outside the monastery building again, sitting at a small round table. They could just see the white stone bridge from where they sat. A sign above a door on this side of the building said, in English, "Gift Shop." Foster assumed that the Chinese characters on the sign said the same. Sitting across from Foster, his hands folded on the tabletop, Robert smiled a symmetrical smile and said, "The exterior of this building and the grounds replicate a Buddhist monastery that I visited often when I was waiting for the study in Beijing."

"I remember this place," Foster said. "You showed it to me." He thought about what to say next, how to find out what they needed to know. He decided it wouldn't hurt to try the direct route. "Robert," he said, "where should Laverne go to make the pickup? Of the drug. The ALS drug. Where should Laverne go to pick up the ALS drug?"

Robert kept smiling.

Foster tried a different tack. "We found these little suitcases," he said. "Carry-on size. They look just like the one Tori Mahoney gave me for Laverne. To make the pickup."

Robert tilted his head, as if in thought. "I'm sorry. I didn't get what you said."

"Suitcases," Foster repeated. "Carry-ons. We found three of them. There was a note in one, but—here's the thing. Robert, is there a note somewhere that says where Laverne Slatchek should go to make the pickup? Is that what we're looking for? A folded note? In a suitcase?"

"Let me check on that," Robert said.

Foster knew he should just wait patiently for more information, but like the geezers who couldn't keep themselves from hitting the submit button twice, he tried again. "Are there more suitcases? What are the suitcases for?"

"The location is indicated inside," Robert said.

This was promising. "The location of what?"

"The location you are seeking."

"I was hoping for something more specific," Foster muttered.

"I'm sorry," Robert said. "I didn't get that."

"So the location of what we are seeking is—where again?"

"The location is inside the first suitcase."

"The first suitcase you open?"

"That's right," said Robert.

"No matter which one it is!" Foster exclaimed. "But the note in the first suitcase said Black Ops."

Robert brightened. "Black Ops is the beginning of the most interesting path through the *Next Level*. Did you follow it here?"

"Did I—? No."

"Did you use the folded map?"

"Yes. Sort of."

"Did you catch the ball?"

"Yes!"

"And here you are."

"Wait. Are you saying that *you*—this conversation we're having? *This* is the Easter egg we're looking for?"

"I have been waiting here for you," Robert said.

This choice of words stopped Foster for a moment. Then he said, "All right, now that I'm here, can you tell me where Laverne should go?" When Robert didn't answer, Foster rephrased the question. "Where does Laverne go for the pickup?"

"I'm sorry," Robert said promptly. "I don't have that information."

"What do you mean you don't have that information?" Foster said. "Laverne Slatchek is on her way to China! What is she supposed to do when she gets there? Where is she supposed to go?"

"Speaking of Laverne," Robert said, "there she is."

A character who looked like Laverne Slatchek had just come out of the gift shop door, rolling a hard-sided tortoise-shell carry-on along behind her. She sat down on a bench not far from their table and looked around, as if she were waiting for someone.

As soon as he got over his initial surprise, Foster called, "Laverne!" but instead of looking his way, she seemed to spot the person she was looking for. Foster turned to see who it was. He was surprised (again) to find her husband Bill waving to her as he stepped off the white stone bridge. She jumped up and hurried away to meet him, still pulling the suitcase behind her.

"Laverne!" Foster called after her, and when he got no response— she was moving at a good clip toward Bill—Foster tried, "Erika!" instead. Laverne kept going. She and Bill met alongside one of the cedar trees. They embraced—as they always did when they met in *The World of Pondside*—and then off they went, crossing the bridge. "Laverne!" Foster tried again. He stood up to follow them. "Laverne!" He thought they looked as if they'd slowed down a bit—Bill even glanced back over his shoulder—but Laverne plowed on until the two of them reached the other side of the white stone bridge, where, like Robert earlier, they disappeared.

In the library, Foster looked at Erika, who looked back at him over the top of her laptop screen.

"That was weird," she said.

Duane Lotspeich rolled backward to the PC he had abandoned. "On *this* computer," he said, with an appropriate amount of disdain for the machine, "Laverne is with us in the restaurant. She's right there at the table."

Erika consulted her screen and said, "Right. She's still me." She toggled two keys. "I'm waving my hand. See that?"

"Well," Foster said, thinking about it, "there's no reason why you couldn't have a player-controlled Laverne in one part of the game—played by you, Erika—and a non-player Laverne in another part." *Like the two Roberts*, he thought, *one under the cottonwood tree, one at the table*. Of course, neither of *them* could be player-controlled, not by Robert anyway, because Robert was—Foster slapped his forehead and said, "Of course!"

Duane Lotspeich and Erika looked at him.

"We can't ask Robert where *Laverne* should go to make a pickup. It wouldn't make sense to him. To the program, I mean." Foster realized that he didn't like remembering he was talking to a program any more than the geezers did when they were hanging out with their loved ones in *The World of Pondside*. "Robert wouldn't know that *Laverne* is on her way to China."

"That's right!" said Duane.

Erika asked, "Why not?"

"Because he thinks—thought—would think—his *mother* would be making the trip," Foster said. "He didn't know she would be in the hospital. That happened *after*—after Robert died. She's the one who was going to make the pickup. She always makes the pickups, she said. She had her ticket already and everything."

"Tori Mahoney bought her that ticket," Duane put in.

Foster frowned at him. "How would you know that?"

"She used the computer in the library. That hunk of junk right there." He nodded toward the PC in the corner. "I came in here to try the ducklink a couple days ago and the screen still said, 'Your purchase

is complete,' and all that. For passenger—what's her first name? Susan—
Susan Kallman. It was her what-do-you-call, itinerary."

"For a ticket to China?" Foster said.

"And back," said Lotspeich. "And that's not the first time she used
that computer to buy airline tickets. Her purchase history was on there.
All you had to do was scroll through it."

"Which you, of course, did."

"Lotsa money spent on tickets to China," Duane said. "One for last
week. Somebody must have gone back and forth not long ago."

"Maybe that was another pickup," Erika said. "Or maybe it was the
same one, and they rescheduled it." She glanced at Foster. "Because of
the tragic events."

Foster asked, "Who was that ticket for? The one last week."

"I don't know. Tori Mahoney came running back into the library
to close the screen before I had a chance to see."

"Did she seem—?"

"Bent out of shape because I saw her stuff?" Duane shrugged. "She's
bent out of shape about everything lately, don't you think?"

"Did you tell the police about this?" Erika asked.

"I figured they knew. The police hardly talked to me anyway." He
sounded a little hurt about that.

"Why would the *police* care about who went to China?" Foster said.
"They don't know about the drug pickups."

"No," Erika began, "but maybe that's why the FBI—"

"Besides," Foster said, "Tori Mahoney worked for the Kallmans.
She's probably been ordering tickets and stuff for them for years."

Something was happening, Foster thought. Events were going down
a path he didn't know was there. How much would Robert know about
this pickup anyway? It hadn't occurred to Foster to wonder until now.
Mrs. Kallman said they'd heard from the contact in China. "They" meaning herself and Tori Mahoney? Who else? This guy Keith? Did "they"
include Robert? Mrs. Kallman never said *who* actually heard—or *when*
they heard. What if contact was made *after* Robert went into the pond?
In fact, wouldn't it *have* to be after he went into the pond?

"Maybe Robert didn't know about this pickup at all," Erika suggested.

A little unnerved by the new CNA's mind-reading capabilities, Foster said, "Then what are we here for?"

"Now don't go getting all philosophical on us," Duane Lotspeich said.

"I mean, if Robert didn't know about the pickup, then why did he go to all the trouble of changing the passwords and locking everyone out?"

"On the other hand," Erika said, "if Robert *did* know about the pickup, same question: Why did he change the passwords and lock everyone out?"

Foster looked at Erika and she looked right back at him. Normally, extended contact with a pair of hazel eyes like hers would have rooted him to the spot while clearing his mind of all usable content. At the moment, however, he was too puzzled to be paralyzed. Robert had gone to a lot of trouble to get them to log in to the *Next Level*—locking them out of the "old" *World of Pondside*, sending the new password to Foster (the only person on the planet who knew "who ate the whole thing"), and putting things in the game like the doll and Mrs. Kallman on his grandparents' porch, the Black Ops note, the jelly sandwich, the hot pot—all this to make sure they would wind up where he wanted them. If Robert hadn't brought them—Foster especially—this far to reveal where the ALS drug pickup would be, then why had Robert brought them here?

*I have been waiting here for you.* Even just thinking those words tightened Foster's throat. Had Robert been waiting just to say goodbye? Then why change the password?

"I don't get it," Foster said, mostly to himself. "What could he be up to?"

A small voice from the earbud barely hanging on in his right ear said, "You want to know what Robert is up to? I can tell you."

"Did you hear that?" Foster said as he fumbled to get both earbuds in place. He turned back to the laptop screen.

"Hear what?" said Duane.

In kitchen scrubs and an apron, her hair utterly ruined by the paper cap she had hastily discarded, Kitty surveyed the crowd of residents and visitors and staff who had gathered in the atrium to see how the standoff between Mary McIntyre and the forces of reality would turn out. She, Kitty Landiss, the recently fired administrator of Pondside Manor, was only a little surprised to realize that she was rooting for Wild Mary. *Let her snatch a whole room full of babies out of their expensively appointed strollers*, Kitty thought. Let the Department of Inspection and Appeals— whose agents Kitty had mistaken initially, and yes, a little hysterically, for the FBI—come to the rescue if they could. Kitty was sorely tempted to tell that overdressed pair from Inspection and Appeals that corporate had accepted her two-word letter of resignation, and the crisis was all theirs now. Let *them* figure out how to get Mary McIntyre to hand over the baby. Kitty Landiss no longer had to give a hoot.

It was clear from the start that neither the Department of Inspection and Appeals nor the homicide detectives, who had so unluckily chosen this morning to return to the scene of the crime, were prepared to handle an in-house baby snatching. One of the detectives actually suggested slipping the old lady a sedative.

"What do you have in mind?" Kitty had asked him as he and his colleague from Homicide conferred in the corner of the atrium. "A tranquilizer dart?" It was fun, she thought, not having to give a hoot.

The first responders called to the scene after the snatching occurred took a more sensible approach. One of the police officers—a sergeant by the stripes on her sleeve—said to Kitty, "Look. We don't want to break any bones on the old lady, and we don't want to make her drop the baby. The best plan is to wait this one out. Has she got any family we could call?"

While Kitty left voicemail messages for the two daughters, Mary McIntyre was gently herded into the conference room off the atrium by two paramedics and a handsome firefighter in full regalia. The handsome firefighter looked like he was going to save the day when, after a few baby-pleasing preliminaries, he got close enough to hand Wild Mary his shiny fireman's hat so she could put it on *her* head, causing the baby to grab the brim with delight. The standoff might have ended right then and there, if only one of the paramedics hadn't tried to hurry things along by placing a Chux pad on the conference table and suggesting that little Robert needed a change. Even before she took a sniff, Mary McIntyre recognized this for the ploy that it was, and she immediately put some distance between herself and the first responders, stopping only long enough to toss the fireman's hat onto the seat of the recliner. She retreated with the baby to the farthest corner of the conference room.

She spent most of the morning in there, alternately walking back and forth while singing to little "Robert" in her arms and dozing with him in a rocking chair in the corner. The baby's mother, a freelance hair stylist who often brought the baby with her when she came to give Mrs. Hickerson her weekly shampoo and set, produced a supply of ready-to-feed baby bottles from her giant shoulder bag and placed them tearfully on the conference table, at the end nearest the door. A little later, Jenny Williams delivered a breakfast tray from the kitchen. (Mary drank the decaf and fed the pureed peaches to the baby.) When anyone approached Mary McIntyre with the stated intention of taking the baby for a while so that she could have a little break—"anyone" being (as the morning progressed) Virginia Pinckney, the first-shift substitute for Tori Mahoney; Jenny Williams from the kitchen; Kitty herself; two of the cops (one male, one female); and Dakota Engelhart, CNA—Mary would say that she was sorry but she couldn't give the baby to anyone but his mother. Unfortunately, the baby's actual mother did not fall into that category as far as Mary McIntyre was concerned. Even when her own daughter showed up—the one who had been coming to see her every day—Mary wouldn't give an inch.

"Mom says I should call my sister and tell her that Mom's got the baby and that he's just fine, he's right as rain, and Molly should come and see for herself." Mary McIntyre's daughter reported to Kitty and the sensible sergeant, simultaneously dissolving into tears.

"Have you called her?" Kitty asked. "Did you tell her?"

"I've called and texted Molly multiple times," Mary McIntyre's daughter said. "I've begged her to come down here, but I will *not* tell her that Mom said she has her baby and he's right as rain!"

"Of course not," the sergeant said, offering a box of tissues. "Let's give her a little more time before we call for backup."

"Backup?" Mary McIntyre's daughter and Kitty said together.

The sergeant shrugged. "Basically," she said, "what we have here is a hostage situation."

"Oh my God!" the daughter said, reaching for her phone.

Kitty reminded herself sternly at this point that she didn't have to give a hoot. Still, try as she might, she couldn't help picturing Mary McIntyre in the back of the transport van that delivered her to Pondside Manor less than two weeks ago: a frightened old woman in a wheelchair that was chained to the floor of the van, her sedative wearing off, the wrist restraints making deep red marks on her child-thin wrists as she cried, "Help me!" to no one in particular, while the daughter who had ridden in the van with her wept, and the transport driver waited none too patiently for Kitty to sign the papers and set him free of these two. Mary McIntyre was a hard case. What would happen to the poor woman now?

Luckily for Kitty Landiss, her phone chimed just then. She took it out of her pocket, glanced at it, and texted a swift response before she put it back. Mary McIntyre's unknown fate still worried Kitty. As a suddenly unemployed former nursing home administrator with a decades-old degree in social work, Kitty herself faced a future full of unknowns. There was one thing, however, that Kitty Landiss now knew for sure. She was going to meet Bert Reynolds at Fitness World for a predinner workout at four p.m. on Monday, which happened to be the first day of the rest of her life.

By the time Foster got his earbuds in place, he found himself standing at the great green copper doors that led into the monastery building, face-to-face with the ruggedly handsome guy who had been at the table with Robert, the one who'd given Foster the long look and a faint smile. The guy was leaning back against the closed doors, his arms folded on his chest and one foot crossed in front of the other. His pants were not the fatigues that Foster thought he saw before but the kind of loose trousers that people wear for martial arts.

"So," the guy said, still smiling faintly, "do you recognize me?" His face, which was not as beautifully animated as Robert's, looked familiar, but Foster certainly didn't *recognize* him.

"I don't think so," Foster said. "No."

"I thought Tori might have shown you my picture," the guy said. "She used to do that."

Foster suddenly saw, in his mind's eye, a 5×7 family photo: two boys and their smiling blond mother and good-looking father in front of a Christmas tree. The photo was mostly hidden behind a gallery of school pictures next to the desktop computer in the nurses' station. Foster had carefully picked it up one time and had a closer look, then put it back behind the other frames.

Scott Mahoney laughed. "You know who I am now," he said. "I can tell."

"Yes." Foster's voice came out a whisper. "Are you—?"

"Am I just a bunch of pixels and code, like our friend Robert these days? Or am I somewhere out there in the real world, playing games with you in the—what do you call it?—*The World of Pondside*? Is that what you were going to ask me? Or were you wondering about the face? I'm afraid it's the old one, still my favorite."

*Pixels and code*, Foster thought. They were all pixels and code in *The World of Pondside*. Why not a Mahoney character in Robert's portal? Anyone could be playing Mahoney, anyone "somewhere out there." He took a calming breath. "You said you could tell me about Robert—what he was up to."

"I can. He's in the process of shutting all this down," the Mahoney character said with an open-arms gesture that took in the digital surroundings.

"This portal, you mean?"

"Not just this *portal*. The whole game. *The World of Pondside*, as you know it."

"No," Foster said, although he had been worried about exactly this possibility, hadn't he? He had been worried about it all along. "Why would he do that?"

"He didn't tell you?" Mahoney sounded surprised. "He calls it an update, but the 'update' ruins everything." He turned and reached for the handle on the door behind him.

Just to say something, Foster said, "I've already been in there."

"No, you haven't," Mahoney said as the doors swung open. "You're in *my* portal now."

The grassy field was gone, and so was the gray wall and the restaurant. In their place was a courtyard with a few huge old trees here and there, some shored up by metal poles and braces. Off to the left, a small forest of stone pillars rose from the backs of large stone turtles. Bordering the courtyard on three sides was a wooden arcade painted dusty red, nothing like the gleaming wood of Robert's monastery. The arcade was divided into little alcoves that opened on the courtyard. The ones that Foster could see into from where he stood were populated by painted statues that appeared to be waiting in line to present themselves to a larger, more important-looking statue seated at the deepest point of the alcove.

Foster didn't see any reason why he should tell this Mahoney character that Robert had shown him photos of a place like this—the real-life version of it, which was some kind of temple, Robert told Foster, many centuries old. Not Buddhist, like the monastery with the cedar trees and the white stone bridge, but something else. What Robert had liked about *this* temple, he said, the thing about it that kept him coming back while he waited with diminishing hope for the drug trial to resume, was the way the painted statues gave concrete, visible form to all the worst things that could happen to a person, laying them out in such a matter-of-fact way, the headless and deformed standing in line with the blessed and the hopeful—nobody left out, plenty of room for every kind of fate, good and bad.

Foster followed the Mahoney character around the wooden

arcade, stopping to peer into some of the alcoves. Someone had paid a lot of attention to detail in coding the place, right down to the posted signs identifying each alcove as one of various "departments" that oversaw the comings and goings of life on earth. They passed the Flying Birds Department, and the Department to Promote Fifteen Kinds of Decent Lifestyle, and the Department for Preservation of Wilderness, and even a Department for Bestowing Happiness. Foster didn't recall having seen any of those before. The ones he remembered from Robert's photos were like this one here with the bright-yellow guy sticking his long purple tongue out: the Deep-Rooted Diseases Department. Foster also remembered—because how could you forget?—the Department for Implementing Fifteen Kinds of Violent Death, where the line of supplicants or applicants (or whatever they were) included a decapitated fellow carrying his own head like a basketball, a man wearing a noose, another holding his intestines in his hands, and a droopy-haired, drowned-looking woman. Foster recalled showing special interest in this department and others like it when he was looking at Robert's photos—he remembered thinking that some of the deformed and the headless would make a pretty good zombie-type army—but when he suggested using it in *The World of Pondside*, Robert said, "No."

And yet here it was.

"You made this," Foster said to Mahoney.

"You've got that right," Mahoney replied. "And I don't mind saying that this is the coolest grid in the game. I guess if I have to be stuck somewhere, this is the spot I would have chosen. At least Robert gave me that much consideration."

"You're stuck here?"

"My, my," Mahoney said. "How little our friend Robert has told you."

They had gone full circle around the arcade and paused again just inside the gate, which put them between two larger-than-life figures that were seated, one facing the other, on either side of the path. One figure had flaring nostrils and a long spear in his giant hand; the other, whose mouth was open wide, silent scream style, held an equally long battle-axe in his.

"Meet Heng and Ha!" Mahoney said.

Foster read the sign describing the powers of General Heng and General Ha, Guardians of the Temple: "Heng, by snorting, gives out two white lights strong enough to knock his enemy senseless," the sign said, "while Ha's breath of yellow smoke frightens enemies out of their wits." Anyone entering the main door of the temple would have to walk between these two, braving fierce looks from their round and glaring eyeballs.

"They're fully interactive," the Mahoney character was saying. "Just grab the weapon and he'll go. Which one do you want to be? I'm usually Ha. Robert prefers Heng."

Foster looked from General Heng and his flaring nostrils to the cave-like mouth of Ha. Then he considered the faint smile that was, apparently, the Mahoney character's default expression and asked, "Are you really Scott Mahoney?"

Mahoney's grin seemed to widen. "Are you really Foster Kresowik?"

"But why would Robert want to shut down *The World of Pondside*?"

Mahoney sighed. It was the stiff and jerky old *World of Pondside* way of sighing: shoulders up, pause, shoulders down. "I confess I thought you knew a lot more about the game than you apparently do. I give you a lot of credit, though. You've put together some pretty impressive portals. But you don't have a clue about the update, do you?"

Foster shook his head. (This, he could have pointed out, was an in-game gesture that *he*, his own clueless self, had come up with: toggling *N* and *O* to shake your character's head. Robert had called it "Brrrilliant!")

"Does your friend Laverne know anything about it? Or the knuckleheads in the library? Never mind. I know the answer to that question. I thought if I could get *you* in here, I'd be able to talk some sense—"

"What do you know about Laverne?"

"I know she spends a lot of time in *The World of Pondside*. She's going to be pretty disappointed when she gets back home and finds the whole game shut down. I know Robert says it's an update, but don't believe it. The new version erases everything that matters."

"I don't know what you're talking about, or who you really are,"

Foster said, "but if Robert wanted to shut the game down, then I sure don't see what I could do about it."

"To avoid such a tragedy, all you have to do, Foster, is roll back the update. Revert to the previous version. It's not too late!"

"I don't know how to do that."

"It's the easiest thing in the world!" Mahoney said. "I can talk you through it." He paused, as if in thought. "Better yet, add me as administrator and I can *show* you what to do."

Mahoney's voice was more convincing than his appearance and motion, which were typical for a player-controlled character in *The World of Pondside* as Foster had previously known it. Hanging around in the *Next Level* had raised his standards.

"If it's so easy," said Foster, "why don't *you* do it?"

"I *can't* do it," Mahoney said. "Robert killed my administrator account. He did it while I was in flight, offline, not looking—on my way back from doing his bidding, no less! Not that I could have stopped him, even if I was looking. He's got all the hardware, which put him in the driver's seat—a little bit of irony there, if he told you what happened in Iraq—and so what does he do? He decides it's time to call it quits."

"What do you mean, call it quits?" Foster said.

"Well," Mahoney said, "apart from the obvious, I mean he makes a unilateral decision to shut me out. Sends me a text: *Time to close up shop.* Game over. Just like that."

"But you're here," Foster pointed out. "In the game."

"As a player, yes, but I can't *do* anything anymore. I can't even leave my portal—all I've got is the hutong restaurant and this temple. My contacts? My clients? All gone, their accounts deleted from the game for their illegal activities. Isn't that rich? Coming from Robert? ALS drug smuggler? I can't even *talk* to anybody in the game unless they're here in my portal with me, which is why Tori has been trying so hard to get you to log in. I've been waiting for a chance to talk to you. Waiting in here is about all I can do. I sure can't roll back the update."

"And I can?"

"*Only* you can," Mahoney said. "I'm out, Robert's dead, *you* are the sole administrator of the game." He laughed. "I guess Robert didn't tell you that either. I'm telling you, Foster, you are the only one who can save *The World of Pondside*."

"I'm just trying to find out where Laverne Slatchek is supposed to go, once she gets to China."

"Don't worry about Laverne Slatchek. Laverne is already going where she is supposed to go," the Mahoney character said.

Foster didn't like the sound of that, coming from *him* (whoever he actually was). "What do you mean? Where *is* Laverne?"

"Since she's flying American, I'm guessing she's over Khabarovsk about now. That's in Siberia, right on the border. Just a few more hours and she'll be in Beijing, filling her suitcase with some very nice decorative scrolls."

"How do you know?" Foster said. "Are you making this up?" He wished he knew what airline Laverne was flying. She'd shown him the itinerary. Was it American? He tried to picture it.

"Listen, Foster Kresowik," the Mahoney character said. "Our friend Robert knew he wouldn't be around much longer. He's always thought that my whole operation was a problem. It appears he decided that the only way to fix it was to shut the whole game down."

"And your whole operation is—what?"

"Shipping. I expedite shipping, Foster. I help people arrange delivery of goods that can't be handled through ordinary channels."

"What kind of goods?"

There was a pause here. Then Mahoney said, "Knock-offs, mostly."

"Knock-offs," Foster said. "You mean, like Nikes that aren't really Nikes?"

"Shoes, cellphone components, luxury goods, I don't know what all. Like I said, Robert's the smuggler, not me. I just give my clients a place to meet their customers. Robert was actually smuggling his drug into the country, and using his own mother to do it, until his supply dried up."

"What do you mean it dried up?"

There was another pause here. The game might have been loading.

"Doctors stopped prescribing the drug for MS a couple of years ago—too many side effects or something—so the company stopped making it."

"But it helped people, other people with ALS, not just Robert."

"They weren't making it for ALS. They'd have to do more studies, get it approved. There's not enough money in it. ALS is what they call an underfunded disease."

"But Mrs. Kallman said—"

"Mrs. Kallman doesn't know that Robert's drug is no longer available. He had her do a pickup last year that was as fake as the wild-goose chase your friend Laverne is currently on."

This was a lot for Foster to take in. The question was, could any of it be true? He thought about Tori and Mrs. Kallman—and Laverne— in the hospital room, trying to get him to say that they *might* be able to find out where Laverne should go to "make the pickup" if they logged in to the game. "The secret is *in the game!*" Laverne had said. "It's in *The World of Pondside!*" Mrs. Kallman appeared to agree. But if this "Scott Mahoney" was telling the truth, then Tori, at least, must have known that there was no drug to pick up. "It doesn't make sense," Foster said. "Why would Robert send his mother to China if there wasn't any drug to pick up? I mean, why wouldn't he tell her?"

"Because she's his mother, and she's a very old lady. She could see he was going downhill, but she didn't have to know that it was over. Not yet, anyway." Mahoney sighed again. Shoulders up, shoulders down. "Mrs. Kallman loved making every one of those trips. Not to mention, she was keeping her boy alive."

"And Mrs. K still doesn't know?"

Mahoney shook his head.

"But you just said Laverne would be putting something in her suit-case—scrolls or something."

"Yeah. Paper scrolls on hollow wooden spools that could have drugs hidden inside them—if there were any drugs to hide. Robert's contact has used them for real pickups in the past."

"You must know who the contact is," Foster said.

"Actually, I don't. I know the drug company so I could figure it out, but I don't. Or maybe I should say, I didn't. Robert and I have always kept our business as separate as we could. Frankly, he would have liked to shut me down a long time ago, but that was hard to do without shutting himself down, too."

"I still don't get it," Foster said. "Robert's dead now, and his mother knows it. If there's no drug to pick up, what was the point of all this?"

"*Ha!*" Mahoney cried, and that's when Foster noticed that the air was turning thick and yellow with something like smoke. "Your presence in my portal has been detected!" Mahoney said, still smiling his faint smile. "Our friend Robert has thought of everything."

"Robert's dead," Foster whispered, reminding himself, as the smoke thickened.

Mahoney turned and leaped to grasp the battle-axe of General Ha behind him with both outstretched hands. When he landed, the ground shook under the weight of massive boots, then shook again. Generals Ha and Heng stood facing each other, battle-axe and spear in hand. All that remained of Mahoney was his voice, sounding thin and oddly cheerful as it issued forth incongruously from the smoky mouth of Ha, calling, "What do you say, Robo, old friend? Winner take all?"

# CHAPTER 34

Dakota Engelhart didn't mind filling in for Landiss who'd been filling in for Foster in the kitchen. In the midst of all the drama, it was nice to have a simple task to accomplish, like setting the tables for lunch. (As Jenny Williams in the kitchen pointed out, "No matter what happens, people gotta eat.") He arranged the silverware on the last table in the dining room—the one against the windows that people still thought of as the Kallmans' table—and when he straightened up, he found himself eye to eye with a dark-haired woman standing outside the window. Almost immediately, he recognized the brown eyes and stern brow of Mary McIntyre in the woman's face. Since he'd started working at Pondside, Dakota had gotten very good at seeing the features of an old person in the faces of visiting offspring. Sometimes the resemblance was so strong that it was spooky. The dark-haired woman who was obviously Mary McIntyre's daughter waved at him, put a finger to her lips, and pointed toward the entrance on the front of the building.

More than three hours into Mary McIntyre's standoff in the conference room, the atrium was still heavily populated. Milling around or scattered on the floral-print chairs and sofas were the forces arrayed against her: police and paramedics, Health and Human Services, concerned family members (including Mary McIntyre's other daughter, the one who came to see her every day), the Pondside social worker in her high heels, Kitty Landiss still in kitchen wear, and a team of counselors who were taking turns at the conference room door. The FBI agents, who turned out to be investigators from the Iowa Department of Inspections and Appeals, had forgotten all about the staff interviews they were there to conduct. As a diversion, the baby snatching was a smashing success. No one even looked at Dakota as he slipped through the crowd. By the time he reached the vestibule, the woman was waiting outside the glass door. He punched the right buttons. She came inside and whispered, as if the two of them had planned this meeting, "Where can we go?"

Dakota looked at her for one surprised moment and then he pointed down the short hallway that led to Pondside's four administrative offices. With everyone in the atrium, the office doors were closed, the hallway quiet and dim. The woman ducked down the hall and, after a moment's hesitation, Dakota followed. He was relieved to find the first door on the left unlocked. She could wait here, he thought, in the vacant office of the director of nursing, while he went to get somebody official.

Inside the office, sunlight streamed through a dusty but sizable window behind the desk, illuminating the woman who was even more obviously Mary McIntyre's daughter. Dakota saw that she was older than he thought at first—fiftyish, he guessed, with careful makeup and a long ponytail. Scowling fiercely in the brightness, she looked more like her mother than ever. Either she had allergies or she'd been crying. Before he could invite her to sit, she turned to face him and said, "I have twenty-nine texts and ten voicemails on my phone, all from my sister, all sent in the past three hours, all begging me to come here. She thinks Mom will give *me* the baby. My sister says she's been calling him *Robert!*"

"I know," Dakota said. "That was weird."

He thought he saw a flash of surprise on her face. "You *heard* her call him Robert?"

"Yes!" he said.

Mary McIntyre's daughter dropped into the chair behind the desk. "I thought maybe my sister made that up just to get me here." She looked across the desk to Dakota, who was still in the doorway. "What do *you* think she's doing? Do you think she's doing this to get attention?"

It took Dakota a moment to understand what she was asking, and when he did, he found himself feeling defensive on Mary McIntyre's behalf. "Your mother has dementia," he said. "She's always looking for her 'baby.'" He shrugged. "Maybe she thinks this kid is the baby she lost."

Dakota thought he was offering a reasonable, if unqualified, opinion about the situation—maybe even stating the obvious. He didn't expect Mary McIntyre's daughter to spring up from the chair. Dakota took a step back. Turning her legacy scowl on him, she cried, "*I'm* the one who lost a baby, not her. My God, it's been twenty-five years! And she's still doing this? *Still?* It was *my* baby who died—tragically, inexplicably, *died*—and she comes to the hospital, my dear mother, and she asks me, *What did you do?*" Her nostrils flared. "Can you see what I'm saying?"

It was not a rhetorical question—Dakota could tell by the way her Mary McIntyre eyes burned into him—but the truth was, he had no idea what she was saying. "You mean—she thought you had—ended your pregnancy?"

"What? No!" she cried. "The baby was full term. He was stillborn. And my mother asks me what did I *do*? I'll *tell* you what I did. I ate right. I did all the exercises. I drank nothing—not a beer, not a glass of wine—from the time I learned I was pregnant. We were so happy—everybody was happy—but especially my mother. She had all these baby clothes from my sister and me—she never threw anything away. She had the bassinet we slept in. I took that, but I had to explain why we couldn't use the crib: it didn't meet safety standards, the bars were too far apart or too close together—who knows? Oh, that sent her into a tailspin, like I was accusing her of being careless, a bad mother. She didn't know any better, she said. She grew up poor. Nobody ever told her anything. Her mother ate dirt when she was pregnant. My mother never heard of the cord wrapping around the baby's neck or she would have gone in the ambulance right away! And I came out all right anyway, didn't I? I was fine, the doctor was wrong—oh, she couldn't let go of that when they told me my baby was dead. *They were wrong before*, she said, *they could be wrong again.* Look how big I was. The baby was just ready to come out, that's all. *Don't believe them,* she said. *Pray!* she said. God could bring my baby back to life. And then she asked me what happened, did I slip, did I fall? What did I do that killed my baby, *what did I do?*"

Mary McIntyre's daughter dropped back into the chair. When it swiveled a quarter turn toward the window, she left it that way, looking out into the parking lot instead of at Dakota, angrily swiping the back of her hand across her cheek. There was a box of tissues within his reach on an otherwise empty shelf—the aloe kind in a fancy box that made him wonder if other people came into this room to cry. He slid the box toward her, at the same time easing himself into the visitor's chair on the other side of the desk. The chair squeaked under him. She swiveled his way, helped herself to a tissue. She dabbed her eyes and blew her nose, and when he took a little bottle of hand sanitizer out of his pocket, she used that, too.

"So," she said, more calmly, "just when I needed her the most, Mom went bonkers. She had a complete nervous breakdown over the lost baby. *My* lost baby."

"Really," Dakota said. He thought that explained a few things about Mary McIntyre.

"And you know what my sister told me? The man who drowned in the pond gave Mom that doll they thought we gave her! Not all torn up, though. I guess somebody else did that."

"Robert Kallman gave Mary the doll?"

"That's what the lady who talked to my sister said. Apparently, the doll was *his* idea, the dead guy's. I guess he thought it would make Mom feel better. I could have set him straight on that. And then it turns out that his name is *Robert?*" Mary McIntyre's daughter shivered. She leaned across the desk, toward Dakota, and said, her voice dropping almost to a whisper, "That was my baby's name. *Robert.*"

"Wow," Dakota said.

"I know." Mary McIntyre's daughter sat back. "It couldn't get any creepier."

Dakota had to ask. "Do you happen to know who told your sister about Robert giving her the doll?"

"I don't know her name. The lady with the basket of stuffed animals attached to her walker. She seems a little strange, but my sister said she sounded like she knew what she was talking about."

Dakota couldn't argue with that.

"What do you do here?" Mary McIntyre's daughter said suddenly, squinting at his name tag as if she couldn't quite make it out. "You're too young to be a doctor, I hope."

"Oh, yeah, no, I'm still in school."

"Well, you'll make an excellent doctor someday," she said.

"Actually, I—I'm in education."

"Well, you'll make an excellent teacher then. Do you know why?"

Dakota was still listening to the words he'd just said to her. *I'm in education.* How did that sound, spoken aloud to a stranger? It sounded okay, he thought. *I'm going to be a teacher.* It sounded pretty good.

Mary McIntyre's daughter didn't seem to notice that Dakota hadn't answered her question. "I'll tell you why," she said. "Because you know how to listen. Not many people do. Most people never hear a word you say." With that, she stood up. "I guess we'd better go find Mom and rescue that baby. I hope to God the mother doesn't press charges."

They worked out a plan as Dakota followed her back down the hall. When they got to the atrium, the crowd parted before her—she really did look a lot like her mother—and whispers followed in her wake. Dakota trailed two steps behind. He watched from the doorway as the scene played out in the conference room, the baby's mother hovering at his elbow and a half-dozen people—including Mary McIntyre's other daughter—looking over his shoulder. Mary McIntyre was sitting in the recliner at the far end of the room. The baby had fallen asleep in her arms. She looked up as her daughter came through the doorway, first suspicion and then surprise and pleasure crossing the old woman's face. Her daughter perched on the arm of the recliner. They both looked down at the baby. ("For a minute there, it was like a scene in a painting," Dakota told Erika later. "You half expected celestial choirs to burst forth in song.") Then Mary McIntyre's daughter slipped one hand under the baby's well-padded butt. "Woo," she said, "time for a change!"

That was Dakota's cue. He sauntered through the doorway, saying, "Hey, Miss Mary!" in the calmest, most offhand way he could manage, his heart beating very noticeably in his chest. Mary McIntyre looked up and gave him a smile that wavered but remained a smile. Her daughter slipped her other hand under the baby's back and neck in a move so deft that Dakota wondered why he had thought, while the daughter was talking to him, that she never had any other babies after the one she lost. He wished he'd asked her. He heard the baby's mother, at his elbow, make a soft and indescribable sound as Mary McIntyre's daughter rose from the arm of the recliner, the baby in her arms rising with her.

As the yellow smoke began to clear, the fearsome outlines of Generals Ha and Heng slowly took shape in front of Foster, tendrils and wisps of vaporous yellow still floating out of Ha's open mouth. Foster stood rooted to the spot he had occupied while the two giant guardians clanged their weapons—spear and battle-axe—over his head. At least, that's what it sounded like they were doing. The yellow clouds of General Ha's smoky breath had grown so thick that not even the bright white beams of light shooting (Foster had to assume) from General Heng's nostrils could penetrate the opaque air. Foster expected at any moment to be stomped upon, but despite all the clanging and roaring, when the smoke cleared, he was unscathed.

There was no sign of the Mahoney character. Only Robert stood on the path, dwarfed by the throne-like chair of Heng behind him. The generals were seated once again, spear and battle-axe at their respective sides. Heng appeared to have a stiff yellow flag stuck to the end of his spear—no, it was a folded piece of yellow paper.

"I've copied this part of the portal into the update for you," Robert said. "You can be Heng or Ha and battle the program, or bring in another player and battle each other." As he spoke, the spear of Heng swung downward. "You'll need this to access the new server." Robert plucked the piece of yellow paper from its tip. It fluttered to the ground, unfolding as it fell.

"You said Mahoney died," Foster said. "Why didn't you tell me the truth?"

"Scott Mahoney lost his life when that IED exploded."

"He didn't lose his life. He lived in your house. You went to China with him!"

"I owe him more than anyone knows," Robert said.

"He got a *face* transplant."

"The game has been exploited by unauthorized users."

"Oh, you mean somebody *else* has been using your game to smuggle unauthorized shit into the country?"

"We have to close the marketplace the game has become."

"So now you want *me* to help you shut down *The World of Pondside*."

"We have to update the game."

"That's what he said you would say."

"The update permanently removes all unauthorized users."

Something was going on in the library behind him. Foster could hear somebody speaking quietly but urgently to Erika. Foster couldn't understand what they were saying, but he thought he heard "Mary McIntyre."

"You arranged everything in advance, didn't you, Robert?" Foster said. "You knew exactly what you were going to do, so you scheduled this 'update'—is that what you did?"

"The update is in progress," Robert said. "You initiated the download. All that remains is to install it on the new server."

"What do you mean *I* initiated it?"

"You initiated the download when you ordered at the ballpark."

"The jelly sandwich?" Foster said. "I've been wondering about that. How did you even have time to put that in the game? You had a couple days to get the doll in there—or maybe you had the doll planned all along—but she ate that sandwich after dinner the night you went into the pond. That *same* night."

"She ate the whole thing," Robert pointed out.

Foster pictured it: the tsunami of pureed spaghetti he cleaned up, and later, the nearly deserted dining room, Mary McIntyre with her hands in her lap looking at yet another bowl of glop, and then Robert calling Foster over, saying, *She can't eeeeeat that.*

"Is that why you asked me to make her the sandwich in the first place?" Foster said. "Was that all part of the plan? First step: get Foster to make the crazy lady a sandwich. Next step: go down and roll yourself into the pond?"

"I don't understand your question," Robert said.

"How the hell was I supposed to get your message about the password?" Foster said. "We never use that company email account! I hadn't looked at it for weeks. Maybe *months*. That account is a *trash* heap."

"Recent messages are displayed on the home page," Robert said helpfully.

This, Foster realized with a little shock, was true. The most recent messages were right there on the home page, senders and subject lines displayed in the inbox like newspaper headlines. If Foster had used his password to open the admin site that same day, the day they found Robert in the pond, then he would have seen Robert's message before it got buried by junk. It would have been right there where Foster couldn't miss it. A new message from Robokall. Robert probably figured that was the first thing Foster would do on finding out that Robert was gone. What Robert didn't know was that Duane Lotspeich would take the laptop and that Foster would wait around, afraid to log in, worried about somebody trashing his hard drive, worried about *that*, when all the time Duane had the server in his room.

The commotion outside the door in Library Lane was getting louder, more insistent. Was that Landiss asking if anybody had a search warrant? *A search warrant?*

"All right, I messed up your plan by not logging in," Foster said. "What I don't understand is why you didn't just do it all yourself. Update your own damn game—hell, shut it down!—and be done with it. Why did I have to do it? Because you'd be too busy rolling yourself into the pond?"

There was a pause before Robert responded. "I'm not sure what you said."

"I guess I couldn't believe that you'd just change the fucking password and roll yourself into the pond without some kind of plan B!"

"The plan," Robert said, "is for you to complete the installation of the update on the new server. When you log out of your current session in the game, everything will migrate to the new server."

"What new server?" Foster cried. "I don't know what you're talking about." In the hallway, it sounded as if someone had fallen against the library doors.

"Updated, the game will have no connection to the unauthorized users or portals that have been compromised," Robert explained. "You will be the sole administrator of the game."

"I told you, I don't know *what* you're talking about." Foster heard a weird noise and realized that it was coming not from the hallway, but from *him*. It sounded like a sob. "You told me Mahoney *died*."

"Scott Mahoney lost his life when that IED exploded," Robert said in exactly the same solemn tone he had said it before. "I owe him more than anyone knows."

There was a steady knocking on the library door now. Somebody tried the door handle.

"Robert," Foster said.

"Yes?"

"*Did* you do it? Did you roll yourself into the pond? I just want to know."

"I'm sorry. I'm not sure what you said."

"Maybe I'm not asking it right," Foster said. "When you made this, this program, you hadn't done it yet, but were you *going* to? *Are* you going to? Are you going to roll yourself into the pond? Is that part of the plan?"

"The plan," Robert said, "is for you to complete the installation of the update on the new server."

"You already said that!" Foster cried.

"I'm sorry," Robert said.

"For God's sake, Robert, does that mean you did it? You rolled yourself into the pond?"

"I don't understand your question."

"*Ooga-booga!*" said Foster.

"What was that again?"

"I said, this is one hell of a voice recognition program, isn't it?"

"It certainly is," Robert said.

"Robert!"

"Yes?"

On-screen, Robert's beautifully animated face raised its eyebrows expectantly, the same way Robert Kallman used to raise his eyebrows to say, *Yes? I'm listening, I hear you, I'm in here, Please, I beg your pardon, Wait! Listen! Oh, what's the use? Never mind,* and *Goodbye.*

Foster said, "Never mind."

"Okay," said Robert, as the library doors opened and the voices in the hall rushed in.

Foster had time to pick up the piece of yellow paper that had fallen from the spear of General Heng on-screen. Then he pressed the power key and held it until his screen went blank and blue.

# CHAPTER 35

Laverne wasn't sure how she had lost Keith, to whom she had hardly spoken five words since she boarded the plane in Chicago fourteen hours ago. Now here they were in Beijing, and Keith was gone! She wasn't even sure where she'd lost him. He had been right beside her when they passed the pillars that took your temperature, and she was able to keep an eye on him at the place where they looked at your passport and asked about the purpose of your trip, although they were in different lines. When it was Laverne's turn to step up to the counter and say why she was visiting China, her mind had gone completely blank. "To see the sights," Laverne was supposed to say, and when she failed to say it, the customs official or whatever they were had left off scowling at Mrs. Kallman's passport to scowl at Laverne instead.

"Tourist?" he said.

Laverne heard something like "Two wrist?"—she was lucky she heard anything apart from the pounding in her chest and ears—and she'd looked down at her wrists, which were sticking out of the linen sleeves of Mrs. Kallman's tunic. She was standing at the counter, her hands gripping the edge, one on either side of a small black box with three buttons that invited her to rate the performance of the customs official who had her passport in his hand as Excellent, Fair, or Poor. She let go of the counter long enough to punch the green Excellent button. Twice. When she looked up at the customs official again, she could see that the corner of his mouth was twitching. "Seventy-two hours," he said, trying to help her out. "Not much time. Go to Great Wall maybe? See Forbidden City?"

"Yes!" Laverne had said. "I'd like that."

He had stamped Mrs. Kallman's passport and slid it back to her—with a smile! She more or less fell back into the wheelchair the Chinese skycap had scooted up to catch her in. They rolled on through.

Keith had already gotten his stamp of approval and was waiting for her on the other side. He and the Chinese skycap lingered nearby while she used the ladies'. It was a few minutes later that she lost him. He had been striding along more or less next to the wheelchair on the way to baggage claim—fortunately, the signs were in English as well as Chinese—and then, all of a sudden, shortly after the skycap had slowed down a bit to maneuver through a mob of travelers in matching T-shirts, Keith was nowhere to be seen.

"Wait!" Laverne said as the wheelchair picked up speed, and then, "Excuse me? Can we wait just a minute? I don't see my friend."

The Chinese skycap said something that sounded quite cheerful, but he didn't slow down.

At baggage claim, there was no sign of Keith. Mrs. Kallman's suitcase might have gone by two or three times (based on the repeated passing of a large pink box swathed in bubble wrap) before Laverne spotted the yellow plush duck tied to the handle. The suitcase was a tweedy-looking soft sider. It didn't match the tortoise-shell carry-on at all.

In customs, they waved Laverne and the skycap through, completely uninterested in a white-haired lady and her mismatched luggage, just as Mrs. Kallman said they would be.

At a door below a multilingual sign that read, among other things, "Ground Transportation," the skycap handed her over to somebody Laverne didn't even see, who grabbed the wheelchair handles from behind, hollered something that sounded like "*Choo-choo chuh!*" and propelled her toward a line of taxicabs. It occurred to Laverne that perhaps she was being kidnapped. Opportunity of a lifetime! She was half lifted into the back seat of the taxicab and handed her things, including the carry-on, all without seeing the face of her (perhaps) abductor who was tall enough that he would have needed to duck and lean into the taxi to bring his head into view. Something was going into the trunk—she hoped it was the large suitcase and not the Chinese skycap—and then the door on the other end of the back seat opened and a man slid in.

They looked at each other. The man smiled at her in an oddly lop-sided way.

*Uh-oh,* Laverne thought. This looked like trouble.

The taxi pulled away from the curb.

Foster would not have been surprised if the cops had hauled him off to jail or something after the raid (which is what Kitty Landiss called it) on the library. Nobody got arrested, though, or even taken down to the station, and all they did about the computers, when Lieutenant Stein-hafel arrived, was secure Robert's laptops—the original server and the backup—by locking them up with the other equipment in his room.

To Foster's great relief, when it was his turn to be interviewed (yet again) in the conference room recently vacated by Mary McIntyre, Lieu-tenant Steinhafel didn't ask a single question about the game Robert Kallman had developed. All the lieutenant wanted to talk about was Robert's habit of going out onto the pier at odd hours of the night to make phone calls. They were in the process of examining Robert's cell-phone records, but in the meantime, what could Foster tell them?

"I wouldn't call it a *habit*," Foster said. He was sitting across the big oak table from Lieutenant Steinhafel. A short stack of baby-size dis-posable diapers occupied the seat of a chair on Foster's side of the table and a mostly empty baby bottle stood on the windowsill. "He only did it a couple times, as far as I know. Most calls he made during the day."

The phone, the lieutenant understood, was built into the wheel-chair, on the armrest.

"That's right," Foster said. "On the left-hand side." The side where he could still move two fingers—index and middle—and his thumb, although the thumb had been getting noticeably weaker. "He needed help with the Bluetooth. Putting it on, I mean."

"And this was a regular Bluetooth device, worn on the ear, with the earbud and the microphone all in one?"

"Yes, but Robert couldn't use the mic. He would text and the other guy would talk."

"The other guy?"

"The other person. Whoever he was talking to."

The last time Foster helped him with the Bluetooth, Robert had been calling his mother. "Time to phone home," Robert had said, mustering up the lopsided smile he reserved for talking to and about his mother. Foster's nose prickled. He thought of Robert putting Mrs. Kallman—and the doll—on his grandparents' porch. He wondered if Mrs. Kallman was still in the hospital.

"And you don't know who it was that he was talking to?"

"I know he called his mother and sometimes he made calls to people about equipment he ordered, like that."

"Did he go outside to make all of these calls?"

"Cellphone reception sucks in this building," Foster said.

"Were you aware that some of the calls he made were to a recipient or recipients in China?"

Now here was a question Foster could answer with complete and perfect honesty. He looked at the lieutenant; he was getting this eye contact thing down pretty solid. "No," he said.

"Any idea why he might be calling China?"

This, Foster suspected, was the key question, the reason they were asking him now about Robert's phone calls, which they must have known about before. Maybe they had come across Tori Mahoney's airline travel purchases on the library computer. Did they already know that Laverne Slatchek was over there in Beijing, breaking multiple laws with every step she took? Foster figured it wouldn't take long for some alphabet soup of an agency to hack into *The World of Pondside*. He hoped that whatever Robert had done to update the game would also make it look like the universe of harmless personal fantasy worlds it was supposed to be.

"Mr. Kresowik?"

"Can you repeat the question?" Foster said.

"Do you have any thoughts about why Mr. Kallman would be making calls to China?"

As he searched for a way to answer this question, an observation made long ago by Foster's grandmother popped into his head. She had been called to jury duty during the summer Foster spent in Wisconsin when he was a kid, and they picked her for a trial. She wasn't supposed to discuss the case while it was going on, which just about drove her crazy, so she would come home with more general complaints about the justice system instead. She didn't like how the judge sat up high "where he can look down at everybody. What's that all about? Makes everybody else look like kids getting the riot act read by some authority figure. How can a person look anything but guilty?" She also questioned "this business about telling the *whole* truth. I can understand 'tell the truth and nothing but the truth.' That's doable. But the *whole* truth? Where would a person start?"

Foster realized suddenly how much Laverne Slatchek reminded him of his grandmother. He put on his most forthright face and said, "I guess Robert knows—I mean, he must have known people there."

In the taxi on the way to wherever they were going, the man whose face had given Laverne quite a start introduced himself as a friend of Robert Kallman's. "We were in the military together," he said in perfectly ordinary English. He didn't sound Chinese.

Laverne had looked around enough inside the taxi to confirm that the oddness of the man's face was not due to a malfunction of her brain. That, at any rate, was a relief.

"So, are you the Chinese contact?" she asked warily.

That made him smile again. The muscles in his face seemed to work a little better on one side than the other. "Actually, I'm kind of a go-between."

It was true that he looked sort of Chinese, though crookedly so. His face was round and outlined by one of those narrow little beards that run all along a man's jawline, from ear to ear, leaving most of his chin and cheeks bare. One cheek looked to be higher than the other—in fact, one eye looked a little higher than the other—or maybe he just had a habit of squinting on that one side. On the opposite side, his jawline definitely drooped a little, creating an overall impression of lopsidedness, which is what made Laverne think she might be having another brain event when she first saw his face. A fine line crossed his forehead from the hairline to his right eyebrow. His skin was blotchy in places, as if he'd had too much sun. His eyes—the most un-Chinese thing about his face—were blue.

He'd had a face transplant, he told her while she blinked at him.

"A face transplant!" she said.

"I got blown up in Iraq. Pretty much my whole face was gone. Also one hand. And my legs below the knee." He pulled up his sleeve so she could see the wires and metal where his wrist and hand should be.

"A face transplant," she said again. "You mean they take a face from one person and put it on someone else? Like an organ donor thing?"

"Exactly. You wouldn't be looking at this face if it weren't for an avalanche in the mountains west of Beijing. Six fatalities buried in snow and one of them was just my size. Actually, he was my tissue type. Thirty-six hours in surgery all told."

Laverne continued to blink at him.

"Maybe that was more information than you were looking for," he said.

"It didn't matter that you're not Chinese?"

"Not much. Tissue type is what matters."

Talking to him for a while made his face seem less strange. She felt bad now about how taken aback she must have seemed to him. He probably got a lot of that. Really, though, it had been a great relief to learn that she was seeing his face as it was. "I hope you won't take this the wrong way," she said, "but I'm glad it's your face that's a little off-kilter—and not my brain."

"Not a problem. In fact, *I'm* kind of glad that the look on your face was about something *other* than my face."

They both laughed. Laverne noticed that only parts of his face participated in his laughter. She was reminded of something Tori Mahoney said one time about the mixed blessings of medical science. At the time, she was talking about a Memory Lane lady who came back to Pondside after major surgery with a colostomy bag that she couldn't remember not to pull off multiple times a day. Suddenly, something amazing occurred to Laverne—something so startling that she didn't have time to stop and think before she said it aloud.

"You're Tori Mahoney's husband, aren't you?"

He didn't answer right away. Then he said, "I was."

"Well, my goodness!" Laverne said. "Then you *didn't* die in the war. Does she—?" Laverne stopped.

"Were you going to ask if she knows that I'm alive?"

"I know it's none of my business," Laverne said.

The strange-looking man whose name must be Mahoney did not disagree with that, but he answered anyway. "Yes," he said, "she does." He paused. "We keep in touch."

In a flash, although there was no flash, Laverne saw what it must have been like for the two of them: Tori Mahoney, a person who could put her game face on and calmly handle any kind of horror the human body could come up with, and this strange-looking man, who must have been filled with grief every time she turned to him with her game face on.

Laverne looked out the window of the taxi. She reminded herself that she was in China! It was kind of hard to tell. They were on an expressway, in a middle lane, moving along fast, just as if the traffic weren't almost bumper to bumper. All she could see were cars to the left of them and cars to the right. A green truck with "China Post" on the side of it, in English, pulled up next to them and eventually passed them by. She was surprised when Mahoney spoke up again.

"I was pretty horror-show when they shipped me back," he said. "I scared myself."

"Maybe you're not giving her—and yourself—enough credit," Laverne said. She wondered if he had heard from Foster yet. Or from what's-his-name—Keith.

"Oh, I give her all the credit in the world, ma'am, but you can only be a monster for so long, and then you want to go someplace where nobody knows what's missing."

There was something in his tone that reminded Laverne of her last argument with Bill, the argument he won while she was outside waving the ambulance into their hidden driveway. The real advantage of being a man, she thought, was the way men seemed to believe that they always had the right to do whatever they'd decided to do.

A phone chimed. Tori Mahoney's husband tapped the screen of his cellphone a few times, and then he said to Laverne, "We're in business now." To the driver, he said something that sounded Chinese. The driver started maneuvering the taxi toward the exit lanes.

*The Easter egg!* Laverne thought. They must have found it. "Where do we go?" she asked Mahoney.

"A Buddhist monastery. Not too far from here."

"A monastery!" Laverne said. "The monks don't mind?"

"When we get there," Mahoney said, "you'll go to the gift shop and look around, as if you're shopping. Wait until you see a Chinese woman—a customer—who has a carry-on just like yours. When she laughs and points to the suitcase, you laugh, too."

Laverne could tell that he was about to go through all of the instructions she had gotten first from Mrs. Kallman and then from Tori Mahoney, but in somewhat greater detail. That was okay with her. A refresher course seemed like a good idea about now.

"Will she speak English?" Laverne asked.

"I think so."

"What do you mean, you think so? Don't you know who it will be?"

"When she's gone, you go to the cashier and buy a decorative scroll. They come in boxes like this." He reached under the front seat and pulled out a box about the size and shape of a box of plastic wrap. It was covered in a Chinese-looking satin fabric, rose-and-gold colored. "They have them on display, unrolled, like this." He took the scroll, which was rolled on two wooden dowels, out of the box and let it fall partly open to reveal a fierce-looking bearded face, very intricately cut out of red paper, against a cream-colored background. "They'll be hanging on the wall behind the counter so you can just point to the one you want, and then he'll give you another one—not the display model—in one of these boxes. Give him a fifty—have you got a fifty?"

"Fifty dollars! For that?"

"Fifty yuan. That's about eight dollars."

That seemed more reasonable to Laverne. "So I should pick the bearded man?"

The taxi turned from an exit ramp onto a boulevard that had almost as many lanes as the expressway. Bicycles and three-wheeled delivery carts competed with the cars and buses.

"Pick any one you want. Doesn't matter. Next thing, the cashier will point to your carry-on to ask if you want him to put it in there. Nod your head yes. He'll give you your change, and out the door you go."

"When do we switch—?"

"Right outside the door to the gift shop, there's an ice cream freezer—you know, with a sliding glass top on it, ice cream bars and things for sale."

"Oh, my Lord," Laverne said. "I can't remember all this. I can't remember anything anymore."

"You don't have to remember it. You'll see it and you'll want an ice cream. Aren't you hungry right now?"

She was. The food on the flight had been pretty meager. ("Very small portions," young Eammon had observed.)

"Do you like ice cream?"

She did.

"The woman with the carry-on like yours will be looking into the top of the case. When she sees you, she'll smile and wave and say, 'Ice cream?' Or, if she doesn't speak English, she'll say, *Bing ji ling?*"

"What does that mean?"

"It means ice cream! Lean the carry-on against the freezer, slide the glass door open, and take your ice cream. The pictures on the packages will tell you what's inside. Then you're done."

"Don't I have to pay for the ice cream?"

"Nope. She paid for it."

"When do we swit—"

"Already done. All you do is find a bench or a table in the shade, sit tight, and someone will come for you by the time you finish your ice cream."

Laverne wasn't sure she wanted to eat any Chinese ice cream but decided not to mention that. It seemed like the least of her problems. "What do you mean, 'someone will come for me'? How will I know who it will be?"

"Don't worry," he said. "You'll recognize him by his cap."

"I'll recognize him?" Laverne said. She was on the other side of the planet—opportunity of a lifetime!—she didn't know anyone here. Laverne felt a wave of dizziness as the taxi swerved, slowed, and came to a stop. The driver turned around and grinned at her. He was wearing a San Francisco Giants cap. "This is our stop," he said. It was Keith! When he saw her face, his grin disappeared quite suddenly. "Are you all right?" he asked.

His face had shifted around a bit and the *SF* logo on the cap had vanished, but she said, "Yes."

Both men were looking at her with concern. Mahoney said, "You remember what to do?"

"Yes," she said, although that corner of her mind was suddenly a complete blank.

Mahoney got out, his pant leg catching on the seat in such a way that she saw the metal leg his shoe was attached to. She blinked, thinking the prosthesis might disappear like the logo on the Giants cap, but she caught another glimpse of it before the pant leg fell back into place. Both men came around to her side of the taxi. Keith opened the door for her and helped her out. Mahoney handed her the green hard-sided carry-on, its handle already extended, along with the cane. She was supposed to do something once she got inside—this place, whatever it was. The taxi had stopped across from a pair of fancy metal doors that opened into a walled park.

"Just follow the signs to the gift shop," Keith said. He had taken her elbow to help her over the uneven pavement. They slowed to a stop. "Maybe we should go back to the taxi," he said. "Sit for a minute."

She shook her head. "There's something else," she said, gripping the carry-on handle in one hand and the crook of the cane in the other.

"Yes?"

The broad street seemed strangely deserted. Mrs. Kallman said the sky here was usually gray or milky, the sun nothing but a white circle behind the smog, but the sky was as blue as it could be. For the life of her, Laverne couldn't remember what she wanted to tell the man. She took an uncertain step. If she kept moving forward, everything might come flooding back to her. That was how it worked sometimes.

# CHAPTER 36

The library seemed oddly empty when Foster looked in at the end of the day. The hulking PC on the table in the corner was dark. Somebody had come through and put the tables back the way they were usually arranged, too. He still had the key to the library closet in his pocket, the one that Erika had given him, the one he was supposed to return to Stephanie, the activities director. He crossed the room and glanced around before he put the key in the lock. Robert's Nooey equipment was still inside—the sensors, the tripod, all the various boxes Foster and Erika had put away. No one had mentioned the library closet when the cops were "securing" the hardware. Maybe they thought this stuff belonged to Pondside Manor—some newfangled technology to encourage the old folks to exercise, like Erika said. Well, Foster wasn't planning to set them straight on that. He closed the doors and turned the key, which he dropped into his pocket again.

"Ready to go?" Erika was in the doorway. She had surprised him earlier by stopping in the kitchen and offering him a ride home. He had surprised himself by accepting. "I'll pull around the front," she said, "and wait for you there."

In front of the building, the Hummer stood yellow and gleaming, Erika busily texting behind the wheel.

Foster climbed into the passenger's seat. He said, "I've never ridden in one of these."

"Oh, I know," she said apologetically, stowing her cellphone in a cup holder. "Usually, I bring my friend's car to work, but she needed it. What about your bike?"

"I'll get it tomorrow," Foster said.

He tried to imagine what it had been like riding shotgun in the plywood-lined and sand-bagged Humvee that blew up under Robert and Scott Mahoney, but there was so much leg and elbow room in the Hummer that even Foster's vivid imagination couldn't make it happen— especially with Erika talking to him pretty much nonstop. First, it was all about how a person of his talents should consider getting a degree in game design. He tried but couldn't tell her that he'd have to get his GED first. Then, she said she had a theory about why they'd seen Laverne and Bill and the carry-on suitcase rolling off into the sunset, so to speak, at the monastery in Robert's portal.

"You were asking about Laverne and about the carry-ons, and so that's what the program put together: it was just feeding back what your questions were putting into it. Kind of like voice recognition feedback based on what you just said, but with images instead!" She paused. "What do you think?"

"You might be right," Foster said. Then he laughed.

"What?"

"All of a sudden, it's kind of weird to hear your voice coming out of—well, out of *you*."

She frowned for a second and then she laughed, too. "You got used to Laverne sounding like me!"

"I guess so."

They pulled into a parking space outside Panera. She shifted into park. A silence followed that should have been awkward but somehow wasn't—or if it was, Foster was too busy thinking to notice. When he spoke, it was more to himself than to Erika. "I wonder why he didn't just text me."

"Text you what?" she said, startling him a little.

"The new password." He looked at her. "Why would Robert use the game administrator email to send me the password? He knows I never look at that. I mean, he knew. So why didn't he just text me? If he wanted me to get in there and do whatever. I would have gotten the message right away."

There was another little silence. Then Erika said, "Maybe he had to be sure you didn't get it too soon."

"What do you mean, *too soon*?" The words were hardly out of Foster's mouth before he understood exactly what she meant. He took a couple of breaths. His goddamn nose started prickling. He waited. Finally, he was able to say, "It just doesn't seem like something Robert would do, to go and roll himself off the pier without some kind of plan B."

"Maybe he figured he had a good enough plan A," Erika said. When Foster looked at her, she added, "That would be *you*, Foster. You're plan A." Her phone buzzed and she glanced at it. "Looks like somebody else needs a ride," she said. "I should get an Uber license or whatever. Let me know right away when you hear from Laverne, okay?"

"Okay." Foster managed to open the door without fumbling.

He watched the Hummer move through the mall parking lot to the nearest exit, which it humped through, as if she'd driven over the curb on one side.

He was halfway up the back stairs to his apartment when Tori Mahoney's "Hey, Foster," nearly knocked him back down to the bottom. She was up there on the landing, waiting next to his door. She had a bag from Panera in hand.

"You met Scott," she said.

Well, Foster thought, that answered one of his burning questions. He said, "In the game, you mean."

"Sometimes we get together there. That place with all the statues?"

"I thought you couldn't even look at the game."

"I couldn't, for a long time," she said.

She looked tired, Foster thought. The bare bulb hanging from the ceiling in the hallway didn't do anybody any favors. He said, "He told me there isn't really any drug to pick up."

Tori seemed surprised for a moment. Then she said, "Not anymore."

"And Mrs. Kallman doesn't know that?"

"Oh, no. If she hadn't been in the hospital, she would have gone to China herself."

"He said she loves making trips to China."

"A pickup was the only way Scott and I could think of to get Mrs. Kallman moving," Tori added, as if that was the thing that needed explaining. "She *had* to get you to log in then."

"To find out where to go for the pickup," Foster said. "Supposedly."

"Yes." The word was one long, exasperated sigh.

"But I did log in." It seemed like days and days ago: Duane Lotspeich spelling out *McIntyre*, Mrs. Kallman and the doll on his grandparents' porch, his first sight of Robert coming over the white stone bridge.

"*Eventually*, you did. Scott was trying to get to you before all his—clients—found out they couldn't get into the game. By the time you logged in, he'd probably lost most of them already. At the first sign of something wrong, they're gone. They won't be back." She laughed—the quick kind of laugh with no humor in it. "He was so sure he could get you to open a new account for him. It was quite a shock, finding out that you didn't know anything about the *Next Level*."

*That can't be true*, she'd said. Twice, she had said it.

"But if it was too late and there was no drug to pick up, why did Laverne have to go to China?"

Tori lifted her hands, helplessly. "Laverne taking the trip on her behalf was Mrs. Kallman's idea. I tried to talk her out of it. I said Laverne had health issues, she was old—*old*, of course, didn't matter to Mrs. Kallman—*and* that they'd be breaking the law. She laughed when I said that. She was very determined. They were going to do this thing, make this pickup. For Robert." Tori shook her head. "I still can't believe Laverne agreed to go."

That had surprised Foster, too, at first, but the more he thought about it, all he had to do was picture Laverne at the wheel of Amelia Ramirez's Saturn, barely able to see over the dash, her old-lady hand sliding the gearshift from first to second to third as smooth and easy as a knife slicing through butter, and it didn't seem so surprising after all.

"I wanted to tell them the truth, Foster, I really did, but I couldn't figure out a way to do it. Mrs. K was so excited when the tickets came. She kept saying, *I didn't think there would be another pickup after Robert was gone.*" Tori unrolled the top of the Panera bag and rolled it up again. "I know she half believes that Robert arranged it all for her, to keep her occupied, to distract her. She said more than once that she wouldn't put it past him."

*Neither would I*, Foster thought. Robert was good at arranging things.

Tori looked away, toward the window on the landing. It was dark now. The parking lot lights had turned the dusty glass opaque. Somebody opened a door downstairs, and the smell of cinnamon rolls filled the hallway insistently, making Foster realize that he was hungry.

"They figure a face transplant like his might last fifteen years," Tori said suddenly. "Nobody's had one for that long yet—nobody who's still alive—but Scott is getting close. Robert and his mother have been trying for a long time to get him to meet with a transplant team in Cleveland—to see what his options are." She paused. "That's why Scott was here last week."

"He was here," Foster said, trying it out. Did she mean *here*? At Panera? At Pondside?

"He and Robert argued about the game, of course, but they'd argued about it before. Scott had no idea what Robert was up to. He didn't know until he got back to Beijing and tried to log in."

"You mean that's where he is, for real? In China?"

That made her turn and look at Foster in surprise. "Yes," she said. "That's another reason Mrs. Kallman likes to travel there. She tries to talk Scott into coming home. I guess you wouldn't know that either."

*No*, Foster thought, *I wouldn't.* He tried to picture Scott Mahoney and Robert arguing in Robert's room—or maybe not in Robert's room, maybe out on the pier—and found that he could only see them as they were in the game: Scott with his handsome face, Robert standing on his own two feet, hands in his pockets. Heng and Ha also came to mind. He said, "Why are you telling me all this?"

"Because I want you to know that Scott's flight departed from Chicago Wednesday afternoon, long before Robert went out on the pier that night. The police know that already, but I wanted to be sure that you knew it, too."

What was he supposed to say to that? Foster wondered. "Okay," he said.

Tori turned back to the window, as if there was something to see out there. "I have this dream that someday I'll look at his face and see *him* again. I don't mean that I'll see him the way he used to be. That's not what I mean." She shook her head. "I'm sure Robert was trying to make things right, before the end, but he had no business shutting down the game."

"He didn't shut it down," Foster said hoarsely. "He updated it."

Tori looked at him over her shoulder. "So it's a done deal then. There's nothing left for you to do?"

Foster thought about that. Scott Mahoney's so-called clients were already out of the game, so *that* was a done deal, wasn't it? Foster was supposed to install the update "on the new server," Robert said. And what, exactly, would happen to the game then? Foster was hoping for *Next Level* animation and a multiplayer option, but he didn't know. There was an awful lot that Foster didn't know.

"Well, I hope you know what you're doing," Tori said. Then she held out the Panera bag. "I got you a sandwich. It must be cold by now."

Foster didn't want to take it, but she kept holding it out there in the space between them until he did. He could tell by the softness of the paper that she had been waiting on the landing a long time before he got there. It must have driven her crazy, all the waiting she'd been doing—not just this past week, but for years. Something else occurred to Foster. After everything she'd said, he wasn't sure why. "*You* tore up Mary McIntyre's doll, didn't you?"

"That doll!" she said, more vehemently than he expected. "Robert's mother said you would recognize that little nightmare from the game."

"But why did you tear it up?"

"I was just looking for information at the time, same as you." She turned to go but stopped again at the top of the stairs. "You don't need to worry about Laverne," she said. "Keith will watch out for her. They both will."

It took Foster a few seconds to figure out who they *both* were.

He waited until the door at the bottom of the stairs closed behind her before he put his key in the lock. Inside, he stood there for a moment and thought about *that little nightmare* on the back of his bike, enjoying the idea that Robert had managed to scare the shit out of him from beyond the grave. Then he threw away the sandwich.

There was something a little different about Chinese ice cream, Laverne thought. It wasn't bad. She had been disappointed in the chocolate coating, which tasted more like wax than chocolate, so she was trying to lick the ice cream without getting any more of the chocolate part.

Her head felt much better. She was pretty sure that she must have had another one of those temporary things that were like a stroke, but then they went away. She didn't remember doing any kind of transaction inside the gift shop, although there was something in the carry-on now—it was a fancy fabric-covered box the size and shape of a box of plastic wrap—and she knew that she was sitting here waiting for someone she would recognize. Two men were sitting at another table at the far end of the monastery garden. The one with all the hair looked familiar, but she wouldn't go so far as to say she recognized him. As she turned to look the other way, down the path that led to a white stone bridge over a pond festooned with lotus flowers, Laverne was dismayed to see a chocolate-covered blob of ice cream melting on the leg of Mrs. Kallman's linen pants. She dug around in her big black purse, hoping to find a tissue.

When she looked up again, there on the path was Bill! He was wearing a Giants cap and a black T-shirt—no! it was his minor league jersey, the same one he was wearing in the picture with Willie Mays—and he was crossing the bridge, headed straight for her. She stood up and before she could say anything but, "Bill?" she was in his arms.

"Watch out for the ice cream on my pants," she warned him. "It will get all over you."

"I don't care about any ice cream, Laverne," Bill said. He had taken her by the shoulders and held her away from him so that he could see her face. "I sure have missed you, sweetheart."

"Same here," Laverne said. She peered up into his face. "Are you crying? Why are you crying?"

"Laverne! Laverne!" said another voice.

Laverne grabbed the handle of the carry-on and slipped her arm through Bill's. "Let's get going," she said.

Bill looked back over his shoulder. "That young man is trying to get your attention," he said.

Laverne did not look back. "He must have me mixed up with someone else."

"But he said your name, Laverne."

"Must be some other Laverne." She steered him toward the white stone bridge and the gate beyond it, pulling the carry-on behind her.

He stopped. "What have you got here, anyway?"

She looked down at the fragile-looking hand—it was *her* hand, she thought—holding the handle of a hard-sided rolling suitcase, a small one, carry-on size. "I don't know," she said. "I hope I didn't let someone give it to me at the airport. They tell you never to do that. Over and over, they tell you."

"You were at the airport?"

"Of course I was. How else do you think I got all the way here?"

"All the way where?"

Laverne looked around. She wasn't sure where, but it was a long way from where she started—anybody could see that—and she had a feeling there was no going back.

Foster's teeth were chattering. This was only partly due to the cold air blowing from the open window over to the plastic patio table that served as his computer desk. He had half expected to find the apartment ransacked by *somebody*—the police or whoever—but it looked (and smelled) exactly as he had left it, or maybe a little worse, right down to the peanut butter smear on the doorframe. He used the mouse to move the cursor to the yellow duck in the middle of the screen. He would always prefer the precision and control of a mouse over a trackpad. He was like the geezers that way. He double-clicked the ducklink and entered the new administrator's password that Robert had given him. A dialog box popped up to say, "An update is available for *The World of Pondside*. Would you like to install it now?"

The last three times Foster had gotten this far, he had opted to "Install later." If he didn't do it soon, he would have to wait until tomorrow or risk running out of Wi-Fi before the update was complete. He wasn't sure what was stopping him. A small part of him worried that when the cyberpolice got around to it, they would trace various "unauthorized users"—whoever they were—back to *The World of Pondside*, and he, Foster Kresowik, sole administrator of the game, would be left holding the bag. Another part of him kept thinking about Scott Mahoney, trying to dismiss the nagging worry that installing the update really would ruin everything, like Mahoney said.

Foster's biggest worry, though, was the daunting responsibility of being Robert Kallman's plan A. What did it mean, anyway? Did the game belong to him now? Is that what Robert meant? Or was he just the tech guy? Robert's mother had already sent him an email suggesting that he "set up shop" at the Kallman residence, where he could enjoy uninterrupted internet service, which meant that she must have known all along what Robert was going to ask him to do. Foster reminded himself of what Erika said about him getting a degree. "A person of your talents," she called him. He wished again that he could have come up with something to ask her that would give him a clue as to the status of her and Dakota. Foster hadn't permitted himself to glance at her phone and see who needed a ride; he regretted that now.

Old Dinglebutt had come off quite the hero in the business with Mary McIntyre snatching somebody's baby. When Foster reported to the kitchen after his interview with Lieutenant Steinhafel, Jenny had filled him in. Her sympathies were with the old lady, particularly (Foster thought) since everything had turned out all right.

"I wasn't one bit worried about the baby that whole time," Jenny said. What really tugged at her heart was what she heard Mary McIntyre say to her daughter after it was all over, when they were coming out of the conference room with their arms around each other, leaning their heads together.

"What did she say?" Foster asked. Jenny was already in her coat with her big purse on her arm, about to head out to her second shift job. Foster was up to his elbows in pots and pans from lunch. Finally, Jenny answered.

"She said, 'There must be a place for someone like me.'"

"Someone like her?" Foster said. "Did she mean someone who pulls the shower out of the wall and takes other people's babies?"

Jenny gave him a look. "I don't know what she meant, Foster. I just know it broke my heart to hear it." With that, she hoisted up her purse and added, "To tell the truth, what she said put me in mind of you." Then she had bustled out the door, leaving him to wonder what the heck she meant by that.

Now, at the bottom of the computer screen, Foster saw that he had a new email message. He took the opportunity to procrastinate a moment longer by clicking the little envelope. It was from Mrs. Kallman. "News re: Laverne. Please CALL." Another email from Mrs. K seemed like a good sign—she must be feeling better. Foster wondered if she knew that all caps meant she was shouting at him. He wished she had put the news *into* the email. As much as he wanted to hear about Laverne, he couldn't talk to Mrs. Kallman right now. He didn't have it in him. Not just yet.

The *World of Pondside* dialog box was still waiting. He twirled the mouse around on the screen, making a figure eight that looped around "Install now" and "Later." He found himself thinking about Mary McIntyre dancing in the library, about what it would take to make Duane Lotspeich's Ginger Rogers look like Mary instead. He would have to get some photos of her. He wished he'd seen her daughter, the one Dakota was talking about, who looked so much like Mary McIntyre. Foster won-dered how the daughter would feel about playing her mother on-screen, how both of them would feel about it, for that matter: Wild Mary cut-ting loose with Erika in the sensors' field while the daughter dipped and twirled with Duane on the screen—but why just her and Duane? Landiss had the wardrobe for it. And didn't Laverne say Bill was a good dancer? It didn't matter if he wasn't. This was *The World of Pondside*, after all. Mary McIntyre could do the dancing for all of them. Duane Lotspeich thought they would be locking her up somewhere after she borrowed that baby, but they could take the Nooey to wherever she was. The key to the library closet was still in Foster's pocket.

Also in his pocket was a folded piece of wrinkled paper on which he had written down the new admin password that Robert plucked from the spear of Heng. Foster had copied it off the yellow note as it fluttered to the ground on the laptop screen. He smoothed the paper out and read it again: "The Farmer in the Dell." He wondered if anyone other than Robert even knew that he had the Dell.

As a server, it wasn't particularly new, but it was powerful.

The computer screen had darkened. Foster tapped a key to make it light. Then he swooped down on "Install now" and clicked, half expect-ing—or maybe only hoping—that Heng and Ha would appear, locked in smoky and decisive combat. They didn't. The ducklink promptly became a baby doll dressed in overalls and riding on a tractor. Foster laughed—not out loud, but his shoulders moved a little. For a few min-utes, he watched the bar that told him how much time remained before the update was complete and the weight of all the worlds of *Pondside* landed squarely on his shoulders.

"This is going to take a while," he announced to no one but himself.

He was pretty sure that he only imagined the yellow smoke billow-ing faintly across the screen.

The old man was upset about something, Mary could tell—something besides the fact that she had followed him out the door. All the way across the parking lot, he argued with himself. She had the impression he'd forgotten something that he didn't want to go back and get. Could he do without it, or couldn't he? When he stopped, suddenly, at the point where the asphalt path leading down to the pond began, she almost walked into the tackle box he was rolling along. Even on wheels, it appeared to weigh him down. In his other hand, two fishing rods bounced and swayed.

"What the hell are you following me for? What are you doing out here?" he growled at her.

Mary was not about to admit to this old fart that she had lost the baby. A person could go to jail for things like that. She had seen it happen to Mrs. Carlyle, one of the women her mother sold eggs to. Even back then, you couldn't leave your five children under the age of eight alone while you went into Gray to have your hair done. Mary and her mother had arrived with the eggs just as the sheriff was loading the Carlyle children into the back seat of his official county vehicle, all except for Billy Carlyle, the oldest, who got to sit in the front seat next to the sheriff and looked more than just pleased about it.

At least, she *thought* she'd lost the baby. Isn't that what happened? You let your guard down for a minute, you turn your back, you do the wrong thing—something you never meant to do, never meant to say— and just like that, you lose her! Mary put her hand to her mouth.

"What's the matter? Can't you talk?" the old man said. "You sure get around well enough. I don't suppose you know what a casting rod is. I left it right outside the damn door. Maybe you could go back and— ah, shoot." With that, he lowered his tackle box onto the grass next to the path and tossed the fishing rods in his other hand down beside it. "Damn women," he muttered as he turned and set off across the concrete toward the building, moving pretty fast for a man his age.

Mary looked down the path to the pond. She could see that the pier was empty now. There was something shiny in the water at the end of it. She looked around the well-lighted parking lot, but the man in the wheelchair was gone. She wasn't sure how much time had passed since she took him out there "to make a phone call," she thought he said. Such a nice man. He'd told her to set the baby in his lap, so she could put one foot on the back bumper of the wheelchair and use both hands to tip it up onto the pier. Of course, the *baby* wasn't a baby at all, it was the doll he had given her, but she didn't say anything to correct him. It was nice of him to give her the doll in the first place. He was just trying to make her feel better. Mary had learned that sometimes it was best to play along, especially when people meant well. She hadn't wanted to leave him out there, but he said he was fine in his funny machine voice. Going back to the shore was no problem for him, he said. He showed her how he could put his wheelchair in reverse and slowly, slowly, go up the little bit of a ramp the pier made and bump back down onto the asphalt path, just like that. He had done it many times before, he said.

"Well, make sure you put it in reverse!" she warned him, and they both laughed out there on the pier. At least, she thought he was laughing.

After she left him, she had stopped on the asphalt path and held the doll up, as if to see him out there. She waved the doll's arm and said, "Bye-bye! Bye-bye!" Of course, he couldn't wave back. Mary wasn't sure if she heard her or not, but he did seem to be looking in her direction.

That would have to do. At the top of the path, where it met the parking lot, Mary had found herself face-to-face with a woman who looked familiar. A cigarette glowed between the woman's fingers. Her short blond ponytail was like a little fountain.

"My goodness," the woman said. She was sniffling, and her voice was hoarse. She took Mary's arm. "We'd better get you inside before your baby catches cold!"

Going inside was a good idea, Mary thought. She had forgotten to put on her jacket, and she was feeling a little chilly. She looked back over her shoulder at the man in the wheelchair, down on the pier, who seemed to be watching them.

The woman with the ponytail gave Mary's arm a reassuring squeeze. "Don't worry about Robert," she said. "I'm keeping an eye on him out there."

# AUTHOR'S NOTE

The "ALS drug" and research trials described in *The World of Pondside* are fictional creations. However, ALS—amyotrophic lateral sclerosis—is a devastating reality. At any given time, about thirty thousand people in the United States suffer from ALS, a degenerative motor neuron disease that leads to the wasting of muscles, loss of movement, and eventual paralysis and death. Currently, there are no effective cures or treatments to stop the disease progression, which varies from person to person, making the research to discover effective therapies especially challenging.

The ALS Therapy Development Institute (ALS TDI) is the world's most comprehensive drug discovery lab focused solely on finding treatments for this unrelenting and complex disease. The scientists of ALS TDI have one mission: end ALS.

To learn more, visit https://www.ALS.net.

# ACKNOWLEDGMENTS

It takes more than an author to bring a novel into the world, and I am more than grateful to the many people who contributed their time, knowledge, and experience to the making of *The World of Pondside*.

For starters, my thanks go to Josie Woodbridge, Megan Bixler, Alenka Linaschke, Kathryn Zentgraf, Lauren Maturo, and all my new friends at Blackstone Publishing. I am delighted to be on board with this crew!

I am grateful to my editors: Kathryn Zentgraf, whose attention to detail whipped this novel into its final shape; Dana Isaacson, who always kept the reader in mind; and Liz Huett, peerless guardian of my galaxy of words.

Special thanks go to David Huett, for sharp-eyed proofreading, and to Vanessa Huett, for patiently reminding me again and again which button does what on the game controller.

Additional help came from these early readers of *The World of Pondside*: Susan Aizenberg, Eileen Bartos, Marjorie Carlson Davis, Jennifer Hemmingsen, Marianne Jones, Suzanne Kehm, Deb Mamerow, Judy Polumbaum, Kathleen Renk, John Stefaniak, Lauren Stefaniak, Mary Vermillion, and Ann Zerkel. Thank you, all!

For expert assistance in areas where I am definitely not an expert, I thank Annie Iglehart for reading the manuscript with the eye of a nurse as well as a book lover; Jeffrey Stefaniak and Van Huett for patiently answering my questions and introducing me to the video gaming experience; and my instructors in computer science and game design at Creighton University and Kirkwood Community College. Jason Christopher Hartley's memoir, *Just Another Soldier*, provided essential details about Humvees and about serving in Iraq.

What I know about what it's like to live with ALS I learned from my dear friend Sarah Lamb, to whom this book is dedicated. I am indebted to her and to her wonderful sons, Rob and Tom Corson, who made it possible for Sarah to share her life so fully with friends like me. Long after Sarah was gone, I learned from the often inspiring and sometimes heartbreaking blog posts of *Richard Is Living with ALS*. Some of Robert Kallman's fictional experiences in the novel were inspired by Scott Haren and Ben Harris, who shared their real-life experiences in "Two Men and Their One Voice," on NPR's *The Story* (May 12, 2012).

I am grateful to the scientists and staff of ALS Therapy Development Institute (ALS TDI) for their ongoing webinars that keep people with ALS and their supporters aware of the latest developments and opportunities in ALS research and treatment. The community forum hosted on the ALS TDI website opens a window on the hopes, fears, and daily courage of people living with ALS.

As always, I thank my agent, Valerie Borchardt, who first befriended me and my work more than twenty years ago, and my husband, John, whose unwavering support goes back a lot farther than that.